Beautiful Liars

When two must keep a secret . . .

three's a crowd . . .

ISABEL ASHDOWN

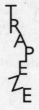

An Orion paperback

First published in Great Britain in 2018 by Orion Books,
an imprint of The Orion Publishing Group Ltd
Carmelite House, 50 Victoria Embankment,
London EC4Y 0DZ

An Hachette UK company

1 3 5 7 9 10 8 6 4 2

A CIP catalogue record for this book is
available from the British Library.

ISBN (Mass Market Paperback) 978 1 4091 6797 6

Typeset by Born Group
Printed and bound by CPI Group (UK) Ltd, Croydon, CR0 4YY

www.orionbooks.co.uk

For my stepfather,
David, with love

PART ONE

PART ONE

A Death

It *wasn't* my fault.

I can see that now, through adult eyes and with the hindsight of rational thinking. Of course, for many years I wondered if I'd misremembered the details of that day, the true events having changed shape beneath the various and consoling accounts of my parents, of the emergency officers, of the witnesses on the rocky path below. I recall certain snatches so sharply – like the way the mountain rescue man's beard grew more ginger towards the middle of his face, and his soft tone when he said, 'Hello, mate,' offering me a solid hand to shake. *Hello, mate.* I never forgot that. But there are other things I can't remember at all, such as what we'd been doing in the week leading up to the accident, or where we'd been staying, or where we went directly afterwards. How interesting it is, the way the mind works, the way it recalibrates difficult experiences, bestowing upon them a storybook quality so that we might shut the pages when it suits us and place them safely on the highest shelf. I was just seven, and so naturally I followed the lead of my mother and father, torn as they were between despair for their lost child and protection of the one who still remained: the one left standing on the misty mountain ledge of Kinder Scout, looking down.

I can see the scene now, if I allow my thoughts to return to that remote place in my memory. I watch myself as though from a great distance: small and plump, black hair slicked against my forehead by the damp drizzle of the high mountain air. And there are my parents, dressed head-to-toe in their identical hiking gear: Mum, thin and earnest, startle-eyed; and Dad, confused, his finger pushing his spectacles up his florid nose as he interprets my gesture and breaks into a heavy-footed run. Their alarmed expressions are frozen in time. There is horror as they register that I now stand alone, no younger child to be seen; that I'm pointing towards the precipitous edge, my eyes squinting hard as I try to shed tears. There are no other walkers on this stretch of path, no one to say what really happened when my brother departed the cliff edge, but the sharp cries of distress from the winding path far below suggest that there are witnesses to his arrival further down.

It wasn't your fault, it wasn't your fault, it wasn't your fault. This was the refrain of my slow-eyed mother in the weeks that followed, while she tried her best to absolve me, to put one foot in front of the other, to grasp at some semblance of normality. 'It wasn't your fault,' she'd tell me at night-time as she tucked the duvet snugly around my shoulders, our eyes never straying to the now-empty bed inhabiting the nook on the opposite side of my tiny childhood room. 'It was just a terrible accident.' But, as I look back now, I think perhaps I can hear the grain of uncertainty in her tone, the little tremor betraying the questions she will never voice. *Did you do it, sweetheart? Did you push my baby from the path? Was it just an accident? Was it?*

And, if I could speak with my mother now, what would I say in return? If I track further back into that same memory, to just a few seconds earlier, the truth is there for me alone to see. Now at the cliff edge I see two children. They're not identical in size and stature, but they're both dressed in bright blue anoraks to match their parents, the smaller with his hood tightly fastened beneath a chubby chin, the bigger one, hood down, oblivious to the sting of the icy rain. 'Mine!' the smaller one says, unsuccessfully snatching at a sherbet lemon held loosely between the older child's dripping fingers. This goes on for a while, and on reflection I think that perhaps the sweet *did* belong to the younger child, because eventually it is snatched away and I recall the sense that it wasn't mine to covet in the first place. But that is not the point, because it wasn't the taking of the sweet that was so wrong but the boastful, taunting manner of it. '*No!*' is the cry I hear, and I know it comes from me because even now I feel the rage rear up inside me as that hooded child makes a great pouting show of shedding the wrapper and popping the yellow lozenge into its selfish hole of a mouth, its bragging form swaying in a small victory dance at the slippery cliff edge. The tremor of my cry is still vibrating in my ears as I bring the weight of my balled fist into the soft dough of that child's cheek and see the sherbet lemon shoot from between rosy lips like a bullet. '*No!*' I shout again, and this time the sound seems to come from far, far away. Seconds later, he's gone, and I know he's plummeting, falling past the heather-cloaked rocks and snaggly outcrops that make up this great mountainous piece of land. I know it is a death drop; I know it is a long way down. I can't say I remember pushing him – but neither can I remember *not* pushing him.

So, you see, I'm not to blame at all. From what I recall of

that other child – my brother – he was a snatcher, a tittle-tattle, a cry-baby, a provoker. Even if I did do it, there's not a person on earth who would think I was culpable.

I was *seven*, for God's sake.

1. Casey

What a morning! What a strange and wonderful morning. It had started so badly, when I woke early after a fitful night's sleep, feeling fat and ugly as I stared into the mottled bathroom mirror, almost beside myself with stomach pains. My eyes were puffier than usual and bloodshot, and in the dawn light of the tiny room I actually wondered if I was getting a moustache. But that low feeling is now a distant memory, because the bright and magnificent thing that happened next quite banished it to the shadows.

I suppose I'm lucky living on this street, unexceptional as it is, in that the post arrives early each day. Not like at home – my *old* home – where the post didn't come until well after midday, and the postman was a grumpy old woman with a crew cut and too many earrings. Postwoman, I should say. Or is it postperson these days? I don't know; these things change so often, it's almost impossible to keep up. I only learned last year that it's no longer considered acceptable to use the expression 'coloured', but apparently that one's been non-PC for years. I count my blessings for the television and the internet, which educate me in these things, or else I'd be getting it wrong all over the place. Can you imagine how mortifying it would be to be caught out like that, to be accused of being a racist simply by not keeping up to date, for not knowing because nobody told you and you didn't happen to read about it and it never occurred to you that these things might change while you weren't paying attention? Not that I mix with a great variety of people these days, despite the fact that London is quite the cosmopolitan city. I don't mean that I *choose* not to mix with them; it's just that I don't mix with *any* people very much, not since my teens, anyway. Oh, but now I think of it there's the chap behind the counter at the local post office, who I would guess must be Indian or Pakistani, although his name badge says 'Harold'. His skin is a deep mahogany and I can't even begin to think what age he might be, though he seems both young and old at the very same time. Is it wrong of me to think of *Harold* as a white name? I suppose it is. Not that it matters at all, of course. I don't mind who serves me at the post office, and Harold is always very helpful and polite. I'm proud to say I've never had a racist thought in my life.

Anyway, the postman who delivers to *this* street is young and male (and white, as it happens) and from the few exchanges we've had I'd describe him as quite the charmer. When I say young, I mean he's about my age, mid-thirties, with the brightest green eyes, and a mischievous smile that makes me blush from my collarbone to the roots of my hair. I don't get too many parcels that won't go through the letterbox, so it's rare for him to have to knock on the door, and the few bits of mail that I do get have usually landed on the mat before I can snatch a glimpse of him through the front window. In the old days, my work documents would arrive in hard copy, thick

12

bundles of A4 enclosed in padded envelopes, often requiring a signature on delivery. So I saw a lot of Ms Crew Cut over the years at Mum's. But in recent times things have changed for the humble proofreader, and now almost all my work comes via email, a condition of my freelance contract being that I own a decent printer to run off documents myself. The whole arrangement seems a bit off to me, because, while these publishers can't be bothered to send a hard copy to me, they still demand that I return my corrected documents to them by post, so I have to go through the hell of a trip to the post office at least once a week, skirting the long way around to avoid passing the old house with its nosy neighbours and difficult memories. If it weren't for my regular postal excursion, I don't think I'd leave the house at all. And why would I? I love it here. I loved it from the moment I laid eyes on the place and decided I would have it. It's never a cause for celebration when someone in your family dies, but without my recent legacy I would never be living here so happily. I'd been longing for my own space for years and Mother's money was a godsend.

Goodness, I'm still sitting here at the table by the front window, gazing out into the morning as my mind jumps about all over the place! I think perhaps it's a symptom of living alone, although I fear it was probably the same when I was living with Mum. At times, when I struggle to focus like this, I will pinch the soft skin of my underarm until it makes my eyes water and forces me to concentrate on just the one thing. Well, the postman is in my thoughts, but of course he isn't the main point of this excitement, delightful as it is to remember answering the door and finding him standing there. He was looking especially chirpy today, and he gave me a wink, and made a pleasing cluck-cluck sound with his mouth as he walked away. 'Have a good day, love,' he called back without turning, and he vanished into the next street on the corner of my terrace. I pressed myself against the doorframe after he'd gone, trying to sustain the physical memory of him, glad that I'd brushed my long hair so diligently last night.

The parcel contained a gruesome biography I'd ordered online about the London killer John Christie, plus a new thesaurus to replace the one I spilled tea all over last week when I drifted off on the sofa. Delivered with the parcel were a few marketing flyers and, to my surprise, a handwritten letter addressed to the previous owner, Olivia Heathcote. How odd, I thought initially, that this was the very first piece of mail I'd ever received for my predecessor, but then it struck me that of course she must have put a forwarding arrangement in place, and, now that twelve months had elapsed, any residual letters would start to fall through my door. I can't say why exactly, but just holding that envelope in my fingers, with its curly handwritten address and its opening flap sealed by the tongue of a stranger – well, it rendered me quite breathless. I placed it down on the table and gazed upon it for a while, running my palms over my painful belly, trying to ease the bloating that had seized me in the night. I'm overweight, it's fair to say, but today my stomach felt even more distended with trapped gas, griping and twisting away inside me like a snake. I'd been forced to open the windows in my bedroom when I rose, just to let out the terrible whiff of it. It's a curse.

Breathing deeply through my discomfort, I went over the logistics of returning the letter to the post office. I had two manuscripts parcelled and ready to go, so it would be no bother to return this item at the same time – but then, I countered, wouldn't it be ridiculous to hand them an envelope absent of a return address? Surely they could do nothing with it? There would be no way of getting it back to the sender, and I'm quite certain it would have ended up in their recycling bin. Finally, I decided to open up the envelope and see if it contained a sender's address within, and then return it. That, I swear, is what I intended to do.

Once I had read the contents, however, my thoughts were taken in an entirely different direction and I realised I'd been handed a gift. And that is why, an hour later, I haven't moved an inch, and I sit here clutching the letter, blinking in astonishment at the last few words: *With love, Martha x*

Dear Liv,

If this letter finds its way to you, I know it will come as a surprise that I'm getting in touch after all this time. I can only say I'm sorry to have left it so long. It's hard to believe that eighteen years have passed, and yet they have. But let me get to the point.

Perhaps you've seen me on TV in recent years? I'm not saying this to brag, but because my latest project is a new show that investigates 'cold cases' – historic police investigations that have either been closed down or forgotten about, but where we believe there's a chance to solve them with fresh evidence or modern forensics. I hope you won't think it gratuitous; after what happened with Juliet, well, I suppose it's made me want to delve deeper into these unsolved crimes, to try to make a difference. The show is called Out of the Cold, *and we've just begun work on our very first programme – and this is my reason for making contact. We're going to be investigating Juliet's disappearance.*

15

I know this will upset you. Believe me, I thought long and hard before suggesting we feature her story – but remember how we all said at the time that there had to be more to it than the police would ever consider? We all knew there was no way Juliet would have disappeared like that by choice, but now, Liv, I really feel there's a chance we could find out exactly what happened and bring someone to account.

I can't tell you much more now – but I'll fill you in on everything once you've confirmed you're willing to talk. This could be in person, by email, on the phone or however you prefer, and all we would be asking you for are your memories of that time. I feel sure that the not-knowing will have haunted you as much as it has me, and I hope with every fibre of my being that you will agree to help. What I can tell you is that David Crown remains a person of interest, so anything you can recall about him will be of help right from the start.

Liv, I hope you are well and happy. I hope above all that you'll forgive me for past mistakes – and make contact.

With love,

Martha x

The morning sun casts fingers of light across the letter, picking out the dust bobs that float in the space between me and the net curtains to the street beyond. There's a tremor running through me, a juddering reverberation like the one I feel when heavy lorries rumble up the road and rattle the glass panes. But this is different. This comes from within. I turn over the envelope, smoothing it out on the tabletop, running my thumb across the handwritten indentations of the address. My address, but not my name. *Olivia Heathcote.*

Martha Benn – *the* Martha Benn – thinks that *I* am Olivia Heathcote. She thinks she is writing to Liv Heathcote, and she wants her help in this unsolved case. It's a case I recall only too well; it disturbed my mother terribly, the idea of that poor girl vanishing so close to where we lived, and for several weeks afterwards she insisted I wasn't allowed out alone, even in daylight hours. It made the national news for a while, until the police concluded that she had eloped with an older man. But I didn't believe that for a minute – and I'm guessing that Martha doesn't believe it either.

I push back my chair and stand shakily, the names swimming across my mind like new friends: Martha, Liv, Juliet, David Crown. I must lie down; it's all rather too much, and for the first time in an age I almost wish my mother were here to share in this excitement. I ease myself into the sagging sofa – my, how it sags – and position my neck against one armrest, catching a waft of body odour as I lug my legs up and over the other. Does it sound dreadful to confess I can't remember the last time I took a bath? The shower hose is broken, but that's no excuse as I've always preferred a bath anyway. If I'm to meet up with Martha Benn – and it's quite possible that this really could happen – I need to buck up my ideas. I'll run a bath this afternoon, after I've had a little rest. I close my heavy eyelids, dropping swiftly into the darkness of slumber, allowing myself to imagine something new. How would it feel to be 'Liv'? I wonder. How would it feel to be someone else altogether?

17

2. Martha

The rest of the team is in the boardroom when Toby Parr turns up for the production meeting five minutes late, and Martha does all she can to keep the irritation from her face as he strolls through the door, pushing back his sunkissed flop of hair and smiling broadly. She hasn't seen him for eight or nine years, but still he exudes the youthful confidence of the privately educated, that self-assured aura of life membership that Martha dismisses as wholly unearned, awarded too freely. Does she feel like this just because of who he is, or would she resent him if they met under different circumstances? He's almost a decade younger than her; he can only be in his mid-twenties. But it's not just that – after all, she's only too grateful that older colleagues were willing to take a punt on her when she was younger and in need of a chance. Well, there you have your difference, she thinks: she *needed* a chance, and really, he doesn't.

'Morning, all!' Toby says, too breezily for a newcomer, eliciting polite murmurs and tight smiles from around the room. Martha takes in the neutral faces at the boardroom table. Many of these people are senior to Toby, and yet there's curious caution in their open expressions.

In the far corner of the room are a cameraman and a sound technician, there to record early footage for the piece. They will film the entire meeting, yet only seconds will be used in the final edit: well-chosen slices that add colour and depth to the documentary, to the mystery. An earnest frown here, a studious turning of papers there. It's not just a documentary they're making. It's entertainment. Martha has a sense of being somewhere outside of herself, looking in on this surreal scene. How is it that she should find herself here, star of a show that may unravel her own past, opening her up to the scrutiny of others? The world knows the Martha Benn she has become, the polished, glossy-haired, media-savvy Martha – queen of the primetime talk show, go-to woman for serious reportage and debate. To her viewers she's clean-cut, a poor East End girl come good. Respectable. Nothing more murky in her past than an early divorce and a couple of tenuous romantic links to minor celebrities. This morning at home, as she prepared herself for the day, she had gazed out across London, sipping strong black coffee – her one caffeinated drink of the day – and again she had been struck by the feeling that she was living someone else's life. There she was in her twelfth-floor apartment, a glass-walled luxury abode overlooking the river, and she wondered how long it would be before she was rumbled.

Sending that letter to Olivia Heathcote had only been the start of it, but reaching back in time like that has unsettled her more than she could ever have anticipated. If the letter has reached her, will Liv even respond? Perhaps, like her, Liv has moved on, reinvented herself; perhaps Liv would rather keep that particular box tightly sealed too. They've all got secrets to hide, of that much Martha is certain. Her

19

new TV show, this investigation, could well be the catalyst to her unmasking. Not that she's ever pretended to be anyone else, or gone out of her way to deceive. Martha Benn is the name she was given at birth; she kept it even during her brief marriage to Denny, much to his family's distaste. And she's never exactly *lied* about her past. But nor has she been open about her earlier life, having long ago become accustomed to skirting over her Stanley House years, skipping straight to the good bits, the bits she can talk about with ease. The life she has constructed is about to change; she knows this without a shadow of a doubt. And there's nothing she can do about it, not if she's determined to unravel the mystery of Juliet. And she *is* determined. Whatever it takes, whether Juliet is found dead or alive, Martha *has* to find out.

Now, at the top end of the table, executive producer Glen Gavin nods at Toby pleasantly, offering a help-yourself gesture towards the trolley bearing drinks and pastries, and rises to close the door and open the meeting. Glen is a lean man, his small frame nipped in by expensive suits, yet his presence is nonetheless large in the room, magnified further by the deep timbre of his Scottish accent. Beyond him and the glass wall of their top-floor office, the London skyline fans out, bathed in the bright white sheen of a winter morning.

'Good morning, everyone.' Glen pauses, his eyes following Toby as he sets down his coffee in front of the one remaining seat and unbuttons his jacket, slipping it from his shoulders and placing it on the back of his chair. It's all done in such a leisurely fashion, Martha could scream – and a flash of flint in Glen's eyes momentarily betrays his mixed feelings about the appointment of Toby Parr.

'So,' Glen says, 'it's hugely exciting to be gathered at the first planning meeting for *Out of the Cold* and I for one am thrilled that we have managed to assemble some of our very best to turn this vision into a reality.'

He falls silent, and it's only when one of the junior researchers releases an awkward, 'Woo!' that the rest of the team realise what's expected. They fall into a wave of polite British hand-clapping.

'Now,' Glen continues. 'Let me summarise our overall plan. The pilot for *Out of the Cold* is provisionally scheduled to air six months from now, so the timings will be tight. It goes without saying that we're relying on the success of this to help us secure the proposed series with the network. Our pilot needs to be a showstopper, and that, my friends, is why you're all sitting around the table.' He rises from his chair and ambles towards the trolley, picking out an apricot Danish, taking a bite and chewing slowly as he eyes each of the team in turn. When his mouthful is swallowed he continues to speak, and he places the pastry on a napkin on the table before him, sliding his chair out to take a seat. He won't eat the rest of it; it's merely a prop. Martha's gaze travels up from the pastry and finds Glen's eyes locked on hers as he says her name.

'We're very happy to confirm that the show will be fronted by Martha Benn, who you'll all be familiar with from her work on ITV – well, across a number of the channels, in fact – with Toby Parr playing a key role as her associate programme researcher.'

Martha nods. Toby raises a hand, like a schoolboy receiving an award from the head teacher. She wonders, momentarily, what they all made of her sacking from breakfast TV last year, when she had been replaced by a younger, pregnant up-and-coming star. *More relatable*, was the way her female boss at the time had put it. *Younger*, was what she really meant.

Glen continues. 'Our pilot episode will investigate the eighteen-year-old case of missing teenager Juliet Sherman,

21

seventeen – who was last seen on a London towpath in January 2000, beside the Regent's Canal, where her abandoned bike was later discovered. Juliet came from what you'd call a nice middle-class family. Dad was a bank manager, Mum worked part-time for a local firm of solicitors. Juliet had one sibling, older brother Tom, who was back from university on his Christmas break at the time of her disappearance. All of them were interviewed at the time, but none of the family was ever considered a suspect. Within a matter of weeks, the police made the decision to scale back the investigation, ultimately concluding that she had run away with an older man . . .' Glen riffles through his papers, glancing towards Martha for help.

'David Crown,' she offers. 'Local landscape gardener and charity worker.'

'Yes.' Glen nods slowly. 'David Crown. All-round good guy.'

There's a ripple of amusement around the table, and Martha bites down an urge to pound her fists on the table, to tell them all to show a bit of bloody respect.

'This is an interesting case, and one that will resonate with the public – not only in the light of recent high-profile abuse cases, but also because our own Martha here was interviewed as part of the original police investigation.'

A murmur rises, a gasp; querulous frowns turn into pleased expressions of surprise.

'Martha, perhaps you'd like to take over from here?' Glen says, and he offers up his palms, gesturing for her to speak as he relaxes back into his chair.

She hadn't expected the surge of nerves that courses through her body, the heart-thumping weight of responsibility she feels in this moment.

'Thank you, Glen,' she says warmly, ever the professional, and she picks up a pen, tapping it lightly on the wrist of her other hand, a movement that apes her own private mindfulness exercises for calm. 'Yes, I was involved in the original case.' Her mind is working fast, and she is careful to keep the emotion from her voice, to state only the facts and none of the profound sadness she still feels. 'Back in 2000, I attended Bridge School in Hackney, along with Juliet Sherman and another schoolfriend, Olivia Heathcote – the three of us had been best friends for over seven years.'

The silence in the room is palpable.

'I think it's important to say that the reason I suggested the new show, and Juliet's case in particular, is because I recently read a local news article about her father's desire to find out what happened to his daughter. He has terminal cancer, and his wife – Juliet's mother – died a few years back, still not knowing. This is a family that has been beset by tragedy, and it feels like the right time to launch a new investigation. Time is running out for Alan Sherman. If we are successful, it will be a good thing we're doing.'

Quite to Martha's surprise, the room breaks into spontaneous applause.

She nods in acknowledgement, speaking quickly to move things on. 'When Juliet went missing, Olivia and I were among the first to be interviewed, in part because of our close friendship with her – they wanted to know if we had any information about boyfriends or family disruptions at home – but more importantly because the two of us were among the last people to see her alive.'

Now Martha hands a photograph down the table for Glen to pass around. It shows the three friends, sitting on the grass on a school trip to London Zoo, taken perhaps a year or two before Juliet went missing. Juliet and Martha have a similar look, both wearing their light brown hair long with outgrown fringes,

23

the difference in their height unremarkable when seated. In reality Juliet had been a good two inches taller than Martha, and, while there was a passing resemblance, Juliet was simply more beautiful, her skin more honeyed, her green eyes more flaming than Martha's dull brown. Looking at that photograph now, she recalls just how much she followed Juliet's lead. Juliet was always the first to risk the latest trend or hairstyle, and Martha invariably followed suit. Liv's appearance was dark to their fair, and she was the smallest of them all. She'd been adopted at birth, and the little she knew of her heritage was that her mother had been Irish and her father Sri Lankan, the physical legacy being her striking combination of dark olive skin and startling blue eyes. At barely five foot one she was tiny, something that had driven her wild when the others were routinely served alcohol at the Waterside Café bar while she had to hide out of sight for fear of being kicked out. Martha feels a pang of longing as the photograph circulates around the table. How could she have forgotten what Juliet and Liv had meant to her? Back then, in their adolescent years, they had been everything to each other.

'And were you able to help?' Toby asks, leaning his elbows on the table, his brow knitted together. He clears his throat, his volume seeming to increase in response to the delay in her answer. 'Were you ever a suspect?'

'*No*,' Martha replies, rather more tartly than she'd intended. Inwardly, she gathers her patience. 'I told the police that I knew Juliet was seeing someone, but I couldn't say who, because I didn't know. Juliet had told me that it was someone her parents wouldn't approve of, but that was all. Of course, the police were particularly interested in that. The last movements we're certain of were just after nine p.m. We'd had a few drinks in the Waterside Café – it was a Friday night – and as we left Liv decided to stay on for another, so I walked with Juliet some of the way along the canal before she headed off to work on her bike. That's the last time she was seen alive – or at least mine was the last confirmed sighting.'

Martha pauses a moment, expecting questions, and when there are none she continues. 'When I say "work", Juliet was a volunteer with Square Wheels, a charity set up and run by David Crown, which was basically a group of youngsters on bikes, handing out food and warm drinks to homeless people sleeping rough along the riverside. According to David Crown and her fellow volunteers, Juliet didn't turn up for her shift that night.'

One of the team, Juney, raises her hand. Her voice is light, slightly lisping, belying the deep intelligence of the young woman. 'And David Crown was a prime suspect? If he *was* a predator, perhaps it makes sense – setting up a volunteer group that brings him into regular contact with young people? It makes perfect sense to conclude that *he* was the mystery boyfriend, doesn't it?'

Martha nods. 'Yes, and I think that's the theory the police were working with. But David Crown's records came up fairly unblemished, and it seems that because it had been such a busy night, with plenty of volunteers on hand, there wasn't a moment that he couldn't account for in one way or another. He had alibis coming out of his ears.'

'But you're not convinced?' asks Glen.

'I just don't know. I helped out with Square Wheels myself on a number of occasions, and, while I agree that the evenings were always busy, it's not true that David was *never* alone with any of the helpers. Usually, once he'd handed out supplies to everyone, we were sent off in pairs – for safety – and if there was anyone left over, they'd pair up with David to do the final handout. On the occasions I was there, Juliet and I naturally

25

paired off, but as I wasn't there that night I think it's perfectly feasible that Juliet doubled up with him, or was at least alone with him at some point in the evening. She was running late that night – she was meant to get there at eight-thirty – so it's quite possible that David Crown was alone at the Square Wheels cabin by the time she arrived.'

'And his wife?' Toby asks, running his finger down the briefing notes in front of him. He's frowning studiously. 'Wasn't she one of his alibis?'

'Yes, but only for later that evening,' Martha replies, glad to see that at least Toby *has* come prepared, has read the overview she sent him last week. 'So, it would have been difficult for David to account for *every* moment between nine and midnight. But on the other hand there were enough volunteers coming and going that night to make it almost impossible for him to have abducted Juliet without someone noticing. The police notes I have tell us that the following morning he and his wife Janet were interviewed extensively. She claimed that he returned home at the usual time, eleven-thirty, give or take a few minutes, and that he seemed completely normal. David had told her that it had been a successful night, and they'd managed to deliver meals to at least forty homeless people along the riverside. There was a hard frost that night, and he was always particularly pleased when they managed to help people out when conditions were so harsh. Mrs Crown said that her husband was in good spirits, and that they went to bed soon after he returned, with nothing seeming out of the ordinary. After the police interview that morning, David Crown went off to his landscape gardening job as usual. But he never came home again.'

'Never?' asks Juney.

'No, he disappeared as completely as Juliet had. Later, it was discovered that on that same morning a large sum had been withdrawn from the Crowns' joint savings account, and when Mrs Crown searched their home she found a number of his personal belongings missing – his passport, a suitcase and several items of clothing. And that's why the police concluded that Juliet and David had been in some kind of a relationship, and had planned the whole thing, with her going into hiding the night before and him following behind once he'd gathered his money and belongings. The investigation continued for a few weeks longer, but with the emphasis on finding a missing "couple", rather than searching for a teenager abducted by a man.'

'How much money did David Crown withdraw?' asks Toby.

'Fifty grand. According to Mrs Crown it was their life savings.'

There are intakes of breath around the table, everyone breaking out into their own thoughts.

'It sounds fairly viable to me,' offers Toby. 'I mean, we've all heard about these cases, haven't we – teacher falls in love with pupil and they go on the run? This sounds similar, except that Juliet was a bit older. I mean, while David Crown wasn't a teacher, he was an authority figure as far as she would've been concerned.' Toby glances around, looking for nods of approval, which he receives.

'That's all fine,' Martha replies, wondering how on earth she's going to tolerate working with him. 'Until you take into consideration Juliet's track record and the responses of every single person who knew her. Juliet was, for want of a better expression, a goodie-goodie. She was an A-star student, hardworking, diligent – a rule-follower. She put me and Liv to shame. She was committed to her volunteer work. She loved her parents, and had a great relationship with them both.'

'It says here that they split up within a year of Juliet going missing,' Toby interrupts, as if this fact makes a difference.

27

'She had a great relationship with both her parents,' Martha repeats, ignoring him. 'And, to be perfectly honest, she never really seemed that bothered about boys. She was a beautiful girl and I remember she was always being asked out, but she just wasn't interested.'

'In *boys*, perhaps not,' says Toby. 'But this was a *man*. David Crown was, what, mid-forties? Was he good-looking? Perhaps she saw something in him that she hadn't seen in the lads of her own age? Perhaps she was attracted to his maturity. Girls often go for older men, don't they?'

Martha feels a rush of anger, hating Toby for what he's suggesting about her friend – and, more specifically, what he's saying about *her*. She knew he wouldn't be able to resist a dig at some point or other, and she avoids looking up to see who else around the room has understood his meaning. She fingers through her papers and slides another photograph into the centre of the table. Backsides lift out of seats to lean in for a closer look, and noises of assent rise up into the room.

'Thanks for that pearl of wisdom, Toby,' she says, delivering her best patronising smile. 'But, for the record, just being OK-looking doesn't automatically make a man irresistible to every woman.'

A ripple of laughter travels the room, which Toby deftly disregards as he brings his finger down on David Crown's face. 'Ladies, correct me if I'm wrong – but I'd say our Mr Crown is a bit more than OK-looking, wouldn't you?'

And to Martha's irritation there's not a person in the room who disagrees. Yes, Martha thinks, David Crown was attractive – but she and her friends had soon got over that, she's certain, once they'd come to know him better. After Martha's first few encounters with him, he had been just David, hadn't he? They'd stopped noticing how handsome he was, because . . . well, just because. He was just *David*.

Glen Gavin reaches out and pulls the photograph towards himself, holding it up high, gaining the attention of all.

'OK, OK, so we're agreed he's an attractive man. But Martha, I think it's fair to say you're not convinced that your friend ran off with this man?'

Thank God for Glen Gavin and his brooding presence.

'No, I'm not. Speaking as someone who knew Juliet better than most, I am absolutely convinced that she came to harm that night. Now I don't know if David Crown is behind it – up until that night I had always thought him to be a good guy too – but Juliet just running away like that, with no note, taking nothing, leaving her bike abandoned on the edge of the towpath? It's out of the question. And, even if they *had* run away together, surely someone would have heard from them or seen them together in the years that have passed. David Crown never made another withdrawal from his account, and his passport was never used, so it's as if *he* vanished from the planet too.'

'Of course it's possible there's no sign of him because he's *dead*, right? I mean, it has been eighteen years,' Toby says, prodding away. He gives a shrug. 'Just playing devil's advocate.'

Martha wants so badly for all these people to be on her side. Not just to make this documentary – but to at last find out what happened to Juliet. To *find* Juliet.

'No, it's a fair question,' she says, maintaining her calm, tucking a strand of auburn hair behind her ear. 'According to the original interviews, his wife believed that he ran away after the pressure of the police questioning – which she made a formal complaint about, by the way – because it brought back memories of a previous false allegation. It turns out that many years earlier he had lost his job as a teacher in Bedfordshire after a sexual assault claim from a female pupil. The girl's claim was retracted completely, so no charges were ever brought against him, but Mrs Crown believes this later suspicion relating to Juliet pushed him into taking flight. She said he was fearful that the police would wrongly put the two events together and try to pin Juliet's disappearance on him. The last time his wife was interviewed was, what, five years ago?' Martha consults her notes. 'Yes, five years ago – it was a local reporter doing a history piece on the Regent's Canal. At that time, Mrs Crown said she continued to believe her husband had simply run away – by himself – and was afraid to return. She still lives alone in the same house, and it seems she's never quite got over her husband's disappearance. In the interview she said she lives in hope that he'll one day come home.'

'So he *was* a teacher,' Toby says.

Glen waves away Toby's comment. 'If he's alive, surely someone would have heard from him over the years?'

'Perhaps they have? It seems Mrs Crown is fiercely protective over her husband's reputation. If she still loves him, I doubt she would let on that he's been in touch. Especially if, in reality, she suspects he *did* kill Juliet.'

'But if she thinks her husband is a killer, surely she would have turned him in?' says Toby.

Martha shakes her head, irked by his naivety. 'People make all manner of bad choices in the name of love. She may have been in denial initially. Or she may have come to accept that he did kill Juliet, but justified it in her own mind. Whatever the truth is, I suspect she knows more than she's let on up to now.'

'And what about the schoolgirl who made the allegation?' asks Juney. 'Do you think David Crown was guilty of that assault?'

Martha glances towards Glen, who is already familiar with her theory. She looks around the room, taking in the eight earnest faces – the researchers and assistants, Jay and Sally, the camera crew – and she says a silent prayer. Please, Liv, please answer my letter so I'm not alone in this.

She nods in reply. 'Yes. I think David Crown was guilty of assaulting that schoolgirl, and I think he was guilty of murdering Juliet – and I think he could still be out there right now.'

3. Casey

This dressing table came from my old bedroom, a gold-leaf and cream piece from the seventies, part of a matching suite my mother and Dad had bought when they were newlyweds, before passing it on to me when they updated their room. It has a swing mirror, with curling, swirling patterns up and around the glass, and even now I'm drawn to run my fingertip along it, travelling the meandering curves from one side to the other. It was one of the few pieces of furniture that I brought with me when I moved, along with Granny's heavy crystal ashtray. As a child, I loved to watch its rainbow of colours on a bright day, when the sun would thread beams of light through the cut glass to dance upon the bedroom wall. The dressing table seemed to be the most important item of furniture to have, knowing how much it had meant to Mum, how many hours she had spent in front of it, rolling her hair, carefully applying her mascara and painting her lips. I would perch on the corner of my parents' bed, watching each action with the greatest attention in case I might one day be asked to repeat the art, although now as I peer into it at my own reflection the idea seems laughable. Once, when I was fifteen or sixteen, I borrowed Mum's crimson lipstick and applied it, just as I'd seen her do so many times, on my way out for a wander in the park to spy on a lad I'd seen there a few times before. As I passed through the living room, my mother did a double-take and laughed, a hard, flat 'Ha!', before calling my dad in to take a look. 'She looks like she's been eating jam doughnuts!' she told him, her hand covering her mouth, and, although Dad didn't reply, I could see in his eyes that he was furious with her. She was heading into one of her low moods, but that was no excuse for such cruelty. Dad saw my tears getting ready to spill over, and he put his arm around me and took me to the bathroom, where he helped me to blot the colour down until it was merely a hint. 'You look beautiful,' he whispered, and he indicated for me to go out through the back to avoid another confrontation. But I don't want to think about that; I prefer the memory of sitting on the corner of their bed, the furrows of the pink candlewick bedspread soft beneath my fingers. I enjoyed the silence of those moments, but at the same time I think I yearned for her to speak, for us to talk and laugh together like all those mothers and daughters I'd seen on TV. I'd watch and wait for minutes on end, but so often she simply continued with her beautifying rituals and afforded me only the briefest of glances, an invitation in her immaculate raised eyebrow. 'You look pretty,' I would tell her, and then the room would brighten with the radiance of her smile.

Now, I lean in and pull down my lower lids, fascinated by the map of veins I can magnify if I blink hard and bulge my eyes wide. My face is round and pale – I'm nothing if not honest with myself – entirely absent of make-up or artifice. Lately I've been noticing the ever-increasing ratio of grey to black in my hair – I must have at least fifty per cent grey hairs – but how strange that they have now started showing up in my eyebrows too. I wonder about down below. I wonder if later, when I'm undressed, I'll be able to bend far enough forward to check there for any changes. It's quite possible that my fat belly will prevent me from getting a good view – that or my bad back, which seems to creak and shriek more and more often these days.

I pick up my bristle hairbrush and run it through my hair, one long stroke from forehead to tip, its length reaching as low as my thigh. 'One . . . two . . . three . . .' I count, automatically falling into the hundred-strokes habit Mum taught me in my early years, and as I gaze at my reflection my mind is once again on Martha and Liv, and the email I started writing this afternoon.

Of course, it was easy enough to set up a fake email address for Olivia Heathcote, but knowing what to say in my reply to Martha was a much harder task. I had spent a good couple of hours Googling Olivia – or *Liv*, as Martha calls her – but there was surprisingly little to be found, only the briefest of mentions about her work as a bereavement counsellor for a local clinic. What I already knew about her was gleaned from the two encounters we'd had during the sale of the house more than a year ago, the first when I visited for an initial viewing with the estate agent, the second a follow-up visit I had requested on the pretext of planning my furniture requirements. In reality, it was not the house but Olivia I wanted to see. It wasn't a crush by any means, but Liv had something about her, such a striking aura. Liv was the type of person who at school would have been popular with the other girls, would have been part of a tight group. She would have *belonged*. I had just wanted another look before I took over the house, and Liv and everything in her life disappeared from mine.

Liv had two children, four-year-old twins called Arno and Jack. They were beautiful too, olive-skinned creatures playing quietly on the faded living room floor, building a world of block towers and animals. Their tawny hair was in stark contrast to Liv's ebony bob and darker skin, but they shared her vivid blue eyes, and I thought how astonishing it was that a person like Liv could produce such fair children. She must have noticed me staring, because she laughed and said, 'You never know how the genes will come out in the wash!' And that's how I learned she was adopted as a baby, taken into this very home at just two months of age by Mr and Mrs Heathcote and their large, boisterous family. Liv was the middle of five, the only adopted child, and the only one 'of colour', as she put it. At one point, she told me, their grandmother was living here too, along with an ever-increasing menagerie of animals and birds. 'It was chaos most of the time,' Liv had told me, laughing at the memory. 'But happy chaos. We didn't have a lot, but my mum and dad were the best kind of people, if a bit gullible. They couldn't say no to anyone, so if someone in the street was threatening to get rid of some old pet or other we'd take it in here. "Hackney Zoo," that's what my friends used to call this place! Bonkers.'

The house is only a three-up, two-down, and I couldn't imagine for a moment how they had managed with so many children to care for in such a small space. But what colourful history! So unlike the details of my own small family, whose genealogy, my mother would proudly claim, went right back to the Domesday Book on both sides: English through and through. I loved that Liv's world was so different from mine, and if I could have stayed there all day long, drinking coffee and asking her questions about her childhood, I would have. Now, in light of my new role as her substitute, I wish I had!

When Liv introduced me to Arno and Jack they smiled so happily, as though greeting an old friend. How my heart had lifted in that moment! I couldn't remember the last time a child had smiled at me with such guileless ease. I'm not the sort of person people smile at easily; I don't have that special thing. On that final visit, I also managed to gather that Liv hadn't been living in the house for more than a couple of years, having moved back in after her mother had died. There didn't seem to be a husband or partner anywhere, but I supposed he was out at work or away on business – until Liv mentioned she was moving out of London altogether, 'for a fresh start'. I took this to mean alone, just the three of them, and this pleased me no end, though now I struggle to understand why it should. That was the last time I ever saw Liv, and a month later I was moving my belongings in, clutching tightly to my very own set of newly cut keys. My solicitor had told me I was paying well over the market price for the place when I offered more to see off another buyer's bid, but I knew I had to have it. And for heaven's sake, I'd thought when he advised me not to rush, what else was I to spend my money on? *This* was the house I wanted.

Today, after hours of staring into my laptop screen (and guiltily ignoring the bleeps of work emails dropping into my inbox!), I finally drafted a reply to Martha.

Dear Martha

How nice to hear from you. What a surprise. Of course I have seen you on the television and I have enjoyed watching your success. You must be so pleased. With regard to Juliet, I would be happy to help you in any way I can, but I am out of the country on business and will

not return for another week. I am a bereavement counsellor and sometimes I have to travel. But if you would
like to email me any questions you have, I can very easily
email you back. I hope you are well, and that we can
meet again some time in the future.

With best wishes, Liv x

I dithered over the kiss at the bottom for an age. Was it too
much? I wondered if I should say where exactly it was I'd gone
abroad, for authenticity – Italy, perhaps? Maybe Germany?
No, better to be vague. Brevity is the key, I concluded, after
deleting much of my earlier version – the details about my
children, my happy place of work and devoted partner – and
now I have this final draft, ready to go. I gave the message
a final read through, aloud, in a clear, confident voice, and
suddenly I was anxious that it might seem too eager if I sent
it straight away. Martha might not believe it's really Liv!
Imagine, if it was all to come to an end now, simply because I
got carried away with myself. So, I will send it early tomorrow
morning, and for now I must be content with the anticipation.
   As I sit facing myself in the dressing table mirror now,
the very thought of this adventure sends a jolt of adrenaline
through my veins. This is the most exciting thing to happen to
me in a long time, and I'm suddenly terrified it might be taken
away. What if the real Liv were to turn up again, confronting
my deception? I imagine inviting her in and offering her a
cup of tea, before bashing her over the head with my crystal
ashtray and burying her under the floorboards, just like old
John Christie in Rillington Place. I blink at my reflection, and
then I laugh, high and loud, clamping my hand to my mouth
to hold in the madness of it all.

4. **Martha**

She's been here before, recognises the still-water tang of the moonlit path, the creaking murmur of houseboats and wooden decking moored along the frozen bank. It's a shortcut home, one they've always taken in warmer months, but to be avoided alone after dark for fear of unseen dangers lurking in the shadows. To her right the frosted path meanders alongside the black water, disappearing into nothing as it stretches beyond the bridge. Her shallow breaths billow out in hot white clouds, misting her vision. To her left a homeless pair sit huddled beneath sleeping bags on the wooden bench, not looking in her direction, more interested in the sandwich packet and steaming tea they've just been handed. 'You're an angel,' one of them says, to no one in particular, his hand raised like that of a stained-glass saint. 'You're an angel.' The swishing burr of bicycle wheels, the ticker-tacker rush of air as they pass – six, eight, ten, twelve – it's hard to know how many there are, but the riders are all young – teenagers, sixth-formers – hair and knitted scarves streaming, ivory teeth gleaming through the darkness, handle-bars festooned with wicker baskets bearing fruit.

'Juliet!' a voice calls out from the followers, a voice chasing after the beautiful girl at the front. 'Jules! Wait!' And Martha realises it's her own voice she's hearing, she who is calling out, the urgency knotting her stomach like rope burn.

Incapable of movement, she watches the cyclists turn sharply where the path grows dim, and they nosedive, bikes and all, one after the other, disappearing like fish from a bucket through the glittering surface of the Regent's Canal. A fracture skitters across the frozen crust, breaking the waterway in two, causing the houseboats to tip and sway. She can't bear it, the motion of the water undulating beneath the nearest boat, the brightest of them all, and she sprints over the crunchy grass and reaches out for its wooden rails, desperate to steady the boat's movements, to silence the night. Her smooth school pumps slip on the frosty bank and she feels herself disappear into the water, fish-like herself, the ice closing up behind her.

It's a dream she's had before, or at least a version of it. Sometimes she's the one on the bicycle, and it's Juliet and Liv sitting on the wooden bench, eating sandwiches. Other times, she's watching, helpless, as Juliet floats by, trapped under ice, her eyes wild. And then there's the version where nothing happens; where Martha roams back and forth along that lonely path, looking, looking, looking, and finding nothing – seeing nothing, hearing nothing. In some ways, that's the worst dream of them all, infected as it is with the intangible qualities of helplessness and guilt.

I should have walked on with her, Martha tells herself, running her hands up and over her sleep-softened face, willing herself to rise from her position on the sofa, where she had sunk into sleep within moments of arriving home this evening. If Martha had walked on with her that night as she'd planned to – if she hadn't changed her mind and left her standing on that towpath alone – would Juliet be alive today?

She's been in the library all afternoon, going back over old newspaper articles about Juliet's disappearance, re-reading the media speculation, the sound-bite quotes from 'close sources'. Her head is full of it, the loose ends and unasked questions pressing against the inside of her mind, and she fears she is destined to dream of Juliet forever, at least until she finds the answers she seeks.

Wrung out, she glances around her living room, a study in contemporary design: a dash of minimalism here, a nod to the baroque there. When she'd signed the papers, Martha hadn't even asked about the decor – it was enough to know it would be new, stylish and easy to care for. Safe. It's a gated community of sorts, the kind Martha would once have scorned as pretentious, but she likes it: she's grateful to be locked in and secure. It's a long way from the damp-curled rooms of her childhood home in Hackney, social housing long since demolished to make way for gentrification. The clock on the far wall tells her it's 9.30 p.m. God, she'll never sleep now, she knows. She's been out cold for nearly two hours.

When her mobile rings, Martha cries out, and without thinking she grabs it from the side table, bringing it to her ear with a brusque, 'Hello?'

There's a rustling sound at the other end, the suggestion that the caller has dropped the phone and is trying to retrieve it. '*Shit*,' the voice says, gravelly, fumbling, his breath laboured and apologetic as he finally sorts the handset out. 'Shit. Sorry, Martha. Shit.'

Dread sinks through her like a weight. Why didn't she check the caller ID before answering? She finds herself frozen, much as she had been in her dream, the sense of helplessness returning like a memory, and her words won't come. Outside, the city roars past and the world keeps turning, life continuing on as ever.

'Martha?' At first his tone is soft and persuasive, but it takes only seconds for impatience to materialise, to betray itself as the stronger emotion. 'Come on, love,' he says, and his words are mashed. Drunk. Growing sing-song nasty. 'I kno-*ow* you're the-*ere*. I can hear you. I can hear the traffic. I can hear you *breathing*. Martha? Martha? *Martha!* Answer me, you hard-nosed cow!'

At his roar she snaps into movement, jerking the receiver from her ear and pressing the red end-call button. It's been months since she last heard from him, a year, even. What does he want with her? She made it clear she was done with him, done with that chapter in her life. She'd given him money, hadn't she? More than enough to set himself up, to make his own way. What more could he possibly want from her?

The following morning Martha and Toby are meeting at the café in the British Library, and when she arrives five minutes early she finds him already seated at a wall table with two coffees steaming in front of him. She started the day in a bad mood, having heard from Juney that they're still unable to establish the name of the girl at the centre of David Crown's school allegation, as it was never formally reported on at the time. Apparently no public records exist. Surely it shouldn't be so difficult to get this kind of information? How hard has Juney actually tried? But perhaps Martha is being unfair: how can she expect Juney to access information that doesn't exist in the public domain? For that, Martha needs an insider. Perhaps it's time to call in a few favours. She'll phone Finn Palin when she's finished here, see what he can do for her.

41

Of course, he's retired now, but Martha knows how the old boys' network operates inside the police force; she's certain he'll be able to track down that girl's name without too much fuss. He owes her that much at least.

Toby rises as she approaches, and she hates him for arriving ahead of her.

'I take mine decaffeinated,' she says, nodding towards the drinks as she removes her winter gloves. The wall lights cast a clean pool of white around him, like a halo, and she catches an amused look on his face as he clocks the spotty Dalmatian print of her gloves before she stuffs them in her bag.

'Decaf?' Toby replies. 'That's what I ordered.' He's unflustered, unflappable, gently pushing the white cup across the small table and taking his seat. 'I got us a flapjack to share too – in case you're hungry?'

Martha could eat a horse, having skipped breakfast to make it here on time, but still she shakes her head. God, she hates herself sometimes.

Giving no acknowledgement of her bad attitude, Toby places the case files on the table between them and flips open his reporter's notebook to reveal a page annotated with small, neat handwriting. He pushes at his floppy fringe. 'Well, I'll save you half anyway – in case you get peckish. So,' he says, taking a sip of his drink, 'yesterday seemed to go quite well, don't you think? The production meeting. I reckon Glen Gavin has put together a really good team. Juney is an excellent researcher. She's given us quite a lot of useful stuff already.'

Us. Jeez. *Out of the Cold* is not some kind of bloody partnership; *Martha* is the lead on this project. Toby Parr is her deputy. He'll get, what, five or ten minutes of airtime if he's lucky, and here he is behaving as though he's her co-presenter rather than some pipsqueak who's been foisted upon her by management. She eyes him coldly, trying to unbalance him, willing him to drop his cheery posh-boy mask and show what he really thinks of her. That she's just an estate girl made good, a poorly educated nobody to clamber across on his trouble-free, well-heeled way to the bloody top.

'Can you give me a summary of what we've got so far?' she asks him. It's a test, and from his change in expression he knows it.

'OK.' He pulls his notebook closer, studies it for a moment. 'First off, Juney has been in touch with the *Metro*, to place that "Can You Help?" ad you drafted. Should go in tomorrow at the latest, to run for five days.'

'Good. I don't hold out much hope of anyone useful coming forward, but you never know.'

Toby returns to his notes. 'To summarise: we have Juliet Sherman, aged seventeen, goes missing at around nine p.m. on a Friday night in January 2000, on a towpath beside the Regent's Canal. Last known person to see her alive is you, Martha Benn, seventeen-year-old school friend. That evening she'd also been with your mutual friend Olivia Heathcote, and her own brother Tom Sherman, at the Waterside Café bar, where you'd all had two, maybe three alcoholic drinks before Juliet had to leave for her voluntary job at Square Wheels. You walked with her along the canal, with your bicycles – it was dark, but lamp-lit – halfway to the Square Wheels cabin, before leaving her to walk the remainder alone as you returned to the bar for your forgotten bag. The roads nearby were fairly busy, with it being a Friday night, and you said you saw a number of other walkers and cyclists along the path, and that Juliet was in good spirits when you parted. As far as we know, no one else saw or spoke to her before she disappeared, but we don't believe she can have gone much further because her bicycle was found the next day only metres from the spot where you'd

43

parted. The person of interest is David Crown, leader of Square Wheels and local landscape gardener, who vanished a day after Juliet went missing, having withdrawn a large sum of money. Ultimately, the police concluded that Juliet and David had been involved in a secret affair, and that they left together of their own accord.' Toby pauses, looking for Martha's approval.

'Which is, of course, bollocks.'

'We know that the police interviewed everyone who saw Juliet that night, including her parents and David Crown, before he disappeared – but no one could shed any more light on the mystery. We now also know that there was a previous sexual assault allegation made against David Crown when he was a teacher, but that it was dropped and written off as a pupil's fabrication.' Toby runs his finger down his list. 'Have I missed anything?'

Martha gazes past him towards the busy foyer of the library café. 'Olivia and Juliet fell out earlier that night,' she says, bringing her focus back to Toby.

'Really?' He looks back at his notes, frowning as though he might have overlooked something.

'It wasn't reported on, because Liv didn't mention it in her interview.'

'But *you* knew about it?'

'I heard them – it was just before Juliet set off for work and the two of them had left the café ahead, while I said goodbye to Tom and a few of the others. When I got outside, I saw them around the corner – Juliet was unlocking her bike – and they were having a heated argument. *Really* heated. Liv was trying to stop Juliet from leaving, grabbing on to her coat, but Jules shook her off, pushed past. It stopped the minute they saw me.' Martha can see their panicked faces now, their rage quickly shutting down to avert her questions.

44

'You didn't mention this in the meeting yesterday.'

'No. And I didn't tell the police at the time either. Liv asked me not to.'

Toby's eyebrows furrow. 'Really? Didn't you think it was important to let them know? It could have been vital to the case.'

'Bloody hell, Toby. Were you ever a teenager, or were you born fully grown? We were *seventeen* – our best friend had just vanished, and we were terrified and guilty and grief-stricken. Liv didn't want anyone to know that they'd argued because she was just so ashamed that her last moments with Juliet were bad ones.'

'Do you know what the argument was about?' Toby asks.

'No,' Martha replies. 'I asked Juliet at the time – as we were walking away from the bar – but she dismissed it. Said Liv was just being a drama queen and it would blow over. She made it clear the subject was closed, so I didn't push it.'

Toby looks unconvinced.

'I was fine about not telling the police they'd been arguing. I mean, I knew Liv didn't have anything to do with Juliet's disappearance. But it always bothered me that Liv never told *me* what the argument was about. Those two – Juliet and Liv – their relationship with each other was always just that bit tighter than it was with me. They went back further, they'd known each other since primary school – I met them at the start of secondary. Of course, they bickered from time to time, but it never got serious or nasty. I don't think I'd ever seen them exchange cross words before that night.' She picks up her coffee cup. 'Or ever again.'

Toby adds a few neat lines to his notebook. 'You've written to Liv, you say? We really need to speak to her next, don't we? Find out what they were arguing about – see what else she might know. That's got to be a priority.'

'I'm on it,' Martha replies, suddenly irritated, sensing a suggestion that she doesn't know what she's doing. Scowling, she adds, 'And I'll give the orders, thanks, Toby. You do *know* I'm the lead here, don't you?'

There's a moment's silence as she stares him down, challenging him to disagree.

'Martha,' he says in a soft voice. 'I think we need to get this out of the way, don't you? Look, I really want this to work, and I really want to do the best I can for the show – for you. But it's going to be hard if you're going to pick me up on every little thing. It feels as if you don't trust me.'

'You have to *earn* someone's trust,' she replies, feeling her cheeks flush as she realises how uptight and clichéd she sounds. 'How can I trust you when I don't even know you?'

He smiles, not unkindly. 'But that's not true, is it? And even if it were, would you be as hard on someone who, well, who came to the job without any connection to you at all? Some graduate, or a junior from outside the team?'

She feels shame creeping beneath her collar, and she hides behind her coffee cup, stalling for time to think.

'Is it because of my connections on the board? Because everyone else seems to have got over that particular elephant in the room.' He gives a small laugh, self-conscious to have brought it up.

'Have they?' she replies, reaching across the table to break off a corner of the untouched flapjack. 'Everyone knows you leapfrogged several perfectly capable junior researchers to take this role – most of them women, I might add – and there's not a person on this project who thinks you got that job purely based on your qualifications or experience.'

'And there's not a person on this project who thinks you got this job without sleeping your way to the top.'

Martha would have made a show of alarm if Toby hadn't beaten her to it.

He clamps his hand to his forehead and curses, a whisper of a word. 'Crap. Martha, I'm sorry. That was a low blow.'

Now it's her turn to laugh, and she's not even sure whether it's relief or embarrassment she's feeling. 'So that's what people think, is it? That I slept my way to the top? Do people actually say that?'

Toby shrugs, looking as though he's about to retract his words, then shrugs again, defeated.

Well, I got what I wanted, Martha thinks, with no sense of victory. Good boy Toby tells it like it is.

'I've heard it said,' he murmurs, his shoulders dropping, his eyes downcast.

Wow, Martha thinks, she really has knocked the wind out of his sails. At once she feels like the school bully, and she hates herself all over again. 'So, exactly how many executives am I supposed to have shagged to reach these lofty heights?' She allows a humorous lilt to break through, a show of forgiveness, perhaps. Something.

Toby's eyes flicker up beneath his furrowed brow, and Martha sees the slightest glimmer of hope reignite.

'One?' she ventures. 'Two? Five? Ten?' He doesn't answer, but a slow smile starts to spread across his features as the number rises. '*More?!*' Martha demands, breaking into incredulous laughter and slumping against her chair back in disbelief.

Recovered, Toby stands and picks up their empty cups. 'Just the one,' he replies.

Martha rolls her eyes and snaps off another piece of flapjack, nibbling the corner of it like a petulant teenager. She blanks him, scrolling her forefinger down her phone, checking for new messages.

'I'll get us a refill,' Toby says, and if she didn't know better she'd think he was stifling a laugh. 'And then, please can we agree to a fresh start?'

He has her in the palm of his hand, Martha knows. What's the expression? Kill them with kindness? Well, he's slaughtered her. And despite herself she finds she likes him, and she has no choice in the matter when she agrees.

'OK. Fresh start.' Ignoring the chime of an email alert on her phone, Martha picks up the rest of the flapjack and takes a bite. 'What are you waiting for?' she asks through a full mouth. 'Fuck off and get those coffees. We've got work to do.'

5. **Casey**

I've barely slept a wink tonight, worrying myself into a state of high emotion over the email I sent to Martha this morning. As I lay in the darkness I ran over the words in my head, searching for clues that I had got it wrong. Had I misjudged what Martha wanted? It was true that there was some urgency in her original message, wasn't it? My stomach knotted and turned; at this rate I would be stuck on the toilet for most of the morning while my insides cleared out. It's a curse, I reminded myself, passed on from my mother. 'A delicate constitution,' Mum had called it. 'Irritable bowel syndrome' was the doctor's diagnosis, but not before I had endured over two decades of its tortures. Perhaps I should get up and take a tablet, I considered as I lay there biting down on my lower lip, fighting back the tears. But I must have carried on lying there in pain for at least another hour, writhing against the twist in my gut. Sometimes I think I must like it, to allow myself to suffer for any longer than I need to. Do I like it, the pain? Surely not.

Shortly after 3 a.m. I abandon sleep to make myself a cup of tea and swallow two of my anti-spasmodic tablets. The stomach cramps should ease in the next fifteen minutes or so, and in anticipation I cut myself a chunk of fruit cake to have with my tea, placing it on the side table as I fetch Martha's letter. Wincing, I lower myself on to the sofa to re-read it and reassure myself that I haven't got things muddled, haven't got it all wrong. Next, I open up my laptop and review my own – or rather Liv's – reply, and with a mixture of relief and impatience I feel satisfied that my message to Martha was well worded. *Appropriate*. So why, then, I'm wondering now as I bite into my cake, hasn't Martha replied immediately? I look at my watch, the small Timex that Dad gave me on my fifteenth birthday. It's a child's watch really, its pink leather strap now balding and cracked, and straining at my wrist on the last hole. Really, I ought to get the strap replaced, but I can't bring myself to part with the old one. It would seem so wrong to throw it away like any old rubbish.

I'm drifting again.

I sent the email to Martha at just after ten yesterday morning, and here I am almost a whole day later, and still no reply. To distract myself I've been researching her on the internet, and I'm surprised at how private she appears to be, skirting over her childhood in interviews and no mention of her missing friend Juliet anywhere to be found. I've added what I can to my notebook, and made a mental note to spend more time delving into Martha Benn's past. She's really quite the mystery! When, by the time I went to bed last night, there was no reply from her, I thought with irritation: Well, it can't be *that* important. I wrap my quilted gown closer, rearranging the belt with a cross tug. Maybe Martha has exaggerated the importance of Liv's role. Maybe she's playing games. Or more likely, I think with a sudden flash of embarrassment, she's a busy woman, and she hasn't had a chance to pick up her emails. Perhaps she's at one of those red carpet events you see in the glossies – an awards evening or a charity gala – or perhaps she's been out all night, wining and dining and signing autographs. That'll be it, I think now, feeling the pain in my stomach subside as my heart rate slows and my eyelids grow heavy. That'll be it. As sleep tugs at me, I imagine myself in a schoolroom, dressed in a smart uniform to match my three best friends, sitting together on a table of four: Martha, Liv, Juliet and me.

I remember my first year at infant school with clarity. I was four, one of the smallest and youngest in my class, and even now I can recall the overwhelming sense of being on the outside, separate from the other pupils in some unspeakable way. They slotted together naturally, even those who came from other places, the ones who arrived speaking in different words and accents, handicapped by language, perhaps, but not by character as I was. I am aware how harsh on myself I sound, but these are simply the facts. Of course, I didn't know it at the time, but many of these children were already acquainted from playgroup or nursery or from simply living in the same neighbourhood. That was always going to count against me, wasn't it, being a newcomer? And even if those children were previously unknown to each other, there was a thing – a 'sameness' about them that I lacked. A straightforward, easy-talking child-ness about them. It was a thing that allowed their arms to rest easy at their sides, their eyes to scan a crowd without fearful anticipation. A gift that let them be both noticed and blissfully unnoticed all in the same moment. I have never possessed that gift, then or since. Somehow I manage to be both invisible and horribly stand-out all at once. I sometimes think this lack in me is the source of everything

51

that is wrong in my life, every lurch of anxiety, every seizure of fear. How do you acquire that good, 'easy' thing? Is it something you can be taught? Is it something I could learn now, given a fresh chance to mix in the world?

To begin with, despite my awkwardness, the other children were pleasant enough. They were so young, and looking back it seems to me now that a child's default setting is probably one of kindness – just like those adorable Heathcote twins – until someone steers them off that path. In those first few days, some of them even tried to coax me into their playtime games of horsey or chase, but I must have put them off somehow, giving off that scent of discomfort and fear that popular children sniff out so quickly. All it had taken was one child to call me out – a beautiful boy with deep almond eyes – and I was marked as 'the one'. After all, I know, there always has to be a 'one', doesn't there? This is what we see in films and on television, what I read in my paperbacks and magazine short stories. Every group needs a 'one' – an imperfect person to shine light upon their own perfections, an ugly person to hold up a mirror to their beauty. Well, I was the one. 'Poopy Head!' was that boy's war cry in the concrete playground of St John's infant school, and he ran from me, archly pinching his nostrils and whooping a loud, 'Poo-poo!' as he went. Others joined in his dance, and soon there was a small army of them waiting for me in the playground at each break, prancing at my rear like merry shadows, plucking at their noses and giggling to the chorus of 'Poo-poo!' It stuck. If the teachers or playground monitors noticed, they showed no sign, and so it went on for weeks and months in its various guises, only stopping when my mother removed me from the school at the end of the academic year, never to return again. Thank goodness for Mum. She was hopeless in so many ways, but there's no denying she rescued me from that particular hell. She stepped up to the challenge when it really counted. 'We don't need *them*,' she told me as we marched back home on that last day, her back straight, her aquiline nose raised to the sky. That evening we sat at the kitchen table and made plans for my home schooling, my mother growing more excited with every jot of her pen, every plan that she hatched. 'And we'll have school trips to the science museum, and the planetarium – and Sea Life!' she told me, as Dad cooked spaghetti bolognese and wordlessly laid out the cutlery around us. 'Just you, me and a packed lunch for two!'

Mum looked lovelier than I'd ever seen her. She loved me so much that I thought she might explode with it, and me with her.

I stretch my leaden arms high above my head, easing out my aching limbs. I must stop dozing on the sofa like this; it plays havoc with the weakness in my neck, and taking painkillers only aggravates my delicate tummy. Shunting up to the edge of the cushions, I lift the lid on my laptop, resolving to do a bit more research on the girls. I've been building up a scrapbook of details, saving them to a special Pinterest board where I can view them as a whole. It's a bit like one of those police wall charts you see on TV, where the investigating officers stick up photographs of suspects and pieces of evidence, scrawling arrows and connectors between Post-it notes, building up momentum towards the inevitable eureka moment. My Investigation Wall is virtual, and visible to me alone. Already I've managed to track down a Year Ten photograph from a Bridge School alumni page I discovered on Facebook, although I'm struggling to work out which of the girls is Olivia. So many of the girls have that same generic nineties look: heavy-fringed and sulky, their ties worn short and stubby, loose at the neck. Martha I recognised straight away, so familiar am I with her famous face and that thick, flowing hair – though of course she wears it darker now, cut in a sophisticated bob – and Juliet, well, it was impossible not to notice her, so strikingly beautiful was she at fifteen. Like Martha, her hair is worn loose and gently wavy, a light honey-brown against so many bottle-dyed blondes and Morticia blacks. She is a natural beauty. Hers was the first face I was drawn to, and images from historic newspaper reports were easily found online to confirm it was her. I feel a sudden urgency to track down more details for them all, to further populate my Investigation Wall, to build up my case. I've always harboured secret ambitions to write a crime novel and I think perhaps all this research will serve me well as practice! At any rate, if Martha does get back to me, I need to make myself useful, to come up with some nugget of information she'll appreciate – something that will make me indispensible. It's vital that Martha continues to believe this is Liv she's talking to, that it's Liv she's confiding in. I'll start with a bit more digging on Martha and see where it takes me.

Just as I type the words 'Martha Benn' into the search bar, an email alert pops up in the top right-hand corner of the screen. 'From Martha Benn' it announces. Well, what are the chances of that, I marvel, and already I'm wondering if it is evidence of a connection deeper than either of us could ever know. I switch screens, hovering over the message for one delicious, tantalising moment of hesitation, enjoying the pain, before I click Open.

6. **Martha**

The email from Liv had taken Martha by surprise yesterday morning. She hadn't expected a reply so quickly – Liv's family might have moved on from her childhood address long ago – but the pleasure of the quick response had been dulled slightly by its formal tone. Martha had at least thought she might recognise something more of the old Liv in it. Olivia Heathcote had been the joker of their group, the one most likely to swear and tell dirty jokes and scribble graffiti on the toilet walls at school. She was the daring one, the chancer, the one who had made her and Juliet take themselves less seriously.

Liv's family had been big and noisy, a world of difference from the hushed void that was Martha's home after her mother's departure. Liv had complained endlessly about lack of privacy, having to share with an older sister, and then – the horror – having to give up her bed for a confused grandmother who called out in the night as Liv slept on the camp bed across the room. 'In the pantry!' Nanna had taken to shouting in the night. 'The eggs are in the pantry with the plums!' Liv's impersonations were hysterical. Every morning as they walked to school, she'd update Martha and Juliet on the previous night's nocturnal wakings, clutching at their sleeves and rolling her head back in a pose of fitful sleep. 'Me smalls are on the line!' she'd shriek. 'I'll 'ave 'is guts for garters if 'e don't sort the sink out!' Sometimes Liv's stories could leave Martha and Juliet gasping for breath, the joy of their laughter enough to eclipse the loneliness Martha had left a few streets away in Stanley House. Thank God for Liv and her crazy family.

'Gordon Bennett,' she groaned one morning in a mimic of her mother. 'The twins are toilet training at the moment. Mum left Frankie on the potty while she made the porridge, but he got off it when her back was turned and laid one down on the bottom step of the stairs.'

'No!' Juliet and Martha screamed, neither of them having experience of so big a family.

'All of a sudden Nanna shouts from the hall, "Joyce! What the 'ell are you feeding them? Could've broke my neck on it! Slippery as a whelk!" Right up between her toes, it was. Dad had to leave his breakfast half eaten, he was retching that bad.'

Martha recalls having to stop on a bench, laughing so hard she thought she would actually wet herself, and the three of them sat for a while, catching their breath and sighing before sprinting the rest of the way to school to avoid missing the bell. *Slippery as a whelk* became their catchphrase, to be called out to one another over the toilet cubicles at school, a code for anything stinky or ugly or grim. When cauliflower cheese was on the canteen menu, Liv would make vomit fingers at it, silently mouthing, 'Slippery as a whelk.' When Gina Norris brought her ugly little baby to show off outside the school gates in Year Eleven, the three of them whispered to one another that only a mother could love a face like that, what with it being 'as slippery as a whelk'.

Martha misses that laughter, the camaraderie of a well-worn joke, the ability to communicate with another human being in so few words. There's only her and Liv now; surely they owe it to one another to rekindle their friendship? She can't have forgotten, can she? Not when they shared so much. Liv and Juliet were more than just her best friends; they were the closest thing she had to family.

The message had come through during Martha's meeting with Toby yesterday, and she'd had to read it over several times, hardly able to believe she was so easily back in contact with her old friend. When Toby had returned with their coffees she'd handed him her phone, inviting him to read it too. 'That's great,' he'd said, and at the time she had agreed, yes, it *was* great that Liv was happy to help them. But something had unsettled her all the same. She supposed it wasn't unimaginable that Liv's formality was simply her unease making its way into her written words. Certainly, Liv would be shaken up by her letter, so it was natural her tone might be a bit off-key. But did Liv harbour any ill feeling towards Martha? Their relationship had all but evaporated with the disappearance of Juliet. Was it possible that Liv held Martha in some way responsible? Or was this just Martha's own guilt rearing itself, making her question herself and everyone around her?

She had slept on it, and by the time she rose at five this morning she'd got it straight in her head. *Of course* Liv sounded different: eighteen years was a lifetime ago. *I've* changed, Martha told herself. Liv has changed. Everything has changed.

She had tapped out a brief response, purposely warming up her own tone, trying to inject something of their old dynamic into her words:

Liv! So great to hear from you! I can't tell you how
relieved I am that my letter found you. So you're a
bereavement counsellor now? Wow, that really is impressive, though it doesn't surprise me at all. You always
were a good listener. Totally understand about your work
commitments, so yes, why don't I put together some
starter questions and send them over to you in the next
day or two? Perhaps we could meet up when you're back
in the country? Mart xx

Mart. No one but Liv and Juliet ever called her Mart. She
hated it if anyone else tried to abbreviate her name in the
same way; it sounded over-familiar coming from anyone
but her best friends. With them it had been different. Olivia
was Liv, Juliet was Jules and Martha was Mart. Martha feels
reality tip every time she allows herself to voyage deeper into
the memories of that era, and her breath catches as the train
she's now travelling on comes to a halt and Toby nudges her
to get off.

Toby has made contact with Juliet's father, and together
Martha and he have taken the Northern line as far as Archway,
following Toby's mobile app to navigate the twenty minutes to
Mr Sherman's new home on foot. It's a ground-floor flat in a
good terraced street, but not a patch on the nice detached place
Juliet's family owned when the girls were growing up. Martha
feels a rush of relief that they made the decision to hold off
on the camera crew until they'd had this first interview with
him; it would seem so wrong, turning up here mob-handed
to rake over his tragic past. Martha has been dreading this
meeting more than any of the others they hope to line up
over the coming days. So far they have been able to establish
that Mr Sherman – Alan, as he asked to be called when Toby

60

and he spoke on the phone yesterday – took a sabbatical from his work as a bank manager around five years after Juliet's disappearance, to return to the family home and care for his ex-wife. It was a late diagnosis of breast cancer, for which she refused any kind of treatment, and so after four months Mr Sherman had found himself a widower of sorts, living alone in a four-bedroom house, with no income. A year later, the old family home had been sold, and he had moved here.

'How did he sound to you?' Martha asks Toby as they stop outside the front door, her finger poised over the button labelled 'Sherman'.

'He sounded like a nice guy,' Toby replied, pushing at the roots of his hair. Martha suspects this is something he does when he feels uneasy. 'But profoundly sad. Like a man who's had years to become that way, if you know what I mean? Lonely, perhaps. He seemed happy to talk.'

Martha presses the buzzer and they wait for only a few seconds before Alan Sherman opens the door, shakes them by the hand and gestures to the back of the hall where the door to his flat stands open. Martha is struck by the reduced size of him. Her memory of him was as a tall man, straight-backed and broad-shouldered, always in a shirt and tie, even at weekends. She would never have recognised this man as Juliet's father. This man is stooped, all-over grey, dressed in shapeless tan cords and a brown V-neck jumper, and as she walks along the hall she wonders if she can make out anything at all of the Mr Sherman she once knew. It seems as though his illness has altered him almost beyond recognition. But when she enters his tidy little home and he closes the door softly behind them, he turns and she sees it there, unmistakable. The same haunted look in his eyes that she saw on their very last encounter, a day eighteen years ago when he'd stood on her doorstep, pleading with her to tell the police if she knew who Juliet had been seeing. To think that that look has never left him; that Juliet's disappearance has haunted him across the years, and lives on in him still.

'We want to find out what happened to Juliet, Mr Sherman,' Martha says. This is not how she had planned to start this conversation, this interview, but it seems suddenly imperative that she's clear with him about their intentions. She has to say this now, now that she perhaps has the power to *do* something, to change something. 'We want to find her. We won't sensationalise it, I promise. The show . . . well, the show will simply give us a louder voice. It'll make people listen.'

The three of them are standing close in the small space of Alan Sherman's living room. He scrutinises them each in turn, like a man deciphering another language, and then he unclasps his hands from where they rest at his sternum and pulls Martha towards him in a fierce embrace. From nowhere, a sob rises up in her chest and she's a teenager again, stifling the sound against Mr Sherman's woollen jumper, grateful for his arms around her, mourning more than just the loss of her best friend. They all lost so much that winter. In losing Juliet, they lost their connections to one another, and over the years they must have forgotten what those connections really meant. They must have forgotten, all of them, otherwise why else would they have let them go so easily?

Mr Sherman had always been kind to Martha. There had been an unspoken acceptance that he knew how things were for her at home, having unintentionally witnessed Martha's family at its worst one Friday night when he'd called by to pick up a textbook of Juliet's that Martha had borrowed. Martha's dad had been on one of his benders, roaring his rage from the far end of the flat as Martha fled through the front door, straight into the chest of Juliet's father before he'd even had a chance to knock. Even now, she recalls the shame of that collision, the lies that poured from her mouth as she tried to explain that her parents were just mucking about, that it wasn't a real argument, just a bit of harmless fun. Behind her the fury continued, audible even through the closed door, and she had steered Mr Sherman away, agreeing to walk back to Juliet's house and join them for their fish and chip supper.

It wasn't always like this, she'd wanted to say. Remember my old house? Remember when Dad wasn't so bad?

'The textbook can wait,' Mr Sherman had said, and even at thirteen she had understood the kindness he'd shown in just those few words.

'I'd forgotten . . .' Martha starts to say as she pulls away, but she doesn't know where she's going with the sentence and she trails off with a shake of her head.

Mr Sherman gives a small nod as he releases her, and indicates for them to take a seat while he puts the kettle on for tea.

'Are you OK?' Toby whispers when they're alone, but Martha waves his sympathy away with a flick of her hand, telling him to get his notes out. Stiffly, she sits beside him on the pale leather two-seater.

The room is warm, the heating on at full blast. Martha loosens the collar of her shirt and shrugs off her jacket. I can do this, she tells herself, drawing strength as the adult Martha returns, the grown-up, primetime Martha. It's something she unwittingly mastered in childhood, the ability to go from broken to unbreakable in a matter of minutes, to present a smiling mask of resilience to the outside world while beneath the surface all might be far from well. I can do this. Within moments she is focused again, and quietly she and Toby run through the questions they have prepared, ready for Mr Sherman when he returns with the tea tray. He places it softly on the coffee table between them, and takes the armchair opposite, sitting on the edge of his seat as he pours tea and offers them biscuits. It's such a civilised scene, slow-moving, punctuated by the soft ticking of a wall clock, that it seems wrong to launch into questions of so dark a nature. But that's what Martha is here for, and she fixes her gaze on his face, anchoring herself to the job at hand: the task of finding Juliet. A momentary flash comes to her: the tabloid suggestion that Juliet's father was responsible for his daughter's disappearance. Why had they suggested that? He must have gone in for questioning early on and, after all, didn't police always treat the parents with suspicion until they could be clearly ruled out? But it had made it to the newspapers, and she can see the headline in her mind's eye – *Missing Juliet: Does Dad Know Where She Is?*

'Are you happy for me to get straight down to the interview?' Martha asks.

'Yes, please.' Alan Sherman's faded expression is attentive, businesslike. As he perches on the edge of his seat, only his hands give away his emotions, his fingers turned under as they grip on to the soft velour fabric of the armchair, his knuckles pale.

'Here's how it will work,' Toby tells him. They have rehearsed this. 'Initially, Martha and I will be talking to everyone connected with the case, hopefully building up a clear enough picture to persuade the police to share more of their initial findings with us. Once we have a stronger argument, and the police on board, we'd like to return with the cameras, to re-interview you as part of the programme. This way, you'll know what to expect – and, if necessary, we can tailor your interview to appeal to members of the public who may have information to share with us.'

64

Alan Sherman nods, and Martha feels as though he is fading before her very eyes, his skin growing more sallow, the lines of his shape growing translucent against the backdrop of his neat living room. He's a ghost, she realises. The real Mr Sherman left years ago, soon after his daughter. This man is nothing but a ghost.

Toby pauses, waiting for Martha to pick up the thread. When she doesn't, he continues, seamless as the most practised understudy. 'The programme could go one of two ways: a) we build up a clearer history and reconstruction of events, and use the programme to appeal to witnesses, or b) – our preference – we solve the case and present the investigation as a finished outcome.'

Alan Sherman listens carefully, nodding throughout.

'How does that sound, Mr Sherman?' asks Toby.

'Alan, please.'

'Sorry, of course. *Alan*. Are you happy with that approach?'

Alan Sherman turns to Martha. 'Are *you* happy with it?' he asks, and she fears there is criticism in the question until she reads his face and sees his need. He just wants her to tell him what to do.

'I think it's a good approach,' she says. 'The more we can find out from the people who actually knew Juliet, the more likely the police are to give us an audience. At the moment, they're resisting.'

He sighs deeply and gestures towards the modest plate of biscuits between them. They're bourbons – Juliet's favourite. 'Then I'm happy with it.'

They start with the easy questions, the ones they already know the answers to, a warm-up of sorts. How did Juliet seem on the night she disappeared? *Normal*. Did he notice any changes in her behaviour leading up to her disappearance?

No. Was she a good time-keeper? *Yes.* Was Juliet in the habit of keeping secrets? *No.* Were there many family arguments – with her parents or older brother? *No.* How often did she volunteer at Square Wheels? *Once or twice a week.*

A couple of times he hesitates before answering. 'You know this, Martha. You were there.'

And Martha can only nod, and agree, yes, she was there, but they need it in his words.

'Did Juliet have any boyfriends?'

Here, Alan Sherman pauses. 'Well, we didn't think so. But then there was the letter we found in her wastepaper bin.'

Martha stares at him blankly.

He frowns, tilting his head. 'Didn't the police ask you about it? They said they'd be asking her friends.'

She has no idea what he means. 'About a letter? No – I mean, they asked me if I knew who Juliet was seeing, but they never mentioned a letter. I don't know what to . . .' Her mind buzzes with confusion. 'Who was it from?'

Alan pushes out of his chair and leaves the room, returning a moment later with a sheet of crumpled paper in his hand. 'I dug it out earlier. I thought you might like to see it. It's not a letter she'd *received*, it was one she was writing – but, as you can see from the state of it, she'd obviously had a change of heart about sending it.'

Martha takes the letter from him, placing it down on the coffee table between them, gently smoothing out its bumps and ridges. Her pulse is racing, her fingers shaking.

'Do you mind if I read it aloud?' Toby asks, reaching across for the sheet.

Thank God, Martha sighs inwardly. She doesn't think she has the strength to do it herself. With a small hand gesture, Alan Sherman tells Toby to go ahead.

'*My one love,*' he reads, '*I don't want us to argue. Please can we stop? I want us to be out in the open too, holding hands when we want to, and no more secrets, but we have to be patient. Too many people could get hurt – think about your own family. I'll be eighteen in a few months' time and I know it will be easier to talk to my folks then. Can't we just wait and look forward to when we will be together ALL the time? Before we know it we'll be free of all this, travelling the world where we won't have to hide! Please understand. Love you love you love you xxx.*'

Toby stops reading and places the letter back on the table-top. 'Do you know who she was writing to?' he asks.

'Not David Crown,' Alan replies. 'That's what you're probably thinking. Am I right? That's what the police thought. But Juliet would never—'

'Did she ever *mention* David Crown?' Martha asks, finding her voice again. This letter – what on earth did it mean? What secrets had Juliet been keeping from them, from her family, her best friends?

Alan's expression is tired, resigned. 'She liked him, but not in the way the police would have people believe. I think Juliet really admired his dedication to the charity. She told us that he ran his own business as a landscape gardener, that he was a good man, that he was fun to be around. He always made sure the volunteers went off in pairs for safety, and he always helped them give their bikes the once-over before they set off, to make sure there weren't any slow punctures or loose chains. You were a volunteer there too, Martha?'

'I was,' Martha replies quietly. 'But it was a bit sporadic, if I'm honest. I wasn't there every week like Juliet. Liv and I both helped out quite a bit the summer before, but we lost interest as soon as the good weather tailed off. But I'd have agreed with Juliet's assessment of David Crown. He seemed like a decent guy to me. On the surface.'

Alan raises his eyebrows and takes a deep breath. 'I never met him,' he says. 'It's one of the things that has troubled me ever since. I mean, what kind of father doesn't go and check out something like this? I should have gone down there, introduced myself, found out what kind of set-up he had going on. Juliet thought he was a decent fellow, but she could've judged it wrong, couldn't she? Maybe I would've spotted it, you know, if he wasn't what he said he was?'

Martha shakes her head sadly. 'You're wrong. If David Crown *was* responsible – if he was this bad person we think he could be – none of us saw it. He was really *nice*. He looked normal, he was kind, caring – a charity worker, for God's sake! Meeting him wouldn't have made the slightest difference, Alan, I promise you.'

Alan Sherman picks up his mug, takes a long drink of his tea. A solitary tear escapes from the outer corner of his eye, travelling down over his sharp cheekbones and into his collar. He doesn't seem to notice. 'You just wonder, don't you? What you could have done differently. I've often thought over the years – if I could just roll back time and change things somehow . . . ?'

Martha knows this feeling only too well. Even as he speaks, she's asking herself: How did I not know about this person Juliet was writing to? Why didn't I question her harder when I knew she was keeping secrets?

'What about her fellow volunteers?' she asks, clenching her jaw, trying to not be moved by his quiet grief. 'Do you recall any names?'

Alan crosses the room and fetches a photo album from the bookcase, barely making a sound on the carpet. 'I've got a couple of photos you can borrow, if they're any help?' He slowly turns the pages, stopping at a pair of photographs, sliding them out and passing them to Martha before sitting again. 'The first one was taken by the local newspaper – I think Square Wheels won some kind of community award. And the second one was from a boat trip out with David Crown. A reward for some volunteer work, I think?'

The newspaper photograph shows the group posed with food-laden bicycles, David Crown in the centre, flanked by two volunteers on either side, the Square Wheels banner overhead, nailed to the side of the wooden hut where the sandwiches were prepared. It must be winter, because they're all dressed in coats and hats and scarves, their skin showing the cold glow of exertion. Juliet stands on the right side of David, to her right a girl whose face looks unfamiliar to Martha, and to David's left are another girl and a boy. The caption reads: *Local Heroes Scoop Community Award.*

'Do you know the names of these other volunteers?' she asks.

Alan reaches across the coffee table and points to the faces in turn. 'I don't know the one next to Juliet but this very thin one on the other side of David Crown, I seem to think her name was Karen, and the boy beside her – don't you recognise him?'

Martha scrutinises the picture more closely. 'Oh, yes! God, I can't believe I didn't see it at first. Tom!' She turns to explain to Toby. 'Tom was – is – Juliet's brother. But I don't remember Tom being a volunteer?'

Alan smiles and shakes his head. 'I don't know how well you knew Tom at the time, but he was never a sticker. He did help out there a handful of times, but that's all. He just happened to be passing on the evening the newspaper guy took that picture, and they needed another body. Typical Tom: all the glory and none of the work.'

'Do you think we could talk to Tom? Ask him if he can think of anything particular about that night? He was there, at the Waterside Café, the night Juliet went missing.'

'I'm sure he'll be happy to talk to you, but you know he's living in Paris now? We sold the house, after his mum, well—'

'Oh, yes,' Martha interrupts. She's ashamed not to have mentioned it before. 'I was so sorry to hear about Mrs Sherman. I didn't know about it at the time, but she was always so lovely. You both were. It must have been very hard.'

'You know we'd separated by the time she died? I only moved back in towards the end, to help Tom, really, although Ann and I still loved each other, if we're honest. But it's difficult to carry on together, when something like that happens. *Juliet*.'

Martha nods, wondering how Alan Sherman keeps on going. How does he keep getting up in the morning and dressing and feeding himself and telling himself everything will be OK? How can he believe everything will be alright, when his entire life is living proof that life can turn out very bloody far from alright?

'How is Tom these days?' she asks. 'I haven't seen him for years.' Since that night.

Now Alan Sherman's face breaks into an unexpected smile. 'He's very happy. Works as a sommelier – wines, something of that kind. Married, with a baby on the way. Imagine – I'm going to be a grandfather.'

And there Martha sees it: hope. That's what keeps him going. Hope that the next day will be better than the last, that next week will be an improvement on the one before, that next year will be happier than the year just gone.

'Congratulations,' she says, and can't find more words, stunned into silence.

'I'd almost given up hope – of a grandchild.' He smiles, and he swipes away another tear, his eyes shining with the pleasure of this piece of joy. 'They think it's a boy.'

'When's it due?' Toby asks, and Martha is glad to have him beside her more than she could ever have imagined possible.

'May. Spring baby. Good time of year.'

Same month as Juliet's birthday, Martha thinks, and their eyes meet in this unspoken knowledge.

Mr Sherman smooths down his trousers and gives a brief bob of his head. 'I'll give you Tom's details before you leave.'

'And this other girl? You definitely don't remember her?' Martha asks, returning to the photograph and pointing to the girl beside Juliet.

'As I say, no idea. I don't recognise her at all. I think they had a fairly fast turnover of volunteers. Juliet said a lot of people came along and never returned once they realised it was hard work and bloody cold.'

'Like me and Liv,' Martha says, grimacing.

Alan smiles warmly. 'She called them "the lightweights". This girl could've been one of them.'

Martha turns her attention to the second photograph and feels her insides flip. The image is of a summer's day, four youngsters on a riverbank, wet-haired in underpants and T-shirts, smiling and waving at the person behind the camera. Three of them sit cross-legged beneath a tree on a picnic blanket, surrounded by sandwiches and drinks, while Juliet's brother Tom hangs like a monkey from the branch overhead, his sinewy legs kicking out. The three on the picnic blanket look equally carefree: young, vibrant, beautiful.

'Remember this one?' Alan asks, dewy-eyed again, and Martha finds she cannot speak.

The three on the blanket are unmistakable. Juliet, Olivia and Martha. And the terrifying thing is, until now, she'd forgotten all about that day, forgotten about that boat trip with David Crown and her closest friends. But, even as the details of the trip remain just beyond her reach, Martha can't shake the feeling that by the time that day was over, nothing would ever be the same.

7. Casey

I love Fridays, because this is the day the man from the supermarket comes. Having my weekly groceries delivered has changed my life, really, in so many ways – and would you believe it, I have Liv to thank for introducing me to the idea. It was during that second house-viewing last winter, when we stood in her kitchen as she made me a cup of coffee, just how I like it, milky with two sugars. Miriam, the estate agent, was there too, but she has faded to a shadow in my memory, because it was Liv and I who were deep in conversation, leaning casually against the worktop eating ginger biscuits. I felt as though I'd known her forever! I'm not used to meeting people as short as me, but she carried it off in a petite, stylish way, and I felt inspired that perhaps *I* could improve myself and be as graceful as her. Liv seemed to know how to dress in a way that suited her exactly. I can see her now as though it was yesterday, wearing quirky patterned leggings and an oversized emerald-green jumper that looked quite stunning against her dark skin. On her wrist was a silver bangle exactly like one I've got at home, and I admired it, and that made her smile. She asked me all sorts of questions about my work, showing an interest that was so sincere that I knew I was in danger of boring the socks off her as I talked through the various books I'd proofread over the past year, showing off over my early access to some of the most hotly anticipated scientific journals of the year.

'What an interesting job that must be,' Liv had said. 'And how great that you're able to work from home. I'm quite envious.'

Her face showed me she meant envious in the good way, and I thought. My word, that someone like Olivia Heathcote – someone as faultless as her – should be envious of me! I put my hand over my mouth, conscious of the ugly snaggle tooth that rears up whenever I smile too widely, and suppressed a giggle.

There was a knock at the door, and I recall feeling quite irked by the idea of interruption, and Miriam and I stood in awkward silence for the few seconds it took for Liv to answer and invite her visitor in. To my surprise, a young man appeared in the kitchen doorway, bearing multiple bags of grocery shopping, and wearing a Sainsbury's staff uniform.

'Just the weekly shop,' Liv explained. 'The twins are a nightmare to take around the supermarket, so I order it online now.'

The young man bobbed his head at us, placing the bags on the floor beside the fridge and heading out again to fetch the next load. The back of his neck was smooth and tanned, the closely sheared hair growing crooked where he was due for a haircut.

'Can you do that?' I asked, amazed. 'Order your groceries online?'

'Yes! I can't tell you how much time – not to mention stress – it's saved me over the past couple of years. They don't charge delivery if you order over a certain amount.'

Well, I decided there and then, I shall do that. One less reason to leave the house. One more visitor I can call my own. I checked my watch and made a mental note: 2 p.m. on a Friday.

And that's what I've done ever since I took over the house as my own. Every Friday at 2 p.m. Carl arrives with my weekly shop. I stuck to the same slot as Liv in the hope that I would get the same driver, and nine times out of ten it has been him. I feel we know each other quite well now, and I'm certain he doesn't mind at all that I call him by his first name. He, on the other hand, insists on calling me by my formal title, and he won't be moved. Perhaps one day!

Today when Carl knocks on the front door I am right there, already with my fingers on the handle, because I don't want to miss a moment of our time together. I closed my laptop over an hour ago, stopping for a brief lunch of scrambled eggs on toast, before tidying myself up in anticipation of his visit. I brushed my hair for an additional fifty strokes, despite having already brushed it thoroughly this morning, and I dotted Mum's 4711 cologne liberally about my person, on my wrists and behind my ears like I've seen her do so many times in the past. I even put a dab or two around my panty line for good measure. It made me smile, having a little secret like that! The smell of it is so fresh, it lingers in the air around me, and I'm certain I can see Carl's nostrils quiver when I invite him inside my home.

He greets me in his usual way, and as always I say, 'Please, you must call me Casey!' and as always he laughs and carries on through to the kitchen, placing the bags down by the fridge, just as he had when Olivia Heathcote lived here. Without a word, but with the loveliest of smiles, he returns to his van and brings back a second load, and then a third, finally offering up his clipboard and asking me to sign at the bottom.

'There are two substitutions,' he says.

I hold his gaze.

'We didn't have tinned mackerels in tomato sauce, so you've got brine.'

'That's an excellent choice,' I reply, sweeping my long hair over one shoulder.

He looks uneasy, and I think how endearing it is that he doesn't wish to disappoint me. Then he says, 'And, er, there were no Always Super Pads – so you've got Bodyform.'

Well, I could die of shame, and all thoughts of inviting him to stay for a cup of tea fly from my mind as I scribble my name in the box and thrust the clipboard back at him, nodding that yes, those substitutions would be absolutely acceptable. In an instant he is out of the door and I am left in a cloud of apoplexy.

For the briefest of moments, I hate Olivia Heathcote for putting me through this. If it hadn't been for her I would never have started taking home deliveries, and this humiliation would never have occurred. But then I talk myself down – I've always tended towards overreaction – and I realise I'm being hysterical. If it hadn't been for Olivia Heathcote, I wouldn't be living in this wonderful house, and I'd still be running the gauntlet of the weekly shop and all the horrors and public embarrassments that the checkout can bring. Without Olivia Heathcote, I wouldn't have Carl, or Martha, or *anything* to look forward to.

I take a deep breath, smooth down my ruffled dress and head into the kitchen to unpack my shopping. I have a lot to do today. For starters, there should be a box of hair dye somewhere in today's order, which I've been excited about for days. I've decided to sort myself out, get rid of this ugly grey hair and spruce up my appearance a bit. The shade I've chosen is so dark it's nearly black, not dissimilar to Liv's, and the instructions say it's as easy as 1-2-3! And then there's the list of questions Martha has said she will email to me, which, when they arrive, I will do my very best to answer as well as Liv herself would. Over the past twenty-four hours I have uncovered yet more treasures of information regarding Juliet and David Crown, and I will bring them into play so that Martha might never guess that I'm not who I say I am. She'll never guess that I'm just a big, fat liar! I like being Liv, and I vow that next time Carl comes I will try to be more like her, more serene and graceful. I can be beautiful too. *A beautiful liar.*

8. Martha

Toby calls for Martha early and together they drive out to the canal, aiming to walk the waterside route that Martha and Juliet took that night, to take a look at the spot where her abandoned bicycle was found. Toby is hopeful they might also establish the location of the Square Wheels picnic shown in Alan Sherman's old photograph, though Martha is less optimistic.

When they arrive at Regent's Canal, Sally and Jay are already waiting on the footpath, drinking coffee from paper cups, there to film some background footage and straight-to-camera pieces. It's a bright, sharp morning, and Sally and Jay are dressed in matching parkas and skinny black jeans, their hoods pulled up against the icy air.

'Can we do the distance stuff first?' Martha asks them, anxious to find her bearings, to mentally warm up before putting herself in front of the camera.

She feels strangely apprehensive this morning, having suffered a restless night's sleep as she went over things in her head. Who *was* Juliet writing to in that letter she never sent? Martha can see how the police jumped to the conclusion

78

that it was David Crown – the secret relationship she talks of, the fact of her turning eighteen seeming important in their timing of coming into the open – but still, something doesn't ring true. It just wasn't in Juliet's nature. *Was it?* As she lay awake in bed, Martha's mind had kept lighting on snatches of forgotten conversations with her friends, nothing to do with Juliet's disappearance, just murmurs from a past they once shared. She'd conjured up the memory of that trip to London Zoo in Year Ten, when Dippy Stephens had got his ankle wedged in the railings near the monkey kingdom and Liv had tried to work it free with a dollop of cherry lip balm. In the end they'd had to leave him to wait for one of the first-aiders to arrive, and Liv had whispered, 'That's the last time I do a good turn. He smells of wet biscuits and Dairylea.' Martha and Juliet had howled with laughter, and they'd all bought Twister lollies and lounged on the neat lawns of the picnic area, soaking up the sunshine and watching the world through their fringes. Dippy had plucked up the courage to ask Liv out on the walk back to school, and she'd said no as nicely as she could, careful to avoid Martha and Juliet's teasing eyes. How the mind plays tricks, Martha thinks now, the way it effortlessly reveals useless snippets like this while so often concealing the memories we seek.

At the waterside, Sally and Jay stand side by side, sipping at their steaming cups. They've worked together for so long now they've become androgynous versions of each other, beachy-haired late thirty-somethings, casual in their easy confidence with the task at hand. Martha has worked with the pair for years, on and off, enabling the trio to bypass unnecessary small talk and get straight down to work.

'Why don't you trail me and Toby along the towpath, and when I spot anything of significance I'll give you a wave?

See that yellow dinghy – the one near the bend in the path?' She points a hundred yards down the walkway. 'Wait till we reach it, then start to follow. It'll give a nice wide view of the location – set the scene.'

The camera guys get to work prepping their kit, and Martha and Toby head off along the path. The verges are muddy with winter rainfall, and Martha tries to recall if this stretch was always paved, or whether it ran to grass back in Juliet's day. The quiet activity of the morning plays out around them: houseboat dwellers emerging from below decks, morning commuters cycling into town, groups of children on their way to school. There's nothing sinister about the towpath in the bright light of a Friday morning, when all of life continues around them, everyday movements of everyday people. But everything changes after dark, and night and day are two different worlds. As children they steered clear of the canal at night-time, afraid of its shadows, warned away by their parents and teachers fretful to keep them safe. What alters in those teen years, to make us so reckless and brave? Is it a chemical change, something we have no control over that makes risk-takers of the most sensible of us? Makes us believe we're untouchable, invincible, immortal, even? Martha pauses by the small yellow boat, a jumble of images throwing confused lines across her conscious thoughts.

'They're on the move,' Toby says, turning to check on Sally and Jay, and Martha raises her hand to silence him.

She's grasping for a thread: she sees Juliet on that dark night, not far from here, smiling and insisting *I'll be fine* – reaching out to squeeze Martha's forearm as she says goodnight. A reassurance, a gesture of affection. But there's a feeling of wrongness about the exchange, because the reason Martha's given for deserting her friend is a deceit, it's all mixed up. She sees the frosty path again, through her own seventeen-year-old eyes, the path away from Juliet, back the way they came. She sees the flash of Juliet's flowing hair as she heads away on her bicycle, and she feels relief as another Square Wheels volunteer passes in Juliet's direction, mixing with the guilt of her lie. Now, Toby stares at her, waiting for her to speak. But what can she say? I lied that night? I lied to Juliet. *I lied*, but I don't recall how or why, or what it even means. She takes out her phone and photographs the cluster of bankside dinghies, turning in circles as she captures the street beyond, the footpath, the meandering movement of the canal.

'What are you thinking?' Toby asks, unable to contain his curiosity any longer. 'Have you remembered something?'

'I told her I had to go back for my bag,' she says, more to herself than Toby. That *was* why she'd left Juliet on the towpath alone, wasn't it? 'I'd left my bag in the Waterside Café.' Martha shakes her head, trying to bring her thoughts back, and sighs. 'I don't know,' she replies truthfully, turning back to wave at the camera guys. She points out the boats as worth filming and then she continues along the path below the flyover bridge. Something has shifted in her, and her discomfort is acute.

Her phone buzzes, breaking her concentration as she takes it from her pocket, checking the caller ID, crestfallen to see that it's him again. She fumbles with the handset, trying to reject the call, failing to gain purchase through the thick fabric of those stupid spotty gloves, and the phone slips from her hands, skittering along the grass verge.

Toby is a step ahead of her, scooping it up before any real damage is done, and still the ringtone blares out as he returns it to her, stealing a glance at the screen as he does so, a question in his eyes.

'Who's "D"?' he asks. 'Is someone bothering you? Martha? What's wrong?'

'I . . .' she begins, swallowing hard, but she can't seem to get her thoughts into any kind of useable arrangement.

Toby puts a halting hand up to Sally and Jay, and steers Martha to lean against the railings for a while. 'You're very pale,' he tells her. '*Something*'s upset you.'

If she didn't feel so shaken, Martha would be furious with herself for displaying such open vulnerability. But, right now, she feels close to nausea and there's no point in pushing him away, in being the uptight cow she's so comfortable with.

'I just need a minute,' she says, running her hands up over her face, breathing deeply. 'It's something and nothing – it's some memory of that night, here, and there's Juliet and me and someone else, and it feels fine, unthreatening, but I'm leaving her on her own and . . . and . . .' She looks at Toby aghast, and speaks in a low hush. 'Was it my fault, Toby?'

To her astonishment he takes a firm grip of her shoulders and looks at her steadfastly, through eyes that are so familiar to her she's rendered speechless. 'No,' he says resolutely. 'No, it's not. You didn't snatch her, did you? You weren't to know what lay in store for Juliet. You were kids – and you need to stop this. You'll never get to the bottom of her disappearance if you fall apart now, Martha. Come on, you're tougher than that.'

All the breath she's been storing up seems to leave her body in a rush and she blinks, signalling for him to release her. It's a strange dynamic; rather than feeling reduced by his strength, she feels strengthened. She had a moment of weakness, and he steadied her, that was all.

'Ready to carry on?' he asks, and he gives Sally and Jay the thumbs-up and they continue on their way. 'So, any sign of that picnic location?' he says after a few minutes of walking in silence. He's trying to lighten the atmosphere. 'Or anything else?'

Of course Martha isn't sure exactly where that picnic site is, although she *does* recall it in part now, the detail of it is so vague. She can remember that they ate egg sandwiches on a red tartan blanket, but not what she wore, or where they moored up to eat. In her mind's eye she can see Liv threatening to push Tom overboard when he kept twanging her bra strap, but she can't recall how they came to be on the trip in the first place. How much is considered to be a normal amount of recollection, she wonders? Surely no one remembers *everything* that happened to them every day of their life. And how can we ever compare our powers of recall with those of someone else, when we can never live in each other's heads, never really experience the same event, even when it's a shared one.

'Look, it was a long time ago,' she says as he asks her again if there's anything she recognises at all. 'I only volunteered with Square Wheels for a few weeks that summer. Do you remember everything you did when you were a teenager?'

'Most of it,' he says, tugging at the collar of his jacket, loosening it against the growing warmth of the sun. 'Except for some of the drunken bits, I suppose. Some of those memories are a bit of a blur.'

A blur, she thinks. If only. She *was* drunk for a large part of that period. Blind drunk. At the time it was just one of the things that had started to push the friendship group apart, and even now she feels the shame of it. She has an oddly clear memory of a different moon-hazed summer evening, the London streets softly murmuring with the sounds of homeward drinkers, the distant clunk of car doors and pub landlords shutting up for the night. The low, meandering slap of the water's edge. Juliet and Liv, sitting either side of her on that canalside wooden bench, holding her hair and rubbing her back as she heaved up on the path between her feet. They'd stuck by her that evening – and so many others like it – way after their own curfews had passed, until she was sober enough to be delivered home, ever hopeful that her house would be quiet with sleep. But that was just a blip, the wilful bingeing of a lonely girl, dealing with her sadness and confusion the only way she knew how. It wasn't just because her parents were boozers, though she's sure there are plenty of psychoanalysts out there who'd like to bundle it up in so neat an explanation. Lots of kids go through binge-drinking phases – even Toby, by the sounds of it – and Martha was just one of them. She's always scoffed when others said, conveniently, that they couldn't remember a thing after a night's drinking; Martha nearly always knew what had happened when she was drunk. That was the problem. In fact, that was why, in her late twenties, she gave up drinking once and for all. By then, she didn't have a problem with remembering her misdeeds; it was forgetting them that she struggled with.

'Well, perhaps that was it,' she replies with a forced smile, pushing the images back into the shadows. 'We were probably pissed.' She stops at a point on the path where the hedge opens up to the street beyond. 'This is it,' she says, taking in the old bench that marks the first of the houseboats moored along the canal. 'Where the bike was found.' She approaches the bench and reads the inscription: *Clara May Avery, beloved wife*. It's the same bench, the same inscription.

Toby looks up and down the path, bringing out his phone to take pictures from various angles as Martha points to the grass verge at the hedge opening. 'There were photos of it in the newspaper at the time, when the police were investigating.

The bike was here, on its side with the wheel obstructing the path. Apparently the area was combed, but there was no useful forensic evidence collected at all.'

'How do you know that?' Toby asks.

'I've got a contact in the Met – I spoke to him briefly last night and he's agreed to help us as far as he can.'

'Was he on the original case?'

Martha nods. 'Crime Squad. On the sidelines, but he remembers the case well. His name's Finn Palin, but we're going to have to tread carefully. He's retired now and a lot of what he's already told me is strictly off the record. So keep it to yourself.'

Toby pulls a face, suspicious.

'And no, I didn't sleep with him to get the info, if that's what you're thinking.'

'I never said—' Toby starts to protest, before noticing the smirk on Martha's face.

She shoves her hands into her pockets, pleased they've managed to move on to steadier ground. 'He knew my dad.'

'Your father was in the police force?' he asks.

Martha simply nods, giving no invitation for Toby to probe further. 'So,' she says, back to business. 'The bike was here, just three hundred yards from where I last saw her, according to the police interview I gave the following day.'

Toby stares at the empty space where Juliet's bike had once been. 'It was hardly hidden, was it? If I were going to snatch someone here, I think I'd probably push the bike out of sight so as not to raise the alarm while I made my getaway. Maybe push it into the canal? I wouldn't leave it sticking out like an advert.'

Martha turns to Sally and Jay as they catch up. 'I think this is a good spot for a straight-to-camera piece. If the programme turns into a public appeal, this location may jog memories.'

Sally removes her parka, tying the arms around her waist like a teenager. 'You think this is where it happened?' she asks.

'Maybe,' Martha replies. 'Although one of the wheels was found to be flat. So it's also possible that someone else picked the bike up further along, with a view to stealing it, but found the tyre was bust and dumped it. Someone unrelated to Juliet's abduction. There were several sets of fingerprints found on the handlebars, none of them a match to anyone on the police database.'

Jay is setting up the camera to face out towards the houseboats with the bench and path in view. He works silently, a stub of pencil sticking out between coffee-stained teeth, giving Martha a brief nod to indicate when they're good to go.

Toby appears deep in thought. 'Did she normally lock it up?'

'Always. It was a standing joke, because it was such a crappy old bike. Liv used to say no one would nick it even if you tied a ribbon around the handlebars with a sign saying "Help Yourself". Juliet was a creature of habit, though. She *always* locked her bike.'

'So the fact that it was found dumped and unlocked seems pretty clear evidence that Juliet was taken by surprise. Wouldn't you say?'

'Completely. And this is one of the reasons we – Liv and I – were so upset about the police's conclusion that she'd run away. I know it sounds weird, but *even if* she was planning to run away, Juliet would still have left her bike neatly padlocked somewhere. She had a strong sense of order about her; she liked things to be a certain way. She was predictable, I suppose. When I heard that none of her belongings had gone from her room, I knew the theory was bullshit. Juliet would *never* have left without planning it very carefully and precisely – or without leaving a note to draw a line under things. Apart from anything, I know she would never have run away in the first place.'

'Can you remember the last thing she said to you before you went your separate ways?'

Martha closes her eyes for a moment. 'Yes. From the moment we left the Waterside I'd been nagging her to tell me what she and Liv were arguing about, but she wouldn't budge. I'd been feeling left out for a while, and I guess I was annoyed that she was keeping secrets from me. "I thought we were best friends," I told her, "but you spend more time with David bloody Crown than you do with me these days."' Martha stops talking for a moment, shocked by the sudden and lucid outpouring, trying to think what would have made her say such a thing. There's just a blank space where that knowledge should live.

Toby tells her to go on. Sally and Jay keep their distance, clearly reading the situation sensitively and awaiting their instructions.

'I remember how guilty she looked when I said that, but it wasn't like I thought she and he had a thing going – it was more like I was jealous that she'd rather spend all her time volunteering than spend it with me. I don't know, Toby, I might be getting this all wrong.' She focuses in on the memory. 'After that we walked in silence for a while – until I said I had to go back to the café for my bag. She said, "It's really not a big deal, Mart, but come to mine tomorrow afternoon and I'll tell you everything." She said she was sorry for being a crap friend, and then she hugged me and that was it.'

Martha takes a deep breath and meets Toby's eyes. 'I hadn't forgotten my bag,' she says in a hushed whisper, not wanting Sally and Jay to hear. 'I think I must have just wanted to punish her, for leaving me out. I just wanted to show her I was angry, to make her tell me the truth.'

How could anyone think that Martha *wasn't* to blame, at least in some small way?

9. **Casey**

Dear Martha
Re: Initial Questions

I've had a chance to go through your email now I'm back in the country. I don't know how much use I'll be as it was all such a long time ago. But I will do my very best!

In your notes, you mentioned that my police statement said I'd last seen Juliet in the Waterside Café before you two left for the night. Yes, I think we did have a little falling out, but it was such a small thing, I can't imagine what it was about. That's probably why it didn't come up in my statement. It was really nothing, I'm certain.

Juliet's brother Tom — to be honest I can't remember much about him that night. You say he was very drunk? Do you think he had something to do with it? I've been thinking, if it was a Friday night in the Christmas holidays, everywhere in London would have been busy, and strangers – visitors, tourists and so on – would certainly have been passing through. I've always thought that it might have just been a chance meeting with a stranger on the towpath.

And of course I remember David Crown – I thought he was a really nice man. He did all that charity work, didn't he? I think he ran the marathon too one year, for the Samaritans. I know he went missing around the same time as Juliet, but I can't believe he was responsible. Do you have any other suspects?

I hope this email contains something useful, and please do not hesitate to contact me again.

Best wishes, Liv x

I pored over my reply to Martha for hours this morning, wanting to get it exactly right. She'd sent me a list of questions about Juliet and the time of her disappearance, so particular that they required some further research. I'd come across an article about David Crown running the marathon, in some local-interest website, so I dropped that in for good measure, and I said I didn't think he could have done it, because having been through the cuttings from that period I think it's the conclusion that anyone with half a brain would come to! She'll thank me, I'm sure. It's narrow-minded to focus on one suspect alone. I would think Martha knows that very well herself.

Some of her questions were easy to answer. For instance, I know the Waterside Café because I went there once or twice with my parents in my early teens, for Sunday morning coffee. I wonder if it's still there? From memory, it was quite a relaxed place during the day, but in the evenings it was a favourite haunt for East London's trendies – with a reputation for serving underage drinkers. Thanks to my excellent Pinterest board, which has now grown to quite an impressive size, I was also able to draw on information about Juliet's disappearance that I had gleaned from the newspapers at the time. But in other areas I was utterly flummoxed. Tom, for example! I had had no idea that Juliet had a brother, or, if I did, it certainly hadn't registered. It made me realise I need to dig a bit further, to fill out the details of their wider family. It would be terrible to get caught out on a simple detail like that. The devil is in the detail, as they say!

When it came to my thoughts on a suspect, well, I was quite torn. What was I meant to say? It seems rather unfair to make alternative suggestions, but my reply had to feel authentic. I couldn't risk Martha doubting me in any way. As I worked on this email, dipping in and out of my research, adding to the story, building up a picture of myself as Liv, I knew I hadn't felt so fulfilled in a long, long time. My greatest fear at this point is that if Martha *does* successfully find Juliet's killer – for everyone surely now believes that she is dead – our correspondence will come to an abrupt end. And I'm not sure I could bear for that to happen.

So I threw a few other ideas into the pot. I dropped in the thought that Juliet's brother Tom could be a suspect (this was genius, as Martha had suggested no such thing!). I also introduced the theory that it was a stranger, a tourist passing through who had grabbed her from the path. That perhaps David Crown was entirely innocent, a victim himself, if you like. Perfect.

After what felt like a hundred redrafts, I finally pressed the Send button.

I think colouring my hair has had a profound effect on me. I feel quite changed, not just when I look in the mirror at the new, younger me, but in my very core too! Who would have thought I could be so creative, so inventive? Certainly not my mother, who believed all fiction was a waste of time! She was Queen of the Glossy Magazine, filling her mind with the vacuous tales of the rich and famous, while I preferred to escape inside imagined worlds, worlds where I could be anything or anyone I wanted to be. My resolve to one day write a novel of my own swells inside me, and I celebrate my good mood by eating a generous slice of Battenberg cake and drinking a milky cup of sweet tea.

Now I just have to wait for Martha's reply. I can't wait to find out what she needs from me next.

10. Martha

Finn Palin has turned out to be a mine of information. Last night he phoned through details he had lifted from the original notes of the police visit to David Crown, which confirms that at the time of his disappearance they had been unaware of his earlier indecent assault allegation. After some digging, however, Finn was able to tell Martha where the school was and when the trouble took place, but the one thing he refused to give up was the name of the girl in question, despite her begging. 'It doesn't matter how well we know each other, Martha Benn,' he'd said, his tone stern and admonishing. 'You're not getting her name. It wasn't on our patch, and anyway there was no case to answer. The girl dropped the charge. I don't want you or one of your team hassling the poor girl.' Martha knew better than to push it if she wanted his continued support.

This morning, she and Toby have scheduled a Skype call with Jane Needham, the current head teacher of the Bedfordshire school and a close colleague of David Crown's in 1986, at the time of the allegation. They agreed to make the call at Martha's place and now, while Toby unpacks his laptop at the dining table, Martha makes tea at the kitchen island.

'I thought *I* had a good view from my apartment,' Toby says, whistling his approval. 'This place is something else.'

Martha rarely has visitors, and she bristles with embarrassment at his apparent comment on her wealth. *His* place is probably paid for by Daddy.

'I wanted somewhere quiet. Almost impossible in London, unless you go upwards.'

Toby takes the cup from her, pulling out another chair so they can sit side by side in front of the screen. 'I'd never thought of it like that. I always wondered why people were prepared to pay so much for high-rise flats, but, looking out across the city like this, I see it. I could get quite used to a view like that.' He runs a hand through his hair and straightens his collar, looking every bit the public schoolboy as he prepares for his small-screen appearance. 'Ready?'

As the dialling tone echoes into the spacious room, Martha has the gradual sinking feeling that Jane Needham has changed her mind. She'd had no idea just how difficult it was going to be, finding people who were willing to talk about the Juliet case – or David Crown – on record. She's still waiting for a full response from Liv, and she's growing increasingly worried about her reliability. She must be back in the country by now, surely? Martha recalls the way in which Liv disappeared inside herself in the weeks after Juliet had gone and she wonders if perhaps she never really came back. Perhaps, unlike Martha with her newly constructed life and wardrobe, with her upscaled accent and weekly manicures, Liv never moved on from it – and her slowness in coming forward is really a front for her pain. Martha wonders about her own easy ability to close it off, to compartmentalise her childhood

94

and the trauma of losing a friend. Maybe there's something wrong with me, she thinks now, not for the first time.

Just as she begins to give up on the video call as a lost cause, Jane Needham connects, her face coming into view on the main screen. She has an arty look to her: her earrings are large yellow ovals and her white-blonde hair is piled up in a messy twist, a vibrant scarf around her neck.

'Hello?' she says. 'Hello? Sorry – I was having a bit of trouble working out how to do this Skype thing. My son usually sets it up for me when I talk to my sister in – sorry! You're not here to talk about me and my family, are you!' She laughs nervously.

'Hello, Mrs Needham,' Toby says, stepping in to soothe her fluster. He gestures to Martha. 'I'm Toby and this is Martha Benn. Would you mind if we call you Jane?'

She smiles, and instantly Martha knows she'll be a good witness, an honest voice.

'Of course!'

'We're so grateful to you for talking to us, Jane,' Toby says, switching the charm up a notch. 'As I explained on the phone, we're looking into an unresolved crime that took place in London eighteen years ago, and we're particularly interested in asking you about one of the key suspects in that case, Mr David Crown.'

Jane nods, her face easing into a more grave expression. 'Yes. I knew David quite well.'

Martha raises a finger. 'Before we go on, Jane, are you happy for us to record this call? For the programme? We won't use anything without gaining your consent first, but we thought it might save us time filming you all over again later on.'

Jane's hands fly to her cheeks. 'Oh. Oh, I hadn't thought about . . .' After a moment's hesitation she laughs lightly. 'I mean, yes, I'm fine with that.'

95

'OK, so David Crown,' Martha continues. 'He worked at your school between 1983 and 1986?'

'That's right. It was his second job, I believe, and we were in the same department – history. It was an all-girls' school back then, not mixed as we are now, which can in some ways raise more difficulties for teachers like David.'

Martha leans in closer, as though Jane were really just across the table from her. 'Teachers *like David*?'

'Well, David was a very good-looking young man. Quite striking. It wasn't unusual for girls like Vicky Duke to get a crush on a male teacher.'

Martha can't believe how easily the name has tripped off Jane Needham's lips. She jots it down casually, without taking her eyes from the screen.

'Do you think that's what happened here?' Toby asks.

'Well, yes, it's possible. Although in Vicky's case she had an enormous chip on her shoulder to start with, and from what I understand David had given her a hard time in class only the day before she made her allegation. I think it's fair to say that Vicky was a bit of a handful. Her parents were separated – she lived with mum and four siblings – and I recall she had a reputation among the teaching staff as a troublemaker. An attention-seeker, you might say. She was constantly in and out of detentions, or wagging off altogether. Anyway, in this case she'd been turning up consistently late, not handing in her homework, giving bad attitude and so on – and on that particular day David had had enough. He told me – straight after that class, actually, because he was cross that he'd let his emotions get the better of him – that he'd told her she wouldn't amount to anything if she threw away all her hard work for the sake of impressing her friends. When she told him to eff off, he gave her an after-school detention for the following evening. It was then that the "assault" was supposed to have taken place.'

'Were they alone during the detention?'

'No! In a school this size you'll usually have at least a dozen pupils at after-school detention every night. But she claimed that when he dismissed everyone at the end he asked her to stay behind.'

Martha feels sick inside. The story sounds so very plausible. If a girl came to her and told her this story, she'd probably believe it, wouldn't she? She'd believe the girl over the man. 'What exactly was he accused of?'

Jane looks down at her notes. 'I've got the ex-head's statement here, from back in 1986. I can read it out, if you like? It says, "Vicky claims that the moment the classroom was empty Mr Crown told her to take a seat beside his desk, close to him. It was at this point she claims he put his hand up her skirt, inside her knickers (roughly) and told her, 'That's all you're good for,' before dismissing her to go home". It doesn't make for very comfortable reading,' Jane says with a frown.

'Jesus,' Toby whispers. 'If it's true, he sounds like a dangerous man.'

'But that's exactly it, you see,' Jane says, her gesticulating hands causing the screen to momentarily blur. 'He was the *sweetest* man. We'd never before had any kind of complaint – quite the opposite. Everyone liked him: pupils, staff and parents alike. I know the head at the time was delighted with him – even then, male teacher numbers were starting to reduce, and she was glad to have a bright young man like David on the staff. It was clear some of the girls were smitten by him, but he appeared oblivious to it. He was happily married, and from what I recall he was a first-class teacher.

I think you're going to find it difficult to find anyone who'll say David Crown was anything other than a very nice man.'

And he *was* a very nice man, wasn't he? Martha's memories of him are of someone at ease around others – whatever their age – a person who others were drawn to and confided in. Was that who he really was – a good, kind altruist, happy to help others in need? Or did this trustworthy demeanour, more obviously, it seems now, give him all the necessary tools he needed to be a dangerous manipulator?

'But the case never went as far as the police, did it, Jane?' Martha asks. 'Vicky dropped the charge?'

'That's right. I'm not sure of the exact circumstances, but yes, she dropped it. There's a handwritten note at the bottom of the head's statement, saying Vicky retracted her allegation without reservation. That was just a few days after she'd made the original claim.'

After their Skype interview with Jane Needham, Martha sees Toby to the door before picking up her mobile phone, intending to phone Finn Palin for a further conversation about David Crown. Standing at her windows, she looks out across the city, desperately trying to somehow connect the details of her recent conversations and discoveries, to find something – anything – that points them in a positive direction. She is suddenly overcome with exhaustion at the sheer scale of it, and for the first time she actually wonders if they'll ever come close to a breakthrough. It's only a matter of time before the television network starts to put pressure on them for some kind of an update, and really, how much further on are they?

Before he left, Toby had asked Martha if she'd ever seen anything to suggest Juliet and David were an item, and she'd said no. She has the sudden urge to take another look at that Square Wheels photograph, and she spreads her papers out across the dining table, locating it, taking it to the window to scrutinise it closer. There's something there: Juliet, dressed just as she is in this picture, her hair loose, the white volunteer's tabard stark against the dark shade of her coat. A small moment presents itself to Martha, growing in clarity and strength the closer she zooms in on it.

After Martha had stopped volunteering for Square Meals in the summer of 1999, Juliet had continued, and in fact so had Liv for a while. Liv *did* give up eventually, before Juliet went missing, but it was only a matter of a week or two earlier, rather than the months that Martha had originally misremembered. Liv's family needed her around more and more, what with all the younger ones needing watching while her mum was on night shifts, and so by early December Juliet was the last of the three still working there. She was unshakeably dedicated to her work at Square Wheels, despite the lack of pay, often forgoing weekend nights out in favour of a two-hour shift with David Crown and her fellow volunteers. Why had Martha given up so much earlier than the others? They did everything together, so it made no sense. She makes a mental note to ask Liv in her next email.

On this particular night in mid-December, Martha had cycled to Juliet's just after nine – she recalls hearing the title music for the evening news as she left, playing out in the living room above the post-pub snoring of her father in his armchair – only to find Juliet not home.

'She's doing Square Wheels tonight,' Mr Sherman told her, standing in the open doorway, checking his watch. 'She was on the early slot, so I think she should be finishing up about now. Why don't you go and meet her?' he suggested, adding that she was very welcome to stay the night if she wanted.

Mrs Sherman popped her head out of the living room to give a little wave. 'There's fish pie keeping warm in the oven,' she called as Martha turned away. 'Enough for both of you!'

Martha had cycled down to the canal, following the darkened path towards the Square Wheels cabin, lit up like a beacon in the distance. It was a ramshackle old place, a basic garage-type construction, donated by a retired tradesman who no longer needed the space for his carpentry work. Its corrugated sides were decorated with an artwork of salvaged bicycle wheels and a hand-painted wooden sign similar to those you'd find attached to the sides of houseboats along the waterway. As Martha drew nearer, she noticed just two bikes leaning up against the adjoining railings, and she recalled how Juliet had told her that volunteer numbers always dropped off during the holidays, just when they were needed the most. Although Juliet hadn't meant it as a dig, Martha felt ashamed to be one of those winter drop-outs, and as she approached the cabin she was feeling nervous about seeing David Crown again for the first time in months, worried what he might think of her for disappearing as abruptly as she had the summer before. She'd hate him to think badly of her.

Her brakes squeaked loudly as she came to a clumsy halt outside the open workshop doors, the noise causing David Crown and Juliet to look up from what seemed to be a close embrace. There was shock in Juliet's tear-streaked face, but not in David's, and for a moment Martha was utterly confused, seeing something that seemed so clear, before it vanished like a wisp of smoke. David smiled warmly, entirely without malice or guilt, inviting Martha in with an incline of his head, before smoothing the hair from Juliet's damp face and saying, 'OK?'

That was all. *OK?* When Juliet bent to retrieve her bag, David Crown turned his gaze on Martha again and he gave her a wink – not a slimy or suggestive wink, but one that said, *I'm glad you're here, Martha. See your friend home safely, will you?* It made her feel good, that wink. It made her feel useful, grown-up, worthwhile.

As they left Juliet gave David a small shrug of her shoulders and she slung her rucksack over her arm and steered her bike around to walk back along the canal path at Martha's side.

Once the cabin was out of earshot, Martha asked, 'What was that all about, Jules? Why was he hugging you?' Was she jealous? Worried? What was it she had been feeling? She had no idea, but there was anger there, or something similar. 'What's going on?'

'I can't tell you,' Juliet replied, glancing behind, then back at Martha sheepishly.

Martha glowered. 'What d'you mean, you can't tell me? You were . . . you and him . . . were you—?'

'No!' Juliet hissed before Martha's words were even out. 'Don't be stupid, Mart! Oh, my *God*, no! We were just, you know, talking. He's a really good listener. We were packing up and he asked me if I was alright because I'd been a bit quiet tonight, and like a complete idiot I burst into tears. He was just comforting me, that's all.'

Martha gave her another suspicious look, before realising she hadn't even asked Juliet *why* she was so upset. God, did she always have to be so selfish? Perhaps her father was right, she *did* always think about herself first, didn't she?

'Soz, Jules,' she said now. Everything felt so wrong these days – her dad, the drinking, her crappy school, the uncertainty of her future. Everything felt off-kilter, and Juliet's weirdness tonight only added to her hopelessness. 'I don't know why I said that. Jules? *Sorry*. But why can't you tell me? I thought we told each other everything?'

Juliet's eyes moved along the inky line of the canal, before turning back to Martha. 'Alright. Look, I can tell you what, but not who.'

'*O-kay*,' Martha replied, and she bit down on her lower lip, preventing herself from complaining further.

'I'm seeing someone.' Juliet waited for Martha's reaction, and got no more than Martha's unblinking stare pressing her on. 'It's been a few months now, since the end of the summer holidays, actually, and, well . . .' She brought her thumb up to her mouth, nibbling on its nail as she gathered her words. 'And we love each other.'

Martha was stumped, completely at a loss for the right reaction. For the briefest of moments it occurred to her that the end of the summer was when she had stopped volunteering at Square Wheels. Was it someone Juliet had met there? Was that how she had managed to keep this a secret from her for so long? Juliet had never had a boyfriend before, nothing more than mild flirtations with fellow pupils. Liv had had plenty, most of them fleeting and uncomplicated, and she had a wicked way of reducing their significance with her tell-all humour, quick as she was to kiss and tell. Martha had had a few fairly innocent hand-holding relationships at school, followed by a series of drunken and shameful encounters over the past year, after losing her virginity in the alleyway by the Waterside Café to a boy called Jamie, whose subsequent phone calls she refused to answer. But Juliet? Nothing. She'd never talked in that way. Martha had even begun to wonder if she was one of those people who just wasn't interested in sex or romance at all.

'So what's the problem? Why all the secrecy if you love each other?'

Juliet shook her head. 'It's not that straightforward, Mart. My parents wouldn't approve.'

'Do I know him?'

She didn't answer and Martha swallowed her hurt. '*Why* wouldn't they approve?'

Still no reply.

'What is it? Is he older? A bit rough? A druggie? What's so bad that your parents would disapprove?' When Juliet silently started up along the path again, Martha lost her temper. 'For fuck's sake, Jules! I thought we were friends! *Best* friends! Does Liv know? Have you told Liv?'

Juliet shot her a glance, and there it was, that look. *Caught out.* She'd told Liv all about this mystery boyfriend, but she couldn't tell Martha. Even David bloody Crown seemed to know more about it than she did. They stood together at the opening to the pavement where their routes divided, their bicycles nose to nose, the rage blooming between them. Martha didn't want to go back home tonight, whether it be to face her father's alcohol-fuelled fury or the morose silence of his post-pub slumber. But nor could she return to Juliet's now, despite Mr Sherman's invitation, not with this between them.

'I'm sorry,' Juliet whispered, the tears flowing freely again, and she climbed on her bike and rode off into the distance.

Martha gazed after her, before pushing away and cycling in the direction of the Doe Street corner shop, where they'd serve alcohol to anyone with money, no matter how young they looked.

Martha consciously halts the memory here; there's no point trying to remember an evening that almost certainly ended badly. Staring at the palms of her hands, she plays the scene over and over in her head, until the nuances of the evening are as clear as a recent memory. Where was Liv in all this? Had Martha later pressured Liv into telling her Juliet's secret?

She certainly would have tried. And yet she can't retrieve the scene of it at all.

'Where the hell are you, Liv?' she says into the empty space before her.

As if in answer, Martha's phone alerts her to a large number of backed-up emails, and nestled among them is one from Olivia Heathcote, marked as high priority, with the subject header: 'Re: Initial Questions'.

At last, Martha thinks. Perhaps now the pieces will start to slot together.

11. Casey

I wasn't always this sad, introverted soul. And I wasn't always fat. I often wonder how things might have turned out if I'd had a sibling or two, someone else to help care for Mum so that I hadn't had to do it alone. These days, I lie in my bed some mornings, running my hands over the mounds and folds of my flesh, and I barely recognise myself, even though I've been this way now for more years than I care to think about. I try to recall what it was like to feel the firm set of my hipbones beneath the skin, the tracks of my ribs, the dips of my collarbones. Sometimes I try to fool myself into believing that perhaps I am still that thin young woman, merely trapped inside this soft covering of flesh, but I know that's not true because I don't care enough to take steps to return to that body. I never diet, or deny myself, or exercise or exert. This is who I am now. 'Obese,' the doctor said six months ago when I visited to discuss my irritable bowel. 'At risk.' I laughed when he said that, putting my hand to my mouth to shield my teeth, and the doctor looked at me as though I was quite mad. He examined me behind the vinyl curtain of his clinic

105

room, and as he pressed firm fingers against the dough of my stomach, I allowed myself to imagine him slipping them below my elasticated waistband and inside my underwear. Was it wrong of me to have those thoughts? I asked myself later as I lay in the bath reliving the moment, my own fingers moving in the way I had imagined his. Was it wrong to think of a stranger in that way? But his touch, as professional and curt as it had been, was the first physical contact I had had in a long time, and it had released something unexpected in me.

My mother would have been disgusted to hear the inner workings of my mind. She despised any talk of that kind, berating the slipping of standards on British television, the *anything goes* attitude of today's youth. 'Filth,' she would utter if she inadvertently tuned in to *Hollyoaks* or some unexpected erotic scene on TV, and if ever homosexuality was alluded to, or, worse, portrayed in a programme, she would tut breathlessly and switch channels. Goodness, if she could have seen my thoughts, which are certainly far worse than anything she'd ever seen on the telly! She would have thought me a sex maniac – despite the fact that I have never actually been with a man. I haven't even had a boyfriend, though I like to think I've come close. Since I've been on my own, I've been pondering on it more and more, how I should be open to the idea of new experiences, and I suppose this is why Martha's appearance in my life has become so profoundly important to me. Of course, Carl visits once a week too, and he features highly in my waking dreams, as well as my sleeping ones. I fantasise that one day he will deliver my shopping, as he does every Friday, and with the final bags he will push the front door shut and turn to me, taking me by the hand and leading me upstairs to the bedroom. I'll be shy, telling him it's my first time, but he'll reassure me with gentle hands, stripping me of my clothes, laying me across the bed like a sacrifice, legs brazenly apart, my small breasts rising and falling. For a while he'll just stand there, looking at me, enjoying the expanse of me, before sliding his rough hands over the soft creases of my thighs towards my secret place. When we make love, he'll keep his uniform on, and afterwards he'll tell me I'm beautiful, and finally he'll leave me there, draped across the bed, spent and glorious in my nakedness. Lately I've been imagining the scene with lovers other than Carl. Sometimes it's the postman; sometimes it's that nice man from daytime TV. Just lately I've even allowed myself to imagine it's Martha. I'm thinking these thoughts when Martha's next email comes in, sounding out from my laptop on the dressing table across the room, forcing me from my bed when I might easily have lain here all morning.

Now downstairs, I sit in my dressing gown at the small table beside the front window and open my inbox. There's a fine drizzle trickling down the windowpane, obscuring my view to the street, where the rest of the world carries on: the workers, the schoolchildren, the dog-walkers and runners. It strikes me how separate I am from that place beyond the doorstep, how the few rooms inside my little terrace have become my universe. To my delight, Martha has responded to my last message with more observations and questions, but best of all she attaches two photographs of Juliet and her friends at Square Wheels, taken not long before she disappeared. The first, Martha's message tells me, is taken from a local article about the Square Wheels charity, showing David Crown with Juliet Sherman and her brother Tom, and two other volunteers, one of whom is 'possibly called Karen'. The second is a more relaxed image, of four teenagers picnicking beneath a tree alongside the waterway: Juliet, Martha, Liv and Tom.

Martha believes that David Crown took this picture, though she confesses she can barely recall the occasion.

Do you remember that boat trip along the canal, Liv? she asks in her email. *Juliet's dad says he thinks it was a reward trip, something to do with helping David Crown out one weekend on some gardening project. I have a feeling it was something to do with the school pool renovation? I'm struggling a bit – I thought you might be able to tell me more about it?*

She goes on to tell me that before he became a landscape gardener he was a teacher in Bedfordshire. Well, this is news to me, and I'm annoyed at myself for not having known. I *should* have known that. How could I have missed something so vital to his history? Martha tells me she's spoken to the head teacher of his old school, where an allegation had been made against him in the 1980s but later retracted by the pupil in question. This old colleague of his was apparently adamant that it was completely unfounded, though ultimately it led to his leaving the school and giving up teaching altogether. Poor man, I think. People are always so ready to think there's no smoke without fire.

Martha has also been speaking with a 'source' from the police force. When she tells me this information is 'strictly between the two of us' and that his identity is a secret, I could cry with happiness! Look at me, I tell the spectre of my mother, look at me in my new, exciting life. Best friend to television's Martha Benn; collaborator; *insider*. They have yet to convince the police to reopen the investigation to Juliet's case, Martha explains, and she's getting nervous that the television network will pull the plug if she doesn't present them with something more compelling in the next week or so. The thought throws me into such a flap that I spend the next hour researching further – visiting social media groups, newspaper archives, family databases – looking for anything that I might present to Martha as a means of keeping the project afloat. It doesn't have to be the truth, it just has to keep them interested. Fortunately I'm able to find a few more nuggets of information to add to my private Pinterest board, and subtly I weave these into my reply to her.

This time my answers come swiftly, with a fluid certainty they lacked before. The very fact of Martha's difficulty in remembering gives me the freedom to expand on my replies with no fear of getting the details wrong!

Dear Martha,

Gosh, it sounds like you've had a busy week! Thank you for those photographs and oh yes, the boat trip! From what I recall we helped David Crown with some weekend digging work at the old school swimming pool, where they were building a new garden. I think his project was running behind, so he asked us four to help out with the groundwork to bring it back up to speed. The boat trip was his way of thanking us. I recall he brought a picnic along – sandwiches, crisps, apples, and even a can of Coke each – and he borrowed the boat from a man at the canal. He was quite friendly with some of the house-boat residents, what with him having the Square Wheels cabin there. I remember we paddled in the water – I think you and Tom even swam – and it was getting dark by the time we got home. It was such a good day (apart from getting sunburnt on the tops of my shoulders!).

You asked what I can tell you about Juliet's 'secret boyfriend'. I honestly can't think of anything at all. I'm certain I would have said something to the police at the time if I had known. Are you sure you've got it right? Like you said yourself, Juliet never had boyfriends, did she? It is such a long time ago! Perhaps she was pulling your leg or saying she had someone just to impress you or make you jealous? You're not thinking of Ethan, are you, one of the homeless men she used to talk to on volunteer nights?

Yes, of course, I'd love to meet up with you now I'm back in London. Just let me take a look at my diary and come back to you.

Hope to hear from you again soon.

Love, Liv xx

I shut the lid on my laptop, pleasantly exhausted. I'm not sure how much longer I'll be able to put Martha off about meeting in person, but I'll worry about that later. I'm very pleased with my invention of 'Ethan', as it's bound to divert her, and may be just what she needs to keep the TV bosses interested. Right now I feel strangely perky – mischievous, even – strengthened by my insider knowledge of Juliet's story. The answers to Martha's questions had come to me so effortlessly, so convincingly, that I almost believed I was there in that photograph, sunning my legs, laughing up at the gangly boy hanging from the branches above. I head into the kitchen to fetch the family pack of cheese puffs that Carl delivered on Friday, and return to bed, where I daydream the afternoon away with thoughts of that boat trip along the waterway. It's so very real, I can almost feel the warmth of the sun on my skin, the cool water at my toes.

Tomorrow I may share with her a photograph of David Crown I recently uncovered, the one of him in his teenage years, arm draped around his girlfriend's shoulder, cigarette in mouth, the great plateau of Kinder Scout rising up behind them. It's 1970, but the girl wears a rather old-fashioned dark beehive, a classic sixties shift dress and neck scarf; he's in baggy trousers and braces, his shirt sleeves rolled up casually to reveal sinewy, tanned arms. It took a lot of digging to find this one, and I know Martha won't have seen it before. I'll tell her that David gave it to me when we were volunteering at Square Wheels, and see where that little lie takes us!

12. **Martha**

Toby offers to drive the four-hour journey to Castledale so that Martha can read through their progress notes and plan the next steps. It's a Sunday, but with the hours they've been putting in lately, the significance of weekends has all but vanished.

Last night *he* tried to call again, leaving a sorrowful message on her voicemail, telling her he loved her through slurred vowels, begging her to get in touch before it was too late. Had he told her? he asked. He was dying. 'No bullshit this time,' he'd said, resignation in his voice. 'I really am dying.'

Does she believe him? She doesn't have a clue what to believe, she thinks hopelessly, her eyes fixed on the road ahead. Is he telling the truth, or is it just another one of his lies, one of his wretched cries for help that come when he knows his tactics of bullying or persuasion have failed? How can she ever know? The man is so wedded to self-delusion, his ability to separate truth from lies so terminally broken, it's no wonder she sees his every plea as a ruse, a trick. The last time she actually responded to one of these SOS calls was over a year ago, and she went to him, perhaps hoping to find comfort, to give comfort. But all he'd wanted was money. He hadn't wanted her care or affection or love; he'd barely hugged her back before getting down to the real business of his call. He wanted her money, and a lift to the nearest off-licence.

Martha swallows this resurrected anxiety into the pit of her stomach and returns to the paperwork. 'Why on earth would David Crown have given *Liv* a picture of himself?' she says. 'Especially one of him taken years earlier, and with an ex-girlfriend of all things? Liv hardly knew David Crown. Out of all of us, she had probably spent the least amount of time with him.' She held the printed image at arm's length so that Toby could snatch a glance as he drove. *Liv* and David Crown? Martha could barely allow the idea to germinate in her mind. Impossible. She would have known. One hundred per cent. She *knows* she would have known. But *why* won't Liv commit to meeting up? It's driving Martha insane. She resolves to force the issue when she gets back to London; maybe she'll even spring a visit on her.

'Reminds me of the Moors Murderers' photographs from the sixties,' says Toby. 'It's a powerful image.'

Martha continues to gaze at the black and white photograph, trying to recognise the David Crown she once knew. The one in the picture could only be, what, late teens? Martha hadn't met him until his mid-forties, and he was quite altered by then: stronger of jaw, taller perhaps, a solid man as opposed to a lean teenager.

'If he's around seventeen in this picture, it would be about 1969 or '70 by my estimate. I'm hoping this could be useful if we bump into any locals who knew him back then. Might jog a few memories, perhaps give us some insight into the kind of young man he was before he moved away.'

Tomorrow they have a meeting with a Mrs Thatcher, neighbour of the Crown family and the only person they have so far been able to locate in Castledale who knew David as a teenager. Other than that one appointment, they're taking a punt on this trip, hoping they might find a few others who can tell them a bit more about the kind of young man he was back then.

Toby indicates, taking the slip road on to the M1, shrugging his shoulders against the back of his seat as he settles into the journey. 'He left Castledale altogether not long after that photo, didn't he?'

'Yep. After A-levels, he got a place at university in Cambridge, going straight on to teacher training and from there into his first teaching job. High achiever. According to Finn Palin's notes, he married quite young – he and Janet met at Cambridge – and she described him as loyal, hardworking, gentle. The "perfect husband". Everything in his history suggests he was reliable and steady – apart from that blot in his second teaching job, at St Cuthbert's in Bedfordshire.' She reaches into the carrier bag at her feet and brings out a supermarket sandwich, peeling back the wrapper and offering half to Toby. 'It's interesting that he moved away *and* changed career direction so completely after St Cuthbert's. That suggests to me a man starting over, someone wanting to put the past in a box and forget it. A guilty conscience, perhaps.'

Toby chews a mouthful of sandwich thoughtfully. 'He was only in his early thirties when that allegation was made against him. If I was a teacher and that happened to me, I think I'd respond in one of two ways. If I were guilty, I reckon I'd thank my lucky stars for a close shave, move away and look for another teaching job – especially if I was a serial predator, looking to put myself in contact with more young women. But if I were *innocent*, I think it would wreck me. I think I'd

114

fall apart for a while, and I'm pretty sure I wouldn't want to stay in the teaching profession. I'd be terrified of it happening again, no matter how innocent I was.'

Martha hands him an apple, polishing her own against her trouser leg, considering his words. 'So, what, you think he's innocent?'

'I've no idea,' Toby replies. 'But it would be interesting to get hold of his medical records from that time. I wouldn't be surprised if he'd had some kind of breakdown before he moved to London and retrained. You said there's a gap in his employment history between Bedfordshire and retraining as a gardener in London. That would explain it.'

It's an interesting idea, and one which on the surface makes complete sense. But if David isn't their answer – if he isn't their man – then who is? What about this *Ethan* who Liv mentioned? Could it be him?

'A breakdown doesn't automatically make him innocent,' Martha concludes sharply, tearing open a multipack of KitKats and flinging one into Toby's lap. 'A breakdown might just mean he's got a whole mountain of stuff to feel bad about.'

'Maybe,' Toby replies, returning the chocolate bar to Martha with a shake of his head.

'Oh, don't tell me,' she says with a groan, 'you're one of those sugar-is-the-devil types?'

He looks perplexed, his attention fixed on the road. 'No, not at all.'

'Then what?' she demands.

'Bloody hell, Martha,' he laughs. 'Are you always this arsey? I just don't like KitKats!'

She folds her arms across her chest with a huff, all the while trying to suppress a smile. 'Alright, clever clogs. Now don't disturb me for the next hour or so, please. I need to gather my thoughts.' With that, she closes her eyes and lets the motion of the car lull her into light sleep.

The Peak Inn is a traditional stone-built pub in the centre of the village, standing on a street that tapers out to showcase the majestic hills and dales of Derbyshire. The landscape here is so vast, so unencumbered by urban sprawl and around-the-clock traffic, the sky so near and rolling. Even the drizzle on Martha's face feels like welcome relief from the dark intensity of the past few weeks in London.

A sharp recollection comes to her as she stands in the cool, dimming light outside the pub: geography class in Year Nine at school – the rain tapping hard at the metal-framed windows, condensation misting the glass – her, Juliet and Liv leaning over a worktable, laughing and chatting as they marked up a diagram of Derbyshire's Peak District. Limestone; millstone grit; white peak; plateau. Strange, the way the mind lets these long-forgotten memories slip in, unbidden.

'Right, let's check in,' Toby says, appearing from the side street where he's parked the car.

Martha takes her overnight bag from him and they enter the public bar to the welcoming heat of an open fire. It's just after 3 p.m., and the pub is quiet apart from a couple of solitary drinkers around the bar and an elderly border collie sleeping at the hearth. A heavy-set man in his seventies rises from the seat beside the fireplace, offering a closed-mouth smile and stepping behind the bar. Martha can tell by the way he holds her gaze for a moment too long that he half recognises her and is trying to place the face.

'Hi,' she says, putting down her bag. 'We should have a booking for tonight – under the name of Benn.'

'Ah,' the landlord replies, his expression at once falling into a friendly one of recognition. 'Miss Benn!' He reaches across the bar to shake her hand, and Toby's, though this seems to be an afterthought. 'Anthony Laight, landlord. *Ant*. Pleasure to have you here!' After another few seconds of starstruck staring, Anthony Laight refers to his booking diary. 'Now, then, is it two rooms for you – or a double?'

'*Two*,' Martha replies rather too firmly, avoiding looking at Toby as she knows he'd find the suggestion amusing.

'*Definitely* two,' Toby adds, and Martha swivels her eyes towards him, a silent reproach.

The staircase to the first floor is creaky and narrow, with local photographs of the village displayed all the way to the top. Many of them are old and faded, relics from the Victorian age, and every one of them features the main high street with the mountainous landscape clear in the distance. Ant leads the way, insisting on carrying Martha's case (but not Toby's, she notices with childish pleasure), pausing briefly at the top step to catch his breath. At the end of the narrow landing he unlocks the first room, holding the door open for Martha to enter. It's small and neatly decorated in whites and neutrals, a double bed taking up much of the space.

'It's our best room – see the views? Hope this will suit you, m'duck?'

'It's great,' Martha replies, feeling uncomfortable at the close proximity she now shares with Ant and Toby, who has stepped inside to have a nosey.

'And you, young man,' Ant tells Toby, a hand on his back, 'are just next door.'

Martha had hoped they might be a few doors apart. Somehow the next room seems far too intimate, and she wonders if his headboard backs on to hers.

'Want a look?' Toby gestures to his room as Ant makes his way back along the hall.

Martha scowls from her open door. 'Not especially.'

As Ant reaches the bottom step, he calls back up. 'Oh, are you lovebirds joining us for dinner tonight?'

Martha and Toby make wide eyes at each other. 'Cheeky sod,' she whispers.

'The special's beef and ale pie. Seven o'clock. I'll save you a table in the lounge bar if you're interested?'

'That'll be great,' Toby replies without consulting Martha, and he bats away her protests and retreats into his room.

'*Cheeky* sod,' she repeats to herself as she closes the door to her own room, kicking off her shoes and reopening the file notes before spreading them across the bed. The Square Wheels photograph sits on top, and Martha taps out a brief message to Juney: *Any luck getting names for those two unidentified Square Wheels volunteers?* Surely if they locate those two other girls – women now – they may be able to help piece together a bit more from the evening of Juliet's disappearance, or at least give an insight into Juliet's relationship with David at the time. Were they fly-by-night volunteers, like so many, or were they friends of Juliet's – friends Martha knew nothing about? It unsettles her, the thought that Juliet had a life beyond the one Martha knew.

Martha scrolls back through her inbox, knowing there's something bothering her about Liv's recent email. It's only when she reads it again that it strikes her so obviously. Why would Liv suggest Juliet wanted to make Martha jealous? Liv, more than anyone, knows that Juliet didn't have a spiteful bone in her body. She would never have tried to make Martha jealous over something so trivial as a boyfriend. And furthermore, Liv claims to have had no knowledge of this secret – but

118

Juliet said that Liv knew, that Liv had known for several weeks. Could Liv really have forgotten something as significant as this? For the first time, Martha allows herself to consider a new possibility: that Olivia Heathcote knows more about Juliet's disappearance than she's letting on.

Just before seven, Toby knocks on Martha's door. 'Care to join me for dinner, m'duck?' he asks, aping Anthony Laight's soft Midland tones.

She gathers up her notes and returns them to her bag, locking the bedroom door as she leaves. 'Does he seriously think we're a couple?' she whispers as they descend the stairs.

'Dunno, but he went to great pains to tell me there's a connecting door between the two rooms.'

'Locked, I'm glad to say,' Martha replies. 'I checked.'

'Charming!' Toby laughs and stands back to let her enter the lounge bar before him.

The pub seems to have come to life over the past couple of hours, a reassuring hum of chatter now rising up throughout the place. The lounge and the public bar merge into one, with Ant's counter separating the two, and all but a couple of the smaller tables are occupied by groups of customers drinking and placing food orders, their laughter and conversation creating a warm, relaxed ambience.

'You happy to have the pie?' Toby asks Martha, heading to the bar to order.

She nods, taking the table that Ant has pointed out to them, scanning the room as she tries to work out which of the customers are locals, assessing whether any of them might be worth a chat with.

Toby hands her a tonic water and she takes a first sip, savouring the lemon cool of it on her tongue. She's silently grateful to Toby for not interrogating her when she asked for a soft drink, for not pulling a face or trying to persuade her to have something stronger.

'Cheers,' she says, clinking glasses. 'To Juliet.'

'To Juliet,' he echoes, and for a moment they sit in contented silence, taking in the atmosphere, enjoying the moment before the first autograph-seeker appears at their table. She's a casually dressed woman in her late fifties, her hair bundled into a loose bun – not your average fan. Martha squiggles her autograph on a menu card, trying to smile away her irritation. She never asked for any of this; she loves her job, but not this, dealing with the public's reaction to a face from the telly. As the woman walks away, Martha grimaces at Toby but he raises a finger and calls out, 'Excuse me!'

The woman turns back, surprised.

'Are you local? I don't suppose you know the Crown family, do you? I think they lived here up until the sixties or seventies.'

A look of recognition crosses the woman's eyes, but then she shakes her head. 'It rings a bell. Want me to ask about for you?' After a beat she adds in a whisper, 'Is it for a new programme or something?'

With the hint of a smile Toby replies, 'No,' while meaningfully nodding his head.

'Ah, got you,' the woman replies knowingly. 'I'll see what I can do.'

'Bloody hell, you're good,' Martha tells him as she takes another sip of her drink. 'Very slick.'

Over the next couple of hours, the woman – Jenny – pops back with a series of disappointing updates. Most of the people she knows are too young to remember much from the period David Crown would have lived in Castledale, and many of them are incomers to the village. As they eat their supper and discuss their plan of action for tomorrow, they give up hope of finding any answers in the local pub, instead relaxing in each other's company, he drinking pinot noir, she moving on to sparkling water.

'So you went to boarding school?' Martha asks Toby, whose posture is measurably more relaxed after a second glass of wine. 'How come? I mean, why boarding?'

He picks up his own glass, scrutinising the contents before putting it back on the table without drinking from it. 'I didn't want to go – I was terrified of leaving home so young. But it was a family tradition. My older brothers and my father – and his father – all went to the same school, so it was always part of the plan. But it also meant Dad could concentrate on his work rather than bringing us up.'

Martha frowns. 'What about your mum? What did she think about it?'

'She buggered off altogether when I was thirteen, so that kind of sealed my fate. I haven't seen her in years.'

'Mine too,' Martha says before she can stop herself. 'My mum. She left me and my dad when I was fifteen.'

'Tough, isn't it?' And that's all he says on the matter.

Martha silently chastises herself for the unfairness of her earlier assumptions and prejudices. They're not so very different after all.

The pub is clearing out now, and with most of the diners gone, only a handful of drinkers remain. The lights around the lounge are soothingly low, the dark wood of the place like a cocoon against the cold wind that whips along the street outside.

Ant calls to them from the bar. 'Can I buy you lovebirds a nightcap?' he asks with a smirk that tells them he really is just winding them up. 'Cognac? Scotch?'

121

They leave their table seat and join him at the bar, sliding on to age-worn wooden stools to accept his offer. There's another man, perhaps a few years younger than Ant, on the public bar side, facing them. He glances at them briefly before turning his attention back to his pint. A small cluster of younger customers are in the fireside seats and a middle-aged couple remain in the lounge bar, drinking after-dinner coffees, snatching the occasional peek at Martha. The mood of the pub is entirely different now, hushed and ancient once the noise has been stripped away.

'I hear you want to know a bit about the Crown family?' Ant says, sliding two small glasses across the counter.

Martha raises her eyebrows in surprise. Of course – why hadn't they asked Ant in the first place? Pub landlords know *everyone*. The man across the bar looks at her for a moment too long, and it's clear he's tuning in to their conversation.

'I went to school with their younger boy – Dick. They had Blackdog Farm over beyond the copse; been in the family for years, for as long as I remember, anyways. Nice family. I used to go back there for my tea sometimes, when my mum was busy. Mrs Crown made the best fruit scones this side of the Peaks.'

Toby has taken the notebook from his back pocket, and he scribbles down the details as quickly as Ant speaks them.

'*Fuck's sake*, Ant.' They're interrupted by the sound of the man's empty glass slamming down on the bar. 'They're not here to ask about the woman's bloody scones, are they?'

Ant raises his eyes to the ceiling before turning to address the man. Martha switches her full shot glass with Toby's empty one.

'Go on, then, Eddie,' Ant says. 'Get it off your chest.'

'They want to know about that lass he killed, don't they? David Crown and that lass from Pleasley. Tilly Jones.'

PART TWO

A Death

I had been sitting on that wooden bench for a while by the time the two girls came strolling along the darkened canal path, wheeling their bicycles between them, flawless in the fractured shades of evening. I strained to tune into their conversation as their soft tones drifted towards me on the winter air, tried to make out their features as the flash of lamplight illuminated their young skin and flowing hair. Silently I left the bench to disappear myself into the shadows of the hedgerow, where I might remain unseen, invisible as a ghost. Look at them! I marvelled. They glide with the carelessness of creatures accustomed to their own beauty, for they've never known anything different, have they? Since their first breath, one imagines they have been told it. What a *beautiful* baby, strangers would have said. What a *beautiful* little girl. What a *beautiful* young woman. The one I had my eye on reminded me so much of another I'd once known, a lifetime ago, in a different place, a different time altogether. It occurred to me in that moment, as I tracked those unsuspecting fawns, that beauty is surely the strongest currency – the most potent of lures. What unsightly man or woman in possession of a great fortune wouldn't readily swap a large part of it for just a little of that magic?

Before long, the girls paused where the footpath opens out on to the main street beyond, now only a short distance from me, continuing to speak in hushed tones.

'It must be more than that,' the girl in the striped hat said, turning her bike wheels towards the exit path. The elegant lines of their bodies, the juxtaposition of the two bicycles at opposing angles, seemed almost balletic in its arrangement. 'It's not like Liv to lose the plot so easily. Me, yes – but not Liv.'

The taller girl lifted one delicate wrist, pushing back her thick hair, a swirl of white breath drifting from her mouth like mist. 'Honestly, I haven't got a clue. It isn't just you she's been funny with lately.' She tugged at the white tabard she wore over her winter coat, readjusting its hem to bring the Square Wheels logo into clear view.

'She even had a go at Tom earlier,' said the other. 'I still reckon she's got a thing for him. She seems to be hanging around your house a lot more lately.'

The Square Wheels girl laughed raucously, betraying her real self, and I swear I saw the brightness of her sputter like a flame in a draught. 'No, I already asked her. She said she'd never be interested in Tom – and anyway, he's just started seeing some girl at uni.'

It was strangely exhilarating to listen in, unseen, to hear them talk of boys in this casual, disposable fashion. I almost forgot why I was there, what it was that I came to the water-side to do. To my irritation a rush of traffic passed beyond the hedgerow, drowning out their words, though it was clear to me there was tension between them when their voices drifted back into my earshot. The striped hat girl turned her bike around to face back the way they've just come.

'Can't you leave it until tomorrow?' asked the other. It sounded like a complaint.

'No – the café doesn't open up until mid-morning, does it?' There was impatience in her voice now, her words slurred. They'd been drinking, that much was clear. 'Anyway, I don't want to risk someone nicking it.'

Another cyclist zipped by, going one way; a dog walker passed along the path in the other. The girls lowered their voices and I could feel the strained atmosphere between them as I struggled to listen in. But all I could make out was 'tomorrow', delivered with resignation in its tone.

'Promise?' the other one said in reply, and they embraced stiffly before the girl in the hat cycled away, her figure disappearing into the night.

For just a brief moment, the lone girl paused on the frosty path, her eyes resting on the gently rippling surface of the water, and I saw something shift in her expression. What was it? Sadness? Regret? Whatever it was, it was fleeting, vanishing entirely as she mounted her bicycle and pushed away, sailing past me, flaxen locks streaming behind her like spun gold.

'Oh, hello!' I called after her, feeling a surge of panic rising as I stepped out on to the path and adrenaline flooded my veins. 'Hi!'

She came to a stop, jerkily hopping on one foot as she twisted to look back at me, her mouth breaking into a broad, gleaming smile. 'Hi!' she called back lightly, and she seemed pleased to see me. She had the power to paralyse, that one. 'I'm late, aren't I? Has everyone else headed off?'

'No, you're fine,' I replied, beckoning her over. 'Actually, I'm glad you're here,' I said as she approached, indicating towards the shadows at the foot of the bench. 'I'm having a bit of trouble with this . . .'

127

As she bent to take a closer look I glanced up and down the empty towpath and hooked the fishing rope beneath her beautiful chin, tugging her up and towards me, crossing my wrists to close up the circle and shut off her breath.

Right up until that moment, I believe I had only meant to talk with her. Of course the rope was coiled and ready in my pocket, and one might gather from that alone that I had waited on the path with the sole intention of extinguishing that girl's life. But that wasn't how it was: the rope was merely a precaution – something I'd picked up in the cabin earlier that same evening, sliding it into my pocket without malice or plan. Even as the girl took her last gasp, as her mittened hands fumbled to gain purchase on mine, her writhing legs slowing to a weak judder, I regretted not talking to her as I had planned. If I'd just spoken with her, as I'd intended, things could have worked out quite differently. I know that now. I know now that I got a few things wrong. A little mixed up, you might say.

But I've always been somewhat rash; it's a curse.

13. **Martha**

The next morning, Martha and Toby have an early breakfast in the quiet of the Peak Inn lounge bar, discussing last night's revelation. According to Eddie's account, in the spring of 1970 a seventeen-year-old girl called Tilly Jones was brutally murdered and left in the copse close to David Crown's family home at Blackdog Farm. The girl, new to the village, was known to David, as the parents were old family friends who had moved in from Mansfield way only a few weeks earlier. On the day in question, David had been asked to show Tilly around and together they had gone to a local café, watched a film at the cinema and got chatting with a few of David's friends before he walked her home. But Tilly Jones never made it home, and when she was found dead at the copse the following morning, David was the first to be questioned.

This extraordinary piece of news has kept Martha tossing and turning most of the night.

The rest of the breakfast area is empty, and when landlord Ant brings their food, he pulls up a seat.

'The girl in that photograph you showed me last night,' he says. 'I phoned my brother – he's a few years older than me. Her name was Hattie Brown – Harriet, I suppose – and he can't remember much about her, other than the fact she was going out with David back when he was doing his A-levels. What he did say was that she – the girlfriend – was the reason David didn't get charged. Turns out Hattie was with him when he walked Tilly home. Lots of folks, like Eddie, for example, didn't believe it, thought she was just covering for him, but then, sometimes people just want to believe the worst, don't they?'

'Do you know where she is now?' Toby asks.

'Again, the family moved on years back. Stew said they lived in the big house on Dale Road, but I can't picture her. I think she was away at boarding school most of the time.'

Martha makes a note to get Juney on the case to trace this old girlfriend. If she *was* with him that night, she would be able to provide vital insight into David's involvement – or otherwise – in the murder of Tilly Jones.

As they settle their bill, Jay and Sally arrive, having driven up early from London to film the location shots. In separate cars, they all set off in the direction of Blackdog Farm, just a mile outside of Castledale, stopping off several times en route to film some straight-to-camera pieces. Since the latest revelation, Martha has cobbled together some additional scripts, which she delivers to camera against the backdrop of the Derbyshire peaks.

'When we arrived in Castledale last night, we were in search of more information about David Crown, missing London gardener and charity worker, and the main suspect in the case of vanished student Juliet Sherman in 2000. Less than twenty-four hours later, and our enquiries have uncovered more questions than they have answers, presenting us with a second cold case from three decades earlier – the unsolved murder of teenager Tilly Jones. Two seventeen-year-olds, missing or dead – a coincidence, perhaps?' She hesitates for a beat, unblinking. 'Perhaps. Except for the fact that our missing charity worker David Crown was a person of interest in both cases.'

She waits for Sally to give her the nod, then snaps her notebook shut and jumps back into the passenger seat.

'Bloody hell,' Toby says, indicating and pulling away. 'You really are a pro, Martha. I've never seen someone nail a take so quickly.'

She laughs, and decides she'll let him do the next one. It'll be good for him, both the experience and the exposure. After this short period of working with Toby, it's clear to Martha that she had been wrong to judge him so harshly. Any reservations she had about him were more to do with her own insecurities than his ability to do a good job, and she makes a mental note not to be such a tight-arsed cow in future.

For a Monday morning, the drive from Castledale couldn't be more different from a morning's commute in central London, and as they pass through hedge-lined lanes and alongside mist-shrouded fields, Martha wonders how she would fare in the countryside. As beautiful as this place is, she suspects she's a city girl through and through.

Toby slows down as they approach a lone house on the edge of farmland, a tall brick building, a little shabby around the window frames and doors. 'This must be the neighbour's place. What did you say her name was?'

'Thatcher,' Martha replies, and she checks the time on her phone. Ten o'clock. They park the car in a lay-by, and Martha instructs Jay and Sally to carry on up the road to capture some footage of the Crown place as it looks now.

'We'll see you there afterwards,' she says. 'Just a couple more speaking pieces and then I think we're done.' She looks up and down the road. 'Jay, see if you can get me and Toby walking towards the neighbour's house – and the neighbour answering the door, if possible?' She checks her watch. If they get a move on with this interview, they could all be back in London by three or four. She taps out a text to Finn Palin, asking him to meet her later today. 'OK, let's go.'

The woman who answers the door is elderly, dressed in a faded floral dress beneath a floury apron. Her white hair is rolled neatly around her small head, and she has all the appearance of a traditional fairytale grandmother. Martha takes care to position herself in such a way as to allow Jay and Sally a clear shot. She'll ask for permission later, once they know whether it's relevant or not.

'Hello, Mrs Thatcher,' Martha says. 'Martha Benn. You're expecting us?'

Within minutes they are seated at the woman's round farmhouse kitchen table, looking at photographs of the two families enjoying a celebration in the garden here, the views overlooking Blackdog Farm. There are only a few pictures, but it seems the Thatchers and Crowns knew each other well, before the Crowns moved on.

Mrs Thatcher places a teapot on the table, inviting Toby to pour. 'I'm a good few years older than David, but of course, who could forget the murder? It shook the community. For a long time people stopped walking home late at night. No one wanted to let their kids out of their sight.'

'Do you think David Crown killed Tilly?' Martha asks, the tea poured, the niceties done.

Mrs Thatcher tuts, her friendly demeanour clouding for a moment. 'David didn't kill Tilly Jones. I know all about the rumours, but the poor boy was just in the wrong place at the wrong time. And anyway, he was with his girlfriend, wasn't he? She told the police she was with David, and that was that. But you know how people like to gossip.'

'Did you know her well?' Martha checks her notes. 'Hattie Brown?'

'Not really. She was only ever here in the holidays – I think she was away at school the rest of the time. Pretty girl. The Crown family sold up a couple of years after all this, when the father died. That place of theirs was enormous – it's a country hotel now.'

'And David was never charged?' Toby asks, steering the conversation back.

'There was nothing to charge him with. David told them the truth – that they'd walked Tilly most of the way home, and said goodbye to her at the edge of the copse, where her house was in sight. That's the worst part of it: she was murdered just yards from her family home.'

'It must have been awful, for all of you,' Martha says. 'Do you recall if there were any other suspects?'

The woman sighs heavily. 'There was plenty of speculation, of course – not all of it helpful – but as far as I know no one else was taken in. You get a lot of walkers through here, all seasons, heading for the Peaks. That seemed to be the favourite opinion, that it was a stranger, some maniac who chanced upon her. You know her skull was completely crushed? Poor love.'

Martha is momentarily derailed, wondering what kind of person has the capacity to crush a person's skull. To crush them to death. Could David Crown have done something like that?

Toby steps in to ask the next question. 'Why do you think he – David and the rest of his family – moved away so suddenly?'

Mrs Thatcher stands momentarily, picking up oven gloves and fetching a tray of scones from the dark range cooker that dominates the far wall. She places the tray on the top and returns to sit at the table. The smell is so comforting. Martha breathes it in, savouring the reassuring warmth of the homely kitchen.

'Oh, it wasn't all that sudden,' the elderly woman says, reaching across to top up their teacups. 'David went first because he had a place at university – Cambridge, I think. He was a clever boy. Most of the youngsters move away from here eventually, looking for something new.'

'And the parents?'

'They'd had enough of farming,' she says sadly. 'And the gossip. They'd had enough of the gossip.'

When Mrs Thatcher sees them to the door, she hands Toby a rolled paper napkin containing two warm scones. She rests a hand on Martha's arm and smiles kindly. 'You know, David – and the rest of the Crown family – they were some of the nicest people I'd ever met. I don't think there was a bad bone in that entire family. Until that business with Tilly Jones, he'd never had a moment's bother, you know? Bright as a button and meek as a mouse. If you want my opinion, David wasn't charged back then for the very good reason that he was innocent.'

By four o'clock they're back in London, and Toby drops Martha and her overnight bag close to where she's meeting Finn Palin. For most of the journey she's been revisiting last night's conversation with Ant and the man at the bar, and today's visit with Mrs Thatcher – wondering how the police could have missed so fundamental a coincidence when they were investigating Juliet's disappearance thirty years later.

Martha had hoped to find out more about the young David Crown on this Derbyshire trip. But she hadn't anticipated a breakthrough of this gravity: another dead girl. Another seventeen-year-old girl murdered, and David Crown once again in the close vicinity. Surely they had to be connected? At any rate, one thing was clear: Derbyshire had presented them with more questions than it had answers.

Now she's sitting in the café, and when Finn Palin enters through the steamed-up glass door, Martha feels an unexpected rush of emotion. She's been speaking to him regularly since starting on this project, but she hasn't seen him in the flesh for a good few years. He's aged, in a good way, his serious expression having softened into sun-weathered creases that gather around his eyes. She rises, and he wraps her in a strong embrace.

'Look at you.' He smiles as he releases her and pulls out the chair facing hers. 'All grown-up.'

She raises her eyebrows. 'I'm thirty-five, Finn. I've been grown-up a fair few years now.'

'Thirty-four,' he replies with a crinkle of his face. 'Still, you've got some way to catch up to me. Sixty-five this year.'

'Same as Dad. You're looking good, by the way, in case that was what you were fishing for?'

Finn laughs, as though that wasn't what he meant, but looking pleased all the same. They've chosen an inconspicuous greasy spoon, halfway between Finn's old patch and Martha's home, somewhere he knows other coppers won't frequent and where she won't attract too much unwanted attention. The woman behind the counter brings over two mugs of tea and a Danish pastry, which Martha ordered when she arrived. Martha slides the pastry across the formica table.

'My favourite,' Finn says.

'I know,' Martha replies. 'It's on me.'

'So, what can I help you with, love? It goes without saying—' he starts to say.

Martha holds her hands up. 'Your name will never come up in this – but are you happy for us to quote "police sources"? I mean, you're retired now, so it shouldn't come back on you in any way. But I don't want you to put yourself at any risk.'

'Just keep my name out of it and I'll do whatever I can to help. This is all a bit "below board" for me, Martha, but I know what it means to you. A couple of Crime Squad lads who came up under me have said they're prepared to help with a bit of historical info, so long as there's no trace back to them.' He stirs a sugar into his tea, and Martha is grateful for his matter-of-fact approach. 'Any joy with your old friend? Olivia, is it?'

Martha releases an exasperated breath. 'I'm not sure what's going on there. She's been fairly forthcoming in her emails, but impossible to pin down to a face-to-face meeting. She's living in the same place in Hackney, so it's not as if it would be difficult for her to meet up. I can't help wondering if she's hiding something, something to do with Juliet's disappearance that she just doesn't want to tell me. Maybe I should just drop in on her. Force the issue.'

'Sometimes an element of surprise is your best bet,' Finn agrees. 'Though you run the risk of alienating her if she's not happy about it.'

'That's what I'm worried about. I emailed her again last night, but I guess I could leave it a few days and see if she warms to the idea.'

'Or you could try appealing to her as a friend,' Finn suggests. 'Old loyalties die hard. Why else d'you think I'm here, love?'

Martha smiles at him and opens up her work book, placing two newspaper articles on the table between them. She points to the first, a national press cutting from March 2000, stating that the police had called off their search for Juliet. 'OK. So, as you know I've been investigating Juliet Sherman's disappearance from 2000, with the prime suspect being David Crown, who disappeared the next day. Obviously, at the time, the police wrote it off as the pair having run away together, but we – I – believe that has to be wrong. I'm certain Juliet was killed – and I'm pretty sure David Crown is still out there.'

'It's a long time since I had anything to do with the case, and you know I was never directly involved. You say he's never been heard of since? No bank account activity, no passport renewals, no traffic offences and so on?' Finn bites into his pastry, moving his jaw thoughtfully. 'Obviously we can't rule out the possibility that he's dead.'

'Yes, but people change their identities all the time, don't they? I mean, how hard would it have been for him to set up a life elsewhere with a new name and back story? Especially with fifty grand in his back pocket?'

'Not that hard,' Finn agrees. 'I double-checked the file notes for you, and that was a strong theory when the investigation was closed – when it was decided that Juliet might have left willingly with David Crown.'

'I can't believe they'd write off a seventeen-year-old girl so easily. None of us, not a single one of her friends or family had previously suspected Juliet was having a relationship with David. So why did the police jump to the conclusion so quickly?'

'There was an anonymous tip-off,' Finn says. 'A phone call. My guy's only just spotted it in the files – for some reason it had become separated from the rest of the case notes.'

'What? What did the caller say?'

'It was a female caller, claiming to have seen Juliet and David Crown together in the Square Wheels hut a week or two earlier. Kissing.'

Martha is shaking her head now, trying to bring this piece of information into some kind of order. Juliet and David Crown? Kissing?

'No,' she says firmly. 'Not Juliet. I don't believe it.'

Finn gives a small shrug of his shoulders. 'As I say, it was anonymous, and as such would have been treated with some caution. The caller didn't say she knew Juliet, just that the girl she saw matched the pictures of Juliet released by the press at the time. I think the phone call, along with the love letter found in Juliet's bin – and the fact that David Crown had withdrawn his life savings before disappearing – would have presented a pretty persuasive argument to believe Juliet had left with David Crown under her own steam.'

'But she was seventeen! Shouldn't they have been trying to find her, whether or not they were having some kind of relationship?' Martha is incensed, both at the police's relaxed attitude to a young girl's safety, but even more at herself, as she realises she's beginning to consider whether this might actually be true. *Could* Juliet have run off with David Crown? Even now, with this new body of evidence, she can't bring herself to fully believe it. 'Jesus, Finn,' she says. 'What the hell were the police thinking?'

He folds his heavy arms on the table, his mouth tugging down at the corners. 'Things have changed a lot since my day, love,' Finn says. 'And I'm certain Juliet's case wouldn't have been closed down so quickly if it happened now. I'm ashamed to say it, but in an overstretched police force *some* officers would look to move caseloads from their desk with as much speed as possible. And if that meant shutting down

138

a few as "unsolved" – well, I think it's fair to say, every now and then the wrong ones were passed over.'

Martha knows the police aren't infallible, but despite her dad's less than unblemished final years with them, she has always believed they are there to protect and safeguard. The thought of them treating crimes in this way is too much. Would her dad have been one of those lazy officers, quick to extinguish an investigation for the sake of a quiet life?

'She was just a teenager. Would you have passed over a case like this, Finn?'

'No,' he replies. 'I wouldn't. And before you ask, neither would your dad. I don't need to remind you, love, but when Juliet Sherman went missing, Eric had already taken early retirement. But I remember how much the case upset him, what with you girls being so close, and he was spitting feathers when he heard they'd scaled back the investigation. Like you, he thought it unbelievable to suggest she'd run off with David Crown.'

'But Dad barely knew what I was doing or where I was going from one day to the next. He was so wrapped up in his own stuff I'm surprised he even knew I had a best friend called Juliet . . .' Martha trails off, focusing on bringing down the accelerating thud of her heart, inwardly berating herself for letting him get to her, even now.

'Your dad was more interested in you than you think, love,' Finn says, chucking her beneath the chin to force her to meet his gaze. 'I remember he had me run a check on that lad you got hitched to, when you first brought him home.'

'Denny? He had Den checked out?' She can hardly get the words out. 'The sly bastard. What did he find out – that Denny was a useless waste of space?' Martha's making light of this, but really, she wonders, how on earth didn't Dad spot that in him? Looking back, it seems so obvious to Martha that Den was a lost cause, but then hindsight is a wonderful thing.

Finn laughs, the sound wholesome and warm. 'No, he thought he was a good lad. He was so happy for you when you got married, and heartbroken when it all fell apart. I was sorry to hear about you and Denny, love. Sorry it didn't work out.'

Martha stirs her drink unnecessarily. 'He was a big mistake, Finn. God knows how I managed it, but I went straight out of the frying pan and into the fire. I guess I was in such a rush to get away from Dad and his drinking that I would have said yes to anyone who offered to take me in. Anyway, by the time I left Denny four years later, things weren't so good.'

'Did he hit you?' Finn asks, straight to the point.

Martha replies with a dismissive jerk of her chin. She's never told anyone about the extent of Den's problems, and it feels like a relief to let it out to someone like Finn, someone who understands.

'Christ, you poor kid,' Finn says, shaking his head sadly. 'I had no idea.'

'My own fault. I knew, really, but didn't want to see the signs. I'm just thankful I got away from it all when I did.'

'You did the right thing,' Finn tells her, softly patting her hand. There's a silence between them, but it's not uncomfortable. Eventually Finn breaks the pause. 'I tried to keep in touch with your dad for a long time, Martha. Until he got so bad that he hardly knew it was me . . . Well, you know, don't you, love? The last time I saw him was when he was admitted to hospital, and the man I knew was all but gone. But it was always clear to me just how much he loved you.' It seems this is something Finn has wanted to get off his chest for a long time, and that he too has carried the guilt of failing to cure the self-destructive Eric Benn.

Martha sighs. Why couldn't her father have been one of those dads who communicated in simple terms, spending weekends with his family and telling them he was proud. Why couldn't he have loved her as much as he loved Friday nights at the Anchor?

'I know,' she replies, for Finn's benefit alone. Even hearing it from Finn Palin, her father's oldest and most loyal friend, the one who had stuck by him through thick and thin, she still can't quite believe it to be true. She's not sure if her father ever truly loved anyone.

Inwardly, Martha shakes off all maudlin thoughts and channels her mind on to the subject at hand. David Crown. She rearranges the newspaper cuttings on the tabletop, and Finn pushes his shirt sleeves back, leaning in.

'Go on,' he says.

'So, we're agreed that it's possible Juliet *didn't* run off with David Crown. We're also agreed that David Crown could be alive and well, living under an assumed identity.'

'Agreed. In theory.'

'However, we then have the problem that everyone we've spoken to tells us that David Crown was the model citizen. Everyone we've interviewed recently concurs: David Crown was a great teacher, a loving husband, a selfless charity worker, a pillar of the community. There *was* that Vicky Duke allegation, but even that was retracted – so on paper, he looks like a bloody saint.'

'And you don't believe that?'

'Something smells off,' Martha says. 'I was starting to think I might be chasing the wrong lead, until we visited David Crown's home town of Castledale this weekend – in Derbyshire – and met a few of the locals who'd known him as a teenager.'

Now she brings a finger down on the second article, entitled: *Hunt Continues for Murderer of Local Tilly.*

'This girl, Tilly Jones, was murdered just weeks before David Crown left Castledale for good – and, according to some of the villagers who knew him at the time, he was the unofficial prime suspect in the case. But he was never charged, never named in the papers, and ultimately the general verdict was that Tilly was killed by a random stranger, a stranger who was never brought to justice.'

'Why was David a suspect? He wouldn't have been much more than a kid himself at the time.'

'He was seventeen – arguably old enough and strong enough to kill a young woman. He was also the last person to see her that afternoon. She wasn't a girlfriend, just a family friend – my source said David had walked her home from the cinema as a favour to her parents, and said goodbye to her at the edge of the copse where she was found. But no charges were ever brought, because his girlfriend at the time provided him with an alibi. She said she'd met him and Tilly before walking to the copse, and they'd waved off Tilly together before the two of them headed back into the village. It sounds pretty watertight. But you know young love – what if he'd persuaded his girlfriend to lie for him? It would be great to track that girlfriend down – Hattie Brown – and talk to her now.'

Finn slips on his reading glasses and takes a closer look, turning his attention from one article to the other.

'Notice anything interesting?' asks Martha, tapping her forefingers beside the separate images of Tilly Jones and Juliet Sherman.

Finn looks up over his spectacles, fixing her with his steady pale eyes. 'They could be sisters,' he says.

'Exactly,' Martha replies. 'I think our David Crown has a type.'

*

142

On her way home, Martha has a strong urge to stop off at her old school. It's late, and as she stands in darkness at the wire-fenced perimeter it's hard to make out the grassed area that served as their playing field. A fox streaks along the playground, setting off a security lamp and casting light over the portion of the field that leads to the Garden of Reflection. A jolt of recollection passes through her. There was a weekend in the summer of 1998 when several of them did some paid work for David Crown as he started preparing to landscape the new gardens. The gardens were to be developed on the site of the old swimming pool, a mildewed old construction that smelled of moss and stone, a relic from the 1950s that had been condemned long before Martha started at the school.

Now, the details of that weekend become clearer: it's a Saturday and the sun is shining. More than that, it's scorching. Juliet's the only one who thought to bring sun lotion and she's handing it around, offering to rub it into the back of Martha's and Liv's shoulders, telling shirtless Tom he's an idiot when he declines because 'lotion is for girls'. Martha recalls his skin shedding like a snake's in the days that followed, and the laughs they'd had at his expense when he had to sit in the shade while his tender back recovered. It's not just them in this scene, there's David Crown leading the group and Mrs Tomlinson from school and a few other youngsters. She doesn't know their names, but they are a similar age, maybe a bit older; other volunteers from David's Square Wheels team. Martha tries to train in on their faces, but she can't see their features, not like with her friends, who she can see as clearly as if it were yesterday. David has them each focused on particular jobs, working in twos, just like at Square Wheels, and Martha is with Liv on shifting duties. They each have a wheelbarrow, which they're

143

filling with tiles and rubble from the pool, which Tom and another boy are busy breaking up, before wheeling it across the barge boards and up the ramp into a skip on the edge of the playground. Martha's hands are moist inside thick builder's gloves and she feels the sweat from her hairline trickling beneath her vest, into the waistband of her running shorts. The teams working on digging over what will become the flower borders are in flip-flops or sandals, but David insisted Liv and Martha cover their toes if they're working with hardcore. They've been lugging debris for several hours now and Martha's starting to get hot and tired, the shoe rule growing in size as the final injustice.

David is nearby, marking out the ground where the new Garden of Reflection will be. Juliet works with him, following his instructions, holding the end of the tape measure, running back and forth to make chalk marks and stand still when he says to stand still. It's a piss-easy job, and Martha, grubby and damp with sweat, is irritated to note that Juliet looks as fresh as she did when they arrived four hours earlier.

'Can I swap with someone else after lunch?' Martha shouts over.

'If you like,' David replies absently, jotting on his notepad. But he doesn't look in her direction. He's still talking earnestly with Juliet, their heads close together.

Martha is at once furious. 'Maybe Juliet can take over from me?'

Juliet's eyes shoot towards Liv then, a fleeting glance. 'No, I know what I'm doing now – David won't want to explain it all over again to someone new.'

Someone *new*. The bloody nerve.

'Liv must be tired too. Maybe you two could swap out with the other team?' David says with his customary tact, and before she has a chance to argue, the tinny sounds of 'Greensleeves' announces the arrival of the ice cream van on the asphalt, and David claps his hands together, indicating that it's time for a break.

He's arranged it, of course, asked for Antonio's to make a special visit on his usual rounds that day. The workers all gather at the brightly painted van as David Crown and Mrs Tomlinson order '99s through the serving hatch and hand them back to each of the parched labourers. There's a party atmosphere in the air, and momentarily Martha forgets her bad mood, joining in with the others, laughing at herself and the filthy mess she's got into. One of the Square Wheels lads is flirting with her, telling her she'd look good whatever state she's in. The girl beside him grimaces at Martha in sympathy and says, 'Alright, Romeo,' making a puking motion with her finger, and Martha knows the heat in her cheeks isn't just from the sun. Tom's skin is already turning pink, and Liv is running in circles, squealing and flapping her arms because Mrs Tomlinson just pointed out that she has a slug attached to her bare shoulder. Liv is screaming for someone to get it off her, but everyone's laughing too much to offer any help, and they're all looking in that direction, so that Martha almost misses what happens next. Juliet has to see this, is the thought that pops into her head, and she turns towards Antonio's van at the very moment David Crown passes Juliet her ice cream, cheekily daubing the end of her nose as she reaches to take it. Juliet smirks and sticks out her tongue, and attempts to lick away the mess he made. It's a playful, intimate moment, and Martha is the only one who sees.

The rest of the memory evaporates before Martha can close in on it. But that last clear moment between Juliet and David Crown – it feels so heavy with significance that Martha is left reeling, trying to comprehend how it's taken her until now to recall it. She anchors her eyes on the shadowy path towards the Garden of Reflection, plunged back into darkness as the security lamp shuts off. Does she now believe Juliet and David *did* have a thing going? Is that what's bothering her so much? Perhaps, but that's not what unsettles her the most.

What's disturbing her is the raw emotion she conjured as she relived that memory, unmistakable in its meaning. In the midst of her amusement, as Martha turned away from Liv's comedy to share it with her friend, she had witnessed that small, daft moment with the ice cream, and she had been jealous. Martha had felt jealous of Juliet.

14. Casey

I woke up this morning in turmoil after a short email arrived from Martha late last night, pressing me for a time and date to meet up. As a result, I've been tossing and turning since the early hours, and in the cold light of day I understand that guilt is at the heart of my anxiety.

Martha's message read as though she'd typed it in haste:

We think David Crown may have killed before. He was linked to a murdered girl in Derbyshire back in 1970 but never charged, and if you ask me it's one coincidence too many. Also, you know that Square Wheels photograph? We've found out the name of one of the other volunteers is Jo Clement – did you ever come across her? We're trying to trace her, as well as the other girl, to see if they recall anything about DC or about that night. Listen, Liv, when can we meet up? You're the only other person who knows what it was like during that awful time, and even if you don't want to talk about Juliet and the case, I'd love to see you. Please? I could really do with a friend right now.

I'm frightened that I'm in too deep. This latest revelation about the murdered girl is horrifying to me, and I don't want to believe it, not after I've gone to lengths making out that I – in my guise as Liv – think David Crown couldn't possibly have anything to do with Juliet's disappearance. I'm scared that I'm making things worse for everyone and, with Martha's constant insistence that we need to meet, I'm scared of being exposed. Mostly, though, I'm scared of losing Martha. *I could really do with a friend right now*, she'd said. How can I let her down at a time like this? I butter my toast as I go over these things in my head, and I know all I really want is to be left alone.

Sometimes, when I was very young, my mother would inform my father that she needed some 'alone time'. There was no explanation required, for it invariably followed several days of oppressive sadness in our home, a wordless building of uncertainty, not unlike the roiling pressure of a thunder-storm in waiting. I have no memories of Dad railing against the demand, and, far from feeling rejected by these banish-ments, I would feel an inward excitement, anticipating an adventure of sorts on the horizon. Over the years, Dad and I visited all sorts of places for these mini-breaks, perhaps two or three times a year, free to leave on a whim, as a family unrestricted by the timetable of conventional education. It was at times like these that I truly valued the commitment my parents had made in home-schooling me, and in my father's good company I didn't miss the presence of other children even slightly. In fine weather we would camp where the walking was good – in the Lake District, the Highlands, the Pembroke coast, the South Downs Way. It seemed to me that Dad was excellent in a crisis, adept at thinking on his feet, because whenever Mum's demands were voiced, he was ready, unfazed, and within hours we'd be bundling our tent and sleeping bags into the back of his van and heading on our way – journeying off to wheresoever he chose for us on that occasion.

One of my favourite places was Uncle Richard's small-holding near Burton, a ramshackle cottage in the countryside, set within an unkempt paddock on which he kept a donkey, two alpacas, a pair of pigs (pets, not bacon, he assured me) and more free-running hens than I ever managed to count. Uncle Richard had always lived alone and Dad said his house was 'a health hazard', so we would pitch our tent facing out towards the open fields, venturing inside only as far as the downstairs bathroom for our hasty ablutions morning and night. By day we would drive out to explore new hill walks, stopping en route at the village bakery for filled rolls and a sweet treat to picnic on, returning by nightfall to build the campfire and wrap up for an evening outdoors with Uncle Richard. Dad cooked over the open fire or a camping stove, and my uncle seemed always glad to join us, gleefully confiding that the only time he ate a square meal was when we came to visit. 'What do you eat when we're not here?' I asked him one white misty morning in May time, as my dad served up bacon and eggs and sweet, milky tea. We were sitting around the camping stove watching the sun's steady rise over the fields and hills, on faded canvas chairs that had soaked up the early dew. 'Spaghetti hoops on toast,' Uncle Richard had replied, and he'd laughed so uproariously that we couldn't help but join in.

When we returned from our travels, Mum would be a changed woman, transformed by her 'alone time'. The smell of her baking was the thing I looked forward to the most. She'd always go to great trouble for our homecoming meal, and as we entered the hallway in our three-day-old clothes and unkempt hair, she'd fuss around us, kissing our fore-heads and telling us to take baths before supper. It was like entering an entirely different home, a parallel universe of sorts, and I grew to love the going away for the sheer joy of the coming home. This home was a bright place, where my mother was more beautiful than the last time I saw her, a place where the colours were sharper, the passage of air smoother in my lungs.

As a grown woman, I understand my mother's need for 'alone time'. Perhaps, after all, there's a little of her in me. Much as I would like to have friends in my life, I too find it hard to be around people for anything more than short periods of time. Before long, the spectre of anxiety rears up inside me, the self-doubt whispering in my ear. Even when people are faultlessly kind to me I wonder: do they mean it? Behind their smiling eyes, are they actually mocking me? Are they thinking up horrible words to use against me? I'm not being hysterical when I consider these things, because they're words I've heard before, insults I've taken, wounds I've had inflicted – not just from those early playground taunts but, more recently, from the cruel keyboards of chat-room trolls and haters. *Fatty. Loser. Ugly bitch.* It's why I'll never again use my real profile picture or name when interacting online, instead employing the reassuring mask of a cartoon avatar and a well-chosen pseudonym, something I can shut down at a moment's notice if the situation demands it. Online, I can be whoever I want to be – Ruby-Boo, Susi-Lee, Marilyn2000, Sunny-Kay. I've tried so many names out, I've lost count! Online, I can interact with others on level footing, without the prejudice so readily aimed at the less-than-beautiful. Beautiful people, like Martha and Juliet and Liv, have no idea what the world feels like to people like me. No idea at all.

Today I try out 'DebbieT' for size. I create a new profile, and within minutes I'm logging on to 'MisPer', a chat room dedicated to missing persons and their families. I've done this kind of thing many times before, so I know exactly what to do, exactly how to pitch it to get fellow users on my side. I click on the tab that allows me to start a new thread.

Hi, I'm Debbie and I'm a MisPer newbie! I hope someone out there can help me? I'm looking for sixty-five-year-old David Crown, last seen in Hackney in January 2000. If anyone has any information regarding David and his whereabouts, I'd love to hear about it. I'm an old friend, and I know it would mean the world to David's family to hear news of him. I've included a picture taken around the time he was last seen, when he was a group leader for Square Wheels charity. Any help or advice from you lovely MisPer peeps would be greatly appreciated – thank you! Xxxx

There now, I think happily as I post the thread. *There.* I'm helping. With any luck I'll be able to come back with some useful information in a day or two. I know I should probably stop all this Liv business right now, but perhaps if I can give Martha something new to focus on she might stick with me a while longer. Ignoring the growing number of impatient work emails that are now clogging my inbox, I decide to shave my underarms with the new razors I ordered along with my hair dye. I need to kill a bit of time before I log on again, and I want to be fresh for when Carl comes later in the week.

Six hours later I log on to MisPer again, this time using another new profile 'CrownieD', claiming to be the missing man himself. I just need to get a good conversation going

153

between Debbie and Crownie and then, somehow, I'll pass the whole thing over to Martha.

There's nothing wrong with what I'm doing, I'm quite certain. I've been reading and re-reading the articles about Juliet's disappearance, and last night I sat studying the photographs of David Crown for several hours. He's got such a kind face, and his life's work was a testament to his goodness, and I'm more convinced than ever that he's innocent of everything they say. Martha, the silly billy, is barking up the wrong tree, and if I can show her the error of her ways through these MisPer conversations, then I'll be doing her a service. I'll be doing everyone a service.

Marvelling at the smooth texture of my freshly shaved armpits, I pull on my nightie and go to bed, imagining how it will feel to be interviewed by the newspapers: the upstanding citizen who saved an innocent man from a grave miscarriage of justice.

15. **Martha**

This afternoon Juney phoned to tell Martha that she'd finally managed to get hold of David Crown's wife, Janet, and a meeting has been set up for her and Toby to visit tomorrow morning. They already know that she's still living in the same house, as is so often the way in cases of missing persons, when families are fearful of moving away lest their loved one returns and finds them gone.

After preparing a set of questions for Mrs Crown, Martha gets to bed late, and she lies awake for a long time, her mind racing as she tracks back over the years, trying again to visualise the places of her youth. Eventually, sleep eluding her, she gives up and heads to the kitchen to make a cup of cocoa. She can't quite work out where the Crowns' home is in relation to where she had lived at the time, and while the milk is warming she fetches a battered box from the top of her wardrobe, hoping to find an old street map she remembers picking up years back. Inside the box are all sorts of odd things, a dwindling collection of keepsakes that have accompanied her from place to place over the years, seldom looked at, almost forgotten. There are no photo albums, but a dozen or more Kodak photo wallets containing pictures from the early eighties through to the end of 1999. She skips past the early childhood photos, going straight to the ones that might contain pictures of Liv and Juliet and her, though she knows there won't be many. Liv was the one usually snapping the photographs; Martha could barely afford the film, let alone the processing costs. She picks out a picture of the three of them, a pre-mobile selfie, their faces not quite in frame, squinting against the sunlight. Liv's blue eyes shine so brightly that they look unreal against her dark skin, and Martha recalls a time when Liv had a stand-up row with Miss Khan in Year Ten after the teacher had tried to give her a demerit point for wearing coloured contact lenses to school. Another is a picture of the three of them together in Juliet's back garden, probably taken by Tom or one of her parents. They're in school uniform, maybe aged fourteen or fifteen, Liv with her tie wrapped around her forehead, her socks pulled high, striking a dumb pose, her tongue pushed down between her teeth and lower lip. Juliet is blowing a kiss at the camera and Martha is bent double, laughing. There's a jug of orange squash on the garden table behind them, and a tray of bourbon biscuits. She'd forgotten how often they were there. It was like a second home to Martha, wasn't it?

In contrast to Juliet's comfortable home, Martha's family lived in Stanley House, a block of flats within a wider warren of social housing that would some years later be razed to the ground following safety concerns. By the time the Benns had moved in, the area had already been classified a 'problem estate', with a good number of the buildings emptied for refurbishment, meaning direct neighbours were scarce and community spirit virtually absent. To young Martha, who had come from a 'nice' street half a mile away, the place appeared derelict, a concrete holding tank for those without choice. It was a shock, a slap of shame that never quite left her, after their own terraced house was repossessed, her parents having defaulted once too often on the mortgage repayments. 'But isn't your dad a copper?' Martha was asked by schoolfriends more times than she'd care to recall. 'Surely *he* can afford a better place than Stanley House?'

Stanley House was meant to be a temporary stay, a 'halfway measure' while they got back on their feet again, while they 'sorted stuff out.' 'Dad will get a promotion soon,' Mum would tell her in the early days, her eyes spongy with crying. 'And I'll find something more up my street. Things will get better.' But *halfway* morphed into *full-stop* over the ten years that Martha lived there, and in all that time she never viewed it as home. Stanley House was the hole Martha's family disappeared down, and she cited their arrival there as the beginning of their end. It was there that her mother descended further into despair and her father nurtured his rage at his enforced early retirement from the police force. It was a place of chaos and uncertainty, of discomfort and lack. Ultimately it was the place Mum had run from. Are there any good memories from that time? Martha wonders. Any at all? She lies in her large bed, eyes anchored to the neon of her digital clock, straining to remember, when a picture comes to her, clear as a film scene, long forgotten: Liv, Juliet and her, stretched out beneath the stars on the flat roof of Stanley House, the heavy cloak of summer draped across the night. What had they been doing there, when Martha *never* brought friends home, never exposing herself to the shame within? Why were they there? Of *course*, she realises now. She'd had the flat to herself.

They were just sixteen, and Martha's mum had left in the spring, packing her bags and vanishing during school hours, never to return. She'd returned home to Scotland, she later had the goodness to tell Martha via a crappy postcard of the Forth Bridge, and she wouldn't be coming home. *Your dad and I are no good for each other,* she'd written, and Martha had hated her for her cowardly words. *You're happy there,* she wrote, by way of justifying why she hadn't taken her daughter too, and Martha wondered exactly what planet her mother had been living on for the past few years. *Happy*?

Fuck her, had been Martha's overriding emotion, an emotion that got her through the toughest of times, when all she really wanted was her mother back. Not once did she allow herself to imagine Mum's new life in the Scottish borders; not once did she allow herself to imagine a different place for herself. Her mother's departure was a blessed relief, she told herself. She was a waste of space. One parent like that was enough, Martha reasoned as she hardened her shell. But two? No one should have to handle two drunks in so small a family.

That starlit evening on the rooftop of Stanley House was a once-only moment in time, a simple day and night of joy and laughter, of sunbathing and secrets and dreamless sleep. Liv and Juliet had arrived in the afternoon, bringing with them sleeping bags, music, Bacardi Breezers and crisps. For the entire morning before they arrived, Martha had cleaned, prising open the rusted metal windows to air the damp flat, scrubbing and bleaching the toilet bowl and stained sinks, running a wet cloth over every city-blackened surface her friends were likely to see. She brushed and dusted and tidied and polished, and, even though she knew it still looked like a shitty little flat in a shitty estate, Martha thought the place had never looked or smelled better.

But how was it she had come to be having her friends over? Where was her dad? Ah, yes. Her father had been admitted to hospital the night before, having taken a knife in his side while in pursuit of a thief. At least that was what he said in front of his stony-faced senior officer who was preparing to leave as Martha arrived. 'It's not life-threatening,' the nurse told her, 'but he's lost blood and he needs to stay in another night.' His face against the starched hospital pillow had been a lifeless shade of grey, and for a moment, before he'd opened his eyes and seen her there, she'd really believed him to be dead. 'Bad luck,' he called it when his eyes focused on hers, when he turned a blind eye to the unspilled tears she was fighting to contain. Pissed, more like, was her silent verdict, the words held captive behind clenched teeth. She had cycled away beneath a gathering cloud of loneliness, back home to an empty flat, where she'd slept on the sofa, fearful of the future, common sense telling her that this night must surely mark the end of her father's career with the police.

That night on the roof, Martha knows, she drank until she passed out, and the three of them slept beneath the stars, the summer warmth of their friendship strong enough to keep the cold away. Did Liv and Jules ever suspect the truth about her father's absence? Did they ever suspect her of lying? Probably, Martha thinks now, as she places the photographs back in the box, returning it to the darkness of the wardrobe. Because that's what true friends do: they recognise the lies that are important to you, and they let them slide.

When Martha and Toby knock on Janet Crown's door, they are shocked by the figure who answers. Mrs Crown is tall but slight, dressed in a crimson dressing gown and silk-screen-printed headscarf, and the dark shadows beneath her eyes show her to be a woman concerned with more than just the whereabouts of her husband. Her cheekbones are chiselled, and Martha can tell she was once beautiful, but now Janet Crown looks like a woman close to death. A painfully thin slick of bright red lipstick slashes across her mouth, and her hairless eyebrows appear drawn in with a shaky hand.

'Come,' she says with an elegant drift of her hand, leading them through her neatly conservative home, out to a small extension at the rear of the house, a sun-room furnished with wicker chairs and an abundance of glossy hanging plants. There's a hint of cigarette smoke and mint in the air. Martha notices the terracotta ashtray on the garden table just beyond the glass door, a single lipstick-stained butt upended in its centre. On the wicker coffee table is an open lacquered box containing a stack of old postcards, the top one picturing the Eiffel Tower at night, beside which is a cigarette packet and a large silver lighter, the kind you might see in old movies. Unsmiling, Mrs Crown gestures for Martha and Toby to take a seat, and Martha is unsure whether her cool reception is a sign of resistance or upset.

'We'll sit out here, if you don't mind,' she says, releasing a long, slow breath as she lowers herself into her own seat, placing her arms lightly on the wicker side rests. 'It's warmer. Since I've been ill, you know.'

Martha sits forward, elbows on knees. 'Oh, I'm sorry to hear that, Mrs Crown. May I call you Janet?'

Janet Crown neither agrees nor objects, but merely raises her hand, fingers poised to join thumb and third finger in the unconscious pose of a smoker. 'I understand you've been trying to contact me for a while now? Yes, I'm sorry I've been so impossible to get hold of. I don't keep a mobile phone, and they only released me from hospital a few days ago. *Cancer*, dear,' she says, dropping her voice to a whisper, as though her illness were some great scandal. 'Isn't it always, these days? Cancer, cancer, cancer. It's everywhere.' Janet addresses all this towards Martha, to the exclusion of Toby, who shifts in his seat, unaccustomed to being overlooked.

'How is the treatment going?' he asks, and Janet swivels her eyes towards him, as though surprised to see him there at all.

After a beat, she replies. 'Who knows? I'm a fairly hopeless case, if the truth be known. *Apparently* I'm tight within in its terminal grip!' She laughs at this, her face at once radiant, and Toby starts in his seat, rattled. 'Oh, ignore me!' she says, and she smooths the velvet of her gown over the lengths of her skeletal thighs, easing out the material's wrinkles.

'Mrs Crown – Janet,' Toby says, opening up his notebook, obviously trying to regain his footing. 'I think our researcher explained on the phone why we wanted to meet up like this?'

'Yes, you're doing a television programme.'

'Exactly. We realise that this is upsetting territory for you, but perhaps, if you'd be happy to answer a few questions for us, we might find some new clues that the police missed the first time around?'

Janet turns to Martha. 'So where are the film crew, then?'

Martha suddenly understands the effort Janet Crown has gone to this morning: the crimson gown and co-ordinated scarf, the red lipstick and pencilled brows. 'Oh, I'm sorry, we should have explained – it's just me and Toby today, and then, if you're in agreement, we'll be back with the camera guys to follow up. We just thought this first time you might . . . well, you might find it a bit difficult. A bit upsetting?'

Mrs Crown reaches towards the coffee table for the cigarettes, finding the packet empty and casting it aside with limp fingers. 'It's fine, really,' she replies with what seems to be

161

exhaustion. 'Don't misunderstand me: it *is* upsetting, desperately upsetting. But really, I've done most of my crying. For years I think I did nothing but cry. But, at some point, life must go on, dear, don't you agree? Now, more than ever, I take each day as it comes. Ask me whatever you like, Martha Benn.' She fixes Martha with an unblinking gaze, her pupils huge and black in her shadowed eyes, and Martha wonders what cocktail of medication this poor woman must be on. She's only in her mid-sixties but her ravaged appearance would have you believe she was ninety, such is the effect of this illness upon her.

Just as Martha is about to speak, Janet raises a finger and turns to Toby.

'Young man, would you be a dear and pop to the shops for a packet of Marlboro Menthols? I'm struggling to concentrate, and they do so help. You'll find a newspaper shop at the end of the street.'

Martha gives the slightest of nods and Toby is on his feet and out of the room.

'Now we can talk,' Janet says when she hears the front door closing behind him. Seeing Martha's surprise, she adds, 'I'm not terribly good around men, dear. Out of practice.' She gestures towards Martha's notes, urging her to get started.

Realising that time is of the essence if she's to engage Janet Crown fully before Toby returns, Martha launches straight in. 'Yes, of course. I completely understand. If you're happy then, Janet, I'll just ask away?'

Janet nods, and Martha's finger trails down her notes to the first question she has prepared.

'Janet, do you think David had anything to do with Juliet's disappearance.'

'Absolutely not,' Janet Crown replies, unmoved.

'How was David on the morning before he disappeared?'

'Well. After the police had been around, he was in a terrible state. Really upset – and frightened, as you would be. Such a dreadful thing to happen to that girl in the first place, and then to be under *suspicion*! But after a while he seemed to pull himself together and he got ready for work like any other day.' She looks at Martha for a moment, before adding, 'Of course, he never came home.'

'Where was he working at the time?'

'Oh, I can't remember.'

'Where do you think he went?'

'Well, he ran away, didn't he? But I don't know *where*.'

'Do you know *why* he ran away?'

'Like I say, when the police came asking questions about that girl—'

'Juliet,' Martha interrupts, bristling at Janet Crown's use of 'that girl'.

'Yes, that's it, Juliet. Well, I was there when those two officers spoke to David and I can tell you there was a definite air of bad feeling from them. They were asking what kind of "relationship" he had with Juliet, whether they spent any time together outside of the charity work, if he'd been alone with her the night before. It was shocking, the tone they took, as though I wasn't even in the room! The female officer was the worst. She glared at him throughout, as if she was trying to unnerve him, to catch him out. As if she'd already made her mind up that he was guilty.'

'And how did the police leave things after that interview? Did they say they wanted to see him again?'

'They asked him to report at the station that evening, to make a written statement. If you ask me, they wanted him to sweat it out during the day. I think they *really* believed that he'd murdered the girl! That poor girl,' she says now, her eyes misting over. 'And her *parents*. Her mother and father. You never get over something like that, you know?'

The sun breaks through, throwing light across Janet Crown's frail figure, and Martha sees something new in her, a softer, more vulnerable side. She's been carrying the weight of her husband's disappearance with her for all these years, Martha realises, never able to start afresh, never knowing what really happened, or where he went. Surely that must be worse than if he had simply died? A death is at least an event, a full stop. When people say it's time to move on, perhaps it's possible after a death, given enough time. But a disappearance is something else altogether. For the first time, Martha sees that Janet Crown too is a victim in all this. It's no wonder her manner is a little odd, her reactions somewhat clipped and unemotional; she must have suffered enormous torment over the years. Perhaps this is what has aged her so prematurely, more so than even the cancer.

'Were you happy together?' Martha asks, returning to her questions. 'You and David.'

'Very.'

'Did you love him?' A similar question, a different emphasis. As she asks it, Martha hopes Mrs Crown doesn't feel she's trying to trick her.

'More than life,' Janet answers without pause. 'He was my everything. And I was his.'

'You didn't have any children . . .' Martha continues.

'Yes,' Janet Crown replies, dropping her voice to a whisper. 'I did. *We* did. But. . .' She breaks off, bringing a curled hand to her mouth. 'Not any more.'

'I'm so sorry to hear that,' Martha says, genuinely shocked by the news, and ashamed that she'd managed to miss this fact in her research. 'It's a terrible thing, to lose a child. Do you think that's why David wanted to help out in the community? With Square Wheels? A sense of doing something good in the world?'

Janet's smile is bright and instant. 'Yes – *yes, I do*. Such an insightful young woman. That's *exactly* what he wanted to do. David was the kindest man you'd ever meet. You ask anyone who knew him. He was thoughtful, caring, hardworking. I couldn't have hoped for a better man, and that's why it was so devastating for him to come under such bitter suspicion like that. The police couldn't have been more wrong.'

'But why would David flee, when he had nothing at all to hide?'

Janet hesitates, before patting her lap lightly, as though making up her mind to confide. 'When we were younger we lived in Bedfordshire, where David was a teacher in a girls' secondary school. We'd met in Cambridge, and had been married for eight or nine years, but we were still like newly-weds, with everything ahead of us. We'd just started a family, and David getting this job was the icing on the cake. We loved it there! *Such* a happy home. Really, we thought we'd stay there forever. Over our first year or so, we got to know several of his colleagues quite well, and David was a wonderful teacher by all accounts. But then there was an incident, an allegation – quickly proven to be entirely fabricated – and, despite there being nothing in it, it forced David to leave his job and we relocated here.'

'Vicky Duke,' Martha says, and Janet Crown blinks at her. Martha had finally spoken to Vicky just this morning, only for Vicky to refuse to discuss the allegation, warning Martha that if she or her team persisted she would report her for harassment.

'Yes, that might have been her name,' Janet says, looking as though she's lost her thread.

'She made it up?' Martha prompts, smiling, urging her to continue.

'Yes! Yes.' Her eyes roam the room, landing on the empty cigarette packet and up towards the doorway. She clasps her restless fingers in her lap. 'So, that morning, after the police had come here asking about the missing girl, David went into a blind panic. He was convinced that they had put the two things together and jumped to all the wrong conclusions. He was terrified. I tried to tell him there's no way they could know about what happened at St Cuthbert's, but he wouldn't have it. I tried to tell him the girl – Juliet – would turn up, that she'd most likely just stayed at a friend's house overnight, that he needed to calm down. I'd never seen him so scared, but after a bit he seemed to pull himself together, agreed that I was probably right, and headed off to work. That was the last time I ever saw him.'

Martha's pulse is racing. Could David Crown really be innocent? Everything his wife says, the way she says it, the love she still has for him – it sounds so compelling.

'And now,' Martha ventures, wondering how Janet will take this last question. 'It's been eighteen years, without a word from or a sighting of David. Janet, do you think it's possible that your husband is dead?'

'Oh, no, dear!' Janet smiles, half-closing her eyes and resting her head against the back of the seat. She looks corpse-like in the cool morning light, and Martha worries that she's worn her out before she's had a chance to get to the end of her questions.

She slides forward in her seat, reaching out to touch Janet Crown gently on the wrist. 'You *don't* think he's dead?'

Janet lifts her head and fixes Martha with a surprised expression. 'No, dear. I *know* he's not dead.' With great effort she reaches over the coffee table and pushes the box of postcards towards Martha. 'He's been sending me these for the past sixteen years. From all over Europe, they are. The most recent one arrived just last week.' If Mrs Crown notices Martha's stunned expression, she doesn't acknowledge it. 'And guess what, dear? He sent it from right here in London!'

16. Casey

I know exactly where Martha will be today, because she told me in her email this morning. She said, *We're off to visit Janet Crown this morning in Craig Street – it's only a few streets from you, isn't it? Maybe we could have that coffee afterwards? Give me a call if you get this message in time. We should be done around midday.*

I'll ignore the message for now, but I'm afraid it really is only a matter of time before she loses patience altogether and cuts me from the team. Later on I'll find a way of alerting her to the MisPer conversation I've been working on – perhaps an anonymous call to that helpline number she told me about – and invent some reason or other for not having been able to meet up today. I could tell her I had to take an emergency appointment, with a client in distress. A suicidal one, even. Yes, that's good. That should stall her for a while. 'Stall her'. I can't help but laugh. I've even started to think like a private investigator! Right now, I'm sitting on a wooden bench at the end of Craig Street, opposite the newsagents and with the house in view, feeling glad I wrapped up so thoroughly before I set off, though my thoughts were more on disguise than warmth. Not that Martha would recognise me, what with my not actually being Liv, but still, you never know who might be out and about, and it's best not to draw attention if you can avoid it. I'm wearing a dark wool beret, with the lower half of my face obscured by my scarf, and I feel quite the Secret Squirrel. Underneath my duffel coat is the emerald-green jumper I ordered online – nearly the same as Liv's – and, even though only I know about it, it gives me a kind of strength to be dressed a little like her. I tried to get some patterned leggings too, but couldn't find any in my size that were even close. If only I could have asked her where she bought them.

I arrived here at eleven o'clock, hoping to catch a glimpse of Martha entering the property, but it's now coming up for quarter past and there's been no sign. My mobile phone is in my gloved hand, poised to take surreptitious photographs if I can. But it's not long before I'm starting to feel cross with myself as I realise I've arrived too late. Martha must already be inside.

'Bobbins,' I curse beneath my breath, feeling the chill of the cold bench beneath my backside. Five more minutes pass, and then at last the door to number 14 opens and I'm surprised to see a tall young man exit, carefully pulling the door behind him before looking up and down the street, as though in search of something. Where's Martha? I want to shout out to him, but as he turns and walks in this direction, apparently heading for the shop, I realise – aha – this must be Toby. Martha's second in command! Within moments we are level, he on one side of the street, me on the other, and the breath inside my lungs is caught tight. I'm not sure whether to come or go. He can't possibly know who you are, the rational part of my brain tells me, while the neurotic side rears up, screaming at me to run!

As he reaches the shop entrance, he glances in my direction, so briefly, before pushing in through the door and out of my line of vision. I allow my breath to escape my lips in a long, slow breath, white as cigarette smoke.

Well, Martha Benn, I reflect now that I'm getting my nerves under control, you kept that little detail to yourself! The mysterious Toby, it turns out, is dazzling. 'Quite the dish,' my mother would have said in her day. 'Quite the heartbreaker.' No sooner have I entertained this thought than I'm batting away fantasies of Toby exiting the shop and meeting my eye, of him crossing the road to join me on the bench, where we'll strike up a conversation – awkward at first but growing quickly more effortless – and I'll invite him home with me, for tea or coffee. Or more. But the door to the shop remains firmly closed and I look down at myself, at the great big stinking lump of me, and I think I must be insane. Why would a man as beautiful as Toby ever look at a monster like me?

Once upon a time, I was thin as a rake. When I was thirteen, Dad tried to encourage me to join a local youth theatre, to get me to mix with other girls my age, he said, to 'broaden your horizons and spread your wings.' I only went along with it to please him, to show him that I could do anything if I put my mind to it, to reassure him that I wasn't just this weird, reclusive kid with no friends and no outside life. The truth of it was, I was all of those things and worse, and on the morning of the first session at Theatre Plus I was terrified. I don't think I'd spoken to another child in at least three years, not since his last failed attempt to join me up at the music club on Blaine Street where, crippled by shyness, I'd sat alone on the bench until my mum was called early to fetch me home.

On this particular Saturday morning, the sun was shining hot over London as Dad and I set off together along the street, leaving Mum washing up and singing along to her Lloyd Webber CD. Dad was trying to make conversation, but I could barely think of an answer, so preoccupied was I by my fears of the new experience ahead of me. Will they make me speak in front of everyone? Will they make me dance? Will they laugh?

'Why don't you take that off?' Dad said, nodding at the pink quilted jacket I'd pulled on as we'd left the house. There was a glistening film of perspiration across his upper lip and brow. 'You'll boil your brains out!'

I shook my head, feeling the cold deep in my bones, and I could tell from the disbelieving look in his eyes that he thought it was because I didn't want anyone to see my body. He and Mum had been talking about it a lot lately, when they thought I wasn't listening: him saying he was concerned about my health, her telling him not to be so dramatic.

'I'm a bit chilly,' I said, suddenly lighting on the idea of illness. 'Maybe I'm coming down with some—' But he cut me dead.

'Oh no you don't, young lady! You're not getting out of it that easily!' He gestured towards the building opposite. 'We're here now!'

A bossy girl called Matilda was assigned to look after me, and as my dad said goodbye and walked away, I felt my heart sink. How would I get through the next two hours?

'Just smile,' Dad had advised me as we arrived. 'Who could resist a smile like yours?' A smile was one thing, but how could I be normal and likeable and chatty and fun? I'd seen how other girls were in films and on TV, so I knew what 'normal'

171

looked like. But I'd never seen a 'normal' I could relate to. I'd never seen someone who felt like me. I'm not just talking 'pretty' or 'ugly' or 'fat' or 'thin'; I mean I'd never seen anyone who seemed to be like me on the inside, let alone the out.

Over in our designated group, Matilda introduced me to Bethany, Keesha and Joy, before tugging at my padded jacket, insisting I take it off before warm-ups. 'It'll restrict your movements,' she informed me with authority, with a smile so straight-toothed and convincing that I was powerless to resist.

And so I acquiesced, revealing my thirteen-year-old self in blue jeans and a yellow T-shirt made for someone far younger than me. Matilda gasped. The group gasped, and, as my eyes took in the other inhabitants of the church hall that was home to Theatre Plus, it seemed the whole theatre company gasped.

'Oh my God!' Matilda whispered, loudly enough for the rest of our group to hear. Her delicate hand reached out and came to rest on my bony wrist. 'You're so thin.'

Within half an hour my mother had arrived, wrapping me up in her warm embrace, returning me to the safety of home. I didn't go back.

As Toby emerges from the shop across the road, I realise my cheeks are wet. Silently, I watch him return along the street, hands in pockets, walking slowly as though killing time, not casting so much as a cursory glance in my direction. Stealthily manoeuvring my mobile phone from my pocket to my lap, I photograph him in a series of action shots along the street, before he knocks at number 14 and an unseen hand opens the door to let him in. Alone on my bench, I watch the world, as though through glass. An elderly man on a bicycle cycles past, his helmet scuffed and wonky. A woman pauses at the far end of the street as her small dog sniffs and pees against an overflowing rubbish bin. On the grass verge at the edge of the green a crow picks at a McDonald's box, turning its head as a toddler runs at it, kicking the air and laughing when the bird takes to the sky. All these things go on around me, and still they seem unreal to me. No one appears to notice my presence, no one really knows I'm here. I wipe my face with the back of my glove and resolve to leave Martha and Toby for now, to return to the safety of home to sleep a while, to gather my strength. 'Sleep is the greatest tonic,' Mum always used to say, when things got too much to bear. 'Sleep can make the worst of days seem better.' Sometimes I forget how much I miss my mother. Sometimes I forget everything she did for me over the years.

17. **Martha**

Martha and Toby are working from her apartment this morning, preparing an update to present to Glen Gavin in the morning, a summary of their progress so far. She's been in touch with Finn Palin to get his advice about next steps regarding the postcard evidence they received from Janet Crown, and he's promised to pass it on to a serving Met detective he's close to, in the hope that they'll consider reopening the case. But the reality is, it's all so flimsy. So what if David Crown has been sending postcards to his wife? It makes no difference at all to the theory that he and Juliet ran away together eighteen years ago; it just suggests that he still has feelings for his wife and wanted somehow to keep contact. What *is* of interest is the variety of locations the postcards are sent from, all over the UK and Europe. If Juliet did go with him, and it's a big *if*, is she with him now as they travel around the world, still together after all this time? If she is alive, is she happy? Martha can hardly stand the thought of it. Is it terrible that she prefers the idea of her best friend dead to her living a life with that man?

She pushes her papers to one side and leaves the table she's sharing with Toby, easing out her aching shoulders and offering to make them both a drink. At the window she pauses to look out over the city skyline, asking herself if she would have taken this on, had she known just how hard it would be to find the answers they're searching for.

'It'll be worth it, you know,' Toby says, reading her thoughts.

She turns to reply, and, not for the first time, she's struck by the beauty of him. There are times, she's certain, when she catches him watching her, and she wonders, is he attracted to her? Surely not. She's almost ten years older, and at her worst a sharp-tongued old boot. She certainly hasn't made this assignment easy for him, and she wouldn't blame him if he'd already written her off as a mardy bitch. And, let's face it, they've got history. She's unsettled every time she allows her eyes to meet his.

'Do you think?' she replies, arms folded, head to one side. At least she's managed to drop the sarcastic tone with him now, though there's no doubt her defences are still high. 'It just seems to me that every time we think we're getting somewhere with this, we meet a closed door. One step forward, three steps back.'

Toby leaves his seat to join her beside the window, breaking eye contact to look out over the Thames and the city beyond. 'But the postcards – that's massive, isn't it? A game changer. Jesus, if they don't reopen the investigation after that, I don't know what will persuade them.'

'*Yes*. But when you consider that those cards contain nothing more than a "D" and a kiss, you can see why the police might not take them too seriously. At any rate, so what if he *is* alive? It doesn't tell us anything we don't already know. The police didn't believe David Crown killed Juliet, and the

176

postcards don't change that. Personally, I'm leaning towards the idea that those postcards are a hoax.'

'But who would bother to keep a hoax going for so long? Eighteen years is a hell of a long time to keep a practical joke going.'

'What about his wife? She could be sending them to herself?'

'I can't see it,' Toby says, sliding his hands into his pockets and leaning against the window frame. 'She seems so frail, and I'm guessing she's been ill for a while. What would she gain from sending herself postcards?'

'Attention?'

'But she says she's never shown them to anyone before now. They're from all over Europe – and she told us she hasn't travelled in years, because of her bad health.'

Martha sighs. 'Yeah, I know. I doubt she's even got a passport. But she *was* a bit of an odd one. I'd like to find out a bit more about the Crowns' relationship before he left. I wonder if they were really as happy as she makes out? She seems like the kind of person who wants to present the world as perfect, even when it's not. Maybe he had a history of affairs? Maybe she never believed he was innocent of that allegation when he was a teacher? Maybe she thinks he *did* run away with Juliet – or worse? Women have been covering up for their men since history began. She wouldn't be the first. You never know, it may have been a blessed relief for her when he disappeared.'

Toby laughs, shaking his head. '*Sexist*. It might help to know where those postcards really came from, though, don't you think? Couldn't the forensics people compare the hand-writing to Crown's?'

Martha turns to face him, realising how near he suddenly feels. 'It's a "D" and an "x", Toby. Even if they thought the letters were similar to any handwriting samples they've got, I'm pretty sure it's not enough to conclusively say it's him.'

He runs his fingers through his floppy fringe, and for a moment, as neither of them looks away, there's tension between them, an increase in the room's air pressure.

Over at the dining table, Martha's phone rings and, grateful for the interruption, she strides across the room to take it. 'Hello, Juney?'

'Hi, Martha. I think I've got something.' Juney's tone is cautiously excited. 'We've just received an anonymous tip-off – from someone who saw our appeal for information in the *Metro* last week – about a conversation thread they spotted on a website called MisPer. Have you heard of it?'

'No. Go on.' Martha switches the phone to speaker mode so Toby can listen in.

'It's a missing persons chat room – where people post up photos and details of their missing loved ones for members of the public to offer information or so that the missing person can get back in touch. There've been a few success stories over the years, you know the kind of thing: someone disappears after a breakdown or family argument, only for them all to be reunited decades later.'

'Yep, I know the kind of thing.' Martha's impatience gets the better of her. 'Alright, Juney, tell me more about this tip-off you've had.'

'OK. As I say, the contact was anonymous, but they pointed us to a thread that was started just days ago by a DebbieT, claiming to be a family friend of David Crown, and asking for anyone who knows anything to get in touch. Well, within twenty-four hours, someone responded.'

'And?'

'And the person responding claims to be the man himself. His username is CrownieD, and he says that he's David, that he's alive and well, and he's maintaining that he did not abduct Juliet Sherman.'

Martha feels a hum of nerves rising through her body. 'Does he say whether Juliet is with him or not?' She can't believe she's asking the question. *Is* it possible that Juliet is still alive? The light of the large room is suddenly too vibrant, too intrusive, and she grabs for a seat, steadying herself as she sits.

Toby rushes to her side, pushing a glass of water towards her and taking the phone from her hands. He places it in the centre of the table and continues. 'Juney? Hi, Toby here. What are your instincts? Do you think it's genuine?'

'I'm not sure, Toby. It certainly sounds plausible – and no, Martha, if this is genuine, Juliet's definitely not with him. In Crownie's reply he talks about Square Wheels and the canal area where he worked, but it's nothing that's not available in the public domain – you know, old news articles, etc. But he does also go on to talk about one of the homeless men they got to know on the Square Wheels circuit, suggesting that he'd taken quite an interest in Juliet – pestering her to go out with him on several occasions, to the extent that David had to step in and ask him to back off. This man's name was Ethan, apparently, and it's Crownie's theory that he is the man the police should have been talking to when she went missing.'

Toby reaches for Martha's hand and gives it a nudge. 'Does that ring any bells, Martha? Did the police ever mention interviewing an Ethan?'

'No,' she replies, absently tapping at the pressure points of her wrists, trying to make sense of this whole new line of enquiry. 'No, but Liv mentioned the same person – Ethan – in an email two or three days back. I passed it on to my Met guy, but he said there was nothing about him in the interview files.'

Toby rubs his jaw between finger and thumb, his face set in concentration. 'We have to get hold of Liv, don't we? What if this Ethan is the key to Juliet's disappearance?'

Martha's anger at Liv's absence rears up, spilling over as exasperation. 'If this CrownieD really is him, and if Ethan really is our man, then David Crown may have spent eighteen years hiding for no good reason. And if Ethan really exists, if he's the person behind Juliet's disappearance, then he could still be out there. Still a danger.' She looks across at Toby. 'Christ, Toby. What if we've been barking up the wrong tree all this time?'

No one speaks for a moment, until the voice of Juney rises up between them. 'Do either of you know who DebbieT might be?'

'Not a clue,' says Martha, gripped by an urgency to get Juney off the phone so they can stop talking and *do* something. 'OK, thanks for all this, Juney. Can you email me the full details straight away? I'll need them in the next hour.' With that she hangs up.

'What now?' Toby asks.

'Now,' she replies, 'I need to run this all past Finn Palin. He'll know what to do. He's got a friend on the inside who's been quietly pulling together the details as we've been feeding them through. I'll ring him now, see if he's got time to meet me today.'

Toby looks at his watch. 'Don't forget we're meeting Geoff Blakely at the Garden of Reflection at five.'

'Shit, yes. Who's he again?'

'Geoff worked for the contractors who took over the landscaping job at Bridge School when David Crown disappeared. Sally and Jay are down there filming some background footage while it's still light.'

'Did you get permission from the school?'

'Yep.'

In that moment, Martha recognises how much Toby's steady presence reminds her of Juliet. The composed quality of him is a lifeline when everything else to do with this damned case feels as though she's all at sea. People are drawn to him in the same way as they were to Juliet, and it's more than just aesthetic, it's something magnetic and intangible. It's *goodness*. Back in the Stanley House days, when things at home became unbearable, Juliet was simply there for Martha, never probing, never judging, just *there* – steadfast, generous, kind. How could Martha ever have harboured bad feelings – *jealousy* – towards her?

Martha pushes up from her chair, drains her drink and walks across to the kitchen sink to refill her glass. 'Good work,' she says, businesslike, and she turns back to face him. 'Why don't you get down there now, see how Sally and Jay are getting on? I've got, what, two hours to catch up with Finn and I'll join you just before five?'

'Sure thing. I'll phone my mate Josh on the way. He's an IT whizz – might be able to help us work out where those chat-room accounts originate from. I'll keep you posted.' With minimum fuss, Toby packs up his papers and, after a brief, searching hesitation in the doorway, he leaves.

Martha stands at her window view, watching the world pass by on the Southbank, mentally preparing to phone Finn. It's only two days since they met in the café; will he mind her bothering him again? Too bad if he does, she tells herself, she's got nowhere else – no one else – to turn to. After a few minutes, she sees Toby emerge on to the sunlit pavement below and she watches him as he lingers beside the railings to tap into his mobile phone. Done, he slides the phone into

181

an inside pocket and carries on along the street, just as an arriving text sounds on Martha's phone. Toby. *You're doing just fine, Martha Benn*, it says. *Just wanted you to know.*

It's exactly the kind of thing Juliet would have said, and Martha feels as vulnerable as a child. A surge of emotion comes at her, confusing and violent in its urgency. This is not good, this blurring of the personal and the professional. Heart thumping, she heads for the bathroom to run cold water over her wrists, to gaze at the groomed, grown-up Martha Benn who looks back at her. What the hell is wrong with her? She's never struggled with this before. Until now her tough shell has been unbreakable, her mask of strength the most vital tool in her armour. But, right now, every fibre of her body wants to give in, to soften in response to Toby's warmth, to show him the yielding Martha beneath. And what then? Weakness must surely follow, and she knows weakness is a luxury she can't afford. She's got a reputation to maintain.

'OK,' she tells her reflection. 'OK. Time to phone Finn.'

When Martha was small, Finn and Helen Palin had been regular visitors to the Benn family home, back in the days before Stanley House, when Sunday lunchtimes were the happy focal point of the weekend. Finn and Martha's dad had remained best friends since they were probationers together, rising through the ranks at more or less the same pace, and performing best-man duties at each other's weddings in the same year. They were 'thick as thieves' Mum and Helen would often joke, but they weren't wrong – the two men were as devoted as brothers. They worked hard and the pressures of police work were not inconsiderable, so, when their shifts coincided, they regularly made time for a few pints together at the Anchor on Dove Street. Long ago, following a worrying night when a worse-for-wear Dad had wandered home the wrong way along the river, an unspoken pattern had been established, whereby Finn would deliver him home at the end of the evening, pushing him through the front door before heading on his way. It was a standing joke, Finn's ability to fare better given the same quantities of alcohol, but on reflection Martha knows Dad's worse state was down to preloading of several sly shots of scotch before his night out had even begun.

Of course, her mum barely noticed when Dad's drinking progressed from steady to heavy, as her own quiet consumption had increased at a similar pace. Hers, however, was stealthy and low, hidden behind unremarkable behaviour and a gentle manner. With the passing of years, the presence of Uncle Finn, once the happy signal of weekend get-togethers and laughter, had morphed into the omen of bad fortune. Nothing changed for *him*; as regular as ever, he'd turn up ready for a night out, bellowing his cheery hello through the hallway, returning Dad to them several hours later, reeling and reeking. But increasingly Dad's end-of-evening merriment switched the moment he stepped back through the door of Flat 1, Stanley House, a ticking time bomb that might go off any time between late evening and early morning.

But how could Finn have known this? How could he begin to imagine what transformations took place when he wheeled his merry friend back in through his doorway? Because, for Finn, nothing had altered. He was just the mild-mannered fellow who enjoyed a few drinks once or twice a week, who treated his family well and did a fine job at work. How could he ever know what was in store for the sleeping mother and child as he walked away from those nights out, pleasantly drunk himself, to return to his own home, where he'd kiss

183

his slumbering wife and drop into smiling dreams, before waking with a conscience as clear as an infant's. How could he know that his best friend was a bad drunk behind closed doors, a cruel-mouthed bully, a broken wreck? How could Finn even imagine how it felt to be woken to the sound of your father raging at your sleep-dulled mother, to hear him weeping alone in the hallway, or gently shaking you by the arm because he 'needs to talk'. Could Finn know how it felt to lie there in the darkness, pretending to sleep; to sit across the breakfast table from your father as his hands shook so violently that you actually wished he'd just get on with it and take that first drink of the day.

Well, Finn should have known, the teenage spectre of Martha reminds her, the bitterness still fresh. He *should* have known, and he should have made it stop.

'It's Martha,' she says when he answers on the fifth ring. You owe me, Finn, she thinks, and for Juliet's sake she feels no guilt. 'Finn, I really need your help in getting this thing moving. We've got some new information I'd like you to take a look at. Are you free right now?'

18. Casey

A pile of unposted manuscripts sits on the table beside the living room window, all parcelled up and addressed, and ready to go. They've been there for days, and the editors I'm working with have been chasing them up for over a week. A couple of them have got quite shirty with me about the delay, but a trip to the post office is beyond me, beyond the realms of my capabilities or the strength of my nerves. I know I should take a bath, but I can barely bring myself to get up from the sofa. I've been here all night long, going over the ways in which I might put an end to this terminal loneliness. There's been no further word from Martha, and I sense disappointment in her silence, as my fear of her abandonment wraps itself around my fear of being caught out. My guts writhe painfully, and beneath my many layers of clothing the sore places beneath my armpits throb hotly and I regret shaving them the way I did, using soap in place of shaving foam. Right now, I couldn't get up if I wanted to. The smell that rises every time I shift position is warm and yeasty, and I'm oddly aware that it comforts and repulses me in equal measure. I wish I'd had the foresight to see a doctor before I reached this stage, to speak of my anxiety in exaggerated terms, to stockpile enough medication to see me off. Though what such medication might be, or might do, I'm too ignorant to know, and I haven't been back to see him since that last time, when he commented on my weight. It wasn't the diagnosis I objected to, it was the tiny curl of his lip, the crease that appeared at the top of his nose that told me I disgusted him, that he'd rather I wasn't there at all.

I'm too much of a coward to take a knife to my veins; too scared of heights to throw myself from the Hornsey Lane Bridge. I've got a small jar of Mum's sleeping tablets rattling around in the bottom of my handbag, containing perhaps enough to knock me out but sadly too few to kill me. What would my mother think if she could see me now? She'd see how much I miss her and need her, if only by the altered shape of me. It was she who kept my eating in check, she who steered me away from those foods that make me so ill, those foods that make me so fat. At home, there were no Battenberg cakes or bottles of pop or jars of peanut butter and chocolate spread. At home, there were 'square meals' and quotas of fresh water to be consumed and lean white meat and steamed veg. At home, there was discipline. But here, there's nothing. No rules, no limits. I buy what I want, I eat what I want, and never have I weighed out my portions or denied myself a second helping. Why, sometimes I'll have three! There's nobody here to tell me *no*, to arch their brows in disapproval or keep me from the food cupboard. There's nobody to stop me. I'm like an articulated lorry with its brakes cut.

It's funny, to think back on it now, lying here as I am, stranded upon my sofa, larger than ever, as I was really just a normal child – neither fat nor thin, but somewhere in between.

Whenever Mum brought up the subject of my size, Dad would argue that I hadn't had my growth spurt yet, that I could rest assured that I was a completely healthy weight for my height and age. If I was carrying a couple of extra pounds, he said, I'd soon shift it with a bit more exercise, and he bought me a bicycle, saying I could join him on his weekend bike rides out along the river and into the countryside. Mum would remain silent during these conversations, her lips a tight line, giving no more than a curt nod when Dad looked to her for agreement. When we were alone, she'd tell me how she *too* was a chubby child, and how she'd never forgiven her mother for not acting on it sooner to help her to slim down.

'But you're not fat *at all*, Mummy,' I'd say, confused as to why she should still be angry at her mother. (Even at ten, I called her Mummy, and never thought it strange until a few years later when someone laughed at me after I'd said it in public.) 'Maybe you slimmed down after your growth spurt, like Dad says I will?'

I remember the face she pulled. It said: What does he know about it? He's just a man! 'There's no such thing as a growth spurt,' she replied. 'You don't stay as slim as I do without considerable effort and willpower. Your dad, quite frankly, is talking nonsense. It's different for men.' The following day, two slimming magazines appeared on my bedside cabinet, and a padlock was fitted to the pantry door. Under the watchful eye of my mother, my meals diminished to the tiniest of portions, and all snacking ended. No more Hula Hoops or ginger biscuits or buttered toast or cake. Even fruit was considered too calorific if I was to make the changes she thought possible for me. In the privacy of my bedroom, morning and night, I followed a strict regime of exercise, as laid out in my *Slim!* magazine, a series of star jumps and jogging and

187

stretching and sit-ups and lunges. I won't pretend it was as easy as I make it sound, because it wasn't. It was a living hell, and many a night I went to bed and wept into my pillow, hungry and tired and too weak to complain aloud.

Within six weeks, Mum had to get out the sewing machine to take in the waistbands of my trousers, and I could balance marbles in the hollows of my clavicles. I had lost a stone and a half! My mother revelled in my rapid transformation, congratulating herself – and me – on making it happen, and I swear we connected in a way we'd never done before. Now we had something in common, a shared project: the project of me. Every time I entered the living room, she'd gasp and call me her beautiful girl, making me twirl for my father as she dabbed at her eyes. But Dad didn't seem to share her enthusiasm, and it seemed the thinner I got, the deeper his furrows grew. I was torn. Surely now I looked better, more normal, more like everyone else? Perhaps, I thought with trepidation, perhaps I could even consider mainstream school in September, when I'd be eleven and able to join at the same time as all the new starters?

With great effort I push myself up from the sofa, desperate to leave these thoughts behind. Why do I do it to myself, returning to painful memories like taking a fingernail to a healing scab? I'm not that person any more: I'm the master of my own destiny, the mistress of this house. Flicking on the radio for distraction, I rummage at the back of the kitchen drawers until I find a pair of scissors and fetch the mirror from the bathroom. Balancing it above the kitchen sink where the light is good and clear, I pick up a first handful of hair, nearly an arm's length, and take the scissors to it just below the ear, drawing sharp breath as it comes away from my head and flops over my fist like a dead snake. Laying the strand carefully on the kitchen worktop, I work my way around, aware that my line is wonky, but continuing all the same, until finally there's a thick pile of my hair arranged on the counter and a different person gazing back at me. My stomach continues to cramp. Carefully, I gather the pieces, tying the cut ends with a length of cooking string before brushing it out and hanging it from the hook on the back of the kitchen door. I'm standing there, admiring it, when a report on the midday news catches my attention.

'Police are appealing for any information on missing school-girl Charlotte Bennett, who was last seen cycling home along the Regent's Canal late on Monday night, near the footpath to the Waterside Café. Charlotte is seventeen years old, five feet four inches in height, with long, dark hair and blue eyes. She was wearing a fur-trimmed khaki jacket, black jeans and white Converse trainers, and riding a black and grey Giant brand bicycle. Police are treating her disappearance as suspicious.'

My griping stomach finally gives way, and I rush for the toilet, making it just in time before my bowels empty them-selves entirely. I slump over my knees, exhausted, confused, not really knowing who I am or where I fit in. If I were to die, if I *were* brave enough to end it all now – to take those scissors and plunge their blades into my neck – who would find me? Who would care?

I think of Carl, poor, lovely Carl delivering my groceries the day after tomorrow, and I know I couldn't do that to him. A person might never recover from a shock like that. It's strange, but the thought of Carl gives me strength, and an idea presents itself to me, so brilliantly simple, it's like a gift. I clean myself up and return to the kitchen, and prepare myself for a long-overdue trip to the post office. That missing girl has given me just the inspiration I needed.

19. **Martha**

With a wide sweep of his arm, Glen Gavin waves to Martha and Toby through the glass of his large corner office, beckoning them in.

'Ah, the Dream Team!'

'Batman and Robin,' Toby jokes, tilting his head towards Martha as he says 'Batman', and she could almost hug him for it.

Glen indicates to the two seats on the other side of his polished desk and they sit, as he presses the intercom and asks Sarah, his PA, to fetch drinks. He checks his watch, loosens his pristine tie a millimetre or two, and places his hands palm to palm. 'So, what have you got?'

Martha tugs back her jacket sleeves, propping her elbows on the desk, talking without notes. 'I think the first thing to say, Glen, is that we certainly haven't solved the case. The way it looks at the moment, the show, when it goes out, will be a "Cold Case Call to Action" rather than a "Cold Case Closed" documentary.'

Glen's expression remains stable, showing no obvious signs of disappointment. On the desk between her and Toby, the screen of Martha's silenced mobile phone lights up with an incoming call: *D calling*. Both men glance at the phone as she hurriedly presses the Call Reject button and flips it face-down on the desk. She knows they've seen it; she knows Toby will be wondering again who 'D' is, will be wanting to ask. She also knows a garbled text message will quickly follow, and dread sits heavy in the pit of her stomach. She ploughs on.

'The good news is that we've discovered plenty of new loose ends, which, if we don't get to the bottom of them soon, will certainly give us a lot to showcase onscreen, in the hope that someone out there will connect them. Toby will run through our key breakthroughs.'

'OK. Number one, we have these postcards, supposedly from David Crown – one a year sent to his wife Janet, from a variety of European locations.' He places a blown-up picture of the postcards, photographed before they handed them on to the police, on the table between them.

'Are they genuine?' Glen asks.

'Mrs Crown believes so, categorically. But we can't be sure. Some of them are very old, and even the newer ones will have been through too many hands to have left any useful finger-prints. There's nothing written on them other than "D x".'

Toby runs his finger down his journal.

'Next, we have the discovery of this chat room, MisPer. Over the past day or so, we've been following a conversation between users calling themselves CrownieD and DebbieT, in which he claims to be David Crown and she – the originator of the thread – claims to be a family friend. Well, we've checked with Janet Crown and she's never heard of anyone called Debbie, so we're wondering if it's a relative, or perhaps an old colleague or ex-girlfriend.'

Glen continues to listen intently.

'Juney's had no joy finding the girl from that black and white photograph,' Toby continues. 'The girlfriend who gave David Crown his alibi at the time of the Tilly Jones murder.'

Martha now reaches into her bag for her notebook, opening it up to refresh her memory. 'We know from a local landlord that her name was Hattie Brown, but he couldn't tell us much more, as she moved away from the village years ago. We want to get her version of the afternoon Tilly was killed. If she's still alive, could she be posing as this "DebbieT"?'

'Doubtful.' Toby shakes his head. 'She's an ex-girlfriend from, what, nearly fifty years ago? I doubt they kept contact, especially with him having left his home town under a cloud of suspicion.'

Glen raises a finger. 'Is it possible that Debbie might be another Square Wheels volunteer, Martha?'

Martha chews her lower lip. There's so much from that period that's grown foggy with the passing of time. 'It's possible, but it's not a name I remember. And, of course, we have no idea if this conversation is genuine or bogus. All we can do is continue to follow it and see what it throws up. CrownieD is adamant that he – David Crown – is innocent, and he says he suspects a homeless man called Ethan as the real abductor or murderer of Juliet Sherman.'

'And your police contact? Have you passed this all on to him? What's his opinion?'

'Yes, I met with—' Martha stops herself from using Finn's name. 'I met with him last night. He's retired, but very much in contact with serving officers in the Crime Squad, and able to feed in any information we think is of significance. He and I go back a long way, old family friend, and he's willing to do everything he can to help with the case, so long as we keep his name out of it. He's been back over the case notes and confirmed that when they interviewed David Crown on the morning before he disappeared, he never mentioned anyone called Ethan, or any other possible suspects, for that matter. That said, my old friend Liv also mentioned a homeless man called Ethan, so it's a lead we need to look at seriously. But, until I see something on that chat-room thread that isn't re-cycled from public records, I'm treating it with caution. It's possible that this thread has popped up in response to the ad we ran in the *Metro* last week, when we appealed for infor-mation. There are plenty of nut-jobs out there. This lead may turn out to be a waste of time.'

'Agreed,' Glen says. 'And you mentioned your friend Olivia? Has she been of any help?'

'No. I'm increasingly getting the feeling she doesn't want to be involved. I've been in regular contact with her since the start of this, but, while she's been helpful enough in her emails, she's resisted any suggestions of meeting up in person. I think perhaps it's just too painful. But I haven't given up yet. I'm pretty sure I can talk her around.'

If only she felt as confident as she sounds.

'Number three,' Toby continues. 'The Garden of Reflection at Juliet's old school. This was the site David Crown was working on at the time he vanished, the remodelling of what was the old school swimming pool into a floral garden.'

'It was quite a big project,' Martha adds, 'and a few of us, Juliet included, had helped out as volunteers the summer before, while David was getting the prep work underway. The old pool had to be broken up and filled in before any landscaping work could be done. Then the funding ran out and it was all put on hold till December, when the school held a Christmas fair and some other events and raised enough money to restart the work. We met with Geoff Blakeley, the gardening contractor who took over when David disappeared, and he tells us that, according to the school, David Crown had met with the building inspector on the very morning that Juliet vanished, when the footings for the patio area were passed. No one from the school could tell us the order of things, but the new contractor suspects that if the concreting work went ahead as planned, which it did a couple of days after David and Juliet's disappearances, the excavated area must already have been filled with hardcore – rubble to you and me. Geoff took over where David left off, and the concreted patio base was already in place, ready for the garden to be planted up around it.'

When the penny doesn't appear to drop for Glen, Toby says, 'We're quite interested in that patio at the Garden of Reflection. It would certainly have been the perfect place to dispose of a body.'

Glen's eyebrows rise, and Martha is sure she sees the glint of excitement in his expression. 'Now *that* would make good television,' he says, looking from Toby to Martha. 'What will it take to get the police to excavate?'

'Right now,' Martha replies, 'we need something big to happen. We need something that will convince the police that Juliet didn't run away, but was taken. We need to convince them that the Garden of Reflection is a potential burial site.'

20. **Casey**

The waiting is killing me. Every few minutes I check my emails for news from Martha, but there is none. Is she annoyed at me for avoiding her invitations to meet up? Has she given up on me? The parcel I sent should have arrived by now, surely? I sent it first class, but there's no mention of it on the news, no update from Martha telling me she knows about it. Perhaps it has got caught up in the system, sitting on someone's desk, unopened, unnoticed. I've been back to the MisPer chat room, adding in more specific details that might grab someone's attention, but the silence rings out.

If Martha *has* turned away from me, I don't know how I'll have the strength to go on. What is left? If it weren't for the fact that I know Carl will be coming tomorrow, I swear I don't know what I might do to myself. Yes, I'll give it another day, give her one more day to respond. Tomorrow, I will sort out my filing and reply to all my emails. I will restore some order, banish the chaos I've allowed to take over my world. And then, if Carl doesn't turn up, if Martha doesn't reply – then I'll do it.

This time I'm not even kidding. I'll kill myself.

21. **Martha**

By 8.45 a.m., Martha's universe has tilted, with a phone call from Finn Palin.

'Martha, love,' he says the moment she answers the call, urgency in his voice. 'My Met chap's just been on the phone about the David Crown case. There's been a new development you'll want to know about.'

Martha had been about to leave the apartment to meet up with Toby, and now she pushes the door shut again and drops her house keys on the side, fumbling in her bag for her notebook and pen. 'Go on.'

'A teenage girl went missing this week in the Islington area. Charlotte Bennett. Did you hear about it?'

'Vaguely.'

'Seventeen, cycling along the Regent's Canal. Parents say it's completely out of character. Police are treating it as suspicious. She was cycling home around nine at night.'

'Christ. Just like Juliet. It's even the same time of year.'

'*Just* like Juliet. Well, that's what I thought, so I called my pal yesterday when I heard about it on the news, but he said it was tenuous to say the least. There's eighteen years separating the two events – too long to make a strong case for them being connected.'

'OK,' Martha says, wondering then why the urgency in his voice. 'So, how does this help us?'

'Well, that was what he said *yesterday*. Today, however, things have changed significantly. They've taken a look at Janet Crown's most recent postcard, the one suggesting her husband is in London – together with the conversations in the missing persons chat room – and now, with this new bit of evidence—'

'What new bit of evidence?' Martha demands.

Finn laughs. 'Alright, alright! A parcel was delivered to the local police station some time yesterday, containing a typed note, claiming to be from someone called Ethan – along with a long, dark plait of hair. All the note says is, "I took Charlotte Bennett, just like I took Juliet Sherman." No instructions, no threats or demands, just a statement.'

Martha's mind races. This name again: *Ethan*. Could he really be Juliet's kidnapper?

'What do you think, Finn?' she asks. 'Do you think David Crown is innocent?'

'No,' he replies without pause. 'And neither do the investigating officers now. I suggested to them that, if David Crown *is* guilty, this is the perfect diversion – sending a note, claiming that the crimes were perpetrated by someone else altogether. If Ethan is a real person, he'll be almost impossible to locate – if he was homeless back in 2000, he'll be either dead now or living somewhere else altogether. The perfect fall guy. Perhaps David Crown is making plans to return? He'll be getting on a bit now. Maybe he thinks this will clear him of any suspicion?'

'What happens now?' Martha asks, anxious to finish up so she can phone Toby and tell him the news.

'They'll want Charlotte Bennett's parents to identify the hair, and if it looks like a match they'll carry out DNA testing to be sure. Martha . . .' Finn clears his throat. 'The police are heading down to the Garden of Reflection this morning. Finally, they're taking your theory seriously. They've got forensics preparing to search beneath the patio for the remains of Juliet Sherman.'

By ten o'clock Martha is standing at the edge of the police-cordoned Garden of Reflection in the grounds of Bridge School. The moment Finn Palin was off the line, Martha had phoned Toby, arranging to meet him there, before rushing out an email to Liv. In it, she pleaded with her to meet them at the school, informing her that the police were about to dig up the garden in search of Juliet's remains. *This* could be the moment they finally discovered what happened to their best friend. Surely this would get through to her? Liv's place is only a few streets away, so it would take her just minutes to be there. Maybe she will turn up this time, out of respect for Juliet, if nothing else. Martha can only hope.

Now, without emotion, she takes in the scene, like a spectator viewing events from afar. To her rear is the playground, its paved surface marked out for netball and giving way to two four-floor blocks of classrooms, alongside a warren of prefabricated science labs and temporary classrooms. The playing field ahead of her is hemmed in on the right-hand side by ten-foot wire mesh fencing, and to the left and rear by an imposing brick wall, which looks older than the school itself. She can see Jay and Sally beyond the fence, setting up their equipment to film through the wire, having been told by an investigating officer that they weren't welcome at close range. Martha knows they're being lenient in turning a blind eye to her and Toby's presence, so she's not going to argue at this stage. Slightly off-centre of the grassed area is the Garden of Reflection – the site of the old swimming pool – a serene patioed area, surrounded by low box hedges, flower borders and a couple of water features that, from where Martha is standing, seem to have fallen victim to vandalism over recent years.

Over beside the frostbitten flower borders, Toby is chatting to the head teacher, who stands with her arms folded, her face set in a concerned scowl. It's clear to Martha that Toby is doing what he does best: putting the woman at ease, engaging her in conversation and forcing a smile from her. He gestures in Martha's direction, no doubt telling her that the famous Martha Benn once attended this school, and yes, hasn't she done well? Martha quickly looks away, scanning the area beyond the high-vis jackets of police officers and school personnel, out across the lawns towards the streets and houses that surround the school. This is an area she once knew like the back of her hand. If she were to wander the streets now, to take her old walking route back home to Stanley House, would she find it changed? Without a doubt. To the right, there are a number of gawkers hanging around on the other side of the wire fence, trying to catch a glimpse of the action, and Martha studies them carefully, hoping to see Liv's face among their number. She feels an ache of guilt that the Sherman family have yet to be informed about the dig. Finn said that, until there's a clear indication that they've actually found something, they've agreed to tread softly, bearing in mind Alan Sherman's frail health.

At the near corner of the fencing she notices the bike shed, a modern Perspex version replacing the old wooden one that stood there in her day. She can see the original in her mind's eye, as clear as day, bringing with it the memory of Tim Brayer and his bloodied nose. Tim Brayer was two years older and probably Liv's most serious boyfriend in all the years the girls knew each other. Up until that point, she'd only had fleeting passions or one-off dates with boys from her own year, but, Martha remembers with an unhappy pang, from the moment she started going out with Tim, Liv had changed. The jokey, couldn't-care-what-anyone-thinks Liv disappeared, to be replaced by a girl so uncertain of her own place that Martha and Juliet were at a loss to help her. They'd never *seen* Tim do anything to undermine her, but his physical presence was like a force-field, his arm constantly draped about her shoulders, his answers taking the place of hers. He'd crack jokes that weren't directly at her expense but certainly nudged close to it, and, whether she noticed or not, he froze out her best friends as though they didn't exist. Juliet was saddened by the change in Liv; Martha was enraged. But what could they do or say? Anything negative would surely seem like sour grapes on the part of the friends who'd been left behind.

The answer showed itself on a scorching lunchtime in June, when a sombre Liv had left the others in the dinner queue to go and meet Tim at the bike shelter, 'to chat'. Martha persuaded Juliet that they should follow and spy on the couple, to find out what was going on to make Liv so low, and so they skipped lunch, trailing them at a distance until they stood unseen on the other side of the shelter. Through the age-shrunk wooden slats of the bike shed they could clearly see and hear the pair, facing them but unaware of their presence. Despite her tiny frame, Liv had never seemed small in Martha's eyes, her energy more than making up for what she lacked in stature. But now Tim, at nearly six foot, towered over Liv, and she seemed suddenly tiny and indistinct in the shadow of him. As Martha and Juliet watched, Tim pressed his face into Liv's neck, murmuring low as her upturned face smiled. Martha felt sick with the wrongness of their being there, and was about to indicate to Juliet that they should leave, when another boy appeared, and Liv's smile dropped away.

'Go on,' Tim said, stepping back to create a space for the other lad to step into. His shadow fell away, and Liv's dread was clear on her face.

The boy reached out and cupped Liv's small blouse-clad breast in his hand. His startled expression suggested he hadn't wanted to do it. Tim's smile slid into an upturned sneer, and he nodded for the boy to do more. Tim Brayer was grinning as though it was nothing more than a bit of a laugh. The smaller boy awkwardly fumbled with the top button of Liv's blouse, his face now crimson and aggrieved. Liv turned her face away, and for a moment Martha thought she must surely be able to see them standing there on the other side of the wood panel.

'*Fucker*,' Martha spat, unable to contain it, and before she knew what she was doing she was on the other side, violently yanking the boy back by his shirt collar, telling him she'd kill him if he breathed a word of this to anyone. The kid ran across the field without a backward glance.

'Jealous?' Tim laughed.

In disbelief, Martha glanced at Juliet, then at Liv, the word ringing in her ears. And that was when she punched him, so hard she thought her knuckles had split through her skin and into his. His nose, an oily dumpling of a nose, appeared to explode, and for a moment Martha was appalled at herself, envisaging her slurring father's response when the school made the phone call home. *How* could she have been such an idiot?

'You dozy fucking *bitch*!' Tim screamed, high-pitched now as he tried to stem the blood-flow with the heel of his hand. His words were muffled, his eyes startled.

As he went to leave, Juliet, never one to put herself in the way of unnecessary drama, blocked his path and, without touching him, leaned in and spoke softly. 'If you mention this to anyone, Tim, we will expose you as the paedo you really are.'

He blinked, then smirked again, about to retort with some clever-arse comment.

Juliet cut him off. 'Think I'm joking?' She pointed at Martha. 'See Martha there? Her dad's a police officer, and he'd love to hear about you and Liv. You're a *sex offender*.'

'What?' he choked, the colour draining from his skin as he backed away from Liv, from Juliet.

Juliet nodded solemnly. 'She's fourteen; you're sixteen. Work it out.'

When Tim had gone, the three girls huddled together, gathering breath. Liv was the first to break the silence, returning to the fold with three whispered words: 'What a cock.' That was all the thanks Martha and Juliet needed. *What a cock.*

God, Martha could do with a cigarette right now, she thinks, recalling the tobacco smell of that old wooden bike shed. She hasn't smoked for over a decade, but every now and then the old craving rears itself in the same way that her thirst for the oblivion of alcohol is never forgotten. She slips a tab of gum on to her tongue and shuts the yearning back in its box.

Over where they're inspecting the Garden of Reflection it's impossible to see exactly what the officers are doing, and Toby makes a shrugging motion towards her to indicate that he's as clueless as she. Again, Martha checks her phone for messages, then wanders over to the railings to take a closer look at the rubberneckers who are loitering there in hope of a bit of local gossip. She could ask if any of them know Olivia Heathcote, but it's such a long shot that she feels foolish even thinking it. As she reaches the fence her phone rings, displaying an unknown number. With a thrill of hope she takes the call, and moves away from the fence for fear of being overheard.

'Hello? Liv?'

'No,' a man's voice replies, and her optimism plummets as she anticipates the sales patter that will surely follow. But instead the man asks, 'Is that Martha Benn?'

Wrong-footed, Martha looks around her, needing to locate Toby. She just needs to know he's nearby. She spots him leaning against a recycling bin on the edge of the hard-standing. Good. Good, he's still here.

'Martha?' the voice repeats.

'Yes, this is Martha Benn.'

'Oh, good. Thought I had the wrong number for a minute. Martha – it's Tom!'

In an instant she recognises his voice, a flood of thoughts and images rushing through her mind. It's Tom, Juliet's brother. *Tom.*

'Wow,' she says. '*Wow.*'

Tom laughs. 'How are you, Martha? Dad told me you'd been around to see him. How are you doing?'

'Good, really good. Sorry, Tom, I'm a bit . . . It's so good to hear your voice.' Once again she's struck by the absence of these people – Tom and Juliet, and lovely Mr Sherman, Liv and everything that came with her and her crazy animal-mad family. How had they all drifted so far apart? 'Where are you calling from?' she asks. 'Your dad said you're living in Paris.'

'Yes, I'm calling from work now. Thought I should make contact when Dad told me about your show. About the investigation.'

Martha tries to imagine how this must all sound to Tom. He and Juliet had always been so close. 'Are you OK with it, Tom?'

'Yeah, yeah,' he says without hesitation, his voice warm. 'I'm just processing the whole thing, but, Martha, I'm grateful someone's looking at it properly at last. I just hadn't imagined it would be you! Have you made any progress?'

If only you knew, she thinks, glancing towards the garden where a man in a white boiler suit is holding up a hand, halting the machine operator. Toby is jogging over to take a closer look; something's going on.

'I think we have, Tom. Nothing I can tell you about yet, but yes, I think we're on to something at last.' She can hardly tell Tom about the excavation, when even his father doesn't know. When there's no reply at the other end of the line, Martha adds, 'I'll tell you as soon as I can. But I'm feeling more confident with every passing day.'

'Good,' Tom manages, and she can hear the emotion in his voice. How could Liv have even suggested that Tom was involved in Juliet's disappearance? Tom, of all people? He clears his throat, and when he speaks again, his light tone has returned. 'So, Dad said I should get in touch if I thought I could help in any way. Well, I think I've got something. When I helped clear out the old house with Dad, I took a lot of Juliet's things with me, as Dad didn't have the space and, well, to spare his feelings, really. Most of it is of no interest – old bank statements, school files and so on – but when I went through them again this week I found a whole bunch of letters.'

'Letters? From who?' Martha has one eye on the activity beyond the police tape, desperate to get over there herself, but wanting to keep Tom on the line all the same.

'They look like love letters to me. I only opened a couple, but when I saw the nature of them I put them away again. I haven't got the stomach for it, Martha. What if they're from him? What if she really was involved with David Crown?'

'So what have you done with them, Tom?'

'They're in the post – should get to you in the next day or so. They might shed some light on what was going on in her last few months. She was clearly keeping secrets, if these letters are anything to go by. I didn't know she was seeing anyone, did you?'

Martha doesn't know how to answer. Yes, she'd known, but Juliet hadn't trusted her enough to share it with her. 'Not as such,' she says eventually. 'I think Liv knew more about it than I did, and I'm still trying to get her to meet up. I don't think she's that keen.'

'Well, good luck with that. Liv's not the kind of person to do anything she doesn't want to.'

Martha laughs, and thanks him, eager to get off the phone now that Toby is waving to her from the dig site. 'Tom, I've got your number now – I'll keep you posted. I promise.'

She sprints across the grass to join Toby, who updates her in lowered tones. 'OK, the officer in charge said to keep it under our hats for now, but the forensics guys have confirmed that there's a definite area of interest in the top right-hand corner of the patio.'

Martha blinks at Toby, then back towards the huddle of men in white suits. 'Juliet?' she whispers.

'Too early to say. But – strictly off the record – he says it looks very likely they've found human bones down there. He said everything's going to slow down a lot now, while they work out how to excavate the area without damaging any evidence – could take hours. We may not get any answers today, but Martha,' he says, taking her wrist in his hand as she looks at him, breath held, 'this could be just the breakthrough we've been waiting for.'

For several minutes they stand there, side by side, gazing at the activity all around them. The white tent is adjusted to fully screen off the site from the public beyond the fence, and the head teacher is sensitively updated before she returns inside the school building to continue with her day. Just another day for her; for most of the people here. But not for Martha. A sob threatens to rise in her chest and she turns away from Toby, swallowing it down, an empty judder of emotion. She's got her whole life to grieve; right now, she has to keep it together. Now that they've found her, Juliet deserves Martha's full, uncompromised attention. She let her down once before, and she's damned if she'll fail her again.

'What now?' Toby asks Martha.

Resentment takes over. *Liv* should be here. If she did nothing else to help in this investigation, she should have been here, to share in this moment they've all longed for, the moment when Juliet's whereabouts are at last uncovered. If not for Martha, she should have been here for Juliet.

'*Right.* Toby, can you head over and find Sally and Jay – they're just beyond the fence.' She passes him a handwritten script sheet, penned just moments earlier. 'I'm meant to be doing a piece to camera, with the excavation tent and activity in the background. Can you do it?'

'Where are you off to?' Toby calls after her as she walks away.

'I'm going to call in on Liv,' she replies without a backward glance. She bites back her tears as she strides on, tugging up the collar of her jacket, picking up pace. 'She doesn't get off so lightly. I don't care how upsetting this is; Liv needs to be here.'

22. **Casey**

Martha says the police are digging up the gardens at Bridge School this morning, and I'm to meet her there. A *body*. She says they think a body may be buried beneath the foundations of the patio. Juliet's body, she says. I feel sick as I read the words, sick at the thought of a body dumped in the ground like any old rubbish, crushed beneath rubble and concrete, hidden forever from the world and the people who love them. What a terrible thing, what an evil thing.

> Please come and meet me there, Liv. If it is Juliet, I'm
> going to need your support – I don't know if I can do it
> alone and I think she'd want us to be together when
> she's found.

I'm unsettled by her needful tone, the way she pleads with me – with Liv, with her friend. More than anything I want to be there for her. I *want* to be her friend. But I'm not Liv, and only Liv will do, and it makes me angry and scared and lonely to know that I can't rush down there as I so want to, to take her hand in mine and help her through it. For an hour I pace the living room, forcing myself to eat a breakfast I know will rush through me like a freight train, popping anti-spasmodic pills in a bid to ease the morbid cramp that doubles me over. I return again and again to the email message displayed on my laptop screen, wondering what to do next, what action to take. After I've sat on the toilet for a while, the pain in my stomach begins to subside and the answer comes to me. I *will* go to the school, but I'll keep my distance. Then, in a way I will be there for Martha, and the next time I email I can tell her that I *did* go as she asked, but failed to find her, and so returned home. Perhaps I can restore her belief in me, if I just make a bit more of an effort.

Within an hour of receiving Martha's email, I am standing outside the school fence watching the comings and goings on the school grounds, as police officers and men in white boiler suits mill about, shifting tent panels and writing on clipboards. There are others alongside me, locals who have caught wind of the activity and are speculating about the reason for the forensics tent and police presence.

'Someone said it was a stabbing,' a young man with an ugly dog informs his friend. 'Some gang thing.'

'A kid from the school?' his friend asks.

The dog owner nods knowledgeably.

Amazing! How people are so quick to fill in false detail when ignorant of the facts! 'Everyone's an expert,' that's what Mum used to say when she didn't believe what she was hearing. She'd say it to Dad when he tried to encourage me to eat more at mealtimes, telling me I was a growing girl and it wouldn't do me any good to go hungry. 'And what do you know about it?' she'd ask, irritated at him for encouraging me to break my diet. 'Everyone's an expert these days!'

'I heard it was a historic murder,' I tell them, shocked at my own audacity. 'Hence the tent and the men in overalls. They're digging it up.'

Several members of the public make moves to take a better look at me, and I like the way it makes me feel. Authoritative. Visible. That's the way Martha makes me feel too.

I spot her over at the edge of the playground. She's alone and she appears to be surveying the dig scene from a distance, scanning the area as though trying to solve a puzzle. She looks lonely, and again I feel the strongest bond between us, the kind of connection only shared by the best of friends. I long to call out to her, to say, 'Martha, it's me! I came!' But, of course, I won't do that. The timing is all wrong, and it's Liv who she expects to see, not some stranger with wonky hair and a coat that won't do up over her stomach. Her eyes rest on the bike shelter near to me, and when she starts to cross the lawn in my direction, I feel certain that she's worked it all out, because her face is set hard with purpose. Is it anger, or concentration? It's hard to tell, but as she draws closer I see her scrutinising each one of the faces in the small crowd that has gathered on this side of the fence and her lips part, as though she's preparing to speak. My heart is in my mouth! I'm still feeling unwell, the cold sweats having returned as I rushed here from home, and I almost turn on my heel and flee, but then her phone rings and she takes the call, sidetracking her. I hear her say the name 'Liv' and then 'Tom'. Aha, I think, it's Juliet's brother! And then, to my crushing disappointment, she moves away so I can't hear any more.

I'm so thrilled to be this close to Martha that I forget for a moment why we're really here.

'Did you know them?' the woman beside me asks, noticing

my tears as I wipe them away on the back of my hand. 'The person they're digging up?'

'We were very close,' I reply.

She touches my arm with a mottled pink hand. The skin on the back of her knuckles looks chapped and raw, and her proximity makes me feel giddy, but the gesture is a kind one. 'You poor love. Family? Friend?'

I simply nod, enjoying the woman's sympathy. The tears continue to flow, streaming down my hot cheeks and under my chin. 'Yes,' I sob, and I move away from her, to reposition myself further along the wire fencing and closer to where Martha now stands.

I raise my mobile phone and take photographs, unnoticed among so many others doing the same thing, and manage to capture both Martha and the scene beyond. As her phone call comes to an end, she turns her head in my direction and, click, I get her, clear as day: a perfect portrait of Martha Benn looking directly at me. When I look up from the screen, I'm alarmed to see that Martha is sprinting across the grassed area towards a young man who I now recognise as Toby. There seems to be an increase in activity around the tent, an excitement of sorts as the men and women in white congregate at the entrance, pointing beyond the canvas screen and jotting notes on clipboards. One of them is making a phone call; another talks with a uniformed officer and indicates in our direction with a sweeping motion. Martha and Toby stand just outside the police tape, their heads close in discussion. Toby does most of the talking as Martha nods, listening intently, bringing her hand to her mouth as she absorbs whatever it is he's telling her. I'm mesmerised by the sight of her, so close, Martha Benn in action. And then she's running back in my direction, tugging at her jacket collar and calling something back to him as she comes. There are tears in her eyes, and as she nears me I clearly hear her words.

'She doesn't get off so lightly. I don't care how upsetting this is; Liv needs to be here.'

My stomach twists viciously, and again I feel the threat of my bowels loosening. She's got to go around the long way, I think, to make her exit out through the school gates at the front. My mind is racing: if I hurry, I could just about reach home before she does. I can't let her see me entering the house, can't let her know that I'm not Liv, that this whole past fortnight everything I've said to her has been a lie. That I'm not who I say I am.

Pushing past the woman with the red knuckles, I run as fast as my tensed muscles will allow, icy sweat breaking out over my face and chest. Just a few streets, I tell myself, that's all it is. You can do it.

At the corner of my street my vision swims, my consciousness threatening to peter out altogether. I remember a time, so many years ago, when I was pursued by the police through these very streets during that bother with Mark Lynton. There were two of them, and they chased me in the darkness, calling to me as I darted from one street to the next, much lighter on my feet back then, and desperate not to be caught. 'Stalker,' they called me when they gave me a formal caution. But how can it be stalking, I wanted to know, when it comes from a place of love? How can admiration be misconstrued as threat? Even now I can recall the pounding sense of fear I felt as those police officers closed in on me, the sound of their footsteps growing nearer, their voices stronger. 'Miss!' they shouted. 'Miss!' In my mind's eye I'm there again, the darkness gaining on me despite the early hour of the day, and I daren't look over my shoulder, daren't pause for a moment, though I'm

211

aware that now my footsteps are no longer pounding the streets but staggering the last few hundred yards as I hold on to everything I've got to prevent my bowels from releasing right here on the street.

With a cry I force my key into the front door and turn it, dark dots pricking my vision, the relief of home enveloping me as I step inside. But my relief is short-lived. I hear Martha's voice before I feel her hand on my shoulder.

'Hey!' she calls out, and it's over, I think.

It's all over.

23. Martha

The woman standing in Liv's doorway is panting and sweat-drenched, and from the terrified expression on her face, Martha has the strongest feeling she's about to slam the door closed. Martha catches the edge of the door frame with her hand, leaning back to double-check the house number on the brick wall outside. Definitely Liv's house. Definitely not Liv.

'Um,' the woman stutters, her eyes darting nervously from Martha's steadfast hand to the street beyond. She can't meet Martha's gaze.

She's very short and heavy-set, with dark bobbed hair, and for a crazy moment back there, before the woman had turned and Martha had seen that the colour of her skin was all wrong, she had actually wondered if it could be Liv. As she'd watched her stop outside the door, fumbling with her keys, it had flashed through Martha's mind that perhaps *this* was why Liv was avoiding her: that she'd been hiding away, self-conscious of her dramatically altered shape. But this person couldn't be more different from the Liv Martha recalls, the small, dark pixie of a girl who had barely reached her shoulders.

'I'm looking for Olivia Heathcote,' Martha says, her hand remaining hooked on the frame.

The woman nods, almost imperceptibly, and Martha notices the slick of sweat along her hairline. Her face is red and puffy, her breathing laboured. She doesn't look like the kind of person who ought to be running; she doesn't look well.

'Are you alright?' Martha asks, as the woman's eyes roll upwards as though she might pass out. 'Here, let me help you inside.'

Steering her over the threshold, Martha guides her straight through to the small kitchen at the back, instinctively knowing the way. To her surprise, very little has changed. The wall units are the same dark veneer cabinets that she remembers so well, sucking the light out of the room, and the big butler sink is the one Martha recalls the twins being bathed in when they were newly home from the hospital.

'I'm Martha,' she tells the woman as she pulls out an upright chair and helps her into it. When the woman only stares back, she begins to wonder if she has learning difficulties, or has trouble speaking. Could she be deaf? She hunches down, so that the movement of her lips might be seen, and asks slowly, 'What's – your – name?'

'Casey,' the woman replies, locking her fingers together across her lap. There's something off about her, but Martha can't quite fathom what it is. When she raises her eyes briefly, shyly, Martha has a sharp sense of recognition, though she's certain she's never met this woman before in her life. She's so distinctively odd – in both manner and appearance – that she wouldn't easily have forgotten her.

'*Casey*.' There's a three-legged stool beside the sink. Martha pulls it over and sits facing her. 'Do you need a drink of water? No? Now, Casey, I'm looking for my friend

214

Liv Heathcote. I was expecting to find her here. Do you know who I mean?'

Casey tenses her arms about her midriff, her face creasing with pain. 'Yes,' she replies with a grimace. She relaxes her hands as though a spasm has passed. 'I bought the house from her.'

Martha's eyes widen, and she looks about the room, confused. 'But . . .' she starts, and then everything begins to fall into place. You stupid woman, Martha Benn. She's barely able to believe her error. Idiot! Just because she sent the initial letter here, it doesn't mean that Liv has been emailing from here. 'Have you received any mail for Olivia over the past fortnight or so?'

Casey nods vigorously, and reaches out for a tea towel, wiping it across her face to mop up the rivulets of sweat that pour from her. 'Yes! A handwritten letter. I didn't open it!'

'What did you do with it?' Martha asks softly. She notices that Casey's hair is a good half-inch shorter on the left side than the right. There's an unpleasant odour about her, like laundry that's been left to get mildewed in the washing machine.

'I took it to the post office and they told me they had a forwarding address and I handed it over to them and they sent it on to her.'

She says this all in such a rush that it reminds Martha of a child telling a big fib. 'Did they say where that forwarding address was, Casey?'

'No.'

'They didn't say whether it was in London or elsewhere? Did you meet Liv during the house sale? Liv didn't mention where she was moving to when she sold you the house?'

'Oh, yes. Yes, she did say, but I can't . . . Oh, dear. I'm such a useless lump, aren't I?' She looks as though she might cry, and Martha feels bullish for bombarding her with so many questions. Then, quite unexpectedly, the woman says, 'You're Martha Benn, from the television, aren't you?' And her face brightens. 'I watch you all the time. My mum and I – we used to watch you together, when you were on breakfast TV. I don't watch it now you're not on it. It really went downhill after you left. *Really.*'

Martha smiles awkwardly at this sudden outpouring of admiration. 'Yes, yes, I am Martha. Actually, that's why I'm here – it's for a documentary I'm working on. I was hoping Liv would be able to help me with a few questions I've got.'

Casey's full attention is on her now, rapt, her focus fixed on Martha's face.

'You'd be really helping me if you had any information about where I can find—'

The woman suddenly leaps from her chair, clutching at her abdomen and rushing from the room. Martha rises from her own seat in surprise.

'Sorry! Sorry, I won't be two ticks!' Casey dashes into the narrow hallway towards the cramped toilet room that Martha knows is under the stairs, slamming the door behind her with an urgent clatter.

Standing alone in the kitchen, Martha stares at the empty space before her, wondering how she could have messed this up so badly. Why hadn't Liv put her right when she'd first got back in touch, and why hadn't she mentioned she no longer lived in Stack Street? Even when Martha had suggested meeting places that were close to this address, Liv had said nothing. Why not?

Sensing that Casey could be some time, Martha quietly steps out into the hallway and across to the small reception room at the front, where a small, neat window table is laid out with an embroidered tablecloth, held down by a large crystal ashtray and a Royal Doulton tea service. On the dark wood sideboard is a laser-jet printer, a pile of paperwork and an open laptop, its idle screen in sleep mode. Curious as to what this woman's line of work is, Martha leans in to peer at the top page. 'Chemicals and Allergy in the Twenty-First Century', the A4 sheet reads, with a few red pen scrawls along the edges, along with the initials KC. A scientist, perhaps? Or maybe some kind of editor? As Martha turns away, her coat catches the edge of the printer and a sheet of paper floats to the floor. She snatches it up, anxious not to get caught snooping in this strange woman's front room, but as she flips it over to return it, something familiar catches her eye. The Square Wheels logo. She steps into the light of the window and her breath stops in her chest. This picture, printed off *here*, in Liv's old front room, is the same image that Martha had sent to Liv's email address earlier this week – the newspaper cutting of David Crown and the Square Wheels volunteers.

On hearing the toilet flushing along the hall, Martha runs her finger across the touchpad of the laptop, and to her dismay Olivia Heathcote's inbox appears on the screen, open at Martha's latest message, entitled: *Meet me at school*. Was that where this woman had been rushing back from? Had she been among the onlookers at the school gates, craning to get a look at the police action? Sickeningly, it dawns on Martha that she's been the victim of an elaborate hoax.

'What are you doing?' The woman, Casey, is now standing in the doorway, holding on to the wall with one hand, the crumpled tea towel gripped tightly in the other. Again, she mops her brow. 'What are you doing in my front room? This is my office. This is my house,' she says, her voice rising tremulously. 'What do you want from me, Martha Benn?'

217

Martha holds up the printed image. 'Casey, if you passed my letter on to Liv, how did you come to get hold of this?'

Casey reaches out and snatches the paper from her. 'It's a project I'm working on. Quite separate!' Her mouth continues to move, but no words come, and she looks so much like a chastised child that Martha knows she's not quite right. She's vulnerable. This woman can't possibly live here alone.

'Does anyone else live here with you, Casey? Do you have a carer?'

'A carer! What for? Why would I have a carer?'

'I don't mean—' Martha begins, but her sentence is interrupted by the ringing of the front doorbell. When Casey doesn't move, Martha calmly asks her, 'Would you like me to get it?'

'No!' she hisses, her fingers rising to straighten and primp at her hair. 'It's just Carl. It's Carl. Carl. He'll come back later. *Yes.*'

'But surely—' Martha tries again, now beginning to feel uneasy about the woman's erratic behaviour. She needs to get out of here. She needs to call Toby and let him know that half of what they thought they knew is in fact useless. There's no time to lose. They need to find the real Liv.

The doorbell rings again, and Casey lets out a whimper, cautiously peering around the doorway and into the hall. At that moment a text message vibrates silently on Martha's phone, and she glances at it as the woman's back is turned, to find an update from Toby.

> Tracked down Jo Clement – one of the girls in the
> Square Wheels photo. Says she only volunteered a
> couple of times, but remembers the girl standing by
> DC is called Katherine (not Karen) and – get this –
> she's pretty sure she was DC's daughter.

Daughter? No, they've got it wrong. Janet Crown said their only child had died years ago and the police records don't mention a daughter, do they? Martha has to get out of here, to speak to Toby, to find out what this is all about.

'Casey,' Martha says, sliding her mobile back into her pocket, but Casey turns sharply, looking up at her through warning eyes.

'Shh!' she says, a fierce little finger flying to her mouth.

Martha's lips open to speak, but then the visitor calls out, sounding so close as to be almost in the same room.

'Miss Crown?' he calls against the tinny squeak of the letterbox rising. 'Are you there, Miss Crown? It's Carl from Sainsbury's! I've got your delivery!'

Now Casey's eyes fall squarely on Martha's, and they are the eyes of a cornered woman.

'Miss *Crown*?' Martha's mind can't work fast enough. 'Miss Crown – as in *Katherine* Crown?'

Casey shakes her head vigorously, reaching out grasping hands to stop Martha from retreating, but Martha snatches her arm away, taking a stride towards the hallway. But adrenaline is on Casey's side, and, in the afternoon gloom of that small front room, the sparkling reflected light of the raised crystal ashtray is the last thing Martha sees.

PART THREE

A Death

When my hand came down on the back of her head, I wondered for a moment where the rock had come from. A rock in my fist, slick with warm blood. The noise of it was sickening; a solid clunk that quickly gave way to moisture, but that one powerful blow was all it took and she hit the woodland floor as gracefully as a felled sapling. For a heartbeat all sound ceased, as though life itself was paused. No longer the chatter of finches soaring between branches, no coo of the wood pigeons in the canopy above, no creak and snap of squirrel or hare. Gone the peaceful sigh of late summer breeze. Just me, and the steady thud of my pulse, and the silent girl, face down in the moss bed at my feet.

From where I stood, her home was in view, not three hundred yards from the clearing, a large stone farmhouse set against the backdrop of the mountains and dales beyond. Out in the open air, the sun was still warm and bright in the sky, and it would be several hours more before darkness descended. I gazed down at the girl, taking in the way her slender arms trailed at her sides, palms upturned, fingers curled as though in restful slumber. One of her yellow clogs had tumbled away to reveal the soft pink underside of her small foot; the other remained in place, incongruous and ugly. I removed it, placed it with its partner neatly at the foot of the nearest birch. It struck me how young the girl suddenly appeared in death, how the absence of life lifted years from her, and how, lying there in her pastel summer dress, her skin sun-kissed and downy with fair hair, she seemed no threat at all. Where was her power now? In life she was bewitching, I knew that much just from watching the way she was with *him*. A coy flick of her hair, a come-hither glance from beneath lowered lashes; she could inspire jealousy in the purest of hearts. But now, what? Nothing. Her gold-tipped tresses fanned about her head, as though arranged that way to hide the broken skull, or as though she were a mermaid, drifting underwater, weightless.

As the sun shifted in the sky beyond the copse, I stole one last glance at the place where she lay, swallowing a scream when, to my horror, I saw her fingers twitch. I thanked God that I hadn't fled the scene immediately, that I had, by some chance of good fate, stayed long enough to witness the flicker of life that remained. It was a terrible thing, but the rock was still in my hand, and I knew it was the kindest thing to do. If she were a rabbit in a trap I would do the same, wouldn't I? I kneeled beside her, momentarily blinded by the piercing evening rays as they descended through the trees, and I brought the rock down on the back of her skull, again and again, with such force that I believed my shoulder might slip its socket. When I stepped away, her hair, like my hand, was crimson, and with one last look at her broken body I fled through the trees, towards the sound of the babbling brook.

Had I intended to kill her? In this instance, and this one alone, I believe perhaps I had.

24. Katherine

Have I killed her? *Have I?* The sight of Martha lying there, slumped face-down in my gloomy hallway, was nearly enough to stop my heart, and the deafening flood of remorse was overwhelming. I hadn't wanted *this* to happen. I'd wanted to help Martha; I wanted her to be my friend. I stared at the crystal ashtray in my hand and saw its corner tainted with Martha's blood. What would my mother say? It's been in our family for years, and, the moment I'm responsible for it, something like this happens! I wiped the blood away with the tea towel I was clutching in my left hand, and carefully placed the ashtray on the table beside the front window where it best catches the sun. Forcing myself to look again, I couldn't bring myself to approach Martha and check for a pulse, in case she really was dead. I couldn't bear to touch the skin of a dead person. Not again. And so instead I made a snap decision, and I hurried to my bedroom to gather my things. From the top room I saw Carl's supermarket van slowly moving away up the street, and I hurriedly threw a few items – a toothbrush, a change of knickers – into my shopper bag and located John's key at the bottom of my jewellery box. Back downstairs I yanked on my winter coat and grabbed up my laptop, shoving it into the bag along with my phone and chargers, desperately trying to work out if there was anything else I might need. The sound of my heartbeat roared in my ears, and while I struggled to think straight, my actions came quickly, and I knew I had to get out of there. This was bad. This was *so* very bad.

Now, as I breathe in the calm air of the Regent's Canal, I turn the key in John's padlock, and I'm thankful of the space to gather my thoughts and consider my next steps. Although the panicky feeling remains deep down in my stomach, my heart rate has levelled, and I am at least able to string a sentence together in my head. With a little shove of my shoulder I push open the door to the houseboat and hurry down the few wooden steps to shut myself inside before any of my riverside neighbours notice me.

The peace envelops me instantly. Everything is exactly where it should be. The red enamelled kettle sits on the gas hob, the bench cushions are neatly arranged, the wooden table is clear but for the woven placemats and gas lantern, the dark floral curtains are drawn. I have so many good memories of this place, and for a short while I just sit, sliding myself on to the bench and resting my head on the table. I just need to close my eyes for a while before I decide what to do.

During my mother's sad moments, this was a place we'd often come, Dad and I. John was elderly, an ex-army veteran, and, Dad said, one of the first people to offer him the hand of friendship when he moved here as a young man. He had moved on to the houseboat twenty years earlier after separating from his wife, and as he had no children of his own he was always glad to see me on our visits, ready to pull out

226

his curled-up old pack of snap cards and challenge me to a game. But Mum couldn't stand him. 'He's so tatty-looking, and ugh, that enormous ginger beard,' she'd say. And, 'Why would a seventy-year-old man be interested in spending time with a young girl, David?' she would badger Dad whenever I suggested calling in on John. 'It's not right. It's *suspect*.'

Dad insisted that John's friendship was with *him*, and that he was just a nice old boy who liked our company. Even though I wasn't sure what Mum meant, I knew her tone suggested something horrible, something dirty. And so our visits became *secret* visits, and that suited me just fine. Dad and I would stop at the houseboat at least once a week for a cup of tea and a cherry bakewell, and as I got older I'd sometimes drop in on my own when Mum needed time to herself. In my mind, I'd pretend to be an ordinary girl on my way home from school, wandering along the towpath in the sunshine, tossing my hair and smiling back at the boys who looked my way. If the weather was bad I'd pick up a packet of biscuits from the corner shop and knock on John's door, asking if he fancied a game of cards. He never, ever turned me away, and I told myself he was my long-lost grandpa, all the way from Derbyshire where my dad had grown up. I'd barely met any of the Crown family, so it seemed perfectly possible to me, perfectly feasible. Perhaps that was why Mum didn't like him, having fallen out with the family years earlier, as so often happens on the TV dramas Mum likes to watch. *Estranged*. John was my estranged grandfather. I liked the sound of it, and fantasised about describing him that way to the friends I'd bring to have tea with him. Sometimes the imagined friends were characters from books I'd read; sometimes they were the teenage girls I saw walking along the canal path in matching school uniforms, or cycling past wearing the Square Wheels tabards my Dad handed out to his volunteers. When I met them for real, albeit briefly, I stored up their names for future fantasies, pulling them out as I ambled alone in the direction of the canal. 'John, this is Juliet,' I would say on their first meeting. Or, 'Meet Martha, she's one of my schoolfriends.' Or, even better, 'John, these are my best friends – Martha, Juliet and Liv.' And he'd say, 'Goodness, KC, I had no idea you were so popular!' and he'd fill the red stove kettle and we'd all have tea and bakewells and sit out on the deck until the sun went down.

KC was John's special name for me, and so it was easy to choose a new name when I started again. *Casey*. Am I Katherine, or am I Casey? Who knows now?

I feel the gentle movement of the water around the boat, hear the soft slap of its motion against the moorings. I wish John were here now, to talk me through this, to tell me what I should do. It was with John that I learned to cook bacon and eggs, to wash and dry up, to sweep the wooden decks and squeegee the windows. I learned to sing 'Do Your Ears Hang Low?' and 'My Bonnie Lies Over the Ocean'. On deckchairs in summertime, he taught me how to tie a slip knot and a reef knot and a bowline and a rolling hitch, while singing his favourite ballad together: *Oh no, John, no, John, no, John – Oh no, John, no, John, no!* Sometimes Dad was there, sometimes he was at work or along the path at the Square Wheels hut, preparing sandwiches and tea. But Dad trusted John to be alone with me, and he was right to, because John was a good man. When Dad had gone I was broken, of course, but I still had the secret of John and the houseboat to escape to when things got too much at home with Mum. But then, two years ago, around the time that Granny – my mother's mother – died, so did John. And I thought my heart would break in two.

The small living area of the houseboat is in near darkness, and I hook back the corner of a curtain to see that late afternoon is falling over the canal. As I blink out at the fading light, I know I must return to Stack Street to check on Martha. If only I hadn't lost my temper like that.

If only Dad hadn't got mixed up with that girl.

25. **Martha**

Martha wakes in a hospital bed, bathed in the clammy sweat of a nightmare. It's not a new dream, but a recurring one in which she awakes in her normal bed, at home in her apartment, overwhelmed by the sense that something is deeply wrong, that someone has broken into the flat. The room is silver and black, the *noir* tones of a 1940s thriller, and, although she knows she's dreaming, the emotions feel so real. There's the toxic smell of stale breath and decay in the air, a taut anticipation of *something* about to happen, a caught gasp of uncertainty in the rooms around her. Terrified, she leaves her bed to tiptoe through the darkness of her room, where she checks on her sealed windows and finds the handles all gone. The other rooms are the same. She slow-sprints through them in the broken half-glow of the moon, running her fingers around the window frames, over the doors between rooms, the spaces on the walls where the light switches should be. She must have it wrong, she keeps telling herself, feeling across the empty spaces over and over until she cannot deny that it's true. The realisation engulfs her that she can't escape.

And that smell – that terrible smell intensifies, drawing her against her will, back into her bedroom, where she is halted by the stark outline of a man laid out beneath her bed sheets. No, she wants to scream out. She wants to scream and run and leave this all behind, but still her feet move over polished wood floors, propelling her onwards, onwards, her reluctant hands reaching out to gently peel back the covers and reveal his face. It's a dead face, always. Eyes open, but not seeing. The colour drained away to a ghostly grey, its lines furrowed deep like healed cuts traced across hollowed cheekbones. And this is where the dream always ends, leaving Martha with the question: why here, a place he has never set foot inside? Why has he come here to die?

Because he has nowhere else, is the whispered refrain.

Toby's face is pale and unsmiling as he draws up outside the hospital in his Mini, a deep line embedded between his brows as he jumps out to help Martha into the passenger seat.

'What are you thinking, discharging yourself so early?' He sounds angry as he fastens his own seatbelt, shaking his head and biting down on his bottom lip. 'You could have died back there, Martha. You should be in *there* right now, being monitored. This isn't safe.'

As he pulls away Martha shoots him an I-don't-know-what-all-the-fuss-is-about smirk that she regrets immediately as pain radiates from the point of impact with every muscle movement. Toby slams on his brakes at the edge of the hospital roundabout.

'*No*, Martha! You don't get to laugh this one off! I'm serious. You might not have noticed but I actually care about what happens to you, even if you don't. I haven't slept a wink, and just as I'm setting off to visit you I get a text saying you want

231

picking up. What did the doctors say? They seemed concerned enough last night – one of the nurses told me you'd be in for a couple of days.'

'I'm fine,' she says, chastened. 'Honestly, they said it was fine for me to go.'

He stares at her face, scrutinising her expression. 'You're lying. They didn't want you to go yet, did they?'

Martha rolls her eyes and turns to look out of the passenger window. She knows he's right, but she doesn't have time to hang around waiting to be given the all-clear. Martha is under no illusions that she hasn't just had a lucky escape. If Katherine Crown hadn't left the door ajar in her hurry to leave, if the grocery man hadn't returned and tried to deliver again, if she'd taken the blow to her skull just an inch to the left – well, it could all have turned out quite differently.

'Alright, *no*. But honestly, I feel absolutely fine – and I promise to let you know if that changes at any point.' She looks back at him, but he doesn't move, just glares back. Is it her imagination or are there tears in his eyes? 'I promise! Now, drive! We don't have any time to waste, Toby. Just drive, OK? First stop, my place. I need to freshen up and change out of these clothes.'

They travel the rest of the short journey home in silence, and Martha is glad of the quiet space to think, to move things around inside her mind, reorganising her earlier 'facts' and filing a new set of questions to follow up on.

Back at the apartment, she showers, leaving the bathroom door ajar so she can hold a conversation with Toby. She feels strangely invigorated despite the constant headache, almost manic with energy as her mind jumps around the many implications of this latest revelation about David Crown's daughter. Toby has softened a bit since they arrived home, and she's left him sitting at the breakfast bar with his notebook and a pile of toast, asking him to fill her in on everything he's discovered since last night.

'So did you phone Finn Palin?' she calls out through the steam of the bathroom. It's the last thing she recalls asking him to do last night, when he visited her hospital bedside soon after she'd been taken in by the paramedics.

'Yes. He said that they've put out a wanted alert for Katherine Crown. They haven't got a recent photograph, but he said they've got something going out on the London evening news. Radio and TV. Finn also said you've done the investigation a bit of a favour, getting hit over the head like that, as the police have to follow it up, what with it being a serious assault. And with the attacker being the daughter of our number one murder suspect. '

Typical Finn, Martha thinks. She can almost hear the humour in his voice as he said this to Toby.

'I can't believe we missed the detail of David and Janet Crown's daughter. How did we miss it, Toby?' She leans her head out of the steaming shower, just making out the figure of him over at the breakfast bar, a pen held loosely between his teeth.

'Well, she *did* make out her child was dead.'

'Yes, but since when do we take important information like that at face value? We should have probed further. Was there any mention of Katherine in the original investigation, did Finn say? Did you ask him?' She steps from the shower and wraps a towel around her hair, wincing at the tender bruising at her crown, the tightening surgical stitches now free of caked blood. The doctors have told her to avoid washing her hair for a while, until the gash has started to heal a little, but there's no chance of her taking any notice of that. She feels better already, through the sheer power of soap and water.

233

'You won't believe it,' Toby replies. 'Katherine *was* mentioned in the police notes, and – get this – she was even interviewed by the police during that visit to David Crown's home the morning he went missing.'

Now Martha pulls back the door to the bathroom, a larger towel wrapped around her body, forgetting her state of undress in her eagerness to hear more. 'They spoke to her? To Katherine Crown? How old was she?'

Toby looks up at Martha then quickly down at his notes, a blush rising to his cheeks. Martha steps back into the bathroom, re-emerging seconds later in a floor-length white bathrobe.

'She was seventeen years old.'

'The same age as Juliet – the same as all of us? Wouldn't we have known something about her if we were all the same age?'

'Finn told me her statement was important in reinforcing Mrs Crown's version of events – Katherine was able to corroborate what time David Crown came home, and how he had seemed at the time. Everything she said backed up what David and Janet Crown had told them.'

'Well, *of course* her version was the same as theirs – she was a seventeen-year-old girl, being questioned at the same kitchen table as her parents. She would have simply agreed with their version, wouldn't she?' Martha fetches fresh orange juice from the fridge and pours herself a large glass. 'And what about the remains found at the school – any news from Finn on that?'

'No, they clamped down on the security soon after you left the school yesterday. Finn couldn't tell us any more either – except to say that apparently they were still on site late last night.'

'So when will they be able to confirm that it's Juliet's body?' She can barely believe that she's saying these words. *Juliet's body*. After all these years of not knowing, of fearing the worst. Will Juliet's father – her family, her friends – be able at last to say goodbye?

'No guarantees,' Toby replies, 'But Finn reckons forensics will be done tomorrow afternoon. Apparently there's quite a backlog of current cases in the system and they're only just getting to Juliet today.'

'And Charlotte Bennett? The missing girl? It's been, what, five days since she was first reported? Any news there?'

Toby shakes his head. 'Nope, and the MisPer chat-room thread has gone silent. Juney even tried adding her own comment to the conversation, to see if it provoked a response. But nothing – and no more info on this mystery Ethan fellow either. Apparently the girl's parents are adamant that it wasn't their daughter's hair in that package. The mother seemed to think the hair sent to the police was dyed, while Charlotte's was – is – natural.'

Putting her glass down on the counter, Martha riffles through the case notes and brings out the Square Wheels photograph, placing it between her and Toby. She rests her finger beside the face of Katherine Crown, the thin, neutral girl to the left of David. Her face is a blank page, neither smiling nor sad, neither pretty nor unattractive. Her dark, straight hair is extraordinarily long, yet there's an unremarkable quality that borders on invisibility, quite unlike the vibrant energy possessed by the handsome man at her side – her father.

'I can't believe this is the same girl as the woman I met yesterday, Toby. And you know, since that bang on the head it's started to come back to me – I'm pretty sure she was one of the volunteers helping out when we were working on the Garden of Reflection that day. I can picture her in the Square Wheels hut too, helping David with the sandwiches. She used to talk in a whisper, so you could barely hear what she was saying. I just thought she was a bit shy, and I had no idea she was his daughter. How do people change so entirely? She's big now, really big, but it's not just that. Everything about her is different. Then, she seemed timid; now she seems damaged.'

'Damaged how?'

'She seems strange, certainly not someone who would easily inhabit the world. She's childlike, but also kind of old-fashioned. There's something really off-kilter about her. I wonder if she's ever done anything like this before?'

'You mean a history of violence?' Toby asks.

Several thoughts collide in Martha's mind: the quiet girl in the Square Wheels hut, silently watching but rarely interacting; the strange creature in Liv's house, all this time pretending to be Liv, acting out Liv's life through emails. The wonky cut of her hair, jagged and asymmetrical, as though she's cut it herself. David Crown with his arms around Juliet, comforting her when no one else was there to see. Mrs Crown in her lonely house, weakened by cancer, devoted to her absent husband, yet denying her living daughter. What *happened* between them? Would Katherine Crown have known Juliet back then? She must have done, if only in passing. Might she have wished her harm?

'OK, Toby. Two priorities. One, we need to track down the real Liv and see if she can tell us anything about Juliet's last movements on that night. Maybe she remembers Katherine – maybe she even knew she was David's daughter? Why don't you see if Finn can get his Met chap on to it? I expect the estate agent who sold Liv's house in Stack Street might be able to help, if it's the police who are asking. While you're at it, tell him to check out whether that hair could actually belong to Katherine.'

236

Toby frowns, but jots it down in his notebook all the same.

'And two, we need to get ourselves back around to Janet Crown's house, to find out what she can tell us about her daughter. There has to be some reason she didn't mention her before. I'm wondering if they've had some kind of disagreement. And I'm wondering if that disagreement has anything to do with Juliet Sherman and David Crown.'

Her phone rings.

'Martha? How's that head of yours?' Finn's voice is instantly recognisable.

'I'm fine, Finn. You know me: it'll take more than a knock over the head to put me out of action.'

'Glad to hear it, love. Are you and Toby up to meeting me at the Anchor in a couple of hours? Quite a lot to update you on.'

Martha gives Toby a nudge and presses the speaker on her phone. 'Like what, Finn?'

'Well, for starters, our missing girl Charlotte has turned up.'

26. Katherine

I was up before dawn, my head full of meandering fears, my most pressing thought being that I needed to put things right somehow, to make amends to Martha for all the trouble I've caused. With my hat pulled low I left the houseboat and headed into the high street, to hide out in this tatty café with free Wi-Fi access and set to work. I have everything I need to work this all through, to sort things out.

The main problems, as I see it, are these. Firstly, I have hurt Martha, something I had never, ever wanted to do. Secondly, I have misled her and potentially damaged her investigation. These are two things that I want to put right, and this can only be done face to face. Thirdly, I have drawn unwanted attention to myself, and as yet I'm at a loss as to how to remedy the whole awful situation. I know this last thing because I tried to return home late yesterday afternoon, only to find the place swarming with police officers and cars with flashing lights. I don't know if I intended to go back in or simply to see what was going on. Perhaps I wanted to see if I'd really killed Martha, because it was all I could think of from the moment I fled and I knew I'd never get a wink of sleep if I didn't put my mind to rest on the matter. When I got there it was already dark, and there were lots of passers-by walking along the diverted footpath trying to get a better look. I joined them, trying to saunter past as casually as possible, without drawing attention, slowing my pace as I passed by an officer leaning against the side of his police car talking into his phone. He was telling them to put out a 'Wanted' communication across the networks! I slowed to the point of almost stopping, and indeed he even turned to glare at me and cock a thumb to indicate I should move on.

'We're looking for a thirty-five-year-old white female,' I heard him say as I made to move away, dallying in the shadows of my fellow pedestrians, safe from his view. 'Going by the name of Katherine or Casey Crown. Yep. Serious assault – paramedics say the victim will be fine, but could've been a different story if she'd not been found. Uh-huh. Run it past the press team, will you? If we can find a recent photograph, I'd like to get it out in the evening news.'

Ha! Good luck with that, I thought, for if there's one thing I do know, it's that there are no photographs of me any later than 2001. Not one! I have a morbid fear of cameras, or at least of cameras being pointed my way. So there, PC Plod!

Here in the café I have my laptop open on the table in front of me, with the Juliet Pinterest board up on the screen to refresh my memory with all the facts of the case. I'm hoping it might help me to decide on my next steps. Remarkably, it does! In a flash of inspiration I congratulate myself on my forward-thinking in obtaining the real Olivia Heathcote's email address yesterday morning. Of course, it hadn't been difficult. I'd phoned Marcia, the estate agent who had dealt with the house sale, and asked her if she knew whether Olivia was still practising out of London. 'I have a friend who is interested in her services,' I lied. Without hesitation she told me that no, she believed Olivia Heathcote had moved to Guildford to work for a new practice there. Easy! It took no time at all to find her new place of work, and there on their company website was a public email address. After creating a brand new 'Martha Benn' email address to send from, I tap out a message, easily mimicking Martha's style from the many she had sent to me over the past couple of weeks – opening with the copied first passage from her original letter, making vital changes in the second half:

Dear Liv,

If this email finds its way to you, I know it will come as a surprise that I'm getting in touch after all this time. I can only say I'm sorry to have left it so long. It's hard to believe that eighteen years has passed, and yet it has. But let me get to the point.

Perhaps you've seen me on TV in recent years? I'm not saying this to brag, but because my latest project is a new show that investigates 'cold cases' – historic police investigations that have either been closed down or forgotten about, but where we believe there's a chance to solve them with fresh evidence or modern forensics. I hope you won't think it gratuitous; after what happened with Juliet – well, I suppose it's made me want to delve deeper into these unsolved crimes, to try to make a difference. The show is called *Out of the Cold*, and we've just begun work on our very first programme – and this is

241

my reason for making contact. We're investigating Juliet's disappearance.

According to the police, you are a 'person of interest' to them. Yes, I know this will be a shock to you – to me too! But I have some evidence that will change their minds immediately, if you are able to meet me here in London tomorrow at midday. I'm sorry for the short notice, but it's the only way we'll be able to prevent the police from following this ridiculous line of enquiry.

I'm out and about for most of the day, so drop me an email to confirm you'll be there? Let's say twelve o'clock, on the Regent's Canal at that bench nearest to the Square Wheels hut. It's right beside a red and blue houseboat called *Dovedale*. I'll take you for a bite of lunch if you have time?

With love, Mart xxx

Once I've sent it, I sit in the same spot for half an hour, checking my watch constantly, watching as the minutes tick by. It's early, not even 9 a.m. Perhaps Liv hasn't checked her emails yet. Maybe she's busy with the twins. Butterflies explode inside me when I realise it's Saturday, and I wonder if it's possible she doesn't have access to her work emails at the weekends. I glance towards the man behind the counter, and something in his expression tells me he's irritated that my bags are obscuring the aisle. Or perhaps he doesn't like that I've been sitting here for so long. It starts to worry me, but then, in an instant, I am invisible to him, as an attractive young woman comes in through the front door and raises her hand, causing his eyes to flash brightly, his mouth to crack wide.

Relieved, I turn back to my laptop, and to my astonishment there it is. A reply from the real, actual, genuine Olivia Heathcote. For a moment I think my mind must be playing tricks on me, but no, there it is! There it is!

Dear Mart,

I'm so happy to hear from you, but also now completely unnerved by what you've just told me. Of course I will do whatever it takes to meet up with you tomorrow, as I know you wouldn't ask me lightly. Do you want to give me your mobile phone in case there are any problems? I will meet you at the Regent's Canal, 12 o'clock, exactly where you said.

Mart, I'm so glad you're on the case for Juliet. She would have been happy to know it's you she's got fighting her corner.

Love you, mate,

Liv

How extraordinary, I think, to say 'Love you' to someone you haven't seen in nearly twenty years. 'Love you'. Other than to my parents, I've never said those words to a soul. Imagine having a friendship so strong that it could stand the test of time, even after everything they've been through. Because I *know* they've been through all sorts of things, I know they have their demons. I might not have said a lot in those Square

243

Wheels days, but I had eyes and ears, and I knew more about those girls than they could ever have imagined.

I've always been a little spy. That's what my mother used to call me, when she'd catch me listening in doorways, or twitching at the net curtains as the neighbours passed by. In some ways I found spying more of a diversion than the dramas on television, certainly more rich and unexpected, and more connected to me. I mean, *EastEnders* bore no resemblance to the world I lived in! Through my silent observations, I knew that Mr and Mrs Jenson along the street never cleared up after their poodles when they pooped on the pavement, except when there were other people about. *Then* they'd make a big show of picking it up in a plastic bag and placing it in the doggy waste bin at the edge of the park. They were what my mother would call 'all show and no substance.' There was the teenage couple who I'd see regularly wandering by hand in hand, their contentment written on easy faces, other times walking side by side, he with his hands thrust deep in his pockets, she stony-faced, arms crossed over her chest. There was Jeanie from two doors down, who many years ago gave up trying to befriend my mother, after popping by once too often when she was in one of her low moods and being turned away by my father on the doorstep. Jeanie has a ginger cat, and she buys most of her groceries from the corner shop, which Mum said must cost her a fortune. Once, when I couldn't sleep at night, the hunger pains in my stomach keeping me awake, I sat and watched the dark street from my bedroom window and saw a fox sprinting along the pavement, shortly followed by a staggering man so drunk he could barely stay upright. It was like watching a blind man navigate the road home. He stumbled to the ground twice before he disappeared from my line of vision and I wondered what his story was, whether he had family waiting for him, or just an empty house to return to.

Of course, there was plenty to spy on inside our home as well as out. Much whispering behind closed doors, low murmurs and suppressed gulps of despair beyond the single wall that separated my bedroom from that of my parents. 'Perhaps we should have had another child,' I heard her say late one night when I was nine or ten. 'We still could,' he'd replied, and I believed he really meant it. 'But I'm no mother,' she'd cried in response. 'Look at me, David, look at me!' At the time, my mind had been galloping so wildly that I'd struggled to keep up with the conversation. 'You're a wonderful mother,' he'd reassured her, but I can't say I recall hearing her reply. I was so consumed by the idea of a second child – a longed-for brother and sister – that I lost the rest of it in the noise of my own thoughts. From there on in, I was on the lookout for signs that my mother might be expecting, listening out for news of my much-anticipated younger sibling. But, of course, it never came, and I've no idea whether they were actually trying, or whether it was even something either of them really wanted. Perhaps it's just one of those things couples say to each other when they're sad, when they're searching for an explanation for why their lives haven't turned out as they'd once hoped. Years later, in a spiteful fit of anger, I asked Mum if that was the reason he had left us: because she'd not been able to give him another child. I suppose that was the beginning of the end for her and me. That and the thing I saw down on the towpath; the *things* I saw down on the towpath.

After setting up yet another fake email account for what I hope Martha will believe is the 'real' Liv, I send a corresponding email from 'Liv' to Martha, telling her that she's just heard from the police about what's been going on with 'that woman pretending to be me'. As Liv, I suggest the same meeting place, the same time, and tell Martha that I have some vital evidence regarding Juliet's disappearance that I need to hand over to her. My words are rushed, as the man behind the counter is getting impatient with me still sitting in the café now the place is suddenly buzzing with people wanting to sit down. I want to stay and wait for Martha's answer to come back to me, but that horrible man keeps glaring at me and reaching over my laptop to take the ketchup for another table, and now two strange men have taken the seats opposite me without even having the decency to ask if I mind, and really, I just have to get up and out of the stinky little place as quickly as possible! With trembling hands, I pack up my things and huff out of my seat, walking as fast as my aching feet will take me, back to the quiet safety of *Dovedale*. It's only when I lie down on my cabin bed that I realise I could simply have ordered another drink, and then that café owner wouldn't have minded me staying one bit. Then I might have stayed long enough to read Martha's reply. Oh, God, oh, God, oh, God, why do I always have to ruin everything? I've been doing it as long as I can remember and I simply don't know how to stop.

All I can do is lie here, trying to control my breathing, trying to imagine what I'll say to Martha and Liv when they get here tomorrow. What if Martha is scared, after our last encounter? What if they try to run away? Well, I resolve, closing my eyes and inhaling deeply, I'll just have to make sure that doesn't happen.

27. **Martha**

By one o'clock they're sitting in a quiet corner of the sticky-floored public bar of the Anchor, Finn holding a pint in his hand, Toby and Martha each with a coffee. It's been fifteen years since Martha was last here, searching for her errant father late one night, and she's shocked to see that it hasn't changed a bit. The dark wood bar dominates, still reeking of the age-old stink of tobacco and dregs, and the same maritime knick-knacks hang from the beams, thick with dust and cobwebs. The faces behind the bar are different, but she could swear the drinkers – or at least the types of drinkers – are not.

Martha fills Finn in on her most recent news: that Olivia Heathcote has been in touch. The email was there in her inbox when she woke this morning. 'Looks like your guys managed to track Liv down quite quickly,' she says. 'She seems to know all about Katherine impersonating her, so I'm guessing they've filled her in on the connection with the Juliet case, because she's arranged to meet me at midday tomorrow, down at the canal where Juliet's bike was found.'

'Should we send Jay and Sally down?' Toby asks. 'To film your meeting?'

Martha thinks for a moment. 'Ye-es, but give us half an hour to ourselves first? It's been a long time since Liv and I last saw each other, and she said she's got some evidence she wants to share. And it'll give me a chance to ask her if she minds appearing on film.' Martha feels a lurch of anxiety. What if Liv doesn't want any part of the TV show; what if she ends up resenting Martha for getting her involved? Martha had replied to Liv's email straight away, but she hasn't heard back in the couple of hours since, and she's got no other way of contacting her to check if she's OK with the camera crew being on hand. She'll just have to wing it. 'Actually, Toby, make it an hour, OK?'

Toby taps into his mobile phone, making arrangements with Jay and Sally for the following day. 'What's the name of the houseboat again – where you're meeting Liv?'

'*Dovedale*,' Martha replies. 'The blue and red one near the exit path where we filmed last time. They'll know where I mean. Tell them one p.m.' She turns to Finn, anxious to hear what he has to say. 'I'm afraid we haven't got much time,' Martha says, rubbing her hands together to warm them up. It's true they're on borrowed time, but more than that she wants to get out of this ghost-pub as quickly as possible. It sets her nerves on edge, makes her feel vulnerable in a way she can't stand. 'We're on our way to Janet Crown's place next.'

Finn takes a gulp of his pint, nodding and pulling out his small police issue notebook. He may be retired, Martha thinks, but he's still Met through and through.

Tapping the top of the page with his pen, Finn begins to run through his list. 'So, as you know, the missing girl has turned up.'

'So what's the story?' asks Toby. 'That's great news – but does that mean her disappearance is unconnected?'

Finn sighs, his mouth turning down at the edges. 'Yup. What her parents didn't say when they reported her missing was that she's gone walkabout a few times before. She's not quite as squeaky-clean as they made out – boyfriends, underage drinking, smoking cannabis, etc. She'd been staying at a boyfriend's house for the past few days, and that bike they found down by the canal turns out not to be hers at all – she had hers with her all along. And obviously the hair wasn't hers either, so I think your theory that it was sent by Katherine Crown looks increasingly likely.'

Martha brings her cup to her mouth, casting a sideways glance at the drunk man who lurches close to their table on his way to the gents. She feels her heart rate rising. It's the one thing that can unsettle her to this day: being in close proximity to drunks. Not drunk people, but *drunks* – those dead-eyed souls already lost to the bottle, beyond caring what the rest of the world makes of them. How does an upright, intelligent human being descend to such depths?

She drags her eyes away from the stumbling man and back to Finn. He's watching her watching, she thinks. He knows what's on her mind. She places her cup solidly on the table.

'OK. So what we need to work out is why would Katherine do that? Why would she purposely mislead us? Why would she interfere with a live police case?'

'Exactly,' Finn agrees. 'I think the most likely conclusion is that she did it to divert blame on to this "Ethan" – and away from her father. I think she's trying to protect the memory – or the reputation – of her father.'

This makes complete sense. It would explain why she took on the Liv role, having been panicked by the nature of

249

Martha's questions. All her responses to Martha during those communications insisted that David Crown was a decent man, that he couldn't possibly have taken Juliet. It was Katherine who had first introduced the idea of a complete stranger – and then of 'Ethan' – way before the MisPer chat-room thread appeared, and before the hair was sent to the police with a letter from 'Ethan'. Now that Martha thinks about it, Katherine even had her wondering whether Juliet's lovely brother Tom could have had anything to do with Juliet's vanishing. Christ, that should have alerted her, if nothing else!

'So do we think that Katherine is behind the MisPer chat-room thread too?' Martha asks.

'Almost certainly,' Finn replies, checking his watch. 'How are you doing for time, love? I've got a couple more things for you.'

'I've got a few more minutes,' she says, glancing at her phone. 'Though we'd better not keep Mrs Crown waiting.'

Toby runs a pen down his own list. 'My mate hasn't had any luck yet working out the IP address of the account that initiated the thread.'

'Well, the police analysts will be on to it now,' Finn tells him. 'They'll winkle it out before you know it. It would help if we could get hold of Miss Crown's PC, but my chap tells me there was no sign of it at her place. Looks like she took her laptop and mobile phone when she fled – so she had her head about her to some degree.'

'You don't think—'

Finn interrupts, reading her thoughts. 'That she might be responsible for Juliet?'

Martha nods, pinching her lower lip. Is it possible? Could the teenage Katherine have been behind Juliet's disappearance – behind her death? She, of all people, would have had access

250

to the building site at the school, what with her father working there. And she was around in that period, they now know.

'What if *she* killed Juliet, and her father was the one who covered it up?'

'Bloody hell, love. Maybe you should have followed in your father's footsteps and joined the force? I've had the same thoughts, but I've yet to be convinced it's not David Crown – especially when you hear the other details I've got to share with you. I suppose it would be another motive for her diverting attention away from her dad, if she knew that our suspecting him might lead us to her. But it doesn't explain why *he* then did a runner so promptly. Why would he have run off like that, if his daughter was the one who killed Juliet?'

'To protect her?' Martha says. 'Perhaps he *did* cover it up for her, and then decided the only way to completely remove suspicion from her was if he disappeared and took the suspicion with him?'

Toby is drumming his fingers on his knee, his face fixed in concentration. 'Yes. But it's hard to completely disappear like that, isn't it? Especially if you haven't had lots of time to think about it. Maybe he did help Katherine cover up her crime, but couldn't live with what he'd done, and topped himself?'

It sounds plausible, Martha thinks. Mad, but plausible.

'What about the postcards to his wife?'

'Katherine?' Toby and Finn say at once.

Martha takes a deep, juddering breath, suddenly aware of the time running away, with so much to follow up on before Glen Gavin starts asking for another status report. 'What about these "other details" you mentioned, Finn?' She pulls on her jacket as the drunk man stumbles past again, on his way back to the bar.

251

'OK. Now mum's the word on this info – I don't want to see this turning up in your documentary, Martha, at least not until you've got official approval to include it. Agreed? I'm going to give you the investigating officer's details, and I want you to contact him with a summary of everything you have so far. He's a good mate of mine, and I've managed to convince him about these connections – and he's expecting your call. He's willing to meet up and see if you can help each other, but it'll be on the condition that you keep everything to yourself until you're given the nod.'

Martha takes the contact card from Finn, slips it inside her wallet. 'Thanks, Finn. I'll give him a call after we've been to see Janet Crown. '

Finn continues down his list. 'After your attack, the police found some items of interest hidden in Katherine Crown's home. They were looking for a recent picture of her to put out on their wanted bulletin. They didn't find one, but they did find a box of old photographs, probably her father's, most of them from the fifties and sixties. We think David and members of his family are the main subjects, because the background strongly suggests a Derbyshire location. Him and his family dog, with his parents, him with a sister or perhaps a girlfriend.'

'That's where she got that picture she sent me!' Martha says, visualising the image of a young David Crown arm-in-arm with his beehive-wearing girlfriend. 'I just couldn't work out why *Liv* would have a picture like that.' Idiot, Martha thinks, not for the first time.

Finn shrugs. 'Makes sense. Also inside that box was a gold cross on a chain, which is unremarkable except for the fact that it has a small ruby gemstone set in its centre.'

'And?' Toby asks.

'And, when our chaps cross-referenced its description with the details of that Castledale cold case back in 1970 – the murder of Tilly Jones – a piece of jewellery exactly matching that description is noted as missing from the scene. The gold cross in David Crown's photo box – in his daughter's home – belongs to our murdered schoolgirl Tilly Jones.'

Martha can't believe what she's hearing. 'So he did it? It's a trophy? David Crown actually murdered Tilly Jones?'

'Looks that way,' Finn says, savouring the shocked responses on Toby and Martha's face. 'And that's not all.'

'Jesus, Finn, there's more?' Martha is almost laughing. This is insane.

'Also in the box . . .' He pauses now, as though uncertain how best to deliver this piece of information. 'It's bad news, I'm afraid, Martha, love. Also in the box was a silver-plated bangle with Juliet's name and the year "1998" inscribed on the inside surface.'

Martha shakes her head, willing her emotions to stay locked down. Her fingers encircle the wrist of her other hand. They each had one: friendship bracelets they'd saved up for together, ordering them at Lamb's Jewellers on the high street at the end of Year Eleven, after their GCSEs. They were a symbol of their unbreakable friendship. After collecting them from the jewellers, they'd sat together, legs dangling from the wooden walkway that edged on to the Regent's Canal, slipping them on to their narrow wrists as they looked out across the sunlit waters. Martha had taken hers off the day the police announced they were halting the search for Juliet Sherman, and vowed that she wouldn't wear it again until the day Juliet was found.

But now they *had* found Juliet, hadn't they? She racks her brains, trying to remember what she did with her own bangle. It seems suddenly of vital importance that she finds it, that she returns it to her wrist where it belongs. Where did she put it? Surely she didn't leave it behind when she finally left Dad and Stanley House all those years ago? A flash of grief fills her mind, a snapshot of her younger self, puffy-eyed, curled up small on her single bed in Stanley House, her sense of loss like a physical pain. Her dad standing in the doorway slurring his reassurances. No Mum; she was long gone. 'She'll be back,' Dad had said when Juliet had been missing just one or two days, but instinctively Martha knew she wouldn't. He'd said the same about Mum, and look how that had turned out. Martha knew Juliet wouldn't just disappear like that, but it was more than just the certainty that came from having known someone well; it was something else, a conviction she can't quite now grasp. *Does* she know more about Juliet's disappearance than she's allowing herself to admit – or was she just recalling the bleak response of a scared teenager? After a week, Dad stopped trying to convince Martha that Juliet would be back. After a month, they stopped talking about her altogether. If only Martha hadn't left her alone on that towpath; if only she'd been a better friend.

'Martha, are you alright?' Toby has his hand on her shoulder, and she has the strongest desire to push against the gentle pressure of his fingertips, to soak in his warmth. 'Martha?'

She turns her attention on Finn, her focus sharpening. 'Another trophy?' she asks.

'I think so, love. We shouldn't rule out the possibility that Katherine is involved, but I think this is pretty strong evidence that Juliet came to harm at David Crown's hands. The forensic results are due in tomorrow morning. Hopefully we'll know a bit more about the "how" then.'

'Will you call me as soon as you know anything?' Martha asks, reaching to squeeze his hand as she stands to leave. One of her spotty gloves drops to the floor, and Toby retrieves it, unobtrusively popping it back into her jacket pocket.

'Of course I will, love,' Finn replies softly. 'Go on, then, you've got things to do. And don't forget to contact the DS – he's expecting your call.'

Martha and Toby leave Finn at the bar, getting another pint in. 'Ease up there, Finn,' she wants to say. But he's not her dad, is he? Finn knows when to stop.

At Janet Crown's house there's no reply, even after they've knocked several times. A few doors along the street, a woman is brushing down her windowsill and she waves to catch their attention.

'Are you looking for Janet?' she asks, holding her brush aloft.

'Yes – do you know her?' Toby calls back.

The small woman, dressed in bright red slacks and a yellow polo-neck jumper, drops down off her low step and hurries along the path to join them. She must be in her early seventies, and looks as though she's stepped straight out of a 1960s television ad.

'She's been taken into hospital!' she tells them. 'The police were here this morning – looking for Katherine . . .' She hesitates a moment, as vague recognition of Martha flickers across her expression. It's something Martha experiences all the time, that shift in people's demeanour when they *know* that they know you, but can't quite place where from. 'Oh, are you police too?'

'No, no.' Toby smiles, sweeping back his boyish fringe and engaging his charm. 'We're friends. Is Janet alright?'

'Well, *no*, I really don't think she is. I'm Jeanie, by the way. Number eighteen. As you know, Janet's very ill. She doesn't like to talk about it much, but I know she's been in and out of hospital for the last few years. Since her daughter left, she sometimes calls on me to feed the cat. You know, when she has to be away for appointments and suchlike.' Martha has the impression that she's adopting a smarter accent in response to Toby's rounded vowels.

Toby makes all the right noises, urging her on. 'Poor Janet. So what happened?'

'Well, I couldn't help but notice the police were here yesterday afternoon – on my way back from the corner shop, I was – and just as I was chatting to the PC at the front door, telling him I hadn't seen Katherine for a long time, I hear one of the other officers shouting out that she just collapsed. Janet. I tried to get in to see her, but they said it was best to wait for the experts. Before I knew it there was an ambulance in the road and she was rushed to A&E.' She lowers her voice now, although there's no one else to overhear. 'Have you seen her lately? Looks on the brink of death. Her poor body must be in shutdown.'

Martha shakes her head in understanding. 'Cancer's a terrible thing, isn't it?'

Jeanie looks confused. 'Cancer? Oh, no, you've got the wrong end of the stick there, sweetheart. Janet hasn't got cancer. She's one of them anorexics. She's been starving herself to death for years.'

28. **Katherine**

There was a hard frost overnight, dusting the roof of every houseboat with a sparkling coat of white. Once again I rise at dawn, and make my way to the high street to see if I can find a different café to pick up Wi-Fi and check in on any new developments. I've already decided I won't be going back to that nasty man's place again in a hurry. His hot chocolate was thin and those teacakes must have been at least a day out of date. Like a complete ninny I've misjudged things, because it's Sunday and there's nowhere except the newsagents open this early on a Sunday morning. It's *so* bitter, and even with my hood pulled up and my top button pinching into the flesh beneath my chin the icy wind seems to get in, freezing me through to the bones and making me want to sob with the agony of it. As ever, my stomach is cramping and twisting, and I've swallowed so many tummy tablets that if you shook me I really think I'd rattle! It's the most miserable feeling, to be cold and afraid and in spasms of pain. I'm thinking I can't just wander around like this, not when there are things to be done, and then I find myself

257

at the end of my old street, where Mum still lives, standing outside the corner shop with its enticing swing board advertising 'Hot Tasty Coffee!'.

I'm so stricken with cold that I consider going inside, despite the fact that the shopkeeper may recognise me from my life here before, despite the fact that my name is plastered up on the billboard that stands on the frosty kerb outside the door. The headline leaps out at me, stark black against white, handwriting huge and menacing.

LOCAL WOMAN WANTED IN CONNECTION WITH SERIOUS ASSAULT

Can they really mean me? Am I that local woman? Slipping inside the entrance, my hood pulled low, I enter the quiet shop and pick up a copy of last night's newspaper, keeping my back towards the till, merely returning a 'Hi!' to the shopkeeper when he tries to catch my attention with a cheery hello. The heat from the overhead blower is a blessed relief, and I feel my numb fingers begin to thaw around the edges of the newsprint.

Police are searching for local woman Katherine Crown in connection with a serious assault in the Stack Street area of Hackney on Friday afternoon. It is believed that a well-known television personality was the victim of this attack, but police sources are declining to disclose further information at this time. Katherine Crown, 35, is described as approximately 5' 1" tall, of larger than average build, with dark hair cut in a distinctively uneven bob. Police are warning public not to approach Katherine Crown as she may be dangerous. If you have any information about the crime, or her whereabouts, please call the *Crimestoppers* number on . . .

258

Dangerous. Me? *Dangerous*. I hope that Martha's been spared the falsehood of seeing this awful headline; I couldn't bear for her to think of me in that way. If only she and Liv knew how I just wanted to be their friend, if they knew how much I admired them, longed to *be* one of them. I've felt that way ever since those early days when Dad first introduced us at the Square Wheels cabin, purposely omitting the detail that I was his daughter so that I might make new friendships on the basis of my own personality and not because of him. 'They're lovely girls,' he'd told me on our way to open up the cabin that night, to prepare the sandwiches and get the urns boiling. To get me out of Mum's hair. But I was sceptical, having encountered 'lovely girls' before, girls who at best blanked me, at worst recoiled. Why should these girls be any different? But these three were, and I knew that, of course, the moment they turned up. They arrived together in a chatter of high spirits, Juliet absently worrying that she had a slow puncture, Liv complaining about the chain oil that had ruined the hems of her new white jeans. Martha seemed to be the glue, the more grown-up of the three, and when Dad introduced us she shocked me by immediately asking if I wanted to help her butter the bread for the sandwiches. Later that evening, Dad paired me up with Liv to take one route along the canal bank, while Martha and Juliet took the opposite direction. It was summer and so the evenings were still light and long, and as Martha and Juliet cycled away I was mesmerised by the sunbeams that haloed about their long flowing hair. Of course there were other volunteers too, perhaps as many as twelve of us altogether, and although I was paired with most of them at one time or another over the next week or so, I can't say I got to know any of them intimately. Or rather, they never got to know me. I was quiet, you see, because I knew from experience that the moment I opened myself up to conversation the judgements were sure to follow. Even in the relatively friendly surroundings of the Square Wheels cabin, I once overheard two of the other volunteers – a boy and a girl – whispering how it was 'disgusting' to be as thin as I was. That it must be an eating disorder or something, because who *chooses* to look like that? I had thought I'd covered my body well, dressed as I was in an oversized sweatshirt and shapeless jeans, but no, apparently not. It seemed that, fat or thin, I was subject to the scrutiny of all and sundry, and none of them seemed to care how their words wounded; how their curled lips and narrowed eyes cut me to the quick. But Martha did. Martha, I always sensed, knew how it felt to be hurt, to be disappointed, and to disappoint. That evening, when the gossiping boy and girl had loaded their baskets and cycled on their way, Martha joined me at the sandwich-making table and without a word began to help me in my task of slicing the tomatoes. 'They're wankers,' she said eventually, just low enough for me to hear, then she patted me on the wrist and went to help Dad pour out more teas. I knew I loved Martha then – and Juliet and Liv, but most of all Martha – and I've followed her life and career ever since. Social media is a wonderful thing when you want to stay in touch from a distance, and on many occasions I've dropped her a tweet under one of my assumed identities, just to let her know I'm there, to tell her how wonderful she is.

Now, staring at the newspaper in my hands, I thank God the police could find no recent photographs! I wonder if I have been blessed with a sixth sense of sorts, some intuition that has prevented me from putting myself in front of the camera for exactly this reason. Aware of the shopkeeper to my rear, I realise that, while he might recognise me from my time living here before, he almost certainly doesn't know my name. People don't tend to ask me my name. I'm safe, I think with relief, and lowering my hood I turn and approach the till.

'I'll have a cappuccino, please,' I say, sliding my newspaper on to the counter as I spot the tray of Krispy Kremes on the worktop behind him.

He must see me looking, because as he starts to prepare my fresh coffee he gives me a big smile and says, 'Krispy Kreme? Fresh in this morning!'

I am *starving*. And those doughnuts look like just about the best I've ever seen. My mouth moistens at the thought of biting down on the sugary coating, my teeth sinking into dough.

'Oh, go on, then!' I giggle, and he winks at me. He *actually* winks, and it's just breathtaking.

'Which one would you like?' He readies a doughnut bag, a pair of bright pink cake tongs hovering over the sweet treats.

'Oh. I'll have the cinnamon bun, please.'

He places it in the bag and looks at me expectantly. The only noise in the shop is the sound of my cappuccino gurgling out through the coffee machine spout and into its cardboard cup. 'Another?'

My hand flies up to cover my mouth, and I don't know quite why I'm feeling so giddy, but I am. Perhaps it's nervous energy, having seen that article in the newspaper, and me standing here so brazenly at the counter, buying coffee and doughnuts with that 'Woman Wanted' headline glaring up at us both, and he none the wiser! Oh, if only he knew!

'OK. I'll have a Strawberry Iced with Sprinkles,' I say. 'And a Seasalt Caramel. For my mum,' I add, lest he think I'm a big, fat, greedy pig. Which I am!

He drops them into the bag and rolls the end closed, handing it to me with a tap on the side of his nose. *Our little*

261

secret, that tap says, and my heart gasps. He has lovely brown skin and a lilting, friendly accent – *foreign*, my mum would say. I wonder how old he is. Maybe thirty or forty? I'm not very good at reading these things, but what I do know is that he *doesn't* have a ring on his wedding finger.

I tap my nose back at him and hand over a twenty-pound note. 'Thank you,' I say, and I do my best to look alluring. It's hard when you're buttoned into a thick padded coat and ruddy with the cold, but I look up through my eyelashes the way Princess Diana used to do, and he rewards me with the brightest smile I think I've ever seen. I've never seen teeth so straight and white!

'What's your name?' I ask him, feeling my cheeks flare up like stop lights.

'Arun,' he replies as he passes me my change, and then he raises his hand goodbye and turns to wipe down the coffee machine.

If I do come out of this unscathed, if I manage to meet up with Martha and Liv and put everything straight, then I will come back here and pluck up enough courage to show him I'm keen. If nothing else, this experience has taught me that life should be seized, that not a moment more should be wasted though fear. I will grasp at every opportunity, and to hell with anyone who stands in my way! Outside the shop I pause. I forgot to pick up sugar for my coffee; there were little paper sachets inside, brown and white, at a counter to the side of the till. I go back in – and that's when I hear it. Out of view, from the back of the shop, I hear Arun's voice, low and conspiring. I move closer to the entrance, just enough to hear him without being seen.

'Hello, Crimestoppers? Yes, I want to report something. The police came in last night asking me to let them know if I see Katherine Crown – the one who attacked that woman in Stack Street? Well, she just came in for coffee. I'm not sure which direction she's heading in, but if they're quick they might pick her up nearby.'

It's like a knife to my chest. Judas! I want to scream, but there is no time for emotion, no time to dally, and I pull up the hood of my coat and head for the park, where I can cut through on my way back down to the canal. There's no way I'm going to be able to sit down in a café to check my emails now, not with the police out hunting me down. If Arun was tipped off to look out for me last night, it's likely that other shops and cafés in the high street had a similar visit. I'm desperate to know if Martha has responded to my email – if she intends to turn up today as planned – but for now I'll just have to lie low, hide below decks back at *Dovedale*, and hope and pray that Liv and Martha turn up. At least I have coffee now. At least I have my doughnuts.

29. Martha

Martha's first thought when she wakes is that Toby is asleep on the sofa in the other room. For a while she lies motionless, tuning in, trying to work out if he's awake too, wondering if he's experiencing the same strange sensation of proximity that she is. The clock on the nightstand tells her that it's just before seven, and she swings her legs out of bed, anxious to prepare herself for her meeting with Liv at noon, and to find out what news Finn has on the police hunt for Katherine Crown. She must try phoning Finn's chap again; she'd tried several times yesterday afternoon without any success.

In the living room, Toby is still sleeping, stretched the full length of the sofa, Martha's Scandinavian throw draped over his legs. From the ankle that protrudes she can see that his lower half is clothed, but his shirt is draped neatly over the back of one of the armchairs, and his torso is naked against the cushions. Martha permits herself a moment to gaze upon him, this beautiful young man, admiring the lines of his chest and long, lean limbs, wondering what it is that *he* sees when he looks at *her*. Why is she even indulging herself in these thoughts? Under the circumstances, it's nothing short of ridiculous.

As she fills the kettle, he stirs, extending his arms, yawning loudly before easing himself upright on the sofa. His hair is all mussed up at the back, no more the well-groomed city boy, and from her position in the kitchen, she thinks, he could be a stranger. She hadn't intended to ask him to stay, but it was gone midnight by the time they finished working through their notes and programme plans, and with today's early start it made sense. They were in high spirits, after Finn had been in touch to let them know that Vicky Duke, the pupil who had made the allegation against David Crown back in 1986, had come forward of her own accord that evening, asking to make a statement to the police. It was likely this statement would put Crown even more firmly in the frame as a predatory suspect. As Martha had handed Toby some bedding, there'd been an awkward moment when their eyes had connected and she'd sensed a hug coming on. 'Sleep well,' she'd blurted out, and she'd turned on her heel and retreated to her bedroom before they could act on it. Was it simple affection or sexual chemistry? She likes to think the former, but she fears – for her part at least – that it might be the latter.

'No sugar, remember,' Toby calls to her, his arm hooked over the back of the sofa, a boyish smile on his lips.

In response Martha holds up the cup she's already made for him and crosses the room to sit beside him. She hands him a packet of madeleines.

'Cake? It's a bit early for me,' he says, passing them back.

'It's what they eat on the Continent – with coffee,' she says, opening the packet and pushing one into his palm. 'Try it!' She dips one into her mug, laughing at his horrified expression. Snatching his back, she dunks it into his coffee and puts it to his mouth. 'Just try it!

265

He obliges, taking it in one bite, chewing thoughtfully as she sips her coffee and awaits his verdict. 'OK, you're right,' he admits. 'They're pretty good. Reminds me of the breakfast cakes they have in Venice.'

He reaches for another one, but Martha's fingers close around the bag. 'They went to Venice,' she says quietly, as much to herself as to him.

'Who went to Venice?'

'Liv and Jules. At the end of Year Eleven, on a school trip. I couldn't afford it . . .' Martha recalls her language teacher trying to persuade her to apply for an 'aid' place, but pride had prevented her from doing so. And even if she could have afforded it, how could she have left Dad in the state he was, with no one else to keep an eye on him? Liv and Juliet had begged her to come too, and she'd fobbed them off, saying she was going to Scotland that same week to visit her mum. Of course it was a lie; there was no trip to Scotland, no trip anywhere.

'Is that relevant?' Toby asks. 'To the case?'

Martha presses her palms against her eyes, trying to take hold of the memories, trying to establish the order of events. That trip had been at the end of term, in 1998, after their GCSEs, right before the start of the summer holidays. It was that summer that Juliet had first started at Square Wheels, followed quickly by Liv and Martha. The summer that everything had started to shift. When they'd returned from Venice, Liv and Jules had seemed to Martha to be more tightly entwined than ever, and, while their trio was still strong, she couldn't help feeling that she had lost them in some way. That she was now somewhere on the outside.

What had *she* done during that week when they were away?

'I don't know, Toby,' she replies, dropping her hands to her lap, turning to face him.

266

There's not a hand's width between them on the sofa, and for just a moment she has the strongest sensation of being separated from her body, watching them from afar: he, bare-chested, scruff-headed and tanned, she free of make-up, her silk-print kimono slipping off one knee, showing the merest hint of her thigh. Neither of them speaks.

'Martha?' Toby is the first to break the silence, his fingers reaching for the side of her face, his index finger resting on her naked earlobe.

She's the one who leans in, who presses her lips to his, soaking in the smooth heat of them against hers, his breath, his scent. His hand slips away the silky fabric, encircling her knee – and the reality of the situation slams her back with a start.

'Oh, God, Toby,' she says, 'I'm so sorry.' She's trying to stand, but he has her hand in his, gently insisting that she stays.

'Don't say that,' he replies, holding on. 'Please don't say you're sorry.'

Now she manages to extract her fingers, and she backs away, gathering up the empty cups, busying herself. Anything but look at him. Every nerve in her body wants her to throw herself down beside him, to give herself up. But she can't, can she? To do so would be to reveal herself, not just her body – that's the least of her thoughts – but *herself*.

'But I *am* sorry! I just . . . I don't know what I just . . . At any rate, Toby, this is a stupid idea, and I'm a stupid woman. Jesus, what was I *thinking*?'

Good, she has regained her control. She stands before him, certain, empty mugs hanging from the fingers of one hand, adjusting the front of her kimono with the other. Toby sits forward in his seat, bare feet – elegant feet, she notices – flat against the plush oatmeal carpet, his elbows resting on his knees, the muscles of his arms strong and relaxed.

His expression is tired. 'Is it because of *him*?' he asks.

'No!' she replies, somewhat too quickly. 'It's nothing to do with him. That was an age ago.'

'I liked you, even back then, you know,' he says.

Martha can't deal with this. It's crazy. She has to shut it down before it all starts to become real in the world. 'OK, that's enough. I'm done with talking about this, Toby. This was entirely my fault, and I'm sorry.'

'But . . .' He rises from his seat, reaching for his shirt.

Martha turns her back on him and strides towards the kitchen. 'I'm meeting Liv at twelve,' she says, fixing her mind on the day ahead. 'I'll use the bathroom first, if that's alright with you?' At the bathroom door she hesitates, glancing back to see Toby already seated at the dining table with his notes, a neutral expression on his face. 'While I'm doing that, I want you to check in with Jay and Sally to make sure they'll be at the meeting point as arranged, no earlier than one o'clock.'

He nods, not looking up.

'And see if Juney can find out the latest with Mrs Crown? We need to reschedule that meeting with her, if she's up to it.'

Toby makes a note.

'Oh, and can you phone Finn, see if there's any news from forensics yet? I've told him that I'd like to go with the police representative to break the news to Alan Sherman, once Juliet's identity has been confirmed.'

Toby does look up now, fixing Martha with a worried frown. 'Are you sure it's a good idea for you to go alone today? I mean, the police haven't located Katherine Crown yet, and judging by your last meeting she's got it in for you. You might be at risk.'

Martha smiles, glad that they're firmly back on to the subject of business again, that they've been able to put this behind them so quickly. 'I'll be fine, Toby. Liv will be there. Katherine's hardly likely to try to take us both on. But if it makes you feel any better, why don't you come down at the same time as the camera guys? Perhaps we can film a few more straight-to-camera pieces while we're there, now we've got more content?'

As she heads into the bathroom, Toby calls after her, 'Jay just texted. He says, "Tell Martha no busy patterns, please. Those spotty Cruella gloves of hers played havoc with the try-outs last week."'

'Tell Jay he's a cheeky sod,' Martha replies, and she closes the door behind her, takes a steadying breath, and sets the shower running.

On the main street, Martha taps out a text message to Finn's police contact, telling him she's meeting Olivia Heathcote at the canal and asking him to phone her as soon as he has a chance. She's left two voice messages this morning, and she's starting to wonder if he's as interested in these cold cases as Finn has made out.

As soon as she turns on to the towpath, Martha spots Liv standing beside the bench in the distance, just as she'd said she would be. She is dressed in a bright mustard coat and fuchsia leggings, heavy boots anchoring her feet to the earth, a swirl of brightly coloured scarf wrapped around her shoulders. She's gained perhaps a couple of pounds, and her shoulder-length hair is more groomed, but she still looks like that pixie of a girl that Martha knew. What will they see when they look into each other's eyes now? What will they *feel*? Liv is facing downstream, looking out across the roofs of the houseboats moored along the canal, her breath pluming white in the winter air.

Despite the hour, the verges and hedgerows are still cloaked in a hard, crunchy frost, and Martha takes care to stay upright as she navigates her way along the towpath, dressed head-to-toe in her trademark black and grey. The spotty gloves and red scarf are her only concession to frivolity, and even they seem a bit over-exuberant on those days when she feels less than animated. The midday sun is a milky yellow above the flyover in the distance, throwing soft shadows out behind Liv and casting her in striking relief. The film-maker in Martha wishes the camera crew were here now, to take in this emotional scene, to capture Liv in the moments leading up to their first encounter in so many years. She slows her pace, purposely savouring the seconds before their reunion, before Liv becomes aware of her presence. Before the years between them shatter, and their grief might be shared.

As though she senses that Martha is there, Liv spins around, releasing her hands from her pockets, throwing them up with a cry. 'Mart!' She breaks into a run, arms outstretched to catch Martha, to surround her.

They're both crying, *sobbing*, and Martha doesn't even care that any old passer-by can see her. They're sobbing and talking and laughing all at once, each of them releasing their grip to look into the other's face, before pulling back in again, crying and laughing some more. Never, in all the years that have passed since the friends separated, has she felt such kinship. Liv and Juliet were all she had back then, more like siblings than schoolfriends, more like family to her than her own. Her own family were shadows; they didn't count. But Liv and Jules – they *knew* her, and they loved her, despite all the shit that came with being her friend.

Eventually they gather themselves, Liv reaching inside her bag to produce a pack of tissues so they can wipe away their tears and mascara, and Martha is reminded that she's a mother now. God, so much has changed.

'Shall we sit here for a while?' Martha asks, hooking her arm through Liv's and walking towards the bench with its age-old inscription to *Clara May Avery, beloved wife.*

The houseboat moored in the water ahead of them is just as Liv described it in her email, blue and red, with the name *Dovedale* etched on its side. Still here. It's memorable because it's the first of the houseboats along this stretch, and back in the day it was the most colourful and best maintained. Martha seems to remember it belonged to an old man with a heavy ginger beard, who pottered about the place in all seasons, touching up the paintwork, tending to his flower boxes or cleaning the outside windows. Now, the paint is peeling, the faded curtains drawn closed inside its neglected windows, and Martha thinks that the old boy must be long gone. It seems symbolic, somehow, that the houseboat remains, the boat they passed by day after day, on the way to school or Square Wheels or the Waterside Café. They've all moved on and changed, but that houseboat has remained, quietly ageing, silently watching the world go by.

'I can't believe—' they both start to say, clasping one another's hands as they laugh.

'I'm sorry,' Martha says, and she doesn't know why she feels so strongly that this is her responsibility, but somehow she does. 'I can't really remember how or when we stopped seeing each other, Liv – but I'm sorry I didn't make more of an effort to stay in touch.'

Liv shakes her head vehemently. 'You've got nothing to apologise for, Mart. None of us planned it this way, did we? After Juliet, how could we ever have thought things would just go on like before?' She brings her hand to her mouth, this

271

time breaking down in grief, not joy, and it's clear to Martha that Liv's pain is as real today as it was eighteen years ago. 'I miss her so much,' she goes on. 'I still have days when I wake up and can't believe that she just disappeared like that. I ask myself, could I have done things differently? Was there anything I could have changed – to have prevented her going like that?'

'You can't think like that,' Martha tells her, knowing her words are false, hypocritical. Hasn't she had the same thoughts and feelings herself, a thousand times before? 'It'll drive you insane. What we have to focus on now is finding out who was responsible for taking her away. That's why I was so desperate to contact you, Liv, to see if we could work together to put things right, once and for all.'

For the next few minutes Martha gives Liv a potted update on the investigation, filling her in on the details of the TV show, about the unsolved murder of Tilly Jones and the recent postcards supposedly sent from David Crown; about the mad woman living in Liv's old house.

'Christ,' Liv says with a shudder. 'She sounds like a complete psycho. What kind of weird coincidence is it that she would end up buying my house? I've got no memory of her from Square Wheels at all – but I certainly noticed she was a bit, well, strange, I suppose, when she came to look at the house.'

'When I spoke with Finn Palin last night, he told me they're now beginning to think that it wasn't a coincidence at all.'

'What do you mean?' Liv looks alarmed. 'You mean she targeted me?'

'Not specifically you, but us, yes. When the police spoke with the estate agent you dealt with during the sale, she told them that Katherine was the first prospective buyer for your house, and that she requested a viewing the day it went on the market. You might recall, two other buyers put in later offers, but Katherine increased hers to get the sale through.'

'Fuck me.' And there she is: the old Liv, potty mouth and all. 'Yes, I *remember*. My solicitor said this buyer was offering way over the odds, and that we should push the sale through as quickly as possible in case she changed her mind. But how would she have known where I lived, let alone that I was selling?'

Martha takes a deep breath. 'Finn thinks she's been stalking us on social media. Have you ever had a Facebook account?'

'Yes.' Liv looks thoughtful. 'I deleted it right before the house sale completed. I, well, my partner and I were separating, and I was moving to Guildford, and I just figured it was time for a fresh start.'

'But up until then, could Katherine have learned much about you?'

'Shit,' Liv replies after a moment's thought. 'Yeah. *What an idiot*. I definitely put up a post about having had enough of London. I think I said I was considering putting the house on the market and moving out. I even mentioned that I lived in Hackney, in case any friends knew people looking for a property in the area.'

'Well, there you go. It's either that, or perhaps Katherine put a call out to all the local estate agents, asking them to alert her to any houses coming up for sale in your street.'

'But why would she want to live in my old house in the first place?'

'We haven't quite worked that bit out. But my bet is it's a case of good old-fashioned obsession. Katherine Crown is definitely not a balanced person, and for some reason she's become fixated on us – it's certainly something to do with the connection between her father and Juliet's disappearance. I think she wants to clear his name.'

'Terrifying,' Liv replies. 'That's it. I'm off social media for good. It's bloody dangerous.'

Martha laughs, pulling her bag on to her lap, hearing the rustle of the unopened morning post she collected on the way out of her apartment. One of the packets, judging by the post-mark, is the bundle of Juliet's letters that Tom promised to send from France, and Martha wonders if now is the time to share them with Liv. But she's just stalling, she knows. She has to break the devastating news about the police discovery of bones, to tell Liv that at last they might be getting close to putting Juliet to rest. On the footpath ahead of them a pair of joggers runs by, a couple in their early forties, the woman athletic and glowing, the paunchy man looking as though he'd rather be doing anything else. The things we do for love, Martha thinks.

'So, Mart,' Liv asks haltingly, 'with all this research you've been doing – are the police any closer to finding out what happened to Juliet?'

Again, Martha reaches for her friend's hand. 'Liv,' she begins. How did you ever deliver this kind of news? Deciding there is no easy way, no right way to do this, Martha forges on. 'Liv, we think we've found her. Skeletal remains have been found buried beneath the foundations of the old school swim-ming pool – where David Crown was building the Garden of Reflection.'

'The garden we helped him to dig,' Liv says, quietly now, her eyes fixed at middle distance, moving slowly left to right as she recalls the scene. She turns to look at Martha. 'That's where she's been all this time?' she asks, and her face is stricken. 'We were there with him just months earlier, clearing rubble from the old pool. Juliet was helping him to measure the patio out, for fuck's sake! Could we have stopped this happening, Mart?'

Martha pulls Liv against her and kisses the top of her head, drawing her back so she can look into her eyes. 'Nobody could have stopped this happening but him, Liv, do you understand? David Crown. He's the one to blame, not us. We were just kids – ordinary kids, making ordinary mistakes – and Juliet got tangled up with the wrong person.'

'Tangled up?' Liv says. 'Juliet wasn't "tangled up" with David Crown. Is that what everyone thinks?'

Martha can see she's upset, that Liv can't bear the thought of her best friend being involved in anything so sordid. 'Well, yes I mean, until recently I never thought it was possible . . .' she says, taking the letters from her bag, holding them up for Liv to see. 'But these might tell us something different. I haven't opened them yet,' she says. 'Tom – Juliet's Tom – sent them to me from Paris. Maybe these will give us a bit more of an idea where Juliet's head was at back then? Tom says they're from that time. He reckoned they look like love letters.'

All the colour has drained from Liv's skin. 'Is *this* why you asked me to meet you?' she asks, her posture stiffening, her tone firmly defensive now.

'Why *I* asked you?' Martha replies, dropping the letters to her lap, pulling back to see Liv's expression more clearly. 'I didn't ask you, Liv – *you* contacted *me*.'

Before Liv has the chance to answer her, a shadow crosses over them and hovers, causing the friends to look up. It's not the camera guys arriving early, as Martha suspected it might be, nor a cloud passing across the winter sky. The person standing over them is Katherine Crown.

30. **Katherine**

Here I am again, the Little Spy, peeking through the cracks in the curtains, watching and waiting for my friends to arrive. The minutes and hours have moved so slowly, sleepily tick-tick-ticking away, every second broadcast from the old wooden clock that John had mounted on the panelled wall above the bench. I finished my coffee and doughnuts hours ago, and I hate myself for not planning this more carefully, for not having stopped off at the shops to pick up provisions before the police started searching for me. But how could I have planned it? When I left home two days ago, after that terrible accident with Martha, I was in a panic so crippling that I wasn't even thinking straight. I wish John were here now, so I could thank him for the gift of this boat. I'll never forget the day when I received the solicitor's letter, and eventually the keys, and I thought that I must be dreaming for such a thing to happen to me. There was a short note too, informing me of the details of his gift. It was brief, so I was able to memorise the whole thing:

To KC,

It wouldn't hurt for you to have a little space of your own, so I'm leaving you Dovedale, *which would have gone to your dad if he was still around. I took it with 80 years left on the lease back in 1967, so the moorings are good to run for a little while yet. Keep the windows clean like I showed you and ask Terry at Rivermates to give it the once-over – I've been a bit lax with the maintenance in recent years, not been feeling as good as I used to. I've left you a few bob to draw on too – it's well overdue for a visit to the dry dock, but Terry will tell you what wants doing.*

Be good.

John

I feel guilty now that two years have passed and I never did any of those things he asked me to, never sought out Terry at Rivermates, never cleaned the windows. The money wasn't a huge amount – just three and half thousand pounds – and apart from the direct debit for mooring fees, I've never touched it, as it was meant specifically for the boat. And I never told Mum about John's gift. It was my secret, something I needed more than ever since John was no longer around for me to call in on when life at home got a bit much. Once I had the boat, I could leave Mum for a few days at a time when she was in one of her lows, instead of hiding out in my room and wishing the time away. No wonder I'm such an avid reader; I've had hours to fill like that, alone and lonely. The boat was a godsend, though of course, since moving into Liv's house, I haven't been back here at all. Looking around at the grimy varnished surfaces and flaking windows, I feel ashamed to have let John down so badly. *Dovedale* was his pride and joy, and somehow I've even managed to ruin that.

A flash of colour catches my attention, and I peer through the crack in the drapes to scrutinise the lone figure that now stands at the wooden bench beyond the path. Can she see me? Impossible, I hope, given that I'm concealed inside the unlit gloom of the cabin, the curtains parted only enough for me to watch through, unseen. She's side-on, her face averted as she looks further along the path, over the roofs of the houseboats and dinghies moored along the way. 'Turn around!' I want to shout. 'Let me get a good look at you!' It's certainly not Martha, so it has to be Liv, but she's so wrapped up in her coat and scarf, her face obscured by dark glasses, that without her turning in my direction, it's impossible to tell. Over here! I scream inside my head. Liv! Over here!

As though in answer to my silent cries, she now turns face-on, lifting her sunglasses and perching them on her head, narrowing her eyes as she studies the boat. And there's no doubt in my mind.

That clear brown skin, that sleek, straight hair, those eyes so blue: it's Liv.

Despite what I led my dad to believe, that initial meeting at the Square Wheels cabin was not the first time that I'd met the three friends, and their lack of recognition was confirmation to me, if any was needed, that I was in fact invisible. I had met them almost a year earlier when, under the enthusiastic encouragement of my father, I attempted to enter the wider world one more time. Between them, my parents had done a good job with my schooling and by the start of that summer I was on track to pass ten GCSEs with A and B grades. My mum was proud of my progress, delighted to have to played such a role in my success, until Dad suggested that as I was such a bright cookie, I should consider studying at the local school's sixth form, with a view to attending university, just as they had. Well, I thought my mother might have a seizure when he first raised the subject! She sent me from the room, hissing at my dad that he was reckless and irresponsible – even going as far as to say that the experience would be the 'undoing' of me, whatever that was supposed to mean! I sat at the foot of the stairs, listening in, fascinated by the war of words that went on beyond the wall, with Mum insisting I was still fragile, and Dad arguing that I was 'over all that'. By 'over all that', he meant that my weight had stabilised in recent months, following a three-week stay in hospital, during which time I was tube-fed until the doctors deemed me well enough to return home. I'd gained a stone in weight during my stay, most of which (unbeknownst to Dad) my mother had managed to get off again through a careful regime of rationing and portion control. The baggy clothes were Mum's idea, I recall. 'You know how Dad fusses,' she'd said. 'Best not to draw attention to yourself when he's around. He'll only march you down to the doctor's again. And you don't want to find yourself back in hospital, Katherine, do you?'

She was right: I didn't. The abdominal scar from my feeding tube continued to bother me at night-time, when I'd scratch away at it in my sleep, causing it to get unbearably inflamed. It upset me, keeping secrets like my eating plan from Dad, but at the same time the secret-keeping paid off, because over the space of a few weeks Dad became more adamant that I was fit enough to enrol for sixth form, no matter what my mother said. This battle, at least, was his to win.

Before long, we'd taken a tour of the school, met with the head teacher and I accepted a place, conditional on my achieving certain GCSE grades. Their conditional grades were a lot lower than those predicted for me, and so throughout the summer Dad and I went ahead with preparations for my start in the coming September. Mum stayed conspicuously outside of the arrangements, and we were careful not to discuss my new school, or anything related to it, in front of her. We'd passed the first hurdle of getting offered a place in the school; the second hurdle, it seemed to me, was getting through the Sixth Form Welcome Ball. The ball was scheduled to take place at the end of the summer holidays, before the start of the new term, and attending it was a prospect so daunting and thrilling that it's a wonder I didn't die of heart failure first. I am aware that under normal circumstances a daughter might go shopping with her mother in anticipation of such an event, but it was my father who accompanied me to John Lewis to choose my dress; it was my father who sat patiently outside the changing rooms, remarking on my various outfits as I twirled and curtsied, seeking his approval. Careful not to show myself looking so thin, I eventually chose a blue strapless fifties dress, under-netted to disguise my shapeless hips, with a neat red bolero cardigan to cover my arms and shoulders.

'You look like a princess,' Dad told me when he dropped me at the school gates beneath a hazy August sky. And for the first time in my life I *felt* like a princess. Despite my galloping nerves (settled only very slightly by a good dose of Fluoxetine) I walked into the school hall to find it already alive with the sights and sounds of what seemed like hundreds of young, smartly dressed teenagers. In that first glimpse, I experienced the sense that maybe I did deserve a place there, that *perhaps* this was somewhere I could belong. I was determined to make this work, as much to please Dad as to prove Mum wrong. I wasn't the fragile creature she described me as; I was a *princess*. I was bright. I was beautiful. I was strong. Inside, I shook like a jelly.

Luckily for me, one of the teachers I had met on my previous visit was at the door to the hall, and she remembered that I was new and beckoned to the refreshments table for one of the girls to come over. I cringed inside, my shoulders hunching instinctively at the burden I was about to become. But all such thoughts evaporated when I saw the girl who responded, smiling and hurrying across in our direction. This girl was, without a word of a lie, everything that I dreamed of being: graceful, bright-eyed and at ease in the world. Her name was Juliet, she told me, and, far from complaining about me being foisted on her, she welcomed me to the school and walked me about the bunting-festooned hall, introducing me to every new face we encountered. The majority of the students already attended the school, having just completed their GCSEs there, and everyone, except me it seemed, knew each other well. I was met with a comforting level of indifference, the boys tending to bob their heads in bland acknowledgement, the girls with a sweeping once-over smile and a 'hi'. There were girls and boys of every height, colour and size; their differences were so strikingly apparent to me that it seemed I had nothing to fear, no need to feel anxious over my own differences at all.

Having done the rounds with me, Juliet left me sitting on a chair at the edge of the hall, while she returned to continue her rota duties behind the drinks table, along with two other girls whom I would later come to know as Martha Benn and Olivia Heathcote. Well, if I had seemed like a princess to Dad on that evening, Juliet and her friends seemed to me like Titania and her fairies, as ethereal and captivating as Shakespeare's own exquisite creations. As the light outside dimmed and the disco-lit room filled up, I revelled in the sensation of disappearing behind a wall of people, but not before I spied Martha, a slightly shorter but no less radiant version of Juliet, sliding a half-bottle of vodka from her shoulder bag and slopping a glug into each of their three beakers. She spotted me watching and pulled a funny face, raising a friendly finger to her lips. Oh, to be in on the secret!

Two hours later I was still in that same seat, cradling the same plastic cup of lemonade, happy just to observe, untroubled by conversation. Juliet and her friends were not the only ones drinking, judging by the shift in mood and decorum as the night went on, and before long ties were loosened and couples were smooching on the dance floor or disappearing through the fire doors out into the warm darkness of the playing field beyond. My eyes followed Juliet wherever I could find her, and when she vanished from view they sought out Martha or Liv. I made it a game of sorts, challenging myself to have one of them in my sights at any given time, quickly locating one of the others when that one disappeared. I watched Martha dancing out through the exit with a pale-skinned boy in a dark suit and bright trainers, and quickly shifted my attention to Juliet and Liv, who were dancing together at the edge of the dance floor, their fingers meshed together above their heads, Liv having to stretch her hands so much higher to reach Juliet's. The music was alien to me, my mother having been someone who only entertained listening to the sounds from her own youth, but these two knew all the words, throwing their heads back every time the chorus rang out '*C'est la vie*', collapsing into fits of laughter as the song came to an end. At the start of the next song, they grimaced and shook their heads, and I watched them as they linked arms, drifting out through the fire exit doors and into the darkness as Martha had done before them.

For the first time that evening I was compelled to move from the safety of my seat. The heat of the crowded room struck me, and without thinking I followed the girls out on to the grass, trailing them at a distance as they ran barefoot towards a derelict-looking building at the rear of the field. As my eyes adjusted to the half-moon's light, I noticed there were small clusters of people everywhere – groups of girls and boys, couples, some of them smoking and drinking, some just hanging out, laughing or kissing. Juliet and Liv seemed so much apart from all this, and as I trod in their footsteps and saw them disappear around the old brick wall, I felt certain that they were seeking out the third of their number, Martha. As I too rounded the corner, I was surprised to find myself at the edge of an old outdoor swimming pool, overgrown with moss, ivy snaking its way through the cracked tile edges and rusting steps. In the pale light, I caught the flash of the girls as they slipped inside the derelict building to the far side of the pool – the old changing rooms, I assumed – and with care I followed the path around the edge of the gaping hole, feeling the chill of late night against my bare legs. What adventures! I thought. They were clearly up to no good, and there was I, in on the action; a fly on the wall; a will-o'-the-wisp! What fun we will have, my new friends and I, when I tell them of the time that I pursued them through the school grounds, chasing them unseen, hoping to catch them out in their midnight mischief! Beyond the entrance to the crumbling old structure I could hear their whispered laughter, their low, murmured conversations. Was that one voice or two? My breath was caught like a butterfly inside my chest, and I dared not release it for fear of capture!

'Mart will be looking for us,' I heard one of them whisper.

The other one tutted. 'Martha will be fine. She seemed to be getting on quite well with Denny Scott the last time I looked.' Now a heart-stopping silence, before she said, 'Forget Martha.'

As I eased slowly around the brickwork I saw those beautiful girls, swathed in the strips of moon glow that crept in through the broken rafters overhead. Their shoulders were bare, their dark and fair skins intertwined like wind-blown saplings, their faces joined in a kiss so tender and taut with longing that I thought the sky might break apart in a burst of stars.

I really had no plan in mind when I arranged for Liv and Martha to meet here; I just knew that I had to see them together and to put things straight with Martha. I'm so, so sorry about hitting her like that. Really, what basis is that for a friendship? I have to explain to her that it was an accident, that I was out of my mind with worry – that I panicked when Carl just wouldn't stop knocking at the front door. She'll want to know why I panicked, and this is something I've gone over and over in my mind since the very moment I took flight from the terrifying scene. Why did I panic? I suppose I was afraid that I'd been caught out. I was afraid that she wouldn't like me, like all the other people before her. But I think, if I'm honest, I was most afraid that she will find out what happened with Juliet all those years ago – and that she'll never be able to forgive me when she does. If she'll just give me a chance to explain things properly, then maybe I can hang on to the smallest hope of our future friendship.

They've been sitting together on that wooden bench for five minutes or so now, and I'm captivated by the affection they share so readily. Even now, Liv's hand is resting in Martha's, their heads closely inclined as Martha draws a bundle of papers from her bag. Clambering above deck as quietly as I can, given my bulky attire, I step from the boat's edge on to the paved towpath just metres from where the two sit. I'm near, but they don't even look up, so absorbed are they in their conversation, in each other. Am I foolish to believe that some day I might experience friendship of this kind? I've no idea what I ought to do next, so I do what my father always taught me in these nervous situations, and I put on a smile. Even as I approach, I'm wishing I had biscuits on-board, or better still a cake. Oh, for heaven's sake – I don't even have milk!

When Liv looks up her expression is confused, as though she's trying to place me; when Martha sees me, she looks alarmed.

'Hello again!' I say as brightly as I can muster. 'I wondered if you two wanted to join me for a cup of coffee on my houseboat?'

Martha and Liv exchange a look, and I feel a flash of exclusion. Why do people look at me in this way? Why must I always be the object of suspicion and ridicule?

'*Katherine*,' Martha says, clutching the papers in her spotty-gloved hands, and I'm not fooled by that wheedling tone. It's the kind of voice that mothers use on misbehaving children. It's the kind of voice that says. *You're not quite right in the head so we'll tread carefully . . .* I'm insulted that she thinks she has to treat me like a child, but then she throws me off guard by sounding more like a concerned friend. 'I've been worried about you, Katherine. Are you OK?'

And I want so much to believe she cares about me that I can't think what to say next. So I repeat, 'Would you like to join me for a cup of coffee on my houseboat?'

Liv shakes her head, moving her hand so that it rests on Martha's forearm.

'We've got to be somewhere,' says Martha, and of course I know she's lying, because the only place she's arranged to be is here with Liv!

And I hate her for lying to me, and I hate her for wanting Liv and not me, and I stamp my foot towards them and lean in close enough to whisper, 'I have a knife in my pocket, and, if you don't both come and have a cup of coffee with me on my boat, I don't know what I might do with it.'

I'm appalled by the change in Martha's expression, as it shifts from concern to fear. She stands, hooking her bag over her shoulder, but she doesn't move away from the bench. She thinks I don't notice the way she glances up and down the towpath, but I do the same, and I know there's nobody there for her to call out to. For once, the path is completely empty. Not a dog walker or cyclist in sight! Perhaps this is serendipity at work. I can tell that Martha is thinking of breaking into a run, because I see the look that passes between the two of them, so I quickly position myself close to Liv and through the fabric of my pocket I press hard against her side.

'We should do as she says,' Liv tells Martha, and she jerks her head towards her shoulder to draw attention to the way I'm standing at her rear.

Martha nods calmly, and, taking the lead, she boards John's old houseboat and descends the wooden steps to the living quarters below. In the far distance, I see a young family wandering along the towpath, and I thank providence that my timing, for once, was simply perfect. I confiscate the ladies' bags, stowing them beneath the bottom step, and invite them to take a seat.

'Now,' I say, doing my best to smile and sound confident as they slide on to the bench behind the narrow kitchen table. 'How do you take it? Milk and sugar?'

If they ask for tea, I'm afraid they're out of luck. I did a taste test with the crushed sleeping tablets last night, and I could definitely detect them in the tea. Coffee's better. They'll never guess I've put them in the coffee.

286

31. **Martha**

It's only when Martha and Liv are seated behind the galley table that Katherine confesses with a nervous giggle that she didn't really have a knife in her pocket. Somehow this news doesn't make Martha feel any less anxious about the situation she and Liv now find themselves in, stowed away below decks with a disturbed woman who is behaving as though they'd just boarded voluntarily.

Now she fusses in and out the cupboards, barely leaving space between one rambling observation and the next. She opens a cutlery drawer and brings out a large knife, pausing to consider it for a few seconds before placing it on the worktop beside a chipped red kettle. Martha feels the panic rising inside her, her pulse racing as she runs through the options in her mind. A sealed shallow window on to the canal is behind them. Their legs are tucked tightly under the table. Liv is to her left, pressed against the wood-panelled wall of the cabin, and to her right is the small kitchen arrangement of sink and worktop, beneath a broad window view of the canal and towpath along which she had walked only minutes earlier. The windows are so grubby, Martha doubts anyone on the path could possibly see them inside, and the quietly formidable Katherine stands between them and the only exit available, up the steps.

They're trapped. Even if they tried to rush at her, the table between them will rob them of the element of surprise they'd need to overpower her. And now, of course, there's that knife. Nobody knows they're here, and Martha can only hope that when Toby and the others arrive they'll notice the glove she dropped at the edge of the path when they boarded. She's afraid, and she's doing her best to mentally convey to Liv that she's to follow her lead, to do nothing until she gives her the nod.

Now Katherine turns to face them with a clap of her hands. 'Actually I've got sugar, but no milk, I'm afraid. I haven't used the boat for a while, you see – not since I moved into your old place, Liv! I mean, I *love* the boat, of course, and I was so grateful – and surprised – when John left it to me in his will, but it's not the same as a house, is it? He died, you know, John? And he left me his boat. It was a gift. A complete surprise!'

Martha smiles politely. Inwardly she kicks herself again. If she were any kind of investigator, she would have found out that Katherine owned a boat, wouldn't she? And for that matter, shouldn't the police have been on to it? Surely it would have been one of the first places they'd have searched for the wanted woman, had they known?

Katherine hooks a finger behind the closed curtain of the opposite window, peeking out towards the towpath and the wooden bench where Liv and Martha had been sitting just a few minutes earlier.

'So, it was you who sent the emails to us?' These are the first words Liv has spoken since they came on-board, and they're uttered robotically. Her skin has taken on an ashen shade, rendering her complexion dull and sickly.

Katherine lets the curtain drop, and looks back, bringing a hand up to cover her smile. 'Oops!' she says, and then she holds up one wrist, giving it a 'naughty girl' slap with the other hand.

Jesus, Martha thinks. This gets more terrifying by the minute. She thinks about Toby, and Jay and Sally, and she glances at her watch, hoping that perhaps they will be less than the hour she had insisted she'd need between her meeting up with Liv and their arriving. Please God, let Toby see that spotty glove, let him recognise that it's hers, let him realise that she's trapped down here with this mad woman.

'So, tell us why you wanted to meet up, Katherine,' she says now, determined not to show her that she is, in fact, shitting herself. 'You went to great lengths to get us here. Well, here we are!'

Katherine finishes making the drinks, placing them on the narrow table between them as she takes a seat on the low vinyl stool opposite. The quarters are cramped; Katherine must find it a squeeze to move about at the best of times, without two hostages crammed in too. Martha's eyes roam the space, calculating how they might free themselves before Katherine can reach for that knife, and once again concludes it's impossible. The only way they'll get out of this fix is by talking their way out.

For a few minutes now Katherine has been silent, nibbling away on the edge of a thumbnail, her eyes darting back and forth, from Liv to Martha to the tabletop, and from the way her lips silently move, it seems possible to Martha that she's rehearsing what to say next.

'Why don't you start from the beginning?' Martha asks gently. When Katherine's eyes meet hers they are glistening with moisture, and she does, indeed, begin to speak.

'Drink up, and I'll tell you everything,' she says, gulping hers down and showing them the empty cup. She's like a child, the way she speaks and moves, and it seems to Martha that the best way to appeal to her is to treat her like one.

'Of course,' Martha says. 'Thank you. It's a lovely cup of coffee, Katherine.' Martha and Liv drink it down, as sweet and bitter as it is, and Katherine clears away their cups, her face brightening as she takes her seat again.

'You won't remember me – very few people ever do,' she says. 'But we've met on a few occasions, and *I* remember you – all three of you – *very* well.'

Martha and Liv remain silent, waiting for her to continue.

'Of course, you now know that my father was David Crown, and I'm certain you won't have forgotten *him*.'

She directs this particularly at Martha, the weighted pause enough to unsettle some buried memory.

'He was the loveliest man. It's important that you know that,' Katherine continues. 'There's all this talk about him, and every word of it is untrue. The idea that he ran off with Juliet! That he killed her! It's all lies. He didn't have a bad bone in his body. I should know! I'm his daughter! Who would know him better than me?'

Martha feels a surge of sympathy for this tragic woman, who has spent all these years convincing herself that her father was incapable of this awful crime, despite the strongest of pointers towards his guilt. In the name of love, and with the passing of time, we can all convince ourselves of anything, can't we? We can convince ourselves that we're not responsible for the misfortunes of others, that we're not culpable in some small way, that there was nothing more we could have done.

'Sometimes people are capable of doing things their loved ones might never think possible,' she tells Katherine. 'We're

292

not responsible for our parents' mistakes. Sometimes good people do bad things.'

Katherine shakes her head vigorously. 'No, not my dad. You didn't know him the way I did. He was a good man. He *is* a good man.'

'Do you know where your dad is, Katherine?'

'Dad and I used to visit John on this boat,' she says, skimming past the question. 'And I think maybe *that* was when I first noticed you. I didn't go to school like other children – so I'd sometimes be at the boat at the end of the day when the canal path was busy with pupils on their way home. The three of you – you two and Juliet – became quite a familiar sight over the years, and really, I almost felt as though I knew you! You were always laughing and talking, and sometimes you'd sit on that bench down there and smoke a cigarette or share a can of Coke.'

The thought of Katherine watching them sends a chill up Martha's spine. She glances at Liv, who appears dumbstruck by the revelation. 'So, was Square Wheels the first time we properly met?' Martha asks now, wanting to move Katherine's rambling account forward.

'No,' she replies. 'We'd met before then. It was at the Sixth Form Welcome Ball a year earlier, when I was planning to join your school to do my A-levels. Juliet showed me around. Of course, I was a bit slimmer back then—'

Now Liv suddenly stirs, leaning forward in her seat. 'Blue dress, red cardigan?' Her voice sounds slow, uncertain.

'Yes!' Katherine shrieks. 'You remember me! Golly, that's amazing!'

'It was *you* in the changing rooms,' Liv replies, but she doesn't expand. Instead, she sits back, pressing her back into the wall, a worried expression setling in her features.

'But I don't recall you after that,' Martha says. 'I'd know if you'd been in the sixth form.'

Katherine shakes her head, clamming up again, and Martha's impatience gets the better of her.

'Katherine, I should tell you that we know Juliet was involved in some secret relationship in the period before she went missing – she told me and Liv as much – but just not who. I hate to say this, but it seems possible – likely, even – that David Crown was her secret lover.'

Liv is crying. 'Martha, stop,' she's saying, and when Martha, confused, looks back at Katherine, she sees the woman's face is now puckered towards Liv in an admonishing, eyebrow-raised scowl.

'Are you going to tell her, or shall I?' Katherine asks Liv archly.

Liv lowers her eyes, not responding.

'Juliet's secret lover *wasn't* my dad, you silly billy!' Katherine points a finger across the table. 'It was Liv!'

With that, she picks up the knife and tip-taps above deck, bolting the door behind her.

Liv covers her face with her hands. 'God, Mart. I don't know where to start.'

How could she not have seen it? The night of the sixth form ball had followed close on the heels of Liv and Juliet's school trip to Venice, when they'd returned home closer than ever before. At the time, Martha had felt left out, jealous, even, and when Liv started hanging around at Juliet's house all the time, Martha had convinced herself that it was because she had a crush on Juliet's older brother, Tom. She'd suggested it to Juliet, who at first laughed it off as a ridiculous idea, but before long she was agreeing with Martha in hushed tones, telling her not to mention it in front of Liv because she'd be embarrassed. Of course it had suited Juliet to let Martha think Tom was the object of Liv's attentions! How could she have been so blind? Flashes of that party night return: the three of them behind the drinks table, topping up their orange juice with vodka; Mrs Matthews and Mr Curtis starting off the slow dance and clearing the floor; an unexpected moonlit kiss with Denny Scott – the first of many more to come. And here she is out among the revellers on the school field, moving from group to group, still clutching her empty plastic cup, asking if anyone's seen Juliet and Liv. She's looked everywhere, inside and out, and it seems as though they've vanished into thin air. They wouldn't have left without her, she knows; they're all walking home together when the party ends. The half-moon is bright in the starry sky and Martha is standing at the edge of the grass, contemplating what to do next, when she sees the flash of red and blue over in the far corner near the derelict swimming pool. It's that new girl Juliet was showing around, she's sure of it. Certain that her friends will be there, Martha drops the empty cup and jogs across the grass, out towards the shadowy brick building, calling their names into the darkness. As she nears, there's no sign of the new girl, but Liv and Juliet appear from behind the brick pillar, laughing, arms linked. 'You found us!' Juliet cries out breathlessly, and she looks at Liv with mischief in her eyes. But Liv's expression is altogether different.

Liv looks as though she's just been caught stealing.

'I'll know if you try to escape,' Katherine calls down through the bolted door. 'And then I'll have to stab you!' Her voice is so breezy, Martha has no doubt that she means it.

For a few moments neither Liv nor Martha moves. Martha's head is feeling fuzzy, and she thinks it's some kind of residual concussion, until she turns to look at Liv and sees the drugged look in her eyes.

'Are you OK?' she asks, and Liv shakes her head slowly.

'The coffee,' she replies, and she rubs the heels of her hands against her eyes, blinking widely, trying to focus. '*Shit*. She put something in our coffee.'

Overhead, they now hear Katherine speaking into her mobile phone, but there's a large vessel travelling up the waterway, making enough noise to obscure her words. Who could she be calling? Martha wonders. And, more to the point, what has Liv got to say about Katherine's revelation?

'I don't know how I didn't see it,' Martha says in a whisper.

She still has the bundle of letters clutched in her hand, and she slides them along the table towards Liv. 'This is your handwriting on the envelopes, isn't it?' *Not* David Crown's.

Liv runs the tip of her finger across the letter on top. 'Juliet and I swore that we'd never tell you,' she says, her words emerging slowly, as though it's taking her greater effort to speak. 'We knew if we did it would have been the end of our friendship.'

'No, it wouldn't!' Martha protests, but she knows that Liv is right. How could a friendship of three survive when two had paired off so intimately?

With great effort she squeezes herself beneath the table and up out the other side.

'Yes, it would,' Liv continues. Martha beckons for her to follow, but she shakes her head sluggishly. 'We never planned it, Mart. Before Venice, we'd always been close, but there, it was like we were in this bubble, where it was just the two of us, in this beautiful city, where we could do whatever – be *whoever* we liked—'

Martha is now standing unsteadily in the small galley space, facing the wooden steps where Katherine has stowed their bags. 'You were different when you came home,' she says. 'I thought you'd gone off me. I thought you'd got fed up with all my boozing. I was a real pain in the arse back then.'

On soft feet, she crosses the floorboards and drags out her bag, retrieving her phone and dumping the bag back where it had been.

'How can you say that?' Liv asks. Her head is now slumped back against the small window, her eyelids closed. 'You were the one that held us together all those years. Don't you see? Whenever Jules and I fell out, it was you who talked us around. You were the one who always talked sense. These . . .' She holds up a wrist, and Martha sees she's wearing her silver friendship bangle. 'These were your idea. Martha, you held us together. You held *everything* together.'

Martha has left so much in the past, packaged up tightly, sealed away. Had she really been so central to their friendship? Only now can she see that it's true; so often she *was* the one holding things together. At home, at school, at work – Martha could be relied on. Martha was strong. Ha, she thinks now. If only they knew.

She stares at the phone in her hand. How long has she been standing here like this?

'A whole year and a half you kept it secret? You should have told me, Liv. If I was so important to you both. You should have told me.'

An apology crosses Liv's expression. 'No, no, it wasn't like that. After the sixth form ball, we didn't know how people would react – our friends, our family. Juliet was so scared of her parents finding out, terrified that she'd somehow let them down. They weren't exactly homophobic –' she stumbles over the word, laughing when it comes out as *phomohobic* – 'but they weren't keen on the idea. Don't you remember Juliet telling us she'd overheard them talking about Tom once? They had some idea he might be gay, and Juliet said the way they discussed it, you'd have thought it was a disease. So we stopped. We tried to pretend it was just a summer fling, a bit of fun – not real life. There was no reason to tell you, Mart – it was over.' She pauses, biting down on her lip. 'But the next summer it all just started up again, and this time we knew it was serious—'

Martha holds up a halting hand, feeling her body sway. A dreamlike image of Liv and Juliet pushes in, at the riverside picnic, the two of them behind that tree, their faces close together, sharing a secret while the others packed up the lunch things. Martha had one end of the picnic blanket, Tom the other, and even now she is reminded of that feeling of envy, of being left out. Martha turned to place the folded rug inside the basket, and she caught it, the moment their faces separated before they ran along the bank and back on to the boat.

She is about to reply, but Katherine has raised her voice. Martha tilts her head to listen in on the conversation.

'I just think you should come, that's all! There are things you need to hear.' Katherine's tone seems to be a blend of pleading and irritation. 'No, of course I don't want to argue. No, I *know* it's a mess.' She's sniffing now, quietly crying, making the occasional noise of assent as the person on the other end of the line continues to speak. Who could she be talking to? Her voice sounds so close, Martha realises there's no way she is going to be able to make a phone call without being overheard. With fumbling fingers, she begins to tap out a message to Toby instead, but when she gets halfway through, Katherine lets out a yelp of distress.

'Dad!' she cries out. 'Of course that's what they think!'

Dad? She's speaking to her father? Is it possible that those postcards really were from David Crown – that he's here in London right now, just as his wife had told them? When she hears Katherine's feet overhead, Martha shoves her phone into her coat pocket, the incomplete text unsent.

She glances at Liv briefly, scared to take her eyes from the top of the stairs. 'So, that last night when you two were arguing outside the Waterside Café – what was that about?' she whispers, her eyes fixed on the cabin door as it opens again.

Katherine's feet appear on the stairs, only reaching halfway down before her phone rings again, and with a tut she returns above deck. Martha feels light-headed. Again she reaches for the phone in her pocket, but is halted when she sees that Liv is slumped, her head on the table. She rushes to her, propping her up, pushing at her eyelids until she's sure Liv is still conscious, her own heart hammering all the while. What the hell has that woman given them? Martha is woozy, but Liv is physically of much smaller build than her, and it's clearly affected her more quickly.

'Don't worry,' she whispers, in a tone of confidence far greater than she really feels. 'Help will be here any minute – I promise. In the meantime, when she comes back we'll just talk to her calmly, reassure her that we want to be friends too. OK?'

Liv swipes a streak of mascara from her face, and she speaks in an urgent whisper now, her fingers hanging on to Martha's sleeve. 'The night Juliet was taken – it was all my fault, you know? I'd had too much to drink, and we were mucking about with Tom when I made a stupid joke about getting off with Juliet. Tom didn't take any notice, but Juliet was furious, and after she'd finished her drink she stormed outside, saying she was late for work. I followed her, on a mission – I'd got it into my idiot head that *now* was the time for us to declare our love to the world. To get it all out in the open.'

Unsteadily, Martha perches on the stool opposite. 'Was that when I interrupted you – by the bikes?' There's a thought in the back of her mind: she was about to do something just now. What was it?

'Yes, but not before she'd told me that if I said a word to *anyone* about us, it was over. She said she'd rather throw herself in the river than tell her parents. I'd never seen her so mad, and I really thought she might do something stupid. So when you said that you'd walk home with her, I was relieved. I thought you'd be safe together.' Liv lays her, head on folded arms.

Martha's own guilt rises again. She had chosen to leave Juliet on that dark path alone. Like a spoiled brat, she had wanted to punish Juliet for keeping secrets from her, and she'd wanted to get back to . . . to what? Oh, God, no. Grim realisation slams into place: the missing piece of the puzzle. She'd wanted another drink, hadn't she? She'd wanted another fucking drink, and she'd left her best friend alone on a dark canal path just to get one. Despite having not touched a drop for more than ten years, shame engulfs Martha.

When Liv manages to raise her head again, it looks as though it's taking every ounce of energy she has just to stay awake. 'If she did something to herself because of me, Mart, I . . . I've never stopped worrying that everything that happened to Juliet from the moment we parted was down to me. *Did* she kill herself, Martha?'

All this time, and Liv has been tortured by the same shade of guilt that has haunted Martha. The shift in what Martha under-stands of the past is so great, her mind is struggling to put it all in the right order. Is it possible that Juliet threw herself into the river, as she'd threatened to Liv? She'd had a drink or two, but

300

she had seemed completely fine when Martha left her, hadn't she? But perhaps, left alone on that dark path her, fear of exposure got the better of her? Perhaps, like Martha, she was concealing all manner of dread. Maybe it was enough to tip her over? But Martha thinks back to that vibrant smile, to the plans and dreams Juliet spoke of with such enthusiasm, and is certain, without a shadow of a doubt, that this is *not* what happened to Juliet.

'No,' she tells her friend, suddenly aware that she hadn't answered her. 'Juliet didn't kill herself.' But the words come out sludgy, unclear.

From her jacket, her phone rings out. Alarmed, she staggers to her feet and pulls it from her pocket, trying to shut off the ringer, bringing it to her ear. 'Toby?' she hisses, desperate to keep her voice down.

Toby's voice is firm. 'Martha, listen, this is important.'

She would interrupt him, but she can hear Katherine unbolting the door at the top of the steps, and she doesn't even know if she can get the words out. Liv is now waving at her, pointing to the stairs, and for a moment Martha feels paralysed.

'Martha?' Toby asks. 'Finn says the police spoke to David Crown's ex-pupil Vicky Duke an hour ago and she told them that she *did* lie about the assault. But before she got a chance to retract her allegation she was snatched on her way home—'

In a flurry of whirling arms, Katherine is screaming down the stairs, dislodging Martha's phone with a vicious wallop across the ear. The phone flies across the room and skitters into the corner with a crack.

'Now sit down, please!' she cries out, her voice high with emotion, the knife in her other hand punctuating each syllable. For a brief second she closes her eyes, and takes a deep, shuddering breath. '*Please*. I'm expecting another visitor, and I want them to see you at your best.'

32. **Katherine**

I'm really cross that she's been out of her seat, wandering about, when I specifically told them not to! This is my boat, and they are my guests, and you'd think they'd have better manners, quite frankly. But then, instead of complaining that I've broken her phone, Martha tells me that I'd given them both a scare with that knife. She was worried that I was going to hurt her again, and that's why they'd tried to get out. I'm so ashamed of myself I don't know what to say. This is not how Dad taught me to make new friends. Whatever happened to 'smile and ask lots of interesting questions'?

'You said you want to be our friend,' Martha says when I point her towards her seat.

I pull the table out a little, so they're not so uncomfortably squashed. It was unkind of me, I know. *I* am the one with the bad manners, I realise, and I feel my cheeks flaming, and it's all I can do to simply nod. My hands are trembling terribly, and I'm shocked at how easily I lashed out again. At least now it appears they are somewhat sedated; Liv looks positively floppy.

'We want that too, Katherine,' Martha is continuing. 'As you say, we've never got to know each other properly – have we, Liv?'

Liv looks uncertain at first, but then she's agreeing with Martha. I have to concentrate to hear what she's saying because she's mumbling terribly. 'I really enjoyed meeting you before. When you bought my house, remember? I was pleased to be selling it to someone as nice as you.'

As *nice* as me? Oh, my goodness. My *goodness*. 'I still use Carl,' I volunteer, but it comes out in a bit of a rush. Liv looks confused. 'Carl from Sainsbury's,' I add and her face slowly shifts in recognition.

'Oh, yes, Carl! Did you keep the same time slot?' She seems to be blinking a lot, and I wonder if she's nervous, but then I think perhaps she's just animated, enjoying our conversation!

'Yes! Exactly the same slot! Two p.m. on a Friday! He was so nice when he delivered your shopping that time, I thought . . .' But then my concentration wavers, because I'm thinking about poor Carl, stumbling in on that terrible scene in my hallway, and Martha lying there, and the blood, and how he must be thinking heaven knows what about me. What must he have thought when he heard them talking about me on the radio, a 'wanted' woman? If he knew the secrets I've been keeping, the lies that I've told . . .

Martha and Liv are watching me intently, and I realise I've been sitting here, thinking about Carl for several minutes, not speaking.

And then, quite out of the blue, Martha asks, 'Katherine, is your dad here in London?'

I stare at her blankly, not wanting to give my emotions away – not wanting to give the game away.

303

'We know about the postcards, you see. Your mother showed them to us when we visited her, and the last one was a London postcard. Have you spoken to him lately, Katherine?'

Her tone is gentle, and I so want to tell her everything, to confide in her as one friend to another. Should I do that? *Could* I do that?

'Will you excuse me for a moment?' I ask them, and I leave them at the table to sit on the bottom step with my face in my hands. I just need a bit of time alone with my thoughts, to get my head straight before we run out of time and I've no longer got them to myself. I'm trying to understand why Mum would have shown Martha those postcards. They were meant to be a secret.

Mum was unreachable for the best part of a year after Dad had gone. She stopped trying to control my meals, and my life, and all my home study for A-levels went by the wayside. It was as though, in my dad's absence, I had ceased to exist too. From the outset, she made it clear that the subject of Dad's departure from our lives – the circumstances surrounding his disappearance, and that of that girl – was strictly off limits. She would not, could not, discuss it, and if I knew what was good for me, I would remain tight-lipped too. If there was one thing I knew about my mother, it was that she couldn't tolerate the idea of scandal, of her life looking anything other than respectable. 'The police are looking for any excuse to sully your father's good reputation,' she told me. 'Do not give them the excuse they need.' If the police were to come calling again, our versions must remain the same: Dad had appeared completely normal when he returned home that night; no, we'd never met Juliet Sherman, the missing girl; and no, we had no idea where he'd run away to or why. My

304

mother coached me so thoroughly on the subject that today I struggle to know what's true and what's not – which events actually occurred over those days and nights, and which are simply memories planted there by Mum.

But, after a year had passed, Mum displayed a miraculous recovery, when she announced to me that life was far too short and that she planned to seize opportunity whenever it presented itself. She joined a local interest group and started going out on day trips with her new friends, enjoying a second lease of life visiting places such as Kew Gardens and Hampton Court Palace – the kinds of places I know Dad once loved to explore with her. It had been their shared passion, gardening, and I thought that perhaps it was her way of feeling closer to him, to get over the trauma of the past year. Before long, I even began to wonder whether she might have another man in her life, because she spent so much time out and about. Instead of growing closer, like so many bereaved or abandoned families do, *we* grew further apart, until we merely existed under the same roof, Mum sharing the occasional gripe about my ever-increasing weight, me biting my tongue and working hard at my distance learning studies. When, on my twenty-first birthday, I plucked up courage to ask her if she'd met someone new, I thought she might never forgive me, so wounded was she by my suggestion. 'No one will ever replace your father,' she told me, before taking to her bed for a week. The following month she updated her passport and flew out to Prague with her group.

On her return, she called me into her bedroom to give me chocolates and a wooden marionette fashioned in the shape of a mouse, and she embraced me with more warmth than I could recall since I was tiny. 'You mustn't worry about your dad,' she said, seating me at her dressing table and running her hairbrush through my long, dark hair. Oh, how I had missed this one small tenderness! 'He'll be home before we know it.' She said it with such certainty, undermining everything I thought I knew about his disappearance. How could I question it?

Two days later a postcard arrived from Prague, bearing nothing more than the letter 'D' and a kiss. 'I've seen him, Katherine,' she told me as I sat at the kitchen table, turning the card over in my fingers. 'I've seen him, and he looks so well, though he misses us terribly. But he's alive and well! Isn't that the most wonderful news?'

'When will he be home?' I asked then, and each subsequent year on the arrival of his postcard.

'Soon, darling,' she'd say each time, adding the postcard to our growing collection. 'Soon, I'm quite sure.'

As I sit here on this bottom step thinking about him and her, about the lies she's told me over the years – the secrets she's made me keep – I allow myself to wonder, is 'soon' now? Could Dad really be coming home?

33. Martha

Katherine is sitting at the foot of the steps, her face in her hands, the knife on the wooden floor beside her. As Martha sees it there are two barriers to their rushing past her to make their escape: the knife, and their impaired motor skills. Even if Liv and Martha did have speed on their side, they'd have to get past Katherine first, and right now her broad frame entirely blocks their passage.

'Do you think she wants to hurt us?' Liv whispers.

'No,' Martha is quick to answer, but in truth she's growing increasingly worried about the way Katherine's attention – and mood – flits from one extreme to the next. On the one hand she says she wants to be their friend, but on the other there is a tone of reproach in the way she addresses them, as though she's working out unfinished business. Martha's also concerned about Liv. She feels groggy herself, but Liv seems so much more so. It was the same when they were younger, she recalls, when Liv would start to show signs of inebriation after just one drink. Right now, if Martha were to make an attempt at overpowering Katherine, she couldn't count on Liv's ability to back her up.

307

'Then why do you look so worried?' Liv asks.

'That phone call she made – I think she may have been speaking to David Crown.'

Liv looks aghast. 'But I thought . . . I assumed . . . you don't think he's on his way here, do you?'

'I don't know—' Martha replies, just as Katherine struggles to her feet, crosses over to the bookcase and pulls out a photo album.

She places it on the table between them, turning it sideways on so they can all view the pages together. The first few pages contain pictures of the young Katherine, on this very boat, some showing her with her father and in others with the large bearded man she must have referred to earlier as John. In all of the pictures, she's smiling, relaxed – sitting in deckchairs, washing windows, waving at the photographer.

'You look happy,' Liv says.

'I was,' Katherine replies. 'We were very close, Dad and I.'

'And John? Did you know him long?' Martha asks, aware that her words are coming out mushy. Even now, she can't resist the urge to investigate, to add lines between the ever-increasing dots.

'Oh, yes. I'd known John since I was quite small. I used to pretend he was my grandfather.' Katherine conceals a smile and continues to turn the pages, pausing when she reaches the familiar news article photo taken at the Square Wheels cabin. She points to each of the volunteers in the picture: 'Jo, me, Dad, Juliet, Tom.'

The next photograph is one of her on a bicycle, a red cardigan visible beneath her white Square Wheels tabard, her extraordinarily long, dark hair fanning out in the breeze. Even through her blue jeans it's clear to see that her knees are wider than her thighs, that there's not an ounce of spare fat on her. She's cycling along the towpath, and the image is so familiar to Martha that it quite halts her ability to speak. A flash of red and white in the darkness. A feeling of guilt and, what – relief? Gratitude? It's there, and then it's gone. Is it the effect of the drugs or simply her rubbish memory?

To Martha's surprise, the next few pages show a full set of pictures chronicling the summer boat trip David Crown took them on as a thank-you for their work on the Garden of Reflection. The details of this occasion have grown clearer to Martha over the past couple of weeks, to the point that she can now remember them all setting off together, having taken instruction from the boat's owner at the canalside. What she also recalls now is that David Crown's wife had been there too, as they boarded. She had been dressed immaculately in a pale lilac shift dress, her dark hair piled into a high twist, her carefully made-up eyes assessing each of them as she passed the hamper of sandwiches and drinks over the side. As David started the motors and they'd set sail, she'd squinted sternly against the bright sunshine and waved them off. It was that image and Liv's whispered words that Martha recalls in particular: '*Blimey*. She looks like she just lost a pound and found a penny.' They'd laughed behind David's back as he steered his way along the lock; laughed at his grumpy-looking wife and joked that it was no wonder he'd rather hang out with a bunch of teenagers. The hairs rise on Martha's arms, and she shudders at the thought.

'I wasn't there that day,' Katherine says, with something like sadness. 'They're Dad's pictures. Mum said I had already over-done it, helping out at the old swimming pool the weekend before. She and Dad had quite an argument about it, but, of course, she won. I was desperate to come. It was so unfair. I just wanted to be part of it all.'

309

Martha and Liv pull the album towards them, for a moment forgetting themselves as they pore over these ancient images of them paddling in the water, climbing the riverside trees, picnicking on the bank. There's the two of them, along with Juliet and Tom, with David Crown only featuring in a couple of the photos, in which case Tom's absence suggests it must have been him taking the picture with David's camera. In one, they're lined up on the boat giving a silly military salute, David in central position in a tatty captain's hat, Juliet and Liv on one side, Martha on the other. All of them smile towards the camera's lens, except for Martha, whose laughing face looks up towards David, as though he's said something hilarious.

Her stomach lurches at the picture, and all at once that earlier image collides with a new realisation.

That night, when she'd walked away from Juliet on the towpath, a cyclist had passed her, travelling in Juliet's direction, and Martha had been relieved to see it was another Square Wheels volunteer. Martha had been a bit worse for wear, and the cyclist had passed by in too much of a blur for her to see exactly who it was, but she'd caught enough of a glimpse to know the girl was wearing a red top beneath her white tabard, with a dark ponytail flowing behind her, as long as a horse's tail.

'It was *you* on the towpath that night,' Martha says, roughly turning the pages back until she reaches the image again.

'What do you mean?' Katherine asks.

'You were there, weren't you? When I left Juliet that night, Katherine – you saw her, didn't you? You saw her on the towpath before she went missing.' Martha's head is throbbing, and she feels nauseous. She wants to ask Katherine what she put in their coffee, but she has to keep her focused, has to keep *herself* focused.

Katherine snaps the album shut and snatches it to her chest, her eyebrows knitting together. 'I saw all sorts of things, Martha Benn!' she barks, a petulant rise in her voice. 'And not just on that night!' She looks like a child, rebuked for stealing biscuits from the jar.

Could Katherine be Juliet's killer? Is Toby's theory possible – that David Crown covered up his daughter's crime before disappearing himself, in a bid to divert suspicion from her? Katherine is certainly crazy enough, and she has a strength and reckless temper that Martha knows only too well. If Katherine *is* behind Juliet's death, she and Liv are in real danger. They have to get off this boat and away from her as quickly as possible.

Overhead, there's a distinct clunk as a hard heel lands on the deck, and with hope Martha visualises Toby clambering over the side in his polished Italian brogues, more suited to the boardroom than the waterside. Is it one o'clock yet? Please, *please* let this be Toby, come to help them out of this mess.

Katherine's head snaps towards the staircase and back to her two captives, warning in her fierce expression.

'Katherine, you can't keep us here forever,' Martha says gently. 'Toby's here now. Why don't I go up and see him, while you make him a drink?'

'It's not Toby, silly!' she replies tartly. 'I *told* you, we're expecting a visitor. Now, please, best behaviour!'

Martha's worst fears are confirmed when she realises that there are no voices as she'd expect if it were Toby and the others, but just a single set of footsteps that have come to a halt beyond the wooden hatch at the top of the staircase. Could this really be David Crown, after all those years in hiding? Does he really think he can just return to the scene of the crime, and start again as though nothing ever happened?

'Who is it?' Liv asks, but Katherine is too preoccupied to hear her, too busy straightening her blouse, running her fingers through her hair.

'Do I look alright?' she asks Martha and Liv, but neither of them replies. Like her, their attention is fixed on the wooden hatch, intent on finding out who is on the other side of that door. Terror courses through Martha as her mind flits about, searching for any possible ways in which they might escape from this madness unscathed. If it is David Crown, what can he want with them? Does he want to silence Martha as he did Juliet, knowing as he must by now that her evidence has caused the police to reopen Juliet's case? But what good would it do him?

The door at the top slams open, and, to Martha's pulse-thumping astonishment, the feet that appear don't belong to David Crown at all. They are the court-shoe-clad feet of his wife, Janet Crown. And, unlike the last time they met, she looks really quite well. And really quite fierce.

34. **Katherine**

'Katherine,' Mum says curtly, hesitating on her way down the steps to bolt the door behind her. She's dressed up, her face fully made-up, her patchy scalp hidden beneath her favourite French twist wig. She pauses at the bottom step and surveys the small space, running her eyes over Martha and Liv, before fixing back on me. 'You've put on weight, I see. And your *hair*, God help us!'

I daren't look at my friends, I'm so embarrassed. I should say something! I should show them, and her, that I'm not afraid any more. That I'm my own person these days, with my own house, making my own decisions!

'That's rude,' I say, but really it's just a mumble by the time it comes out.

Mum walks over to the seating area, tippy-tappy on her shiny shoes, but she doesn't sit down, instead choosing to stand with her back to the sink, her patent handbag still hooked over the crook of her arm. There's a sneer on her face and I know it's because she hates this lovely boat. She always has.

'So that hairy old tramp left this floating heap to you, did he?' she says, because she's only just getting over the news of it. When I called her and told her where I was, she refused to come until she heard I had Martha and Liv here, and that I was going to tell them everything I know. Well, that did it, because here she is now, not half an hour later. She may seem calm and in control, but she must be worried because why else would she set foot on this 'floating heap' as she calls it?

I jut out my chin. 'If you're talking about John, yes, he did. And I'm very grateful for it!'

'So what about that house you bought with my money? How's it working out for you, living on your own? Not very well, I'd say, judging by the size of you.' Now, incredibly, she looks to Martha and Liv, pulling a face that says: Isn't she a selfish girl? Isn't she a disgusting fatty?

'You *gave* me that money, after Granny died.'

'You extorted it from me, you mean.'

Extorted is a little on the strong side, I want to say, and I open my mouth to speak but she holds up a silencing hand. I know what she's thinking. Not in front of the guests.

'I've told you before, Katherine, don't call her Granny. You never even knew the woman.'

It's true. I had a grandmother somewhere, and I never even met her. Mum would visit her once a year, but always alone, packing a small suitcase and disappearing for a few nights at a time. I suspected that Granny was rich, because my mother would return every time with a new outfit and hairdo, smelling of expensive perfume. Once I heard Dad ask her, 'Have you told her about us yet?' and I wondered what on earth he could mean.

Martha is staring at Mum with an intensity that I can't quite read, and I think I need to take control somehow, though I'm not entirely sure how. I have no plan, no clear idea what I think will happen now that Mum is here. All I know is that

314

I want to get to the truth of it all, before I go mad with the not knowing. I have so many conflicting versions of the past, so many adaptations of the same events that now I can't tell which were dreams and which were real, or which were put there by other people. *By Mum.* That's all I want: the truth – that, and Martha and Liv's friendship.

I pick up the stove kettle and refill it at the sink, trying to conjure up some semblance of normality. 'Mum, this is Martha and Liv. This is my mother, Janet.'

'We've met,' Mum says with a cursory hand flick towards Martha. 'She came asking questions about your father. Another vulture, I'm afraid, Katherine.'

'Martha's not a vulture!' I protest, but Mum dismisses my comment with the slow arching of one eyebrow.

'She'd got it into her head that your father is dead. But I put her straight, and showed her all the postcards he's sent to me over the years. You've seen them, haven't you, Katherine?'

'Yes . . .' I reply, but I'm feeling uncertain now, because I know that tone of voice. It's the one she uses when she's trying to make something sound better than it really is. When she's lying.

'What about Juliet?' Martha asks, speaking for the first time since Mum's arrival. 'Do you really believe he had nothing to do with her disappearance?'

'Of course he didn't,' Mum replies. 'Her disappearance was nothing to do with us. What reason could David possibly have for doing harm to that girl?'

'If he wanted to be in a relationship with her,' Martha replies. 'Perhaps she spurned his advances? Maybe he couldn't risk her letting anyone know?'

Mum slams the palms of her hands against the tabletop, thrusting her face forward until it is just inches from Martha's.

Liv has shrunk as far back against the window as is humanly possible.

Mum spits out the words with precision. 'David was NOT interested in that girl! And she did not "spurn his advances" as you so disgustingly put it!'

'How can you be sure?' Martha replies, unmoved.

'Because I can!' Mum shrieks, and she turns towards me, grabbing hold of my coat sleeve and tugging me to her side. 'Tell them, Katherine!' she says. 'You tell them exactly what you told me. Tell them what you saw!'

And now I don't know what to say, because it was all my fault, what happened that night, me and my stupid pride, and my stupid mouth! Mum slaps me hard across the cheek, and it's Liv who screams at her to stop, not me, and I want to throw my arms around Liv and say, thank-you-thank-you-thank-you for being my friend. For taking my side over hers!

'If she won't tell you what happened, then I will,' Mum says now, picking up the knife that I'd left on the side, tapping the flat of the blade against the heel of her hand. 'It was *David* who spurned *her* advances. *She* was all over him, and *he* rejected *her*! There! What do you make of that?' She looks so pleased with herself that I think perhaps she will just leave now, just clip-clop her feet back up those steps and disappear forever. I wish I'd never asked her here in the first place.

Liv is shaking her head, and Martha looks stunned. They don't believe it; they don't believe anything could have happened between Juliet and my dad. And they'd be right.

'Jules wasn't interested in David Crown,' Liv murmurs, to herself as much as anyone else.

Martha's expression grows distant, as though she's searching for something just outside of her grasp. Now she looks at me.

316

'Katherine, what does your mother mean, "Tell them what you saw"?'

No more lies. No more lies, I tell myself. *That's* why I wanted Mum here, so that the truth might come out once and for all. No more lies! 'It was you, Martha,' I say at last. 'The week before Juliet disappeared. It was you I saw kissing Dad in the Square Wheels cabin.'

The bitter cold of that night had been almost intolerable, and Mum was growing increasingly belligerent about the fact that Dad was working so many evenings at Square Wheels lately. He'd tried to explain to her that there had been a new influx of homeless along the riverside recently, that the meals service was needed more now than ever before, but she'd got jealous and spiteful, and I was taking the brunt of it in his absence. Things between Mum and me had deteriorated steadily, ever since I'd had to pull out of sixth form with ill health before the first term had even started, only to find out some weeks later that she'd been poisoning my breakfast with laxatives to keep me thin. To keep me weak. I'd been rebelling, in some small way, spending more time on John's boat, earning a bit of money here and there, running errands for him and his neighbours. Every penny went on feeding myself up again, albeit unconsciously, on doughnuts and crisps and chocolate bars and fizzy drinks. Each mouthful was a victory, a punch in the air, a two-fingered salute; a secret of my own that she could never take away from me. If I'd been less of a coward I'd have confronted her, told her about my secret bingeing, but no, instead I used Dad against her and it all backfired in the most horrible of ways.

I'd been on John's boat that evening, delaying the moment of returning home as I knew Dad would be at Square Wheels until late. I didn't want to see Mum, not if there was a chance she'd still be in the cutting mood I'd left her in earlier. As I cycled along the towpath, it occurred to me I could meet Dad at the cabin instead – I'd help him to clear up with the other volunteers, and we could walk home together. Mum would leave me alone if Dad was with me. She'd be too preoccupied with questioning him to bother with me.

As I approached the cabin, I spotted Dad through the small side window and it looked as if he was there on his own, packing up the last few things before shutting up for the night. I leaned my bike against the hedge and turned the corner, about to call out to him, when I realised he wasn't alone at all. Martha was there too, perched on the corner of the worktop, swinging her legs and watching him clear up. I was surprised to see her there, as I knew she'd given up volunteering a good few months ago. I stepped back into the shadows to watch. Something in her demeanour, the way she swayed, that sleepy, sad smile on her lips, the way she eyed him so directly, told me she was drunk.

'You shouldn't be here, Martha,' Dad said. His voice was friendly, concerned. 'Come on, love. You're in no state to cycle home alone. I'll walk you back.'

He held out his hand to help her off the table, but instead of dropping down she yanked his arm so that he fell against her, his chest to hers. Then she pressed her lips to his, bringing her fingers up and into his hair, cradling his head with her hands. It was a moment of such unfettered passion that I nearly cried out in astonishment. I had never seen Mum kiss Dad in that way. But the moment lasted no more than a second, because now Dad was pulling back, holding Martha by the shoulders and telling her to stop it, to take a look at what she was doing.

'Martha!' he insisted. 'It's me – David! You don't want to be kissing me, love! Come on, let's get you home.' And with that he led her, with her head hung low, out of the cabin and on to the path.

Around the corner, I waited long enough for them to disappear from view, and I cycled home in a whirr of excited shock. Martha! Kissing *my* dad! I could hardly blame her, of course, he was so lovely, but rather than making me feel mad at Martha, it made my anger towards my mother even greater, as it proved what I had known all along. My dad was a wonderful man – a good, kind and caring man – and my mother didn't appreciate him.

I shouldn't have done it, I know it now as I knew it then. But I couldn't help myself, when I arrived home and found my mother glaring and cold at the kitchen sink, spoiling for a fight. I couldn't hold back the bad feelings that had been building in me for the past eighteen years.

'I just saw Dad kissing one of the volunteers,' I said plainly. I wanted to see her pain; I wanted to watch her cry.

'Who?' she demanded, and to my dismay I saw that she was neither hurt nor surprised. This was what she'd been waiting for: proof of his bad nature.

'I don't know her name,' I lied. 'But she looked lovely. About my age, tall and slim with golden-brown hair. It's no wonder he couldn't resist her!'

I didn't stay around to see her reaction. I just walked away, shut myself in my room, and lay in bed, breathlessly waiting for Dad to return and the fireworks to explode. But they never did. Not that night, nor the following day, nor the day after that, and soon I came to fear the worst. She hadn't confronted him. I'd given her this knowledge, and now, I knew, she would use it against him when it suited her best.

Like the stupid fool that she'd always thought me to be, I'd handed her all the power.

Martha looks as though she's taken a punch to the stomach.

'You were drunk,' I told her. 'I don't think you meant to do it – and Dad was really fine about the whole thing. He stopped you, and then he walked you home. Remember?'

I want her to remember – I want her to tell Mum just how wrong she is.

Slowly, Martha nods her head, and I see tears springing to her eyes as her fingers grasp for Liv's. I want a friendship like that; I want a friend I can reach for when I need support. Could Martha or Liv be that friend to me?

Mum is shaking my arm, forcing me to look at her. 'You said it was that other one! Katherine, *you said it was Juliet!*' Her eyes look wild, and I can see just how crazy this is making her, the idea that she got something so wrong – that it was all for nothing.

'No, I didn't, Mum! I never said it was Juliet! I just told you what she looked like – I never said her name!'

Martha's face shifts in waves of understanding. 'Our hair,' she says, 'it was practically the same. Janet, did you—'

But Mum's on her like a wild animal, hooking her fingers into Martha's hair, slamming her cheek against the table, the knife held vertically at the nape of her neck. Martha's hands lie either side of her head, palm down, white with fear. She's too weak to fight back.

'You!' Mum screams. 'All these years I've been watching you on the television, Martha Benn! There I was, enjoying your television shows, and all along, it was *you*? You're the reason I lost David? *You're* the cause of all of this?'

I'm frozen. How has this all gone so wrong? I can't see Martha's face now, but Liv looks terrified, her hands clasped to her chest, and I watch her cast a panicked gaze around the cabin, trying to find a way out of this, a way to get away from my terrible mother. Maybe I should let them go? But then what? What happens then?

'Mum, please,' I try, but the look she shoots me is so furious that I don't know what else I can say.

'Don't you dare, Katherine. You're as much to blame as this little prick-tease.' She sees me flinch at her coarse language, and she purses her lips. 'Do you think it's right that this little slut has been free to walk around unpunished all these years, while I've suffered the life sentence of a world without your dad?'

I stammer, trying to get my brain to work as fast as my heart rate. 'No,' I reply. 'No, it's not.'

'Good,' she says, and she lifts up the knife and brings it down hard through Martha's hand.

I scream as she tears it away again, returning the bloodied blade to rest on the nape of Martha's neck. Blood seeps between Martha's fingers, pooling around her hand like an abstract image.

'Good,' she says again, and now she smiles at me as though I'm on her side. 'We need to finish this, Katherine.'

With those words, I feel the blinkers drop from my eyes, and *everything* makes sense. We're not on the same side, Mum and I. All these wasted years, when I thought that she was protecting me from the world, from what happened that night. But now I realise, with a clarity that swells inside me as strength: she wasn't protecting me.

She was protecting herself.

35. **Martha**

She realises now that she'd never *really* forgotten what had happened between her and David Crown on that winter night, but shame and embarrassment had pushed it to the far recesses of her mind. Slumped here now as she is, her face pressed against the table, a knife at her neck, jumbled recollections stream past her inner eye in a rush of information. She'd had a crush on him, one that had started months earlier, on the day of the summer boat trip – the day that had marked the end of Martha's working at Square Wheels. After their trip, they'd returned the boat to its owner, and the others – Juliet, Liv and Tom – had all headed off home for supper. But Martha, as ever, was in no rush. It was Sunday, Dad's worst day for drinking, and she wanted to stay with David, wanted to delay the moment she'd have to walk in through the front door of Stanley House. Apart from that, she was still bruised by what she'd seen on the riverbank: Juliet and Liv, their faces so close they were almost touching, whispering, leaving her out. When she'd asked them about it, they'd told her she was imagining things. Now, in the stark light of this new revelation, Martha sees it for what it really was. It wasn't a secret they'd shared behind that tree: it was a kiss.

'I'll walk with you, if that's OK,' she had said to David, who was on his way to the cabin to make preparations for the evening's Square Wheels drop.

'Sure,' he'd replied, and he'd handed her the empty picnic hamper to carry. It was August, and the sun was making its slow descent overhead, a pink hue tinting the breezeless sky. She felt happy just to be there beside him.

Inside the cabin, David set about wiping down the work-tops, counting out paper beakers and filling the steel urns for boiling water. 'Hadn't you better get home, Martha?' he'd asked, looking back to where she stood gazing out of the small window, watching a family of ducks plopping down the canal bank and into the water. 'Your dad must be wondering where you've got to.'

'I'd rather stay here with you,' she replied, breathing in the freedom of this quiet space alone with him. She watched as he counted out paper bags and napkins. His shoulders were broad, his movements fluid, relaxed. 'You're much better company.'

He'd laughed. 'Don't be daft!'

'I could stay and do an extra shift,' she'd said then, moving away from the window, and quite out of nowhere she'd imagined herself crossing the cabin floor, putting her hands to his face.

'No need, love,' he had answered without looking up. 'It's been a long day – I expect your dad's got your supper waiting for you back home?'

Martha didn't reply; she didn't know how to reply. She stood, stuck to the spot, and stared at the side of his head, trying to find words. And then she saw the subtle shift in him, the tiniest flinch of regret as he realised the unlikeliness of what he'd said. Which meant that he *knew*. That somehow he

323

knew Martha's dad was a waster. That there would be no hot meal waiting at home for her tonight or any night.

David put down his butter knife and turned towards her, leaning against the worktop. Martha was stranded in the centre of the dimly lit hut, unable to speak. She was adrift, like a boat cut free of its moorings.

'Who told you?' she asked, a whisper.

He ran the heel of his hand over his brow, apology and, worse, pity in his expression, and Martha wanted to die. 'No one told me – no one had to tell me, love. Your dad stopped by here one night, not long after you'd started volunteering. He wanted to check out who his daughter was spending time with, quite rightly. But he was, well, you know . . .'

'Pissed?' Martha offered.

David nodded, and to her deep embarrassment she felt her face collapse into a rush of unexpected tears, and she slapped her palms to her eyes, wishing she could vanish. What would he think of her now? her mind screamed behind the darkness of her hands. Of *course* he'd rather she went home than stay and help him. Why would he want to be around someone like her? *Nobody* wanted her. Juliet and Liv had each other, more so since that bloody Venice trip than ever before, and dad was always so out of it that she might as well not exist. Even her mother had fucked off before the job of parenting was done. Why did she keep on screwing up like this?

Without warning, his arms were around her – David's arms – warm and anchoring, and he was stroking the hair from her face, tucking it behind her ear and saying, 'Shush, Martha. Shush. Come on, now.' Through his cotton T-shirt she could smell the lingering warmth of the sun's rays on his skin, the subtle tang of boat grease and long grass. She wanted to stay there, stay in the heat of his embrace; she wanted to know how it might feel to be kissed by a man like David . . .

'I understand,' he said. 'I really do.'

Suddenly angry, she pulled back, swiping at her tears. 'How can you understand?' she demanded. 'No one can. None of you.'

David's hand still rested on her upper arm, his face soft, forgiving. 'My father was the same, Martha, love. My dad was a drinker too. Believe me, *I* understand.'

But, rather than feeling a kindred connection with him, a fresh sensation of crashing exposure washed over Martha and she knew she had to get out of there. It was bad enough that her best friends suspected her problems at home, but the fact that they could only imagine was of some comfort at least. They couldn't know how bad it was, how it made her *feel* – not just about her father, but about herself. But this was different. David Crown *knew*. Suddenly it was as though he could see right down inside her – could see that she was a fraud, that the neutral face she presented was a lie, that the smile was fake, the laughter forced. He knew, because he'd been there too.

Martha pulled away, apologising through her tears, and ran.

That night she sat in her room drinking her dad's vodka, and vowed she would never return to Square Wheels again. And she very nearly kept that vow, apart from that one spontaneous night to come in late December when, following a fight with Dad, she would stumble, cold and drunk, into David's cabin, only to be rejected. The night that Katherine would see them. The night that would ultimately lead to Juliet's death.

It *was* her fault, Martha realises now. Just as she'd feared – only not in the way she had always believed. Now, she had no choice but to put things right for her friend. She had to get out of here alive, and she had to see justice served. She owed it to Juliet.

'So, it was you, Janet?' she says now. Her voice is thick, her movements constrained beneath Janet Crown's dry palm.

The woman doesn't deny it, just lifts her hand momentarily to slap it back down on Martha's ear, sending a clap of pain running through the tight stitches nestling in the back of her head. From her restricted position, Martha has an obscured view through the windows at the front of cabin, and in the distance she can see them coming. They're running along the towpath, a group of four, and as they draw closer she can make them out more clearly: Toby, Jay, Sally and Finn. The closer they get, the more afraid Martha is that Toby will come charging in, provoking Janet Crown to carry out her threat to plunge this knife straight through her vertebrae and out the other side. She wouldn't stand a chance.

Beside her, Liv is silently shaking, and Martha can almost hear the cogs of her mind turning, searching for some way to distract Janet and get Katherine on side.

Out on the path, the group are gaining ground, but in a flash they're out of sight again, passing the window, moving on to the far side. Will Toby know she is inside the boat? Will he notice her spotty glove and know that it marks their location? Or will he miss it entirely and continue along the towpath, oblivious to their presence?

Janet Crown's grip is surprisingly sturdy for one so frail. Right now, she's the most dangerous of risks: a woman with nothing to lose. Katherine is completely out of Martha's view, but she knows her best hope is to appeal to the younger woman, her contemporary. She senses that Katherine isn't a bad person but a damaged soul, and Martha knows something about that.

'Katherine, did you know that your mother killed Juliet?'

There's a long delay, before Janet cries out, 'Oh, for God's sake, Katherine! Speak up! You're not a mouse!'

'Yes,' Katherine murmurs. 'I saw her do it,' she says, but there's no pride there, no shared victory.

'You poor thing,' Liv says, her voice clearer now, and in an instant I know what she's doing. She's applying her psychology training; she's bringing Katherine over. 'That must have been traumatic. How did you cope?'

Janet reaches over Martha and smacks Liv around the side of her head. '*Shut. Up.*'

'It was horrible,' Katherine says, but then she's silent again.

Martha's thoughts flash and whirr. If she's going to kill me, she reasons, I might as well get the truth out of her now. Someone will come out of this alive, even if it isn't her. Someone will be able to testify to Janet Crown's confession.

'So, Janet, here's what I don't understand,' she says, her voice challenging. 'If it was you who killed Juliet, why did your husband go on the run? Why not you? Did David help you to dispose of the body? Was it David who buried Juliet under the Garden of Reflection?'

'Ha!' she laughs, harsh and loud. 'That girl's not buried underneath the garden!'

'What?' This is not the response Martha had anticipated.

'Juliet Sherman is not hidden under that patio, you fool. Some investigator you turned out to be.'

'Then who is?' Liv and Martha ask at once.

There's an almighty crash as the wooden door at the top of the steps splinters and falls in, followed by the sound of feet rushing down into the cabin. Martha can't see who it is, or how many, but when she hears Finn's voice she releases the air from her lungs in one long breath.

327

'Alright, Mrs Crown. You can let Martha go now. Don't make things any worse for yourself. The police are just along the bank – so there's nowhere to run. Mrs Crown?'

Janet's hand presses harder on the side of Martha's face, the knife tip jabbing at her neck, and it's plain she's not going to give up that easily.

'Martha!' Toby cries out, and just knowing he's alright, that he's *here*, is enough to give her a new surge of courage.

'Janet!' she says, raising her voice. 'What do you mean, it's not Juliet under that patio?'

'Mum?' Katherine asks, and it's clear she's crying now. 'Mum, why is she asking *you*?'

Martha's impatience breaks through the fog of sedation. She doesn't care about anything more than she cares about this: she *has* to find out what happened to Juliet. '*Just tell us!*' she screams, silencing the room.

There's a lingering hush, and the room is so quiet that for a few seconds all Martha can hear is the thump of her own pulse. Finally, it's not Janet Crown who speaks, but Finn.

'She's not lying, love. The forensics team just confirmed it – the remains from the Garden of Reflection aren't Juliet's.'

Uselessly, Martha tries to push back against Janet Crown's hand. 'But, Finn, if it's not Juliet, who is it?'

'It's David Crown, love. The remains belong to David Crown.'

With a frenzied scream, Katherine Crown swipes up the iron kettle and swings it against her mother's head, knocking her from her feet, sending the blade slashing across the back of Martha's neck. Toby is at her side in a second, rushing past Katherine and pressing a clean handkerchief to the wound. Finn is attending to Janet Crown, who now lies crumpled beside the sink, a dark and bloodied bruise already forming at her temple. Katherine sits balled on the floor in the far corner, her hands clasped around her knees, the kettle at her feet.

Dragging the table back, Toby helps Martha and Liv from their seats, guiding them together, woozy and stumbling, up into the winter sunlight above.

The police swoop in in a flurry of noise and activity, arriving on the scene as Toby sits Martha on the wooden bench beside the houseboat. His arm is around her shoulders, his other hand pressing the handkerchief to her neck. 'It's just a surface wound,' he reassures her, pulling her closer, kissing the top of her head as though it's the most natural thing in the world.

Liv stands to Martha's side, watching the activity at the houseboat, a steady stream of tears coursing down her face. She's in shock; they're all in shock. Five minutes ago they believed they had found Juliet, that at last they might put her body to rest. But it isn't Juliet under that patio in the Garden of Reflection, is it? It's David Crown. It's David bloody Crown. Liv sits beside Martha now, clinging to her as though she'll never let go. How she's missed Liv, Martha thinks, fighting the shudder of emotion that threatens to spill out of her. Somehow, she knows that Liv is back in her life now; all that is missing is Juliet.

'Where is she?' Liv whispers, her words still sodden with whatever it is Katherine put in their drinks. 'What did she do with Juliet?'

A fresh wave of anger flashes in Martha. She doesn't have time to wait for Janet to confess in some interview room, to delay this nightmare any longer. More than anyone, Alan Sherman doesn't have time, and, for him, Martha gathers the strength to make her voice heard.

'Janet!' she shouts over as Mrs Crown emerges from the boat, flanked by two uniformed officers. The woman turns to face her, her expression stony, unrepentant. Martha softens her own tone. 'For her father's sake, Janet – please. Where is Juliet?'

Janet Crown studies Martha for a moment, before jerking her chin back towards the houseboat. 'She's under the boat,' she says simply, and then she's led away, her neat head held high.

36. **Martha**

It's getting late, and back at the apartment Toby sits at one end of the sofa, Martha at the other, takeaway curry containers spread out over the coffee table in front of them. The room feels more like home than it has for months, music playing softly from the kitchen, the London skyline glinting as far as the eye can see. Right now, Martha wouldn't want to be anywhere else, or with anyone else, for all the money in the world.

After several hours in A&E, the doctors had patched up her hand and given her the all-clear, handing her over to Toby, who had remained with her the entire time, despite her protestations that he should head off home and get some rest. Before they'd left the canal, she had offered Liv a bed for the night, but once the medics had checked her over and she'd given her statement, her friend had been keen to get back to the twins, and the police had arranged for her to be driven home. When they'd said goodbye, Liv had assured Martha that she'd be back in a week or two for a proper reunion. A *happier* reunion, Martha had promised as they'd embraced at the riverside. Already, she's been on the phone, telling

Martha she arrived home safely, and they'd wept together, the realisation that it was finally over dawning on them both. It feels like the start of something; it feels as though Liv is back in her life for good.

Martha's phone is, surprisingly, intact; in fact, it had saved her. When Katherine had knocked it out of her hand, the connection had stayed open, and Toby had heard enough to call the police before setting off at speed to find her. An hour ago, Finn had sent a text through.

> Police divers have recovered the remains of a female body from the canal bed beneath the houseboat *Dovedale*. We've found her, love. We've found Juliet.

Martha's reaction is strangely serene. Somehow this seems less terrible than the idea of Juliet being buried beneath the concrete and rubble of the Bridge School gardens. The canal was a place Juliet knew and loved, the towpath a well-worn route the girls took together throughout their schooldays; it was the backdrop to their teenage lives. It seems oddly fitting that this was where she had been all those years, silently waiting for them to piece it all together, to be returned. If Juliet could see how this had all turned out, she'd be proud, of that Martha is certain.

Thank you, Finn, she responds to the text message. It's all she needs to say.

Earlier, as they cleared the scene at the houseboat, the police had found an empty bottle of sleeping tablets in Katherine Crown's bag, so at least they know what she put in their coffee. Assessing Liv and Martha's limited level of sedation, the doctors aren't too worried, but Martha is under strict instructions to rest for the next twenty-four hours, especially since she was already supposed to be recovering from that knock on the head two nights earlier. Despite Toby's nagging, she's certain she'll be fine in the morning, when she has arranged to meet Tom Sherman at the Sparrow Hospice, where his dad was admitted yesterday night. It turns out that Alan Sherman has recently taken a serious turn for the worse, and by the time Janet and Katherine Crown were under arrest, Tom was already on the next flight home to be at his father's bedside, unaware of this huge breakthrough in the case of his missing sister. Of course, this is the news they've all been waiting for, albeit bittersweet news, and Martha prays that Alan can hang on until the morning, so that he might die knowing his beloved daughter will at last be laid to rest.

'We did alright, didn't we?' Martha says now, tearing into a piece of naan bread, using it to mop up the remainder of her curry. For the first time in weeks, her appetite is raging.

'Not bad for a jumped-up posh boy.' Toby smiles, reminding her of her snippy earlier self.

God, she had been such an arse to him back then. 'Or a council-flat girl who slept her way to the top?'

'*Touché*,' Toby replies, reaching out to pat her knee. It's a warm gesture, natural and uninhibited. He passes her a bowl containing bhajis and she takes one, biting into it, glad to not be alone.

'Glen was pretty pleased with the outcome,' she says. She'd phoned him from her hospital cubicle, anxious that he shouldn't hear the news of Janet Crown's arrest from anyone else. 'I thought he was going to break into song when I told him that Jay and Sally got the whole thing on film: you and Finn breaking down the door on the boat, the police arrest, my dripping, bloody hand. If this pilot doesn't guarantee us a full series, I don't know what will!'

Toby sits back, pushing his plate away, bringing his socked feet on to the sofa between them. 'Jeez, you had me worried back there, Martha Benn,' he says, running a hand through his uncommonly messy hair. He looks exhausted. 'When Vicky Duke told me what had happened back in eighty-six – about David Crown's wife abducting her like that – it all fell into place. I just knew Janet Crown was at the heart of it all.'

'So, tell me again. She *abducted* Vicky Duke? Janet Crown?'

He shakes his head, as though still making sense of it all. 'Yes. Vicky said she had been about to retract her allegation about David assaulting her – it was a complete lie – the very next day. But on her way home from school that night Mrs Crown pulled up at the roadside and bundled her into the boot of her car. She drove her out to a secluded spot in the woods and held a knife to her throat, telling her she'd kill her and the rest of her family if she didn't drop the charge. She left her there, in the woods, to walk the five miles home alone in the dark. Vicky was so scared, she never breathed a word of it.'

'Wow, Janet Crown really *is* something else, isn't she? Pretending to have cancer, for God's sake! And sending herself postcards for all those years. According to Katherine, her mother went abroad with a social group every May, and the postcards would always arrive shortly after. I think Katherine knew in her heart that her dad wasn't coming home, but her mother kept that seed of doubt alive just enough to keep her on-side.'

'What will happen to Katherine?' he asks.

Martha sighs heavily. 'Finn says she'll be charged with assault and wasting police time, maybe even identity theft. But she won't get long, and with any luck she'll start to get the kind of help she really needs. You can't begin to think what it does to a person, carrying a secret like that for so many years. Imagine knowing your own mother is a murderer?'

'So Janet killed Juliet – we know that much – and then we can only assume that she did away with David when he confronted her about it? She as good as admitted it, didn't she?'

Martha brings her legs up too, stretching them along the sofa so that her feet rest against Toby. 'She can't have known the cement was due to be delivered to the school that week. That was one hell of a lucky break she had. Her husband virtually prepared his own grave.'

Toby reaches for his notebook, scribbling down a few thoughts, a small crease forming between his brows. 'But it blows the theory that David killed Tilly Jones back in 1970, doesn't it? Poor bastard, dead all these years and under suspicion for two deaths he had no responsibility for whatsoever.'

'Tilly Jones,' Martha says. 'Just a coincidence, I guess. Like that runaway Charlotte Bennett. Mind you, thank God she disappeared when she did. I don't think the police would have reopened the Juliet case if she hadn't.' She smiles at Toby. 'Hey, maybe Tilly Jones could be our next cold case?'

'Slow down,' he says. 'Why don't you get yourself better first?' But still, he looks interested, and Martha knows he won't be able to resist getting to work on it the minute this case is over.

She runs her fingers over the lines of her silver bangle, rotating it, feeling the throb of pain returning to the site of her stab wound. Thankfully, the blade had missed her tendons by a whisker, slicing cleanly through the flesh and out the other side.

'Where did you find it?' he asks.

'It was in my memory box all along,' she replies, 'in an envelope with a load of old cards and keepsakes that I didn't even know I had. I found all sorts of things in there – I can't

335

wait to show them to Liv.' She smiles at the sight of Toby at the end of her sofa, at the warmth that radiates from the contact between her feet and his body.

'Martha . . .' he says, hesitating uncertainly.

'You want to know why I didn't say anything about me and David Crown? About the kiss that Katherine saw?'

Toby nods, laying a steadying hand on her foot.

'The truth is, Toby, I barely remembered it. Back then, my life was in chaos. It's not that I'd forgotten, exactly, but at the time I was making so many stupid mistakes – drinking, smoking, getting off with the wrong kinds of boys. Don't get me wrong, I wasn't a slapper or anything . . .'

He laughs.

'I just . . . I just kind of lurched from one disaster to the next. My dad was a full-on alcoholic, and my mum had left home two years earlier. I didn't have siblings, and Juliet and Liv were the closest thing I had to family. When David came along, I think he was just such a nice man that I got a bit of a crush on him. It was nothing more than a bit of mooning about, and a drunken lunge at the poor beggar. It was such a small thing – and I was so ashamed of myself – that I don't think my mind held on to it, especially after what happened with Juliet. I guess the minute that David was under suspicion for her disappearance, it suited me to forget any positive feelings I had towards him. I think I just pushed those memories away.' Martha suppresses a yawn, stretching her arms high, pressing her toes against Toby's side.

'You're tired,' he says. 'Maybe I should go?' But he doesn't move, doesn't go to stand up.

'You don't have to,' Martha replies. 'You could stay.'

Their eyes are locked again, in that way that sends a tremor through her, and she dares herself not to look away. Toby takes a deep breath.

'So, you and my dad,' he says. 'Don't you think we should talk about it?'

They are apart now, the moment of intimacy lost, the atmosphere of ease between them strained, and Martha feels off balance. 'So what do you want to talk about?'

Toby stalls for a moment, shifts uncomfortably in his seat. 'Well, he's been phoning you, hasn't he? My dad.'

Martha puts a hand to her mouth, stifles a smile. 'Dylan? You think *Dylan's* been phoning me?'

'Well, *yes*. All those calls you've been rejecting – from "D" – I mean, you've been so cagey about it, and you wouldn't tell me when I asked who it was. I thought, short of it being "D" for David Crown, why else would you keep it from me?'

Martha waves for him to stop. 'Oh, Toby, you've got it all wrong. Your dad and me – it was a huge mistake. You know that, and it was all done with years ago. He wasn't really interested in me – I needed a distraction from my marriage break-up, and he needed a distraction from the boardroom. It was something and nothing. Anyway, he was *far* too old for me. "D" doesn't stand for Dylan, I promise.' She holds out her good hand, reaching for his.

'Then what does it stand for?'

It surprises Martha when she tells him the truth without hesitation. 'D for dad. It's my father.'

Toby's expression shifts into one of confusion. 'But, I thought—'

'You thought he was dead? Well, I never said as much, but I guess it's easier for me if people think that. I haven't seen him for a few years because he's been a constant problem in my life, and when he started phoning again I just didn't know how to respond. He *says* he's dying.'

'You sound like you don't believe him.'

337

She shakes her head. 'Experience tells me not to. But you know what? This time, I think he might just be telling the truth.'

'Will you see him?' Toby asks.

'I don't know,' she replies, and, for the first time, she thinks perhaps she might. She thinks now about that last desperate voicemail from him, begging her to make contact, telling her his time was running out. He's not dying, she knows, not like Alan Sherman. But he *is* killing himself. She knows she can't save him, but maybe she can show him some kindness at the end of his life. Right now, though, what Martha needs more than anything is to save herself. To be kind to herself. 'Maybe I will,' she says softly. 'So, there you have it. It was *my* dad phoning, not yours.'

Toby's fingertips brush hers, resting in the space between them. 'I know I was only a gawky teenager when you and Dad were seeing each other,' he says now. 'But I always thought you were wasted on him.' Quite naturally, he moves towards her, their fingers never breaking contact.

'Are we about to make a huge mistake, Toby?' she says, but already she knows she's lost to it.

37. Hattie

In the silence of my cell, I have all the time in the world to think about the events that conspired to bring me here, and, strangely, it is some comfort to allow myself to revisit those places in my mind.

In many respects, I regret the way things have turned out, when, for the most part, I had managed it all so well, for so long. I suppose it was Katherine's sudden desire for independence that marked the start of this certain decline, for she became so fixed on the idea of living apart that she used our secret against me. 'If I tell people what you did, I wouldn't *have* to move out. I could live here alone,' she'd said, when my inheritance eventually came through. She was giving me a choice. 'But if you let me have me the money and I *don't* tell, you could stay here, and I could move out.' So I gave her the money, and within six months she was gone. I never received an invitation to visit her new home, and she never returned to see me again. All those years I'd wasted on her, trying to convince her that David might come back any time soon, trying to convince her that the events surrounding that girl's death were not as she remembered them. I suppose it's alright for me to use the girl's name, now that I know she's not the whore I originally took her to be. *Juliet*.

There's a surreal reality that takes hold after an event of this kind, in which all sensations are intensified, while at the same time feeling muted. That night, as the girl – Juliet – lay at my feet beside the bench at the canal, I knew I had only a matter of minutes to deal with her disposal. Ahead of me was the path, the hedgerow at my back. The wind was gathering and a short distance away a loose sheet of blue tarpaulin flapped and swayed, threatening to break loose of the bungee cords that held it in place. Deftly, I unhooked the cords, freeing the plastic sheet, revealing nothing more than a pile of old junk beneath: a small mound of building blocks and sand, a rusty iron anchor and a broken length of guttering. I looked down at the girl, suddenly fearful that she might not really be dead at all. But the life had left her face altogether now, the colour of it grey-white in the dark of the towpath. Her limbs looked strangely dislocated, lying limply where they had fallen, the curled stack of her fingers resting against the toe of my shoe. For a few dreamlike seconds I gazed upon her, until the bubble burst, and I was overwhelmed by the sure conviction that I was being watched. From the shadows, just feet away, I heard Katherine's voice. '*Mummy*,' she said, and she sounded the way she did when as a child she'd tick me off for tugging her hairbrush through a knotted strand. I had no way of knowing if she'd seen me in the act of murder, but one thing was for sure: she would have to help me cover it up if I was to rely on her silence. Before us was *Dovedale*, the houseboat she and David were so fond of. It belonged to that hairy loner John, and beyond its drawn curtains a light glowed, throwing soft illumination over the narrow strip of ground that edged on to the bankside. Between us, Katherine and I untangled the girl's leg from her bike and dragged the body on to the blue sheeting I'd laid out at the boundary of the water, where a shadowy gap presented itself between the houseboat and its moorings. I saw Katherine slip the girl's bangle from her wrist and take it as her own, a swift and subtle action that I might have missed if my wits were not so alert. I pretended not to notice. Let her have it. She was always a little magpie, that one. Thought I didn't notice her squirrelling away things from my jewellery box every chance she got.

I hefted the rusty anchor across the verge and heaved it on to the girl's chest, all the while praying that no one would pass by at that moment, that we would have time to complete our work unseen. I am grateful to say my prayers were answered, and we were able to continue unhindered, undisturbed by either pedestrian or waterside dweller. With some effort, I used the bungee cords to bind the anchor to the girl's chest and after several back-breaking rolls, she was neatly wrapped in the tarpaulin. Katherine appeared stuck to the spot, until I thrust the rope length into her hands and told her to secure the package, using one of those clever knots she was so keen on. 'It must be a tight one,' I told her, hurrying her along, keeping my voice low so as not to alert the boat's inhabitant. 'Tightly, Katherine! It mustn't come off!' She did as she was told, securing the top end of the tarpaulin like a Christmas cracker, winding the rope around the body until she reached the end and tied it in a final knot. The sounds of weekend drinkers sailed in from the streets beyond the canal, and with what I can only describe as inhuman strength, we managed to manoeuvre the body up to the edge of the mooring and down through the gap between the canal wall and the boat. It plummeted like a stone, sinking to the deepest part of the canal, leaving nothing more than an undulating ripple on the water's surface.

A group of pedestrians appeared on the path in the distance, and I knew we had missed our chance to dispose of the bicycle. I could only hope that some miscreant would spot it lying there and thieve it away before morning light; one of David's lost causes, perhaps. Slipping through a break in the hedge, Katherine and I returned home, and I believed the subject would never be raised again. So when David didn't come home at teatime the following night, after those police officers had called in the morning, I went to confront him at the school where he was preparing the foundations for the new gardens. I won't dwell on it, but I knew then that he *knew* – Katherine had told him what had happened – and he could barely look me in the eye.

'Not again,' he'd said, over and over. 'Once, and I could accept it was a mistake – but twice?'

The strange thing is, he just carried on moving rubble with his gloved hands, the builder's festoon lantern throwing long shadows across the grey expanse. He was weeping, I saw, and it was more than I could bear to see this grown man reduced to such depths. I felt so betrayed by Katherine, and so disgusted by David's pathetic refusal to even look at me, so I said, 'For God's sake, David! It was an accident!'

Something in him hardened then; I saw it. He hesitated in his labour, his gaze fixed on the ground, the muscles in his jaw tensing.

'I'm leaving,' he said. '*We're* leaving. Me and Katherine. We'll go to my brother's place for a few weeks, give you some space.' Now, he looked up at me, his face anguished as he used my real name, the pet name we'd agreed he could only use in private. 'Please, Hattie, while we're away, do the right thing this time? Think of her parents, her friends. Go to the police. Because if you don't, in the next couple of days, then I will.'

'I can't,' I said, and when I saw the love he had for me leave his eyes, I seized the metal spade and I smacked him hard enough that he fell and hit the concrete blockwork with the side of his head. The noise was awful, and I knew in an instant that he was dead. It took me the best part of two hours to remove enough hardcore from that corner to bury him from view, along with the bloodied spade and concrete block. I turned off the lights when I was finished, and hurried back to Katherine.

At home, I was shocked to find his travel bag already packed and stowed beneath our bed, his passport and Katherine's documents neatly paperclipped in a brown envelope, along with enough clothes to last them a week or two. After some persuasion, Katherine confessed all, and without prompting she handed over the fifty thousand pounds he had asked her safeguard when he'd seen her at lunchtime. The snakes had had it all worked out! I was wounded, of course, but the money was a blessing, and life, as they say, carried on.

Oh, David, how I miss you! It saddens me that our life together was cut so short. But even now a small part of me laughs at the naivety in those last words of yours – for it was not two that I killed, my love, but three. Of course, you won't know about my little brother, but he was the first, way up high on Kinder Scout, though I like to tell myself that that was an accident. But who really knows how a child's mind works? And arguably that awful mistake with Juliet was not intended, but I'd been led erroneously to believe she was a cuckoo in my nest. Of course, the one that really tested us is the one that no one seems to be troubled by any more, the one *you* knew about and which I committed with absolute malice aforethought. The murder of your little friend Tilly Jones.

When we left Castledale that autumn, you had not a clue about my role in Tilly's death, no idea why I was so adamant about moving on, about changing my name from Hattie to Janet. I told you I wanted a fresh start, that I could never let my parents know we had married, that I had set up home with the man suspected of killing a girl, later that we had a child. Not if I expected to remain in my mother's favour. As you know, she was worth a lot of money. And you, David, were happy to go along with it, for your 'beautiful Hattie'. As far as my mother was concerned, after Cambridge I stayed single, a successful career girl living in the City; unmarried, contented to be childless, devoted enough to visit her on an annual basis. You never complained about the arrangement, my love; after all, how would we have survived without my monthly allowance? Especially after that nasty business that led to you losing your teaching post. *Someone* had to keep the family afloat. But when you came across Tilly's old necklace in my jewellery box, all those years later, I thought my world had fallen in. We were packing up to come to London, and you asked me what it was, what it meant. I was unprepared. 'It's *Tilly's*,' you insisted, and you looked broken. When your eyes met mine, I knew there was no point in denying it. And so instead, I said nothing. I said nothing for the next twelve years, and neither did you.

Thank goodness the police are such useless buffoons! When they came asking questions about your volunteer Juliet Sherman, I told the officers that I had never met her. When they probed further about our private life, I said you and I had first met in Cambridge and they took my word for it. Perhaps if they'd followed it up they might have discovered my earlier life as Hattie Brown, your teenage sweetheart from the Castledale days. Maybe then they would have joined the dots and worked it all out sooner. *Idiots.*

I've had a lot of time to think about our life together, David, and I can't help but feel that if only we'd never had Katherine, things could have turned out so differently. We were in love, weren't we, way back then, before she came along? She was the undoing of us, the one who led me to deal with Juliet – and with you, my poor love – and ultimately, it was Katherine who exposed the whole sorry mistake. She always was a selfish girl.

So you see, David, it wasn't my fault, was it? It really *wasn't* my fault.

Acknowledgements

Heartfelt thanks go to my readers and champions,
and to the wonderful folk involved in making my books
as good as they can be. You are diamonds,
every one of you x

Reading Group Guide

1. The story is told from multiple points of view. Why do you think the author used that technique? How did this shifting structure impact your reading of the novel?

2. What are your first impressions of Martha? Is she likeable? Do you trust her?

3. How does the author ratchet up the tension throughout the novel? Were there particular moments when you were on edge?

4. Katherine's past has left her damaged. Do your feelings towards Katherine change as the novel goes on? Do you empathise with her?

5. Describe the relationship between Toby and Martha. What lies in store for them after the novel ends?

6. Did the revelation about David Crown's death shock you? Or did you have your suspicions?

7. What did you think would happen in the showdown on the canal boat? Did you think Katherine would be violent towards Martha and Liv?

8. Describe Katherine's relationship with her mother. Will they have a happy ending?

9. Were you surprised at Hattie's revelation of what happened on the night that Juliet disappeared?

10. What are your favourite films/tv programmes/books about female friendship?

Author Q&A with Isabel Ashdown

Crime writer **Stephanie Marland** asks Isabel Ashdown about her motivations behind *Beautiful Liars*

The voices of your two main narrators Martha and Casey are very distinct. How did you find the experience of writing these very different women?

I'm fascinated by the differences in people, all those markers that make us individual, that separate us from others – or bind us to them. I spend a lot of time thinking about my characters before I'm ready to write a word of the actual novel – jotting notes and imagining their lives and backgrounds, 'getting into their heads', if you like. By the time I start on the real labour of getting the novel down on paper, they feel like real people to me, and more often than not, the voices flow quite naturally.

Hidden secrets, survivor guilt and loneliness are strong themes within the book, did you start with these in mind or did they develop as you wrote?

The main theme or idea I started with was that of 'false identity'. It began after I'd received a Christmas card addressed to a previous resident, and an image flashed into my mind of a lonely woman – a woman with no family and nothing to look forward to, a woman with more than her share of complications. I thought, what if, in another world, she was to reply to that piece of personal correspondence? How might she feel to be someone else, just for a short while? Where might it lead her? How would she feel about being found out? That woman became Casey. As I wrote, the other themes you mention grew quite organically, which is, for me, one of the greatest joys of writing. That sense that the story has taken on a life of its own.

The conflict between having a well known public image versus the need for privacy and self protection comes out in Martha's narrative, What was it that especially interested you about this aspect of celebrity culture?
Martha is a naturally solitary person – that is not to say she is introverted, but rather she has a strong need for time alone, away from the limelight of TV and celebrity. She is conflicted by her public role, thinking of herself as very ordinary, whilst at the same time being fully aware of the privileges celebrity affords her. I think that feeling of inner conflict is something many of us experience in this modern world, our desire for affirmation perhaps at odds with our need for silence and privacy.

Both your main characters are strongly influenced in adulthood by their experiences as teenagers. Did start with their back stories or did you create the modern versions of themselves and work backwards?
In real life, our past and present is very much interwoven, with pieces of the past often felt keenly as they fracture through, unsettling our everyday lives. My writing process for *Beautiful*

Liars has been a little like that, in that I used the present narrative as a vehicle to steer the story forward, while every now and then snapshots of the past would show themselves to me, and my character's paths would grow clearer.

True crime 'cold case' television programmes like the one Martha is making in Beautiful Liars are becoming increasingly popular, what inspired you to write a story set in this world?
In the early drafting stage, I just had my two main characters: strange Casey, and brittle Martha, both single women in their thirties with an interest in the 18-year-old case of missing schoolgirl Juliet. In the early stages, I like to work closely with my fiction editor, Sam Eades, as I throw around ideas and possible directions, and it was during a conversation with her that we landed on the concept of making Martha the celebrity who would lead the investigation. As soon as I'd established this key role for Martha, I set about researching the world of TV production, and Martha's supporting crew soon followed. I'm an avid viewer of cold case TV myself, so it was no great hardship having to research the field a little further.

Is there a chance we'll see more of Martha in the future?
I've grown rather fond of Martha, and I'd love to write another cold case story for her. I guess the simple answer is, if there's reader appetite for more Martha, it may well happen!

My Little Eye by Stephanie Marland is out now

If you enjoyed **Beautiful Liars,**
discover ISABEL ASHDOWN's
latest twisty, psychological thriller

Lake Child

She thought she knew who she was...
She didn't know the half of it...

Out April 2019

Am I waking from the dead? Every morning *feels* like waking from the dead.

It's like rising up through emptiness, through a blackness I cannot touch or feel or smell or hear, and only when I open my eyes and see the wooden rafters of my attic room do I remember that I'm alive at all. In the forest we understand the meaning of darkness, where night falls like a black cloak, broken only by the rare slivers of moonshine that slip through the dense canopy of spruce and pine; where the deep lake shadows spiral into endless pools of ebony. But descriptions of the living world beyond my attic window are insufficient to express this waking feeling; *this* feeling is blacker – blacker, perhaps, than death itself. In the forest, after darkness comes morning light, clean and bright. Here, there is no such illumination; here, sleeping night simply rolls into waking day, where life lingers awhile before sliding back towards sleep again.

Most mornings I wonder at my very existence, as dreams and half-remembered images tumble across my mind's eye. I free myself of the wires that tether me to sleep, wincing at the flashing pulses of my bedside unit, alerting my parents downstairs to my waking state. Is this real, or just a nightmare conjured up by my fevered imagination? How can I ever know, sealed up as I am in this wood-panelled room, hidden away at the top of the house, with no one to ask – at least no one who's prepared to tell me the full truth. My injuries have robbed me of memories – in particular those of recent events, those of the weeks before the accident. I try so hard to piece it together, to dredge up something that makes sense, but there's nothing to be found. Nothing but an empty hole where that time should live. It's as if that part of my mind has been wiped clean; my head flipped open and the recent past spirited away. My early recollections, on the other hand, are crystal-clear, as sharp as though they occurred just yesterday, and in these endless hours of solitude I yearn for the freedom and lightness of that sun-filled childhood.

If I close my eyes I'm back there in an instant.

I miss the clean, green smell of the pine wood, the cool touch of morning mist on my face, the plip-plopping echoes of fish breaking the water's surface before rippling back into the deeps of Lake Barn. More than anything, I miss my friends, Lars and Rosa – and someone else, a shadowy presence my fractured mind won't allow me to grasp. This person-shaped gap haunts me daily as I peer through the slatted window shutters that hold me in, straining to make out the movements of my mother setting off for work in the mist-shrouded clearing below, my father waving her on her way. I ache to rejoin them in a life outside this room, to breathe freely and turn my face to the summer sun. They tell me that it won't be long now, that I'm almost ready, but that outside there are germs everywhere and I must conserve my energy, concentrate only on getting better. They tell me that I must trust them.

The trouble is, *I don't* trust them. They're lying – it's the only thing I'm completely certain of – and it scares me more than the memory loss or the scars that score the length of my body or the deadlocks that seal my door. There are so many questions unanswered. How long have I been shut away in here? When will I get better? Why don't my friends come to visit? And who is the boy that stands alone at the lakeside, gazing up at the house? It's too far for me to make out his expression, but his posture is one of sadness. Silently watching through the loosened slat in my shutters, I grow ever more dependent on his nightly visits, and, while he is a stranger to me, my heart tightens each time I see him standing there, caught in the watery gold reflection of evening's end. I know better than to ask too many questions of Mum and Dad, or to expect truthful replies, and I'm certain that I can never tell them about the boy, for fear that they might see him as a threat and send him away. For all the questions I *do* ask, the answers I receive are incomplete, the words designed only to soothe and placate – and my parents' pained expressions beg me to stop asking, plead with me to settle down and sleep. *It won't be forever*, they tell me, *soon everything will be back to normal. You'll see.* But then they're gone again and I feel so completely alone, my body weak and my mind racing, with only myself for company.

Despite all this, with every passing day my resolve grows quietly stronger: I *will* recover. I *will* remember. And, when I do, I *will* break free.